"A BARBARIAN," TEDRA MUTTERED IN DISAPPOINTMENT. "FARDEN HELL."

He was magnificent. This was dominant maleness personified, arms, legs, chest, everything larger than anything she'd ever seen before. He wore only a pair of buttery soft black leather pants for clothing, skin-tight and molded to those thick-muscled legs.

"Why are you dressed so, woman?" he demanded, his voice deep and authoritative—and arrogant. "They are the clothes of warriors. You will remove them."

"Well then," Tedra replied agreeably, "if you'll just produce something else for me to wear, I might consider changing. Otherwise, I'll keep . . ."

Her words died as he started walking toward her. At that point Tedra didn't have a single doubt of his intention. Her reasonable offer was not being considered. He'd ordered her to remove her clothes, and since she hadn't, he was going to do the removing himself . . .

Warrior's Woman

Johanna Lindsey

AVON BOOKS ◆ NEW YORK

AVON BOOKS
A division of
The Hearst Corporation
105 Madison Avenue
New York, New York 10016

Copyright © 1990 by Johanna Lindsey
Front cover illustration by Elaine Duillo
Inside cover author photograph by Roger's of Kailua
Published by arrangement with the author
Library of Congress Catalog Card Number: 89-92480
ISBN: 0-380-75301-4

First Avon Books Printing: June 1990

AVON TRADEMARK REG. U.S. PAT. OFF. AND IN OTHER COUNTRIES, MARCA REGISTRADA, HECHO EN U.S.A.

Printed in the U.S.A.

RA 10 9 8 7 6 5 4 3 2 1

TO SUSANNE, WHO SAID GO FOR IT;
SHARON, FOR INSPIRATION;
AND ALFRED, FOR HIS *SA'ABO*.
MANY, MANY THANKS.

Chapter One

Kystran, 2139 A.C. (After Colonization)

The demonstration against boskrat killing had been going on for three days, with ecology students marching in front of the Fanya Science Lab, their projector banners flashing on and off in neon colors, protesting the need for the extinction of another species in the name of science. The anticipated riot had come to pass and was now in full swing, joined by bored and frustrated Fanya citizens on the lookout for a little excitement and tension release.

If it were only the ecology people involved, who had protesting down to an art form, there wouldn't have been any trouble. But the local Stress Clinic had been closed last week for remodeling and extension, and the unattached citizens of Fanya, those not having filed for double occupancy, were more aggressive than usual.

"If they don't get their sex once a day in the clinics, they think their world's coming to an end," Fanya's Chief of Science had complained to Garr Ce Bernn, present Director of Kystran. "These young people don't remember what it was like before we had Stress Clinics in every city."

"Neither do we," the Director had replied dryly, but he'd sent a Sec 1 as requested to pacify the man.

Tedra De Arr was the lucky volunteer ordered to Fanya to take charge of the local Security Division. And she'd known after her first hour there that if the growing crowds got out of hand, there wouldn't be much she could do about it without some serious damage to life and limb involved. The Fanya Security Division was nothing but a bunch of young graduates who didn't know their phazor units from their communicators, the reason that they were never given combo-units. And if the cits decided to get destructive while rescuing the ugly little boskrats, she didn't see much hope in stopping them with the kind of backup available in this small town.

With only forty Sec men on hand and at least a hundred citizens already breaking down the outer doors, Tedra thought about leaving quietly by the rear entrance. That was what those frightened scientists had done, and she didn't give a farden damn about the scaly little creatures they'd left behind for her to defend. Defend, hell. She couldn't stand the creepy things herself. Why would she want to defend them?

With unkind thoughts for the man who had volunteered her for this temporary duty, Tedra lifted the computer link from her belt which gave her a direct line to Martha, her personal Mock II computer. "You know the stats, Martha, and they're breaking the doors down now. What are the odds on their grabbing the boskrats and running?"

"About sixty to one." Martha's very feminine voice came through the small, hand-sized link unit loud and clear. "If it weren't for the Stress Clinic being closed—"

Tedra cut her off with a snarl, literally, returning the compact unit to her belt. "Farden sex," she cursed to herself. "When did it get to be a be-all, cure-all, got-to-have-it-or-I'll-fall-to-pieces—or get violent?''

"Did you say something, Sec 1?"

Tedra turned around to the kid behind her, and he was just a kid. Couldn't be more than eighteen years. Of course, when she was eighteen, she'd been at the top of her class, had been actively working for a year even though she continued her training, and was already unmatched in her field. That was five years ago. Four years ago she had earned her present rank, Security 1, the highest rating for an expert in weapons and hand-to-hand combat. The young man who had spoken wasn't likely even a Sec 5, the lowest rating, though he would have to be to be assigned to her. They shouldn't turn them out for active duty until they are ready, but you couldn't tell Administration that, not when there was such a shortage of Security available. Too many of the new crop of students elected to train for more fulfilling and less dangerous life careers, especially on a planet not at war and in a league of planets devoted to peace and profitable trade.

"No, I didn't say anything to you, Sec 5, but I'll say it now. We're going to let the cits have what they want, because I don't believe a building and a bunch of smelly, ugly boskrats are worth anyone dying for. Stay out of the way and hope they settle for the boskrats. But if they come at you, shoot to stun. If that doesn't turn the tide, run like hell. Pass the word; stun only. If a single cit ends up dead when this is over, you Secs will answer to me.''

She didn't have to add they'd wish they were the ones who'd died if it came to that. A Sec 1 was no one to cross. Using you as a rag to wipe the floor with was the least of what one could do to you, and the Sec knew it.

When the crowd came through the last door into the large, vaulted lab, there were unfortunately few of the ecology students among them. These were the unattached cits who had been denied their daily ration of sex therapy for a week, poor things, and they had no interest in the farden boskrats other than as an excuse to relieve stress and tension in the old-fashioned way, with a heady dose of violence. They went right for the equipment and the Secs, breaking and attacking what they could. Stunning didn't help much beyond the first horde.

Tedra De Arr spent the next half hour doing some breaking herself, on bones and faces. The local med-itechs would be busy for the rest of the afternoon, but at least no one was seriously injured. But she was still angry as hell. She didn't like to break bones and hear men scream while she was doing it, not for no farden boskrats anyway. At least the women in the crowd had stuck to damaging only the furniture and equipment, because she liked hearing women scream even less, and she didn't need anything to put her in a worse foul mood.

But it was still a fiasco and a waste of her talent, and she was still angry about it when she later returned to the temporary quarters assigned to her. That kid, the one she'd just known had had no business being there, had shot his own foot with his phazor unit. What she wouldn't give to get hold of his instructor for five minutes. He wouldn't be releasing students before they were ready after that.

Marching to her door, she slapped her hand against the identilock without slowing her pace, and slammed right into the unmoving obstacle. She cursed a blue streak before calming enough to put her hand again to the lock for the required two seconds for identification. The door quietly slid open then under her fierce glower, but she wasn't pacified, not in the least. The next time Garr Ce Bernn got the idea that she'd appreciate the extra exchange tokens an outside assignment could earn, she'd tell him what he could do with them himself, and she didn't care if he was the head honcho of the whole planet.

She was a Sec 1, and the job of a Sec 1 was to protect and defend the leaders on the planet, not to be loaned out to any farden department. Her own job was the highest-paying in her field, assigned to Goverance Building and the Director himself. But to give him his due, he'd known she'd just bought a house in the suburbs outside the city, and likely thought she needed help paying for it. He thought he'd been doing her a favor. After she calmed down she'd see it that way, and probably even thank him when she got back to Gallion City, but she had to calm down first.

Picking up her pace again, she went straight to the Sanitary wall in the corner of the one-room quarters, pressed the wall activator, and started stripping as the walls slid out to enclose her in a five-foot-square area. The lights came on automatically as the newly created room within a room closed with a soft click around her. Out came the toilet if she should need it, a hair-and-eye changer, and a drawer full of lotions and perfumes and a few male colognes left over by the last occupant. All she was interested in, however, was the bath.

She stepped out of her one-piece uniform, made of all-weather solarcloth in the standard silver-gray that denoted her rank. The body revealed in the mirrored wall to her left was long-legged, tightly muscled, in prime condition. Strength was there without the bulge of muscle, leaving lines femininely curved and deceptive. It was a body that had undergone fifteen years of intensive exercise and training, turning it into a fighting machine. She still regretted the three years that had been wasted as a student of World Discovery, her second choice in careers, before her height finally became apparent and she was allowed to switch to her first choice.

She paused when she caught a glimpse of herself in the mirrored wall and noticed the frown still marring her fine-boned countenance. She needed a tension relaxer but knew the bath wouldn't do it. What she needed was her massager, but as the machines were rare and used only by a few residents on Kystran, they weren't standard in temporary quarters. The apartment had most of the other amenities she would find at home, but a massager wasn't one of them.

She knew what Martha would tell her to do about it, and was glad that Fanya's Stress Clinic wasn't operational, because for the first time she was actually tempted to visit one. The benefits would be the same, just accomplished with a different kind of body pounding, the kind she had yet to experience, though not for lack of offers. Men were attracted to her despite her size, and it was only her Sec 1 rating that kept them from becoming nuisances about it in pursuit of her. She often wondered how bad it would be if she weren't as tall as she was. But she was above average in height, about an inch above the male average of five feet nine inches. Six feet was tops for men on Kystran, but rare, and all of those six-footers were in Security, which would have been nice if she was interested, only she wasn't.

Eventually would come along the man she couldn't make mincemeat out of, and then she would be glad that her body was sleek and nicely proportioned, her breasts an abundant handful, her waist narrower than most, and her hips marginally curved rather than bony or thrusting. The peach-gold skin tone, large almond-shaped eyes, patrician nose, and soft coral mouth were nothing to ignore either. The stern brown hair and eye color were only for effect and not her own today, but they couldn't detract from features that went together just right to from a very pretty package. Tedra didn't bemoan that package. She had just never had a reason to appreciate any of it except for her height, which was one of the main requirements for a career in Security.

She left her uniform where it dropped on the floor, knowing the robocleaner would zip out to pick up after her as soon as the walls opened. No one could accuse Tedra of being tidy, but then robocleaners had been around longer than she had and they tended to spoil a person awful, keeping everything sparkling and sanitary and in its proper place. The machine stood no higher than her hips, moved on silent rollers so it never made a nuisance of itself; in fact, most of the time she barely noticed the thing as it worked around her. Her home unit was even programmed to take her order and bring her meals to her in bed if she felt too lazy or tired to get up and press the buttons on her Meal Provider herself. Hell, the farden thing would brush her teeth if she'd let it.

The solaray bath was smaller than her home unit by about a foot, the tubelike bath about a foot and a half round, just barely adequate for someone her size. The curved door slid quietly shut as soon as both feet were on the floor of the unit, and the tall cylinder filled with a red light that bathed her in scarlet hues. The beam of light turned off by itself after three seconds, the door opening automatically, a silent suggestion that she step out, which she did, squeaky clean now from head to toe, even the dull brown of her hair given a soft sheen in the cleaning. She didn't know how the thing worked, but the solaray bath had come into use more than fifty years ago during what was now termed the Great Water Shortage, and stayed in use because of the time-saving efficiency of the thing. Her home unit, a newer model, was designed to be compatible with the solarcloth of her uniforms, to clean them as well, and since the uniform was thin and comfortable enough to sleep in, too, it saved her even more time in not having to change clothes unless she was going somewhere other than on duty. Few citizens on the planet remembered what it was like to take baths any other way.

But her assignment was finished here now, and so she dialed a two-piece outfit, which the closet promptly delivered, the pants and vestlike top being the only other articles of clothing she had brought with her for her short stay in Fanya. The perfume she favored had been applied only last week, so she didn't need to refresh it. And the little bit of eye makeup she preferred, a thin application of black liner that matched her lashes, and the barest smudge of blusher were permanent. She was done with the nondescript hair color now that the job was finished, and spared the twenty seconds required for a new color, a vibrant lemon yellow that she couldn't wear well with any but the brown eye shade. She kept her long hair in the tight folded roll required by her job, since it was unnecessary to loosen it for cleaning or coloring. A quick swipe with the styler over her shortened bangs to get them off her forehead, and she was ready to depart, the whole process having taken less than five minutes.

The robocleaner was already heading toward her as soon as the walls opened and disappeared in their slots. "Pack me to go, fella," she told it, not having bothered to name a temporary unit, afraid her home model might get jealous if she did. Even though it wasn't a free-thinking machine like Martha, she didn't want to take any chances of upsetting her smoothly run household.

While she waited for her personal items to be collected and bagged, she headed for the audiovisual console to call her boss to tell him she had happily failed her mission. Every single boskrat had been whisked out of the lab when the ecology students had finally stumbled their way over the bodies on the floor to rescue their scaly friends. Actually, she hadn't really failed. The building was still standing, no one was dead, and there was only minor damage to the interior of the lab. No one had said she had to prevent the boskrats from leaving the premises.

Dropping into the adjustichair before the console, which immediately adjusted to her height and contours, she was just about to activate the long-distance channel for direct access to Gallion City, nine hundred miles away, when the three-by-three-foot screen flashed on in front of her, and a man she vaguely recognized filled the screen in vivid color. Her hand stilled in midair and she sat back, a little in shock that the screen was on without having had the voice command of "Answer," nor had the console chimed that there was a call awaiting her attention. People didn't appear on audiovisual consoles without permission, since the viewing was two-way and it would be an invasion of privacy otherwise. Yet there the man was, looking at her, sitting behind a desk in an office she *did* recognize, the office of the Director of

Kystran, but he was most definitely not Garr Ce Bernn.

The shock dissipated before he spoke as it dawned on her that he couldn't see her, that she was seeing what many other people were likely seeing at that very moment—a multiple transmission. She knew it could be done, that every single audiovisual unit could broadcast simultaneously planetwide, but it had never been done before, so she couldn't be faulted for being thrown by it. But the shock returned as he began to speak.

"Greetings, citizens." His voice was modulated. He looked a happy man and likely was, if his message could be believed. "Some of you may remember me from my bid for the Directorship in 2134 A.C., five years ago."

Now she knew where she'd seen him before, with his brown hair an even mousier shade than hers had been, and his gray eyes like chipped steel. The challenge for the Directorship had taken place before she had been transferred to Goverance Building, when she was still a Sec 2, but she remembered how outraged the citizens had been at this man's underhanded tactics in trying to buy votes from the Council of Nine, who were only all-powerful during election time every ten years when it was their duty to decide the matter, and were mere advisors otherwise.

"Whether you remember me or not is of no importance," he continued, seeming to have read Tedra's thoughts. "All that you need know is that I am Crad Ce Moerr, your new Director—"

"The hell you say!" she growled, almost missing the rest, since he didn't stop to allow for her fury.

"—by virtue of might. I have this day taken control of Goverance Building and do not intend to give it up. The takeover was accomplished with ease and a minimum of casualties. And you will be pleased to know your previous Director will not be harmed as long as there are no attempts to remove him from Goverance Building, where he will enjoy a comfortable confinement as hostage for your good behavior during the transition of power, as well as in the years to come. Let me assure you there will be no major changes under my Directorship. Your careers and lives, good citizens, will continue as they are, including those of Security, the only difference being you have a new Director to lead you in peace and prosperity, a new Director to protect and revere. I am he, Crad Ce Moerr.''

The screen went blank, and Tedra's thoughts exploded in a whirl of outrage and disbelief. It was a joke, and in very bad taste. Yet there was that word ''revere,'' which planted the doubt and twisted it around in her gut. Demanding reverence? How utterly autocratic. Garr Ce Bernn *was* loved and revered. He didn't have to demand it. By virtue of might? Security against Security? No! Impossible! But how else?—if it was true.

She flipped on the long-distance channel and keyed Goverance Building direct. Her fingers bit into the arms of the chair as she waited for the screen to flash on again. Security at Goverance Building was the best. How could they be defeated? Bribery? Payoffs? Could she work with men for so long and not know them at all? Damn and damn, why hadn't she been there? She could have done something, made a difference. The screen remained blank, refusing to give answers.

Immediately she tried another location while the channel was still open. On the second chime the screen lit up with the face of one of her closer friends, Rourk Ce Dell, Chief of Relics Hall.

"Thank Heaven's Stars, Tedra, we were so afraid they'd—" He broke that off, running a hand over his blue eyes in a sign of extreme weariness—or relief. Her heart had already accelerated again, expecting the worst after that. "Listen up, babe, and don't interrupt. It's true if you saw it with the rest of us, at least the fact that they've got Goverance Building locked up tight. And the Director was still alive, last we heard. But the rest—nothing but lies. You wouldn't believe some of the things we've heard . . . the farden slime's issuing directives left and right . . . so many changes, and he's getting away with it."

"Just tell me *how,* Rourk."

"I will, as soon as you get here—"

"Rourk!"

"There's no *time* now, Tedra!" he said with as much frustration and anxiety as she was feeling. "I've got to keep this line open for Slaker. He's working magic at the computer lab. When I couldn't reach you, I took the chance that you were still in Fanya and had him list you dead as of yesterday, so there shouldn't be any suspicion. We've worked up new stats for you, too, but there's been some trouble with the Records computer, as if they've already figured out there'll be tampering and have put a lock on the files. But Slaker's working on it, and you know how good he is."

"Yes, I—"

"Just get back here as soon as you can, Tedra, and come straight to my place. Don't even think of going near Goverance Building or the Security Complex, or your new place. Don't talk to anyone else, and try not to worry. Slaker and I will get you off the planet somehow.''

"Off the planet?'' she said in a small, disbelieving voice. "I've got to leave the planet?'

"That or worse, babe. Crad Ce Moerr has to pay his mercenaries with something. Every female Sec they can get their hands on is the first installment.''

Tedra blanched, but got out, "Mercenaries, not Security? Who?''

"The Sha-Ka'ari.''

But the Sha-Ka'ari were sword-wielders, was her incredulous thought as the screen went blank again.

Chapter Two

In her four-seater air cruiser, it took Tedra less than twenty minutes to return to Gallion City. It took several hours to find parking, however, since Rourk's apartment was right in the heart of Gallion, and to find space for an air cruiser was never easy, today almost impossible. She wished she dared zip out to the suburbs to exchange the cruiser for her much smaller Fleetwing II, which she usually used for city travel, but after Rourk's warning, she'd be crazy to try it. She still didn't know what the hell had happened at Goverance Building, and until she did, she'd follow Rourk's suggestions to the letter.

At last another cruiser took off from a parking roof three blocks away, and before enough Fleetwings could zip in to fill the space, she set her craft down. It was likely Crad Ce Moerr's broadcast that had brought such traffic congestion to the city today. Tedra wouldn't be the only one anxious to find out what was really going on.

Her mind was still spinning with it, and it still made no sense. She knew so little about the Sha-Ka'ari, but there had to be tons of information about them on computer file, since Kystran had been trading with Sha-Ka'ar ever since the small planet was first discovered tucked away in the north sector of Centura Star System not too many years ago. All she knew was that they were reputed giants who clung to many of their old beliefs and customs, such as the keeping of slaves and the making of war on their own planet. Despite that, however, they coveted the advanced technology of other worlds to improve their lifestyles, which they had done considerably. But the last she had heard, they were still slaveholders, and still sword-wielding warriors, which really made no sense—unless Ce Moerr had trained and supplied them with modern weapons for the takeover.

Even as the thought occurred to her and seemed to be the only answer, she got her first look at the devils in question, and it was swords attached to their belts, not lazors. Two of them rode the avenue glide, which got the foot traffic where it wanted to go about three times faster than walking would. She was cruising down the avenue under her own steam herself, having wanted to keep a distance from the crowded glides, if just a few feet distant, Rourk's warning not to talk to anyone ever-present in her mind.

Just seeing them, heads above everyone else on the glides, set her adrenaline pumping. They really were bigger than she had counted on, even if they were reputed giants. Kystran men obtained height; at least a few did. But they didn't obtain brawn. The two Sha-Ka'ari warriors were huge in comparison, even the one who was likely no more than six feet himself. His buddy had maybe another four inches to top that, but they were both so muscular it was worth crying over. Heaven's Stars, were they all like that?

But they carried swords, for Star's sake. Again it made no sense. Against a phazor, they might as well be unarmed. Her own weapons were in her carryall, but she could get to them quickly enough if she had to. Against mere swords, she wouldn't even need to. She wasn't a Sec 1 for nothing. She had advanced beyond Security training years ago, and gone on to self-train in some of the more deadly techniques of weaponless fighting. Rourk, who worked in the Relics Hall, supplied her with all the tapes she could ask for. He'd even hooked her on general ancient history, which had become her second passion, next to her job.

If she had thought nothing would come of seeing these two warriors, her pumping adrenaline had told her otherwise. Sure enough, they stepped off the glide in front of her, her height likely having drawn their notice. Big and wide as they were, there was no room to pass around them unless she got on the glide. But they weren't standing there blocking her way for nothing. And being chased after on the glides was not her idea of fun, or any way to keep a low profile just now.

They were grinning at her, as if she were something that had been lost but now was found, and speaking gibberish to each other, probably Sha-Ka'ari, which was really rude when you considered they weren't likely to come invading without having slept on some Kystrani Sublims first, to acquire the language of the target planet. Even if they hadn't come prepared to be understood, they could have been given the language their first night there while they slept. They did sleep, didn't they? Most humanoids did require at least a few hour's sleep a day, and they were definitely humanoids, and damn handsome ones at that.

They wore uniforms similar to Security's, long-sleeved, long-legged one-piecers in a dark blue material she didn't recognize. It was kind of thick, probably to hold in all those muscles that looked like they were about to pop open all available seams. Their boots were standard material, as were their belts, the major difference being they were *sword* belts, designed to hold nothing else.

Even as they talked back and forth, they were paying her as close attention as she was them. But that gibberish was starting to annoy her. She could speak every language in the Centura League of Confederated Planets in the Centura Star System, all seventy-eight of them. Kystran ranked twelfth in the League in the matter of importance, being a major exporter of luxury items like solaray baths, hair-and-eye changers, adjustichairs and beds, air blankets, all the little things that made life more comfortable and efficient, so Kystran received a good deal of Centura League visitors. But Sha-Ka'ar wasn't a member planet. There had been no reason to sleep on its Sublim, if Kystran even had its language on file.

She was about to say something about their rudeness when the taller one spoke, his Kystrani very slow and precise, as if he distrusted the new language inside his head, which was funny if you thought about it. Not many people from lower-tech worlds believed you could learn a whole new language in just a few hours, especially when you didn't even have to be awake and listening to do it. First timers were always skeptical, not trusting the new words in their subconscious to come out in accordance with their conscious thoughts. It took a little longer to be able to think in the new language as well.

"You are a Security, are you not, woman?"

Stars, was it the way she stood, ready to take them both down at the slightest wrong move? Or was it her height? They were only guessing, of course. She'd just have to get them thinking along different lines.

"Security? Me? You've *got* to be kidding, sweet-cakes. Do I really look like a Security?"

She spread her arms wide, which parted the lower half of her vest to reveal a wide expanse of bare midriff. As she had hoped, that was where both pair of eyes went, getting their minds off Security.

"I'm a programmer over at Exports Exchange," she continued, in case there was any suspicion left. "Got transferred there about three years ago, but I'm still not used to living in the city. Stars, the convenience of it all! Plays hell with the body, if you know what I mean. Have to get out and exercise on my off days or I'd go nuts."

"Off days are free days," one warrior said to the other.

But neither was really sure. There were always some words or expressions in a new language that made no sense, because you had nothing to compare it with on your world. Such things took a little verbal explaining if you were going to use the new language for an extended period of time.

"You both must be visitors to our fair city, right?"

It was the logical thing to say at that point, and after all, Ce Moerr's broadcast hadn't mentioned the Sha-Ka'ari, so the average citizen wouldn't know these warriors were the "might" that had somehow accomplished the takeover. She didn't get an answer, and hadn't expected one. Besides the fact that they were probably under orders not to alarm the citizens with knowledge of who they were and what they were doing there, who other than a Sec would push the matter if he didn't get an answer? And she had denied being a Sec, hopefully to their satisfaction.

The taller warrior stepped closer to her, forcing her to bend her head back to keep eye contact with him, a quite foreign experience for her, and frankly a little intimidating. She had never tried her skill on someone his size. Of course, size didn't really make a difference for most of her moves. But there was always that slim chance that he might get lucky. If her hands and feet weren't free for her to use, strength could indeed make the difference. Her training demanded that she not let him get so close where he could use that strength against her, but to move back now might bring their suspicion back.

"We are pleased your time is free, woman. Our time is also free, thus you will share your time with us."

Not "will you" or "how about it," but "you will." She had just learned one new fact about the Sha-Ka'ari. Their arrogance was unbelievable. And she had obviously done too good a job of playing the carefree flake of no danger to them. Then she gasped as the taller one's hand slid through the lower opening of her vest to press flat against her midriff, a hand large enough to cover nearly the entire area, leaving her in absolutely no doubt about what they wanted to do while sharing time with her.

She had an excuse to step back now, to pretend outrage. "Sharing? As in a threesome? What do you take me for, fella, a Stress Clinic worker?"

He was unbelievably fast, grabbing her wrist before she could move back too far. In two seconds she could release her wrist, but she'd be showing them what she could do and the game would be up.

"Hey—" she began, only to hear, "Choose, then."

So they could be reasonable—as long as one of them got what he wanted. Well, that was all right, certainly better than their first idea. She had already made a mistake by being so friendly, so it was too late to change her tune. And their libidos were already working overtime, if the look in their eyes was any indication, so she knew changing her tune wouldn't work now anyway. She was stuck with one of them, and as long as it had to be that way, she would play it safe.

With a grin, she shifted her gaze to the warrior who topped her by only a few inches and hopefully would be the easier of the two to handle. "Are you as good as you look, babe, or am I going to have to try your friend here another time?"

With her choice made, she was released, only to have her "choice" step forward and secure her with an arm about her waist. "If you are as good as you look—babe, we will neither of us find disappointment."

Nothing like getting into the spirit of the thing, she thought with an inward groan, but said aloud, "Then what are we waiting for? My place is just down the street."

He said something to the bigger brute in the gibberish again and they both laughed, giving Tedra the feeling they still had every intention of sharing her since they considered her their own personal find—they'd just agreed to do it separately now. Well, that was for later worry. The taller one got back on the glide, to her relief, but her present worry wasn't letting her out of his meaty grip—and he had come up with a new idea.

"I will be more—at ease—do we go to my ship."

Not farden likely, she almost snarled, remembering in what manner Rourk had said they were being paid. She was afraid the payment wasn't temporary. Sha-Ka'ari were slaveholders after all.

But none of her growing anger was in the sultry look she turned up to him. "You must have been lost, sweetcakes. Spaceport is clear on the other side of the city. Do you really want to wait that long?''

He almost crushed her ribs in answer. ''After you will come to see my ship.''

''I'm likely to be too worn out,'' she said meaningfully, ''but we'll see.''

He must have decided that was the best he would get for now, for he nodded and started off in the direction she'd indicated. She could breathe again—and wondered just how she would take him out. Six feet of confident, arrogant, amorous, *strong* warrior. Her Frimera technique might be her best bet. He wouldn't even see it coming.

And he didn't. When they reached Rourk's apartment and she palmed the identilock, which fortunately had her prints on file, Tedra had one arm already around her warrior's neck. It was just a matter of moving her fingers into place and applying the pressure while he was distracted with the door opening.

Only he didn't go down immediately. He even turned to look at her, and for about four seconds her body went cold with fear. But then he did begin to slump forward, finally to crash onto the floor. So it just took a little longer on someone his size. Those thick neck muscles, probably. Stars, what a scare! But not nearly as much as the scare she gave poor Rourk, showing up at his door with a Sha-Ka'ari warrior in tow.

Chapter Three

"What do you mean you don't want to kill him?" Rourk practically shouted.

"I don't know," Tedra answered with a sigh. "He told me his name on the way here. If he hadn't told me his name—"

"Tedra!"

"Well, the man had his hands all over me and I didn't half mind it. Do you know how long I've been waiting for something like that to happen?"

Hearing that, he simply stared at her. Of all the times for Tedra De Arr to remember that she was a woman, why did it have to be now? For years he had been trying to set her up with one man or another, and all she ever did was challenge them, *beat* them, then never mention their names again.

He knew her problem. They'd been close friends for nearly five years, so he couldn't help but know her problem. And truth to tell, he sympathized with it. He wouldn't feel comfortable himself, filing for double occupancy with a woman who he knew could demolish him in a matter of moments if he ever got her riled. Sex-sharers did fight occasionally. It was inevitable. A man would *not* like knowing that he could end up seriously injured or dead if his partner lost her head. Tedra didn't like knowing it any better. She was waiting for the man she couldn't walk all over to come along. She'd been waiting a long time.

"You're not seriously considering . . . consorting with the enemy, are you?"

She snorted. "I brought him down, didn't I? He didn't stand a chance." But there were those four seconds when she had thought the Frimera technique had failed. And there were those feelings that had come up out of nowhere when Kowan had stopped just before they reached Rourk's and kissed her. Damned warrior. What'd he have to kiss her for? "I just don't feel like killing him, all right?" she fairly growled, not used to feeling this way.

"All right, all right," Rourk agreed quickly, anything to get that growl out of her voice. For a moment he stared at the warrior they'd dragged across the room and propped up against a chair. "There are other ways, of course—agents that could make him totally forget his last twenty-four hours, but I don't have access—"

"Martha does."

Rourk whirled around, his face brightening. "That's right, she does, doesn't she? I keep forgetting she's a Mock II. Stars, Tedra, do you know there are only three Mock II's on the planet? That you got one, and in payment of a bet—"

"Garr never reneges, and he accepted the stakes. But she didn't cost him too much, just the suspension of all import taxes on Morrilian goods for one year."

He chuckled, running a hand through his bright red hair.

"Not much, huh, when Morrilian silk costs a fortune? Well, that solves the problem of your friend there. Come to think of it, Martha can probably get into Records easier than Slaker can. Do you have a linkup with you?"

"Yes, but do you mean to say we've been sitting here jawing when my future's still up in the air?"

"He would have had it cracked by tonight, and it'll take a day or so to get your ship supplied and—"

"You've got me a ship already?"

He shook his head. "We've got to get you on record as a pilot with Explorations first before we can request a ship for you." He waved a hand when she started to interrupt again. "Never mind. Send Martha to Slaker's console and let him take care of the incidentals while I tell you what we know so far."

She did, but of course Martha had to know why first. There was a short discussion over who was boss and who had to do what she was told to do, with Rourk laughing his head off listening to it, before Martha connected with Slaker's computer, likely shocking the hell out of him since he had no idea she was coming.

Sometimes Tedra's top-of-the-line, ultramodern, free-thinking computer was more trouble than it was worth. Hell, most times. She'd had to go through testing just to get it, so it could be programmed to be compatible with her temperament. Naturally, she'd been shocked to find the thing would frequently argue with her, deliberately annoy and provoke her. What had happened to compatible? But she had finally realized those arguments were likely what she needed, an outlet for the stress from her job, since she didn't use Stress Clinics like everyone else, and had been honest about it in her testing.

Tedra turned now, waited for Rourk to wind down from his chuckling, then demanded, "So tell me, how did the Sha-Ka'ari do it? How did they get through Security to Garr? What weapons did they use?"

Rourk sobered completely at the reminder. "Those swords and—"

"Don't give me that! They couldn't get near a Sec with no more than swords, and you know it."

"If you'll let me tell it, then *you'll* know that that's just what they did. Their swords and shields are made of some kind of steel we've never come across before, not that we have much use for steel anymore. It's called *Toreno*, and only their armorers know the secret of producing it. It was there in Records for anyone who cared to look. Crad Ce Moerr must have looked, before he left the planet in disgrace. Nothing can penetrate this *Toreno* steel, Tedra. Everything Security fired at them bounced right off their shields."

Tedra sat back in her chair, feeling a certain deflation. That easy? No secret weapons, no brilliant strategy, just shields to hide behind. And then she squirmed in her chair. It was *her* Security unit that had been defeated.

"So the weapons were useless. But Sec 1's don't *need* weapons," she reminded Rourk. "The day I can't dance my way around a sword, I'll retire, so how—"

"Don't get defensive now. Have you really looked at one of their swords? The things are at least four feet long, not to mention double-bladed. And you're forgetting the shields, which are even longer. Add to that the strength of those giants, their longer arm reach on top of the sword length, the narrow space to fight in, and lastly, that although you'd like it to be otherwise, no one in your unit is quite as good as you are."

He didn't say it, but it was there for her to realize, that she wouldn't have had much chance to do any better. She could picture it, having every blow or kick she threw being met by a farden piece of metal, every technique she knew becoming as useless as the weapons.

Her body slumped a little lower in the chair. "How do we fight something like that? How do we get our planet back, Rourk?"

"We don't—not immediately. It may even take several years before Crad Ce Moerr feels safe enough not to surround himself with guards. Nor will Secs be allowed anywhere near Goverance Building. He'll likely still use them, in other cities, but at Goverance Building, where he's keeping Garr Ce Bernn hostage, there will be only Sha-Ka'ari."

"He'll have to keep himself prisoner as well, if he hopes to stay alive," she growled.

"Just about," Rourk agreed. "We won't be sitting back and playing 'it's all right.' When the opportunity comes to get rid of the farden slime, we'll do it."

"But if there aren't any Secs left in the city—"

"Do you think men have to be Secs to fight, Tedra?"

She colored a little. She hadn't meant to imply he was a coward. But it would take forever if they had to depend on citizens to overcome the Sha-Ka'ari.

"I'm glad to know at least that no one's taking this with a shrug."

"Oh, you can be sure there are those who don't really care. The new Director and his directives won't affect everyone. There'll even be some who'll like the changes. The computers might be wrong in the objectives they've come up with, given all the facts fed to them so far, but it looks like Ce Moerr might have liked the way the Sha-Ka'ari do things. One of the possibilities is that he means to subjugate our women, to get them out of their present positions of power and back to the servile level they broke out of thousands of years ago."

"What the hell has he done that would suggest that?"

"Every single woman in Gallion City holding a job of any importance, and even a few in secondary positions, have already been fired. The next male in line for that position has been given it."

"Without reason?" she gasped.

"None is needed when the directive comes from Goverance Building. You know that."

"What else?" she demanded, in the grips of an anger like nothing she'd ever felt before.

"They've already gone on file as being unacceptable for employment."

"Then what are they supposed to do for exchange tokens? How can they support themselves—"

"That's just it, Tedra; they can't. They'll either have to resort to lawbreaking, in which case the Sha-Ka'ari get them, or they'll have to depend on a man to support them, not an easy thing for some women to accept."

No, it wasn't. She knew she couldn't. To have to ask a man for everything you wanted or needed when you knew perfectly well you were capable of providing it for yourself, to be told no if he felt like it, or be forced to beg and wheedle it out of him. Tedra shuddered, quickly addressing the alternative he mentioned.

"What was that about lawbreaking and the Sha-Ka'ari getting them?"

"You're not going to like it, babe, but I have it from Dexal, who's been watching Goverance Building. Three women were brought in this morning on minor infractions, things worth no more than a hand-slap and a warning. All three were later taken to one of the Sha-Ka'ari ships. That ship has already left planet. It looks like the female Secs aren't the only women the Sha-Ka'ari were promised for their help.''

There it was, what she had feared. "Tavra and Prish from my unit?''

"Both on that same ship. It looks like the Sha-Ka'ari especially want all female Secs, which is why I was going out of my head worrying about you before you called. I think they like the idea of making slaves of what they consider female warriors. The directive already went out, ordering every other female Sec on the planet to report to Goverance Building. And they'll come, unsuspecting, unless we can somehow make known what is really happening. But all traffic has been suspended from leaving the city and no outgoing calls are permitted. The best we can hope to do right now is try and intercept them as they arrive.''

Tedra closed her eyes, letting it all sink in. "You think they mean to eventually enslave *all* Kystran women?''

"I think they'll take all they can get, in any way they can get them without alerting the general populace to what they're doing. The lawbreakers are an easy catch. They can be brought in without questions, and if anyone does inquire about them, they can be told they were sentenced. Several laws have already been changed that will make a good number of women lawbreakers without their even knowing it. You're—ah—one yourself.''

Her eyes narrowed on him. "Am I?''

"Ce Moerr's lowered the women's Age of Consent from twenty-five to eighteen. You are now illegally unbreached.''

She blanched. "He can't do that! I'm not the only woman who's never accepted a man before."

It had been decided years ago that a woman shouldn't be allowed to hold herself back from sex-sharing, that it was somehow detrimental to her health. Tedra was a living example that that just wasn't so, but who was she to buck the laws? So an age had been picked, twenty-five, as being quite long enough for a woman to file for double occupancy, or be on file in one or more Stress Clinics. If she hadn't taken the plunge by then to find out how beneficial sex-sharing was supposed to be, then a partner would be chosen for her, by computer of course, so he'd be ideally suited to her, and allowed to legally rape her if she was still having doubts.

It had been a source of slowly growing panic for Tedra, as she approached the Age of Consent, that even as a Sec she wouldn't be able to get around the law. She would, of course, have chosen *someone* before then, likely Rourk, just to get the farden unfair law satisfied. But she hadn't been looking forward to it.

"Don't frown so, babe," Rourk interrupted her thoughts, just short of grinning. "Your new stats will list you as breached and a member of no less than four Stress Clinics."

She blushed. She couldn't help it. She didn't have many close friends like Rourk, but those few she did have found it a source of amusement how she felt about sex-sharing, especially since they knew she was all for it, that it was only the choice in partners that was giving her trouble.

Fortunately, Martha came back on line then, before she really got to brooding about it. "Everything's taken care of, kiddo." Martha was using her sexy, purring voice for Rourk's benefit. "You're now Tam-ber De Oss, a World Discoverers Pilot with Explo-rations. I suppose you'd like a World Discoverers craft now?"

"That would be nice," Tedra replied dryly. "And if it wouldn't be too much trouble, you might hook up with Supply's computers and requisition enough supplies for a lengthy voyage."

"No problem, doll. Anything else?"

"Yes, I want—"

Rourk's tap on her shoulder cut her off. "You—ah—better do something quick about your friend there. I'll tell Martha what else you need."

Tedra was already rushing across the room to drop down beside the warrior, who was starting to make waking noises. Damn, he hadn't been out very long. "Ask Martha to find that agent and have it deliv-ered," she called over her shoulder, fighting off the hand that came immediately to her when she spoke. "Easy, baby." She pried his fingers from her hair and leaned forward to whisper by his ear, "You're drunk. Too much good Antury wine. But you're having a great time."

He must have thought so, for his head turned and his mouth caught hers just as her fingers went to his neck. Swirls of want and need denied too long came rushing to the surface, almost making Tedra forget to apply the pressure that would put him out again. But she did apply it. Her lips clung to his a moment more before his head fell to the side.

Tedra sat back on her heels, sighing as she stared at him. His hair was short and as black as her original color. His eyes were a lovely amber. She didn't think she'd ever seen a man put together quite so nicely—

well, except maybe his taller friend. It was a farden shame they had to be her enemies.

She'd been able to take this one down, but would it have been so easy if she hadn't caught him by surprise? She ran a hand down his meaty arm, rock hard even in total relaxation. If those arms had wrapped around her in combat, she might have found herself on a ship headed for enslavement. He'd tried to get her on that ship. After he was finished with her, he would have tried again. She wondered how many other women were being stolen in that way.

"Too bad, sweetcakes." She patted his cheek in regret. "But I don't care for slavery, no matter how good-looking the master is. We'd have ended up killing each other."

"What's that?" Rourk asked behind her.

"Nothing. Are you sure he won't remember anything after you give him the agent?"

"Not a thing. And he'll have a sore head to assure him he imbibed too much, if his loss of memory doesn't."

"There was another warrior with him when they stopped me. He's likely to remind Kowan—"

"Then why don't you scratch him or something so he'll have a reason to *wish* he could remember?"

Tedra grinned and leaned forward again, putting her lips to the sleeping warrior's throat. When she finished, there was a small bruise of the like she had often seen on Rourk's neck after Xeta had shared sex with him.

"That ought to make him swear off intoxicants for a good while," Rourk said. "Are you sure you don't want to be breached before you lose yourself in space?"

She glanced up and was shocked to see that he was serious. "Rourk!"

"Sorry," he said, flushing. "I've just never seen you looking so soft."

Had kissing the warrior done that to her? She was annoyed, thoroughly. After all, the farden slime had wanted to make a slave of her.

She got to her feet abruptly, grouching, "You picked a fine time to remember I'm a woman."

He chuckled, now that the Sec was back. "I guess the timing is kind of lousy."

"Did you get me a World Discoverer?"

"No, but I got you a priority rating, so you'll have no trouble clearing port."

"And just what, then, am I going to clear port in? What other single-pilot, long-distance craft—"

"I had to take what was available, Tedra. The Discoverers are all off planet or in repair. I got you a Transport Rover instead. It'll go just as far as a Discoverer, even farther, and faster, too. It's just bigger."

"One hell of a *lot* bigger, Rourk. How am I supposed to pilot a craft that large? I don't know the first think about Rovers. My studies, short as they were, were on Discoverers."

"Not to worry." He grinned. "Tell her, Martha."

"He's right, kiddo." Martha's voice traveled across the room, proving she'd been listening to their exchange. "All you have to do is hook me up to the Rover's on-board computer, and I take over. I'm programmed to fly anything they've got. Why do you think I'm so expensive?"

"I *did* always wonder," Tedra came back dryly, only to hear what sounded suspiciously like a snort from the computer.

"Now, now," Rourk intervened, looking at Tedra with silent laughter.

Tedra just sighed. "Were the supplies taken care of?"

"For a Rover, supplies are regulated," Martha told her. "I only had to give them the date of departure, and the craft gets fully stocked."

"For a full crew? A Rover *usually* takes a full crew, you know. And what about that? Is spaceport going to let me leave without one?"

"You're scheduled to pick up a crew on Tara Tey, as far as they know."

"And once you're gone, I'll have Slaker erase all entries," Rourk added. "The extra supplies might well come in handy, babe." At her raised brow, he reminded her, "It could be years before it's safe to come back. You might as well do a little world discovering while you're out there."

Years, Tedra thought, feeling a little sick. She thought about the new house in the suburbs that she had moved into only last week, all her belongings she'd have to leave behind, her friends . . .

"Stars, my possessions!" she gasped. "Who's going to pick up Martha's controller boards? She's only here on a linkup. Her heart and soul are at my new house."

"You don't think *I'd* forget such important little details, do you?" Martha asked in her voice labeled smug. "Rourk's friend Slaker is already taking care of it. I'll be aboard the Rover long before you will."

Tedra gritted her teeth. "Did you happen to think of Corth and Bolt when you sent someone to collect yourself?"

"Forget my little friends? Me? I'm not the one who

can't even remember that an identilock requires at least two seconds to make identification.''

Tedra's face flamed with color. She wasn't going to ask how Martha knew about her run-in with the door, she really wasn't.

"No comment, kiddo?" Martha purred.

"Not in mixed company," Tedra bit out, sending Rourk a look that dared him to say just one word.

Chapter Four

"Where are we now, Martha?"

"Still in deep space, kiddo, same as last time you asked. If you're going to be so impatient, you should have elected to stay in our own Star System. There are still hundreds of planets unexplored there that you could have amused yourself with."

"And a frequency range that could have got me called home. I am a *female* pilot, remember."

"I'm the pi—"

"Don't argue," Tedra cut in, almost losing her patience for real. "You know what I meant. It's within the laws of probability, and I'd just as soon not take the chance for a while of being put on Kystran's wanted list if I refuse to acknowledge a summons home. And as long as we have some time to kill—"

"We go Star System-hopping."

"What are you complaining about? You thought it was a great idea last week."

"That was when I still had the occasional asteroid belt to play dodge with. This space is so empty a blind man could navigate it."

"Don't tell me you're bored, Martha." Tedra chuckled. "You have to monitor the control stations of every absent crew member. You don't have time to be bored."

"Child's play."

"Don't give me that. You love it, being in such control. You're just trying to pick an argument, aren't you, since we haven't had one in so long? But it won't work, you know. I'm still too delighted with you for raiding the Relics Hall before we left. That was really a sweet, thoughtful thing to do."

Silence. Tedra laughed to herself. Martha hated it when her tactics didn't work. And Tedra had discovered it was a lot of fun, thwarting Martha. But she'd also spoken the truth. When she had found literally hundreds of history tapes in Martha's files, she'd been ecstatic. She had thought she would have to give up her hobby until it was safe to go home. But she had enough tapes to last her several years, if she didn't run through them all on Sublim format.

"Tedra, you haven't fallen asleep, have you?" Martha's voice returned about fifteen minutes later.

"Not yet."

"You're right, kiddo, maybe I am bored. Why don't we discuss your love life?"

Tedra started up, almost taking the bait. But then she lay back down on the adjusticouch that had been widened so Corth could lay next to her on it. She settled back into his arms, but caught him grinning at her, after Martha's off-the-wall suggestion.

She gave the android a stern look when he started to speak, and said to Martha, "Why don't we discuss your love life instead, old girl? How are you and the engineering computer getting along together?"

A very definite snort. Martha was getting good at that sound. "Let's get serious, shall we? There isn't a machine on this ship up to *my* standards. But you've got one there up to yours. I brought the kid along so you could make use of him. So why don't you?"

"I am," Tedra replied, wrapping Corth's arms more tightly around her.

That was all she needed occasionally from Corth,

to be held. Being raised in the Kystran Child Centers left a big void in some people's lives, probably why so many young people started going to Stress Clinics as soon as they were old enough, looking for the love they had lacked in their growing years. The Child Centers were for learning only. They gave you approval, motivation, self-esteem, and any number of other good qualities, but they didn't give you love.

It was a lack Tedra sometimes felt keenly, the reason that she had bought Corth last year. He was an entertainment android, designed to entertain a woman in every way possible. He was free-thinking to a small degree, insomuch as he could follow and participate in a conversation as long as only logical responses were required and the subject was one within his memory banks. He couldn't make decisions on his own the way Martha could, didn't have feelings to bruise or stir up, and Stars forbid he should argue with anyone. Aggression was not in his makeup, but spontaneity was. Tedra had only to touch him in a sexual way and he could become the ideal sex-sharer, totally devoted to her pleasure. Getting him to just hold her in a nonsexual way wasn't as easy, so it had to be verbally requested.

"The Martha is correct, Tedra De Arr." Corth spoke softly behind her. "You do not make full use of my abilities."

"I get as much use as I want of them, babe."

"I would be gentle with your breaching."

Tedra sat up to look down at him suspiciously. "Since when do you pursue a subject that has been dropped, Corth?" She didn't wait for an answer, her eyes locking on the communications console in the center of the large Rec lounge she had taken to spending most of her time in. "Have you been tampering with Corth's programming, Martha?"

"Me?" She had got her innocent-sounding voice down pat. "Why would I do that?"

"Well, you better undo what you didn't do, metal lady, or—"

Corth pulled her back down to their previous position. "Relax, Tedra De Arr. I am incapable of hurting you."

Tedra scooted out of his arms and off the couch, more than a little unnerved by the change in him. After all, as a machine, he had the strength of ten men. And Martha really had given him a dose of aggression.

"I'm going to kill you, Martha!"

"Now, kiddo, he's only a little more lifelike, is all," was the computer's response. "All that sickening agreeing with you was getting on my nerves."

"You don't have nerves, you motherless piece of scrap iron, you have circuits. And those can be turned off."

"You can't shut me down, doll." Martha went for a reasonable tone now that she'd got a rise out of Tedra. "I run the ship, remember, supply your oxygen, your food, etc. If you turn me off, you go with me. I didn't think you were into suicide."

"Oh, shut up!" Tedra snapped. "And you"—she glared at the android, who was sitting up—"don't move another inch, or I'll have to kick you into malfunction."

"Now don't do that, Tedra," Martha said in her soothing voice. "If you break him, who's going to fix him up here in space? The Rover's meditech unit only works on live bodies, you know."

"Then you'd better change him back to the way he was. I won't be raped by a machine."

"He wouldn't do that," Martha insisted. "He's only a *little* more assertive. Reassure her, Corth."

The android stood up, but not to reassure her. "My appearance has not been changed, Tedra De Arr. Do I no longer appeal to you since you met the Sha-Ka'ari warrior?"

"So you filled him in about that, old girl?" Tedra asked with even more irritation.

"We've talked about them enough," Martha replied blithely. "I thought he shouldn't be left in the dark."

"That's your problem. You think too much." And now *Corth* needed reassurance. This was ridiculous.

"I love the way you look, Corth. You're more handsome than any man could possibly be."

And he was. His outer frame was crafted to her specifications, black hair at a moderate cut, lovely light green eyes, half a foot taller than she was, and young in appearance. If he were real, she'd likely beg to file for double occupancy. But she'd never lost touch with the fact that he wasn't real, even when she used him to fulfill her need to fantasize that she was loved and cared for.

"I just don't want to be chased around the ship by you, babe," she continued, only to hear a loud, heavy sigh from Martha's direction. "And *you* can cut that out," she told the computer. "You did this on purpose just to annoy me, and don't think I don't know it."

Martha didn't answer, but Corth was determined to prove how effective his new programming was. "But you would enjoy the breaching more with me, Tedra De Arr."

"No offense, Corth, but . . ." She paused as an unpleasant thought occurred to her. "Martha, *can* he be offended now?"

"No."

A small blessing. She addressed the android again. "It's like this, babe. I'd prefer my first sex-sharing to be with a real man. It's an emotional thing that I want to share with someone who will feel the same emotions I will."

"The Martha can give me emotions."

"She'd better not," Tedra growled, losing her patience. "Now hook yourself up to *the* Martha and rid yourself of the need to argue with me, or I'm going to pull your plug."

He hesitated very briefly, but a direct order from her was still impossible for him not to obey. When he came back to her a few minutes later, she demanded, "Are you as you were before?"

"I am as you want me to be, Tedra De Arr."

She sighed in relief. "I'm delighted. How about a game of Warfare to take my mind off this unpleasantness?"

With a nod he moved immediately to the imaging screen console to activate games mode and bring the screen out of its ceiling slot where it was stored when not in use. Since Warfare was a lifelike simulation of the real thing, played with real-looking people on a real-looking world, the game could only be played on an imaging screen. The one choice to make before the start of the game was the era of weaponry to use.

The Rover's screen was an eight-foot square, but some screens could be hundreds of feet square, depending on their location and size of the expected audience. Since imaging screens were mainly used for story viewing, the imaging computer could create a visual portrayal of any one of the millions of ancient stories in its files, again with very real-looking people enacting the stories. Of course, all stories, even those created thousands of years ago, were updated and made modern, which was a crying shame, since seeing them in their original form would have been like seeing history come to life. But most citizens of Kystran weren't familiar with their ancient history and had studied the modern history of the planet only since colonization, if even that. So few, if any, of the older stories would make sense to them if viewed in their original form.

Tedra took one of the six game chairs before the screen which contained controls for the few dozen games available that needed an imaging screen for play. There certainly wasn't anything else to do aboard a Rover but amuse herself. Had she got a World Discoverer, it would have been otherwise, for she had had enough training in her three years of study with World Discovery to be able to fly the small, one-manned craft by herself. On the Rover, she was left only with the job of ambassador and trade negotiator if and when they came upon any new worlds. And she fully intended to do the job, since she wanted at least something to show for her wasted time away from Kystran. But whatever trade contracts she could secure for Kystran would not be reported for the benefit of the new Director. They would wait until Garr Ce Bernn was returned to power.

Chapter Five

"*M*aybe I should have bought an intelligence model and had him reprogrammed for entertainment," Tedra remarked to herself as her eyes followed Corth about the large exercise gym where he was readying equipment for her use. "Their bodies aren't designed to be so . . . enticing."

"Did I hear that correctly?" Martha's voice purred from the small audiovisual ship's intercom on the wall behind her. "Have you changed your mind about our sweet Corth?"

"No." Tedra sighed and flopped back on the sweat mat, wishing Martha would lower her hearing level. "But if I could have spent a little more time with the warrior, Kowan, that answer might be different."

"Well, well," Martha said smugly. "So you would have let the Sha-Ka'ari breach you. I wonder why. Maybe because he could have bested you?"

"I doubt he could have, but for the first time it might have been close."

"And you think you'll have to settle for close? You've waited this long, kiddo. What's a few more years?"

"My, how you change your tune." Tedra chuckled. "So tell me, how compatible would I have been with that warrior?"

"As a temporary sex-sharer, he would have been ideal if you like brawn, which I happen to know you do. But he wouldn't have suited you for double occupancy.''

''Not even if he weren't the enemy?''

''Not even a little. You forget there are no free women on Sha-Ka'ar. Sha-Ka'ari males know no other women but slaves, and this for several hundred years.''

''So he would have tried to treat me like a slave, is that what you're getting at?''

''Not tried, kiddo. He would have. And it's just not in your makeup to be treated that way . . . not long-term, anyway.''

''What's *that* supposed to mean?''

''You could handle it for a while. You might even enjoy it once or twice for fun and games, as long as that's how you saw it.''

''You multipurpose piece of miswired circuitry, you're really looking for a fight, aren't you?'' Tedra growled low as she came up off the mat to glower at the small intercom screen, which showed a view of the Control Room and the main computer where Martha was housed.

''Just kidding, doll. But I do find it interesting that you'd be willing to consort with the enemy.''

''Women have been doing so since the beginning of time, for one desperate reason or another.''

''The key word being 'desperate,' I suppose?''

''The Tedra De Arr need never feel desperate,'' a new voice said behind her.

She stiffened as she felt Corth's hands on her hips and was very quickly pulled back and pressed against him for a reminder of just how fully functional he could be. Face flaming, she whirled around and pushed away from him.

''Martha!''

But she saw that the small intercom screen had gone blank, Martha pulling a disappearing act now that she'd been found out. That interfering metal nightmare, how dared she ignore a direct order?

Tedra glanced back warily at Corth, but he was merely watching her. "I thought you couldn't lie," she accused him.

"I cannot," he said placidly.

"Can't you? You said she'd changed you back. But she didn't, did she?"

"I am as you want me to be, Tedra De Arr." He repeated what he'd told her two days ago.

"And what has Martha got you believing I want you to be, Corth?"

"Patient. The Martha added patience to my new programming. I can wait until you are ready to use me."

"But in the meantime you're going to keep the pressure on, is that it?"

"If I do not remind you of my eagerness to give you pleasure, you will give no thought to changing your mind about my use."

Tedra rolled her eyes. Stars, how she wished Martha had a neck she could squeeze.

"Patience, huh? I'm the one who's going to have to have patience if I have to keep telling you to back off. You *will* back off, won't you, if I tell you to?"

"Of course."

"Then back off, babe. I'm here to exercise with machines, not you."

He just grinned—until she realized what she'd said, and then her laughter filled the room.

The sudden loud beat of bass drums shook even the walls, and Tedra was half out of bed before she realized it wasn't an invasion, just the music she had programmed to wake her, albeit with a bit too much volume.

"Lower, please!" she had to shout before the noise fell to a bearable level.

"How can you stand that Ancient's caterwauling?" Martha's voice came in with the quiet.

The Ancient's music did take getting used to with its accompanying words that most times didn't make sense, and wild beats and rhythms. Kystran music didn't include words, much less the things called drums. Ancient's music gave most Kystrani headaches, yet Tedra found it stimulating, usually feeling the need to tap her toes or move in some way when she listened to it. Right now her only need was to ignore Martha.

"You wouldn't answer me yesterday, coward. Today I'm not speaking to you," and she promptly buried her head under her pillow.

"Sec 1's are above sulking, kiddo."

She would have to hear that and agree that it was so. She threw off the pillow, and immediately Bolt, her robocleaner, came out to pick it up from the floor. She barely noticed.

Testily, she said, "I miss my bedmate, Martha."

"Then why did you send him away?"

"Because I don't trust him to just hold me anymore since you tampered with him."

Tedra called out the massager and climbed in, enclosing herself in the body-shaped box. It looked much like a meditech unit, only didn't possess so many miracles, just one, the easing of sore muscles, and she had a few after the strenuous exercise she had put herself through yesterday when she became furious over Martha's silence. The hundreds of little rollers and skin-pressers moved over her body from head to toe, almost putting her back to sleep, which was why the massager would open of its own accord after it had diligently worked top and then bottom muscles into loose relaxation.

She heard only the music when the massager opened up, but a glance at the audiovisual console the Commander's cabin contained showed the receiving light still on, so she knew Martha was waiting for her to say more. Tedra kept her waiting while she dropped her sleepsuit and took a solaray bath first, leaving the Sanitary walls open in case Martha showed any signs of impatience. Of course, that didn't take much time, and she was keeping herself waiting, too, to hear Martha's explanation.

"All right," she said at last, moving to the hair-and-eye changer, which had come out automatically when she activated the bath. "Why didn't you change Corth back like I told you to?"

"Because you needed the excitement of pursuit, kiddo."

Tedra groaned. For such a brilliant, free-thinking computer, Martha could be decidedly one-track.

"Then you should have contrived to smuggle Kowan aboard the Rover before we left," Tedra said, not really serious, but hoping to reinforce the fact that she wanted a real man before she ever considered using an artificial one. Though she'd said so, Martha's memory banks were playing forgetful. "I could have kept him in lockup and got all the excitement I could have asked for."

"I thought about it," Martha admitted.

She probably had, which only made Tedra realize she might as well give up. Martha was going to keep involving herself in Tedra's sex life until she had one, and *then* she'd probably come up with a good dozen reasons why Tedra ought to abstain. She'd either have to ignore the computer or go nuts.

She settled on ignoring. "Surprise me," she told the hair changer, and then actually was. "How old-fashioned," she said, seeing her original glossy black tresses spilling over her shoulders.

"How about silver eyes with gold sparkles to go with that?" came Martha's voice.

Tedra glanced at the console to see that the viewing screen had come on so Martha could monitor her. She'd forgotten that Martha could see, too, one of the skills necessary to flying spacecraft.

"No, as long as I've started out old-fashioned, I might as well go all the way with my own colors for a change." And she ordered the eye changer to erase the previous artificial tint. What remained was a clear, light aquamarine. Glancing in the mirror, Tedra smiled. "I'd forgotten how striking my own colors are together. What do you think, Martha?"

"No one would believe you are a Sec, doll."

"So now you know why I need to go bland when I'm working," Tedra replied.

"Too bad. You'd have been breached ages ago if—"

"Cut it out."

"Well, you would have."

"It might have been tried, but it wouldn't have happened without my cooperation. Now, how about leaving me alone so I can clothe myself in peace."

"In another Rover uniform in boring dun gray, which is all I've seen you in since we left Kystran? Not today, kiddo. One of those long slinky things that Supply filled your closet with ought to go over well, something teal with lots of sparkling Canture gems.

Canture does mine the best quality jewels in the Star System.''

"What's with you this morning, Martha? You know I never wear feminine clothing that can constrict my legs and hamper my movements.''

"Then what about one of the short skimpy things that show off so much skin? *They're* certainly not restricting.''

"Would you like to tell me why I would want to wear one of those hot-weather outfits when the Rover is air-cooled? Are you planning on turning up the heat . . . or have you programmed Corth to jump on me if I show him some skin?''

"Neither.'' There was what passed for a sigh. "It looks like I've found you a planet, is all. Thought you might want to dazzle the prospective traders. That *is* what those flashy trade-courting outfits are in your closet for.''

"Of all the . . . Why didn't you just *say* so, Martha, instead of going round the block to annoy me? I *know* that's why Supply stuffed my closet with such outrageous outfits. It's standard World Discovery procedure to impress the natives with a little sparkle. Are we close enough to Transfer yet?''

"We've been orbiting about two hours now.''

"And you let me sleep!''

"The planet's not going anywhere, kiddo.'' The screen went blank, leaving Tedra to swear a blue steak without benefit of an audience.

Chapter Six

"Not bad, kiddo," Martha remarked as Tedra entered the Control Room, the heart of the Rover with its numerous flashing grids and monitors that kept constant tabs on every function of the ship. "I concede to your own tastes."

Tedra raised the coffee cup she carried to acknowledge the compliment. She had chosen to wear a close-fitting, two-piece outfit of pants and long-sleeved tunic that covered her from neck to ankles, the material opalescent pearl with a high-gloss sheen to make it glow jewellike in bright light. If that wasn't impressive enough, she had draped it with a double-strand necklace of large kystrals, the clear crystal mined on Kystran's single moon that was even more prized than Canture gems, because the live crystals would change color upon request to look like any gem imaginable. Tedra had requested blood red in a brighter hue than the fiery red that occasionally appeared to mix with the other colors in the opalescent outfit.

Her long hair was drawn severely back and coiled on top of her head, held in place by a three-inch-long pearl band that lifted it up and away from her head, to then fall in a thick tail down her back. Her low boots were silver, matching the utility belt that already held a combination phazor/computer link unit that would see to all her needs in one innocent-looking rectangular box. Inside the belt was a homing signal so that Martha couldn't lose track of her in a crowd.

Corth had been sitting in the Commander's chair, keeping Martha company. He got up as Tedra entered, but she waved him down, too nervous to sit herself. Now that she actually had a planet to investigate, she'd be using Transfer for the first time, and she still remembered the nightmares she had had for nearly two years after she had first learned about Molecular Transfer, the means to get from ship to planet and back without benefit of spacecraft or landing. One second you stood surrounded by metal walls and flashing grids on board ship, and the next your feet were planted firmly on whatever planet you'd been sent to. It didn't take even a full second to Transfer. Just pop, and you were in a new location.

Transfer was made possible only on crysillium-powered spacecraft, which the Rover just happened to be, crysillium being the highest source of energy known to man, and the only thing strong enough to allow a safe Transfer. It was that word ''safe'' that had got to a child of seven, which was how old she'd been in her second year of Explorations study when the class learned of Transfer, making her active mind imagine all kinds of things that could go wrong, that *she'd* be the only one Transfer wouldn't work on, that she'd end up lost somewhere between Transfers, wherever that was, and no one would ever find her. Switching to Military Arts at eight, she thought she'd never have to experience Transfer, but she'd still had the nightmares about it for another year.

She might be an adult now and know that those childhood fears had been silly, but the nervousness was there anyway. As long as Martha didn't detect it and ride her about it, she'd be all right. And once the

Transfer was made she could relax—until she had to go through it again.

"So where is it?" she asked, walking toward the four observation screens that divided the area surrounding the ship into quarters for viewing, but were all blank presently. And then the left top screen came on to reveal a huge blue-and-green sphere, and Tedra gasped. "It has vegetation!"

"We're a bit far from our own Star System to trade for food, kiddo," Martha felt it necessary to point out.

"I wasn't thinking of trading for it. I just want to see it. I've never thought it was fair that Kystran citizens are forbidden to visit their own space gardens."

"Contamination, doll. If you want to eat it, you have to keep away from it."

"I know." Tedra sighed. "But look at all that green. It's certainly prettier to look at from up here than Kystran's drab brown and gray. So tell me. If there's plant life, there must be other life. Is any of it humanoid?"

"The wide-range scanner indicates it's not an overly populated planet, but there are enough people in small groupings, probably their idea of cities, so you won't have trouble making contact."

"Do I get lucky with a known language you have on file, or will I have to trudge through universal communication?"

"I've spot-checked in each hemisphere with the short-range scanner that picks up voices, and the language appears to be the same worldwide, with only slight differences in accent." Short-range scanning could pick up clear conversations, but only in a five-foot radius. Anything on a larger scale would be just a jumble of noise. "It's a language you've recently learned, too—Sha-Ka'ari."

Tedra stiffened and turned around to glare at the huge computer that took up an entire wall, plus a huge console base in the center of the Control Room. "Did I miss something while I was sleeping, like an unscheduled trip home?"

Martha brought forth her offended tone. "You are fully aware that Kystran is three weeks, four days, eighteen hours, eleven—"

"I know how far away it is, damn it! Just tell me that's not Sha-Ka'ar down there."

"It's not."

"But you're picking up their language?" Tedra asked. "There's no mistake?"

"I don't make mistakes." The offended tone was stronger.

Tedra sighed and looked back at the observation screen. "Sorry, Martha."

"Wait a minute! I'm going to short-circuit."

"Oh, shut up," Tedra said with a chuckle. "You'd think I never apologized to anyone."

"I only think it because it's true."

"Let's keep to the subject, please. Can this find of ours be the Sha-Ka'ari mother planet?"

"Good possibility."

"*Not* good," Tedra groaned.

"Not necessarily," Martha disagreed. "You must remember that the Sha-Ka'ari showed up in Centura Star System about three hundred years ago. They don't remember where they came from, having brought no records with them, and remember very little about how they got to their new planet, only that they were captured to mine for silver, and ended up killing their captors and taking over the planet instead. We can't know how this world here has evolved in that amount of time. Also, the Sha-Ka'ari were conquerors, and conquerors tend to enslave the conquered. It goes with the territory. It doesn't mean they were taken from a slaveholding planet. So you don't really know what you have down there, except it'd be a good guess to expect a warrior class of men . . . and I don't like that look on your face."

"Are you kidding, Martha!" Tedra came back excitedly, the idea falling on her in full bloom.

She had been going nuts with frustration, thinking about all those Kystran women being forced into slavery, friends of hers, women like herself who would fight against it, and keep on fighting until they either were killed or succumbed to madness. They had to be rescued, somehow, and before there was nothing left of their former selves. And here, miraculously, was the how.

"Crad Ce Moerr used the Sha-Ka'ari to take over Kystran," she continued. "It'd be poetic justice if we could use their ancestors to get it back. After all, our weapons were proven useless against them, and we aren't sword-wielders ourselves. But warriors just like them—"

"I only said it was a good guess."

"But if they are—"

"Maybe they can't be bought."

"And maybe they can, so stop arguing with me. I'll find out one way or the other after I go down."

"I wouldn't just jump right in with the big question, were I you. Asking them to fight their own kind might not go over too well, you know."

"I know how to test the waters, old girl. I do have another reason for being here, after all."

"And if it's a 'no-go' after you take the plunge?"

"Then maybe I can trade for *Toreno* steel. Sword-wielding can be learned with practice."

If Martha had eyes, they would have rolled. She settled for a few unnecessary flashes on her display grids.

"The gravity was slightly off, but you've been slowly acclimated to it since you entered my domain, so it won't take you by surprise when you get down there. The air is purer than you're accustomed to, but that won't be a problem."

"How's the weather?"

"Moderately warm directly below, which is in the southern hemisphere. I would suggest a private Transfer, a mile or two away from any settlements. No point in dropping their jaws with a pop into the midst of them. Might get your head hacked off that way."

"Very funny."

"I thought so," Martha gloated.

"And the time of day?"

"Midmorning. But I can have you on the other side of the planet in a flash if you'd prefer to arrive at night, when there's less chance you'll be seen making Transfer."

"I might not be seen, but then *I* wouldn't see much either. Right here's just fine, and if that's it . . . ?"

"Not so fast, kiddo. Where's your lazor unit?"

"The phazor combo will do."

"Not if you have to use it repeatedly."

"I'm officially here to negotiate trade, Martha, not wipe out the planet. And if I start killing them, I'll never get their help. The phazor will go me a long way on stun. It's only when it's set to demolish that the power drains. And the lazor looks too much like a weapon. World Discovery frowns on its use, and

I'm a World Discoverer for now, not a Sec. If I get into trouble I'll tell you, and you can Transfer me back.''

"Then make sure you keep the link open.''

"Not to worry, old girl. That's standard procedure with first Transfer. And your scanners should have informed you that my homing signal has been activated, and it can't be turned off. You couldn't lose me if you tried. So go ahead and Transfer. I'm ready.''

"You are, huh? What's with the face?''

Tedra sighed and unsqueezed her eyes, and found Corth standing in front of her.

"I wish you a safe Transfer, Tedra De Arr.''

"I *really* wish you hadn't said that, Corth.''

But he was on a one-track program. "And until you return . . .''

He picked her up and kissed her, and Tedra had the absurd thought that those couldn't be mechanical lips, they really couldn't. When he set her back on her feet, he was grinning. She didn't have the heart to get mad.

"Okay, babe, you made your point. I'll *think* about it when I get back." And then, "I'm ready, Martha.''

She closed her eyes again and waited, but nothing happened. When she opened her eyes again, she was on another world.

Chapter Seven

*T*he tree limb was becoming uncomfortable to lie upon, but it would not be much longer now. The *taraan* was moving steadily closer, only forty *yarid* away now, and it was large enough that it was worth the wait. With this kill, there would be enough meat to end the hunt and return to Sha-Ka-Ra the next sunrise.

Challen Ly-San-Ter did not often find time to hunt with his warriors anymore. Since he became *shodan* of Sha-Ka-Ra, his duty was to remain in the city to be available to the needs of his people, not to enjoy himself with his warriors, which had been his pleasure before he was *shodan*.

The *taraan* would be his third kill since sunrising, but the two small *kisrak* now tied to his *hataar* would merely provide food for this rising. Challen was, in fact, feeling hunger pangs as he thought of roasted *kisrak*, and willed the *taraan* to approach at a more swift pace, but of course it did not. He was several *reyzi* from camp, so it would be a while yet before his belly could be satisfied, even if the *taraan* could be brought down in the next few moments.

It was perhaps his wandering thoughts of food that caused Challen to miss seeing the woman enter the clearing, for suddenly she was just there, standing in the path between him and the *taraan*. How it was possible for him *not* to have noticed her coming, when the *bracs* and *comtoc* she wore glowed like gaali stones, he could not say. But she was there now. There was no doubting what he was seeing—just that he was seeing it, for women did not cover themselves in the clothes of warriors, nor did they venture out without a warrior at their side, yet this woman was alone.

He would wager his *hataar* she was not of the servant class. No servant would possess such unusual, but obviously fine, clothes, or own jewels of the like around her neck. But she was not from any city in Kan-is-Tra, of that he was certain. The black hair was foreign to Kan-is-Tra. The clothes seemed foreign, too. Perhaps she was of Ba-Tar-ah in the far north. That country was known to have strange customs, and perhaps allowing their women to wear warrior's clothing was one of them. But what was she doing here?

He was still pondering it when the *taraan* also noticed the woman and started to leap away in fright. She turned then, hearing the movement, and pointed with her arm in the direction of the noise. The *taraan* simply fell to the ground—and a low growl came out of Challen's throat. Her unusual presence was one thing. Stealing his kill was another, though he could not begin to guess how she had brought the animal down.

He was about to make his own presence known in a very aggressive way when she spoke, nothing that he understood, and not to him surely, for she still faced the *taraan*. That she did not approach the animal gave him pause, and when she turned away from it, he was pacified. So she did not want the *taraan*. But then why kill it? And *how* had she killed it?

She was facing him again, looking at the trees surrounding the area, perhaps for more animals, and still talking to herself. This time Challen noticed the small white box she held in her hand. Thin and rectangular, could this be what had killed the *taraan?* No, such was not possible. Boxes could not kill, and even if they could, the laws forbade women to carry weapons. It was time he found out just who this woman was.

Tedra was jumpy now after being startled by the deerlike animal. Her instinct for self-preservation had canceled her common sense, stunning the poor thing before she even saw what it was. It would be a long while before it revived, and might become food for something else before it did.

"I don't know why you're blaming yourself, kiddo," Martha remarked, having seen the incident happen from the tiny viewer on the front of the phazor, *and* hearing Tedra's choice swearing over what she'd done. "It couldn't have been helped."

"I shouldn't have had the stun set so high," Tedra said to the larger two-way viewer on the flat side of the unit as she lowered the setting. "I'm in the middle of nowhere, for Stars' sake, and can see anything coming at me with plenty of time to raise the stun if necessary. If that creature had been any smaller than it is, it would have been demolished."

"Look, it's your first time setting foot on another world. You're bound to be nervous, which is perfectly natural, but unfortunately, they aren't likely to have any Stress Clinics down there to help you out."

"Get serious, will you?"

"Just keep your finger off the stun button, and try taking a few deep breaths before your next reaction."

"I'll do . . . oh, my."

"What?"

"Talk about getting knocked off your feet," Tedra said with a good deal of awe.

"Did you fall down, doll?"

"It sure feels like it. Take a look." She pointed the unit at what had dropped down from a tree in front of her not ten feet away.

" 'Oh, my' was kind of an understatement, I'd say." The voice in the box was duly impressed. "Is he as big as he looks from here?"

"Bigger. Stars, he's got to be nearly seven feet! What is he, do you suppose, besides a giant?"

"An accurate guess would be a barbarian, what the Sha-Ka'ari would still be if they hadn't been touched by the advanced worlds in our Star System."

"A barbarian . . . farden hell," Tedra said in disappointment. An arrogant warrior was one thing. A barbarian warrior was another matter entirely. "Maybe I better return to the Rover."

"Aren't you giving up a bit soon?"

"That's a damn big sword he's holding in his hand, Martha."

"That's a damn powerful phazor you're holding in yours, kiddo."

Tedra grinned then. "That's right, isn't it? What do I have to be wary about? And he is magnificent, isn't he?"

That was another understatement. He put the handsome Kowan to shame, in height, brawn, and looks. Even Corth, whose features were artificially perfect, paled next to the barbarian. This was dominant maleness personified, arms, legs, chest, everything larger than anything she'd ever seen before. Dark golden brows sat low over his eyes, with barely an arch to be seen. The chin was square and aggressive, with the slightest shadow of a cleft; the lips a slashing line with no hint of humor. Skin deep gold, only a little lighter than wavy long hair, which fell just short of massive shoulders—bare shoulders. He wore only a pair of buttery soft black leather pants for clothing, skin-tight and molded to those thick-muscled legs. Calf-high boots were in the same soft leather, and from wrist to elbow was strapped an intricately carved arm shield. His only other accessories were the wide sword belt about his hips and a large gold disc the size of her fist hanging down to the center of his massive chest.

She hadn't realized she had been looking him over so thoroughly, or for so long, until her eyes happened to meet his. "Why is he looking at me like that, Martha?" she asked uneasily. The barbarian wasn't exactly frowning, but the whole look of him had turned to one of high displeasure.

"Maybe because he doesn't understand a word you've been saying. Or maybe because he's never heard a box speak. You can bet your krystals he's never encountered anything like *me* before, and you don't come under the heading of normal either. You'd better introduce yourself, kiddo, before he decides you're an evil vision he should try to banish. After all, we don't know how primitive their beliefs are."

His dark eyes had indeed gone to her phazor unit while Martha spoke. His sword came up a little, and Tedra took a step back.

"I think you've hit it on the nose, old girl," Tedra said thoughtfully. "I'm going to turn you off for a while, so you aren't tempted to butt in."

"Now wait—"

The link went dead, and Tedra smiled. She hadn't been able to do that on the Rover with Martha in control of every communications outlet in sight. It was a distinct pleasure to be able to do it now. Martha could still hear what was going on through the short-range scanner which was locked onto her homing signal. She just couldn't talk back.

Tedra's smile had been intercepted, and although it wasn't for the barbarian, his sword tip returned to point at the ground and she relaxed a tiny bit. He hadn't said anything yet, and she had to wonder if he might have seen her pop into his world. He could be in shock if that was the case, or thinking her some type of devil or witch—if these people believed in such things or their equivalent. She'd best dispel that notion if it was there.

"Greetings, warrior." She switched to Sha-Ka'ari to be understood, and it was a safe bet he was a warrior, so calling him one shouldn't offend him. "I hope I didn't startle you with my appearance. If I did, I can explain, but it's complicated and best left for later." No answer, which she could take either way. "I'm called Tedra De Arr."

She raised her hand in the universal sign of friendship. It was wasted on the barbarian, who didn't recognize it. But his expression said he did understand her words. After listening to her Kystrani, he had revealed a slight surprise when she began to speak in his language. But she obviously hadn't reassured him enough for him to put away his sword.

She tried again. "I come in friendship—"

"Why are you dressed so, woman?"

The sound of his voice did some startling as well. It was deep and authoritative—and arrogant. She had given him her name, but still he called her woman. Well, she had known it wouldn't be easy dealing with barbarians. And she could have kicked herself for not realizing a primitive like this would find her clothing fantastical.

"These are the clothes of my people," she started to explain.

"They are the clothes of warriors."

So that was it. He wasn't amazed by the material, just that she was wearing what he would consider the clothing of men only. From her Relics tapes, she knew there had been a time when the Ancients from Kystran's mother planet had held the same primitive belief that women didn't belong in pants.

Tedra didn't care to get into a long discussion about progress, not with him anyway. It was the leaders of his planet, the *shodani,* whom she needed to impress with the wonders of the advanced worlds, not a mere warrior.

To avoid the issue for now, she said simply, "I found it necessary to borrow these."

"You will remove them."

"Now just a—"

"Remove them, woman."

He didn't raise his voice. He didn't have to with that tone. It was an order he fully expected to be obeyed, and Tedra had a moment's inclination to obey him with all speed, which was crazy. She wasn't a helpless female who was subject to a man's will. She was sorry he was offended by her outfit, but that was just too bad. She wasn't removing anything, not for him or anyone else.

"Are you going to tell me your women aren't allowed clothing?" she asked suspiciously. If that was the case, she was leaving right now.

"They wear the *chauri.*"

"Well, then," she replied agreeably. "If you'll just produce a *chauri* for me, I might consider changing. Otherwise, I'll keep . . . what . . ."

Her words died off as his sword came up and around to slide into its scabbard before he started walking toward her. At that point she didn't have a single doubt of his intention. Her reasonable offer was not being considered. He'd ordered her to remove her clothes, and since she hadn't, he was going to do the removing himself.

"Now, look, warrior, I can't let you . . . you'd better stop right . . . I said stop!"

He didn't, and the distance was closing fast between them—too fast. She couldn't think how to reach him with words, if anything could reach something that looked that determined. But she wasn't about to let anything that big get close enough to get his hands on her.

"Farden fool," she hissed under her breath before pointing her phazor and pressing stun.

He was stopped instantly. He even remained on his feet, as big and wide as they were. She was too furious to appreciate that. This wasn't the way to start friendly relations. The barbarian wouldn't realize what she had done to him when he came out of it, but that wasn't the point.

She opened the computer link to demand, "Did you hear all that, Martha? Can you believe such arrogance?"

"Am I to assume you've put him on hold?"

"What else could I do? He was about to steal the clothes right off my body."

"Maybe you should have let him, kiddo. It would almost guarantee some *very* friendly negotiations."

"Very funny," Tedra said, only the possibility wasn't in the least revolting.

She couldn't deny the strong attraction she had felt on first sight of the barbarian. She had been hit with a jolt of sensation similar to what she experienced when Kowan had kissed her, yet the barbarian hadn't even been close to her. She felt it again now, staring at him. And now that it was safe to do so, she was drawn to him for a closer look.

All that bare skin and visible muscle was irresistible, and she gave into the urge, hesitantly placing her fingers to his chest, then more surely. The skin was warm, soft to the touch, but with no flexibility, like velvet-covered rock. As her exploration moved down to his hip, she discovered the leather of his pants was as buttery soft as it had looked, and she couldn't help wondering how a backward culture like his could produce something of a manufactured quality.

The steel wrapped around his left forearm did indeed look like *Toreno,* but she couldn't test that without firing at it when he was conscious, to see if the stun beam would be deflected or put him out again. She didn't think he'd appreciate her using him for testing, and she felt bad enough already that she'd had to stun him at all. Her sense of fair play was outraged at having hit him with something he didn't know was coming, especially since it had only been one on one, where she could have discouraged him in any number of other ways if she hadn't panicked because of his size.

The upper arms, Stars, she couldn't even get her hands halfway around the muscled expanse. Moving to stand directly in front of him, she felt small and vulnerable, an alien feeling it was hard to shake off. But her head likely didn't even reach his shoulders, and that chest was so wide, she had nothing to compare it with.

He really was a good foot taller than she was, and it was a strain on her neck to try and look up at him that close. But when she stepped back to examine his face, the dark eyes made her uneasy. They were probably brown, but such a dark shade they appeared sable black, and they seemed to be looking right at her with an awareness that couldn't possible be there.

"Let me take a wild guess at what all that silence means," came Martha's dry tone through the unit.

Tedra's cheeks scalded. Damned computer. How in the farden hell did she do that, when the unit had been pointed away from the barbarian so she couldn't see what Tedra was doing?

"I'm only human," Tedra grumbled, knowing it was useless to deny she'd taken advantage of the barbarian's unconscious state. "He can't be offended by what he doesn't know, can he?" Silence met that question, and Tedra felt a certain dread, staring at those dark eyes that continued to stare right back at her. "Martha?"

"I hate to break up your party, kiddo, but I seriously doubt the stunning worked properly on such a large specimen as that, not on the low setting I'm reading on your unit. There's something in the atmosphere down there—"

"*What* didn't work?" Tedra cut in, shouting, "He's immobilized!"

"Yes, but I don't think his mind was put on hold. I think he can hear you, feel you—"

"You're heading for the junkyard, Martha, I swear you are! Why in hell didn't you tell me immediately? Are you trying to get me raped?"

"Would it be rape?" Martha came back placidly. "I didn't miss that 'oh, my,' doll."

Tedra was so furious she slammed her fist down on the link button, afraid she'd stomp the unit into the ground if she heard another word from Martha. But worse than her fury was her mortification, and that increased to the limit when she met those sable eyes again, and did feel that they were seeing her with perfect clarity. Awake. The barbarian was awake and aware of everything she had done, and that thought made her jump back so quickly she stumbled. But landing on her backside didn't embarrass her any further. Nothing could be worse than what she already felt.

Looking up at him again, she saw that the eyes had even followed her to the ground, and all she wanted to do was roll over and bury her head. She got up instead and came back to him. She had to take advantage again to explain while he still couldn't move and was forced to listen to her.

"Look, I'm sorry, I really am. I shouldn't have examined you like that, warrior. I had no right, and my only excuse is . . . curiosity . . . yes, that's what happened. My curiosity got the better of me. The men don't grow as big as you where I come from. They're more my size, which can't mean much to you, but was pretty big to me until I began meeting Sha-Ka'ari warriors, but even they weren't as big as you. Wouldn't you be curious about something you'd never seen the like of before?"

He *was* listening. He couldn't help but listen. And that was another thing. People coming out of stun usually felt just a slight disorientation, but no remembrance of being stunned or even of a time lapse. They might wonder about the scene around them being different, like missing people who had been there before, but unless they saw the phazor beforehand and recognized it for what it was, they passed the incident off as being unexplainable and dismissed it. The barbarian, however, being awake, *knew* he couldn't move, knew something had been done to him, and was probably experiencing a lot of confusion and even some fear. He had probably never in his life been so confined, and he wouldn't be liking it one bit, but he had brought it on himself. She wasn't taking the blame for that, too.

"If you had just stopped when I requested it, warrior, I wouldn't have had to stun you. But the condition is only temporary. You'll be as good as new when you come out of it. It was supposed to render you unconscious, but my setting was too low, and you're too big . . . and I figure you'll probably try to take it from me now, though I can't let you do that. I've already raised the setting. Next time it will knock you out, and I'm only telling you this so there won't be a next time. I don't like stunning people any more than they like being stunned, so if you'll just keep your distance from me until we can come to some sort of agreement, I won't have to use the phazor on you again. Is that too much to ask? I'm not here to cause trouble or hurt anyone. I'm here to trade with you people, and maybe more, but that's for your *shodan* to decide. If you could agree to take me to—''

Tedra shrieked, he moved so fast when he came out of stun, too fast for her reflexes to accomplish anything except try to get out of the way. She wasn't quite successful either. He obtained what he was after, ripping the phazor unit from her hand and throwing it a good distance away from him, while she ended up tripping over her feet again. She wasn't usually so clumsy, and it was disgusting that she should be now. She sprawled on the ground, and this time she was looking up at an awake, aware, and *movable* barbarian.

Chapter Eight

Challen was too angry for words, but most of it was self-directed, and none of it showed. He had acted most foolishly in approaching the woman after seeing firsthand what she had done to the *taraan* with her small box. That she had done the same to him was no more than he deserved for that foolishness. How she had done it was less important, since it would not happen again. But he had let a mild annoyance over her clothes get the better of him, something a *shodan* should not have done.

Her—examination of him was another matter. He had not liked it, but only because he could not respond to it accordingly, and the basis of most of his anger now was the simple fact that he still could not give the woman what her boldness had demanded of him. If he had not taken the juice of the *dhaya* plant that morning, as warriors usually did when they had been long on the hunt, she would be under him already and receiving the proper instruction on how to deal with a warrior. But taken undiluted, the *dhaya* juice prevented the need for a woman, in fact made it impossible to take one, which was why it was used on raids to keep warriors' minds from being distracted by female captives, and on hunts. Taken mixed with wine, it served another purpose, that of keeping children from being conceived by just any woman, for only the life-mate of a warrior could bear his children.

This woman intrigued him with her strange way of speaking that ran words together, and her other language that made no sense at all. She was also very pleasing to look upon, something his distraction with her clothing had kept him from noticing fully until she had approached him. And that boldness, by the stones of gaali, he had never known the like of. Women expressed their needs and desires with words and looks, and hoped a warrior would be interested. They did not touch without first receiving expressed encouragement to do so, since their place was to give, not to take.

Challen smiled finally, remembering that the woman was here before him without a man at her side, which made her claimable if he so desired to offer her his protection. She might be a woman of the higher classes, if her raiments were any indication, but the laws pertained to all women, servant and highborn alike. He could claim her or use her, the choice his, her ignoring the law losing her the right to refuse him.

It was a law Challen had never taken advantage of before. Women came to the *shodan* for protection, the old ones, widows, the orphans. There had never been the need to find one to claim, when he had more than made for a peaceful household. Of course, those who sought his protection could not be used, did they not offer themselves for use. But one who was claimed had no say in the matter.

Tedra didn't like the smile that came her way. It was too full of satisfaction to warrant her any good. So the barbarian thought the tables were turned now, did he? She would just have to disabuse him of that notion.

"You might have thrown my phazor aside," she

said as she sat up. "But that doesn't mean I'm defenseless, so don't get any ideas we'll both regret."

His smile didn't waver, and it wasn't hard to tell he found her words amusing. "You are alone, woman, without the protection of a warrior, which indeed makes you defenseless—and claimable. You should have begged my protection immediately, for then I would have been bound to give it. Since you did not, you declared yourself claimable."

Tedra frowned. "If that means what I think it means, you can forget it. I didn't declare myself anything, and I don't need anyone's protection."

That got rid of his smile, though there was no other indication that her words annoyed him. "I am claiming you, woman. Do you mean to resist my claim?"

"I'm not going to let you rape me, if that's what you call resistance."

"There is no rape in a claiming. Your lack of protection denies you your right to resist."

"But I wasn't without protection. That phazor you tossed away was all the protection I needed. It stopped you, didn't it?"

He did not like that reminder. "Your weapon is strange to me, but weapon it is, and women are forbidden the use of weapons. Since they are so forbidden, only a man's protection can prevent a claiming."

She wasn't getting through to him, but that didn't stop her from trying again. "What if I can prevent it?"

He crouched down by her feet, his hands now within reach of her. The urge was strong to draw her legs up and away from him, remembering how fast he had moved before. She remained as she was, however, sitting on the ground, her legs outstretched as if she had nothing to worry about. She had more than her share of worries, though. Martha, who could hear what was going on, could Transfer her out of this situation, but Tedra knew she wouldn't. Martha would be all for her getting raped by this barbarian, probably thinking it was just what she needed. That farden computer was forever deciding she knew best when it came to Tedra's needs.

"You have other strange weapons I have yet to see?" the barbarian asked her.

"Strange by your standards, but not by mine."

She'd caught his curiosity now. "Do you show me these weapons, woman."

"And spoil the surprise? Do I look dumb, warrior?"

He laughed. She liked the sound. She liked him. Too bad he was insisting on this claiming business. She couldn't afford to be claimed by a man on this world when she wouldn't be staying here for very long, and when she had negotiating to do that just might be the salvation of her planet. Her own personal inclinations couldn't get in the way of that.

When his humor had run its course, his eyes came back to her glowing with appreciation. "Whatever surprises you have hidden will be revealed when we have seen to your *bracs* and *comtoc.*"

Tedra didn't try to hide her groan. It was loud and long. "That again? I thought I made myself clear on that score. Didn't you get yourself stung trying to take my clothes before? They're staying on me and that's that. They wouldn't fit you anyway."

He gave a snort, letting her know what he thought of that last crack, but she'd already known he didn't want the clothes for himself. He just didn't want her wearing them. And he was staring at her thoughtfully now, increasing her nervousness with his being so close.

"You are claimed, woman. As well you know, this means you must yield to my will. Yet you continue to defy me, risking punishment. I have never met a woman who would willingly court punishment."

He was either genuinely perplexed by her attitude or subtly letting her know what would happen if she didn't buckle under to his demands. Tedra's tokens were on the latter, and she had never liked threats, subtle or otherwise.

"You still haven't met one, warrior. What you're missing here is the fact that I've never heard of your farden claiming before, so how can I know the rules or regulations pertaining to it? It's a word the Sha-Ka'ari use, so one I know, but not in the sense that *you're* using it. But above and beyond that, I simply won't be claimed. It sounds suspiciously like slavery to me, and I'll kill the man who tries to enslave me— which reminds me of something I should have asked right up front. *Do* you people own slaves?"

She could see he was dying to address some of her other points first, but deigned to answer her question anyway. "We have no need of slavery in Kan-is-Tra. There are servants aplenty in the Darasha, those of this land who were conquered many centuries ago. There are countries to the east that make slaves of their captives, but Kan-is-Tran warriors deal differently with captives."

"How differently?"

"They are treated as claimed women."

"All right," she sighed, "what's the differences between the two?"

"A claimed woman cannot be misused, sold, or killed, as is frequently done with a slave. She can also become the mother of a warrior's children if he chooses to so honor her. What she cannot do is deny her warrior's will.''

''And if she does?''

''You have already been told the consequences of such action.''

''Punishment, when you just said she couldn't be misused,'' Tedra spat out.

''There are ways to punish that cause little harm.''

She'd just bet there were, and he likely knew every farden one. ''Well, I'm glad we got that cleared up. I had a feeling your claiming wouldn't be to my liking, and I was right. You're just going to have to ignore the fact that I didn't come here accompanied by . . . wait a minute.'' She grinned suddenly. ''I don't mean to be rude, but''—she switched to Kystrani—''Martha, I want you to send Corth down here immediately. I don't need the aggravation this barbarian is giving me. I've got a job to do, and I can't do it if I have to fight every warrior I come across who tries to claim me. Corth will satisfy their idea of protection. Martha? Come on, damn it, I know you can hear me.'' She waited a moment more, and held up her hand when the barbarian started to speak. ''Martha, if you cross me on this, I swear I'll get even. I'm not down here to get breached, as much as you'd love to see it otherwise. Now stop fooling around and send me Corth!''

Nothing, and the barbarian was done waiting. ''Why do you talk to yourself, woman, and in words that make no sense?''

''I'm talking to Martha. She's the voice you might have heard coming out of my phazor unit.''

''But you turned the voice off. I saw you do this.''

''She can still hear me.''

"Even though she is not here? Is she a God, then?"

"Yes, I suppose you could say Martha is like a God," Tedra said bitterly, and added in a Kystrani aside, "Don't choke laughing over that one, you farden traitor." Then, to the barbarian again, "She could make me disappear if she chose to, or send me down a male who would pass for the protection you say I need. She obviously chooses to do neither, but to leave me to deal with you myself."

Doubt was written all over him, telling her he didn't believe a word of that. "I had thought you from Ba-Tar-ah in the far north, but the Ba-Tar-ahi speak as we do. From what country do you come, woman, that your other words have no meaning? From this Sha-Ka'ari you have spoken of?"

"Sha-Ka'ari is your language, my big friend, not mine. I come from Kystran, not another country here, but another planet. I'm here to trade with your people, to offer them the wonders of my world."

"Another planet." He grinned, and Tedra knew he still wasn't buying any of it. "How does one come from another planet?"

"In a spaceship," Tedra gritted out, then added much louder, "Which Martha could show you if she'd just realize I'm *making a breakthrough here.*"

"The Kystran woman has a talent for storytelling." The barbarian chuckled. "I am not displeased. I will look forward to more of your amusing tales."

"Damn it, I really am here to trade—and maybe hire some mercenaries if some of you warriors are interested. I need to speak with your *shodan.* Can't you at least hold off with this claiming nonsense until I've had a chance to prove—"

He waved her to silence. "A woman would not be entrusted with such a task, with trade or the hiring of warriors. Too long have you worn these warrior's clothes, I think. They have let you believe you can do as you please, but such is not so.''

He didn't tell her to remove them again. His arm stretched out toward her, intending to grasp her hand to bring her to him so he could see to the matter himself. But Tedra wasn't having any of that. She caught his arm in both hands and tugged, dropped back for the pull, and raised her legs to help send the barbarian flying over her head. It worked, even with his colossal weight, but only because she'd used the additional kick of her legs. She was on her feet the moment the move was completed. The barbarian was now flat on his back.

He stayed like that for about ten seconds, then sat up and looked over his shoulder at her. He didn't look mad. He didn't look surprised either. She had a suspicion the barbarian rarely showed what he was feeling.

"I am going to assume, woman, that you knew not what you were about."

"You can do that, but I wouldn't recommend it. There's more where that came from."

"Then you have challenged me." It wasn't a question, and he gave a short bark of laughter before he got to his feet. "By the stones of gaali, you have solved the problem of your own resistance."

"I have?" she said blankly, then, "Wait a minute. I'm not challenging you, barbarian. All I did was defend my right to keep the clothes on my back."

"A claimed woman has no rights, and you have indeed challenged me. I now accept the challenge. The choice of weapons is mine."

He was serious, she realized, and had a sinking feeling there was no way out of it. He saw this as the answer to some problem he had faced and was absolutely delighted that she'd solved it for him.

"I suppose you're going to hack me to pieces with that sword of yours?"

He merely grinned at her. "You could not even lift a warrior's sword, *kerima*, if there was one here for your use. No, I will choose weaponless combat, of which you appear to have some knowledge."

It was Tedra's turn to grin. "If you insist."

He was not expecting such easy compliance. "You understand the outcome of a challenge?"

"No, but I'm sure you're dying to tell me."

He grunted at her nonchalance. "The victor can demand death or service of the defeated one. No other thing can he demand."

"In other words, the loser can't buy his way free of this service, should service be chosen?"

"There is no avoidance of service if it is chosen."

"What if the loser just simply refuses to go along with it?"

"He would be shamed with the loss of his rights. Most times his hand is cut off, so he can never issue challenge again that he does not intend to honor."

"Who decides that, the victor?"

"Challenge is governed by warrior laws, laws enforced by every warrior. As I said, there is no avoidance of the outcome of a challenge."

"All right, I can see how a warrior thing like this would be backed up by all warriors. So what kind of service are we talking about, and how long does it last?"

"The kind of service is also the choice of the victor, but it can be only one service. Does he need a new stable for his *hataari*, the defeated one can be told to build it, and as this is a specific task, the service will last until it is finished. Most service, however, is usually simple labor, on a farm, or a mine, or even in a household. This type of service is generally demanded for only a month's time.''

''And it can be only one thing? You can't assign him to household duty, then change your mind if you need another farm worker?''

''That is correct.''

She thought it over for a minute. It sounded too easy, a little menial labor for just a short time. What had made him so delighted with her challenge?

And then her eyes narrowed on him suspiciously. ''One of those services to choose from wouldn't happen to be labor in the bedchamber, would it?''

''It has never been demanded because only men challenge—but it can indeed be considered a service.''

So that was what he had up his bare sleeve. He had correctly foreseen nothing but trouble in the claiming of her, but with this challenge thing, he could have exactly what he wanted of her without the trouble.

Tight-lipped, infuriated at how he wouldn't even have mentioned that particular service if she hadn't asked, Tedra said, ''And if I win, warrior?''

''The same choice will be yours, death or service.''

''Very well, I figure it will take me about a month to conclude my business here. You'll make a nice guide or assistant.''

''You truly expect to defeat me, woman?''

The amusement in his voice was natural, she supposed, but still annoying. ''You don't know me, babe. I'm as arrogant in my skills as you are in yours.''

''Arrogance in a woman is not allowed.''

''Why don't you see if it's deserved first before you

disallow it?'' she fairly purred, hoping to rile him, but she was finding to her further annoyance that it was impossible to tell with him.

He simply nodded, allowing her point. ''You will abide by the outcome of the challenge?''

''I hate to put a damper on your confidence, warrior, but fighting is what I do, and where I come from, a fighter is not without honor. You insult me by questioning mine.''

He couldn't have cared less. ''Swear it by—by your Martha,'' he insisted.

''Oh, for Stars' sake.'' She sighed. ''Swearing by Martha wouldn't mean a thing, since she isn't a God, just a pile of scrap metal who's got too big for her circuits, and whom I happen to *despise* at the moment. I'll swear by the Stars in Heaven, which is binding for me. But I don't expect to lose this challenge, babe, so don't say I didn't warn you. You might be as big as all farden hell, but big doesn't matter in what I can do. Do *you* swear to abide by the outcome?'' She got a flush out of him, which made her chuckle that he could react to her barbs after all, and she rubbed it in. ''Fair's fair, babe. You made *me* swear.''

''Then I swear by Droda,'' he growled. ''But I also swear you will regret your taunting of me, woman.''

''That remains to be seen,'' she replied, unruffled. ''Are you sure you want to go through with this?''

''There is nothing that could stop me now, *tyra.* ''

He'd called her witch. My, she really had got him riled, which was all the better for her. One of the first rules of fighting was to stay cool.

''So what are you waiting for? I'm ready.''

Chapter Nine

*T*he strategy was not to let him get his hands on her. Tedra quickly discovered that blocking did little good against those meaty arms, so any frontal attack was out of the question. She got her blows in from the sides, from behind, but that took some fancy footwork to maneuver around him; the barbarian might be big, but unfortunately, he wasn't clumsy or slow. In fact, he could move nearly as fast as she could, which didn't help to get the fight over with quickly, as she had hoped to do.

Finding out early in the game that he was reluctant to actually hurt her was a good thing, because there had been several opportunities where he could have ended it, but she would have had some broken bones to show for it. She didn't harbor any such reluctance herself, not that she thought she could actually damage the brute with the limited blows that distance allowed her. Those kicks she did get in were designed to bring him down; they just didn't. He might be sore later, but as far as she could tell now, he wasn't feeling anything, all that thick muscle cushioning her every blow. She'd either have to go for a running jump kick, wagering all that she could reach his throat as high up as it was, or else wait for an opening to take him from behind with her Frimera technique.

After two successive lateral kicks that he was just short of blocking, Tedra got in a third kick that staggered him somewhat. Elated, she wasted no time in leaping on his back and going for the pressure point on his neck. She could have broken his back in that position, or his neck, by bringing up her feet for leverage and yanking back on his head. Something would have snapped before her added weight toppled them over. But she couldn't bring herself to kill the barbarian. She applied the Frimera technique instead and held her breath, counting those four extra seconds it took to work on someone his size. But four passed, then six, and Tedra broke out in a sweat when eight seconds had come and gone and he was still standing. His neck muscles were just *too* thick, and when she heard his deep, rumbling chuckle, she realized that he could have stopped her at any point, that he had *let* her give it her best shot!

Her only thought at that point was to abandon ship, but she'd known if she got that close to him it'd be all over, and even as she let go of her hold on his back, his hand was there to keep her from dropping free of him. In another second she was dragged around to the front of him by a fistful of her tunic, had only a moment to see the gloating pleasure in his expression, then was tossed upward into the air.

To her credit, she didn't scream. She didn't come to ground either. The barbarian had merely wanted a more secure hold on her, but hadn't wanted to set her down yet. He caught her on the fall with both hands, one on each of her arms just above the elbow, pinning them to her sides—which was a good thing for him. That close, and with his hands busy holding her, she could have broken his nose, smashed his vocals, or done any number of other disabling things if she'd had full use of her arms. She still had full use of her legs, however, but once again he proved how fast he was in blocking her moves, and he went one further and shook her until she decided she'd had enough and just let her legs hang.

"Concede you are beaten, woman."

It was an order, not a question. And it did seem as if she were beaten, without having received a single blow. Colossal strength did have its advantages. His hold was too tight to wiggle lose from, and she didn't care to have her brains rattled again if she tried any more kicks. But concede? Not until her last options had been used, and one of them was to bring both legs up, plant her feet squarely in the center of his chest, and push back.

It worked, but only because he wasn't expecting it. She went sailing backward to land hard on the ground, which was better than having her arms pulled out of their sockets if he hadn't let go. But her push hadn't knocked him over as it should have, giving her the extra moments she needed to catch her breath. Just as she rose she was shoved back down, the barbarian's body pinning her to the ground. Her hands were captured, her legs held down by his, and if that wasn't enough, he let her have his full weight, taking no more chances with her.

Breathing normally became a memory. Tedra had to fight for each breath and he knew it, but he didn't ease even an ounce of the pressure bearing down on her.

"Now do you concede you are beaten."

Again it wasn't a question. And this time there wasn't a doubt in either of their minds. Tedra couldn't move an inch except to nod her head, and the moment she did she could breathe again. But all he did was ease his great chest off hers. He didn't let go of her or move to get up. And he seemed perfectly content to stay that way as he looked down at her. Her own look was filled with disgust, all of it for herself. She'd made one mistake after another with the barbarian, but agreeing to the challenge was the biggest.

"I don't suppose you're going to kill me, are you?" He slowly shook his head. "I'm right handy at cleaning floors," she lied. Again he shook his head, but this time with a grin. "All right, damn it, spit it out. What kind of service do you want from me?"

"This you know already, *kerima.*"

Little one, or little girl, he'd called her, and however she cared to take it, she felt both at the moment. He was so farden *big.* And she'd already had a taste of his full weight. She'd never survive sex-sharing with him, she knew she wouldn't, and yet who was there to stop him? She'd found out the hard way that she couldn't. And even if she could, honor demanded she not try.

"There'll be no assuming here, warrior. I want it spelled out, and to know how long it's to last."

"Very well."

He rolled to the side now, telling her at least that the service wouldn't begin just yet, for which she was more than grateful. She really had worn herself out trying to beat him. And then it hit her with the force of a blow. She'd been beaten. For the first time since she had become a Sec 1, she'd been beaten, and by a man she found utterly desirable.

A wave of vulnerability washed through her, and a thrill that flushed her cheeks and weakened her limbs. Here was a man she couldn't walk all over, one who wouldn't fear her abilities or worry about riling her temper. It seemed as if she'd waited forever for him, and she looked at him now wide-eyed, with a little awe and a lot of anticipation. She'd know sex-sharing at last. Even if it killed her, she'd enjoy every minute of it.

"What is it?" he asked, intercepting her look.

"I . . . Nothing."

She sat up and wrapped her arms around her drawn-up knees. He was sitting next to her, his legs crossed. She couldn't meet his eyes again, but he was having none of that. His hand turned her face to him.

"You agreed to honor the outcome," he reminded her almost sternly.

Flustered by his touch, she pushed his hand away. "Don't go doubting my honor again. I'm still waiting to hear what the outcome is."

"For one month you will give me the service of a claimed woman."

He said that with a certain amount of triumph. But then that *was* why he'd been so delighted about the challenge, because she couldn't resist his claiming of her. And no matter how much she was looking forward to sex-sharing with him, that rubbed her a little on the raw. *He'd* known he couldn't lose, even if she hadn't. If that wasn't underhanded, she didn't know what was.

"You said this means I must yield to your will? In all things?"

"That is so."

"That sounds a bit much, warrior. You also said this service could be a specific task or a certain type of labor, but just one kind only. If I have to clean your cave, cook your meals, *and* warm your furs, I'm afraid I'm going to have to protest. That'd be more than one service, wouldn't it?"

He had to be annoyed with her for pointing that out, but damned if he showed it. She wanted a reaction from him. In fact, she wouldn't half mind if he'd do some of that claiming right now. But all he did was seem to thoughtfully consider her point.

Finally, he said, "Very well, I will choose the service you have yourself named. Your words were 'labor in the bedchamber'; thus wherever I sleep, woman, you will deny me nothing. Is that specific enough for you?"

She almost laughed. He actually thought he was making her regret protesting his first choice, that she'd like this one even less. She'd got a reaction out of him after all, not a typical one, but then he could in no way be called a typical man.

Not to disappoint him, she gave a long sigh. "What can I say, warrior? But you're passing up an excellent floor sweeper."

He grunted. "You would have done better as a claimed woman. It at least is a position of some respect."

Her reaction had obviously been too mild to suit him. He'd wanted her angry, as angry as she had apparently made him by disputing his first choice.

"And a bed-warmer isn't?" She smiled, then shrugged, unconcerned. "Well, then, since I'm having the job forced on me, you'll just have to defend my honor, won't you?"

He shook his head. "You will accept what comes, with no recourse. Service through challenge loss is not meant to be agreeable."

She didn't have his ability to conceal anger when it did show up. Her eyes glittered with it. Her teeth gnashed with it.

"Nice of you to tell me that after the fact," she gritted out. "What other unpleasant surprises do I have in store for me? Some chains and whips maybe?"

Now he smiled, the farden beast. "I cannot know what would surprise you, when you knew so little of challenge."

She waited for him to go on, but he didn't, so she demanded, "What about the chains and whips?"

"For what reason would such be needed, since you have agreed to accept my will as yours?"

"In the bedchamber only," she reminded him.

"Wherever I sleep," he reminded her. "But—" and now he grinned. "You are still a woman, not a warrior."

He seemed much too delighted by that fact. "Is that supposed to mean something in particular to me?"

"A woman, any woman, highborn, servant—or challenge loser—must defer to warriors, especially to the warrior who protects her, whom she must also obey. Until your service ends and you are again a claimable woman, I must give you my protection; thus will you obey me in all things."

For a moment Tedra was too furious for words. Then she shot to her feet, snarling, "Like farden hell! That's what you said about claimed women. Are you telling me every woman on your planet is claimed?"

"I know not the customs in every country," he said as he also got to his feet. "But in Kan-is-Tra, very few women are claimed, since they need only apply to a warrior for protection to avoid claiming. This you were told, and this they gladly do, because Kan-is-Tran women do not care to lose their rights to claiming."

"What rights?" she demanded. "It sounds like they have none if they must still obey—Stars, how I hate that word—every warrior who snaps his fingers!"

"Defer to, woman, not obey," he replied with a sigh. "A warrior can make no demands of a woman under another's protection. He can request such and such of her, but she need not obey him if the request is unreasonable or abhorrent to her. This is her right."

"But she does have to obey the warrior who protects her? I see no difference."

"He who protects her cannot have of her the service *you* will give to me, not unless it is her wish to give such service. Is that difference enough for you, woman?"

Tedra pinkened. "It still sounds too slavish to suit me, but I didn't come here to live, only to trade. Though I'm not forgetting that you wanted *me* in the 'without rights' group."

He shrugged. "You could have requested my protection instead."

"I didn't *know* about it!"

"Ignorance of the law is no—"

"Don't rub it in the ground, warrior," Tedra snapped. "You've already taken more advantage of me than any other man ever has, so let's drop it, all right? Now, are we going to stand around here all day, or what? Why don't you get on with whatever you were doing when I showed up to brighten your day. What *were* you doing out here on your lonesome anyway?"

She got a very clear look of chagrin out of him, which was heartening, proving he didn't always keep his emotions to himself. "I was hunting the *taraan* you killed."

"So that's a *taraan?*" she asked. "Hey, I didn't kill it. It's only in a deep stun, which I wish to Heaven's Stars *you'd* been in, and stayed in."

His only response to that was to ask, "How is it

you know of a *taraan* but have never seen one before?''

"Because it's one of your words that needed a picture to go along with it, but Sublims don't supply pictures, just words.''

"Explain, woman.''

"It's how I learned your language, with a Sublim tape. I know all the words, just not all of their meanings. Your animals, foods, things like that will give me problems until I can match them up with the words I have for them. You'd have the same problem if you were given my language.'' She grinned then. "Now there's an idea. Would you like to Transfer up to my ship to learn my language? It would only take a few hours of your time, and the culture shock would do you a world of good.''

He snorted in answer. "I will see to the *taraan*. You will stay where you are.''

But first he saw to her phazor unit, much to her regret, retrieving it from where he'd tossed it and hooking it on the back of his sword belt after that was also retrieved and put on. There were a few moments when he had hesitated in touching the unit that were worth a laugh or two, but Tedra managed to restrain herself. At least the barbarian wasn't leaving the unit behind so she'd never have a chance to get it back. And she would get it back. But a fat lot of good it would do her for the next month, since she was honor-bound to accept the consequences of her challenge loss—and still looking forward to that despite the barbarian's domineering nature.

Chapter Ten

*I*t was an ugly, huge, shaggy-looking thing, what the barbarian called his *hataar*. Long-necked, long-haired, four-legged, it had a mane that fell on each side of its neck down to its spindly legs, and a tail of hair that nearly dragged on the ground. Its back, which was to be sat on, was as high as Tedra was tall. She knew it now to be an animal for riding, but the Sha-Ka'ari must have had a different name for theirs, if they had any, for *hataar* was not in their store of words. The Kystran Ancients had a similar animal for use as transportation, but not nearly as big and ugly, and long since extinct.

The barbarian's *hataar* was black in body coat, with a white tail and mane that surprisingly showed no discoloration. It had been tied at the end of the tree line, or the beginning, depending on which direction you were coming from. Tedra had immensely enjoyed walking through those low-limbed, lovely green trees, savoring the smell of verdant earth and growing things. All vegetation had died on Kystran during the Great Water Shortage, which had led to the invention of solaray baths. By that time all Kystran food was being grown on the space stations or imported from other worlds, and wood had long since become inferior as a building material, so the loss of greenery on the planet hadn't been considered a serious catastrophe or an urgent problem to solve. And when the scientists had got around to solving it, the land was extremely desertlike, good only for being paved or built on. A Kystran park consisted of a great expanse of brown solidite paving, dotted with gigantic metal sculptures of trees and plants, a far cry from what she was seeing today.

The barbarian had carried the poor *taraan*, which was still living only because it was still in ştun. He had been glad, though, that he could avoid leaving a trail of blood behind him. Tedra refrained from asking why that should matter. She'd yet to see any of the wild animals on the planet, but that didn't mean they weren't around.

There was a harnesslike contraption around the neck and chest of the *hataar* that reins were attached to, and which sported a handhold in the center to use for mounting, since the beast was saddleless and merely covered with a thin fur blanket. A long fur sack and two small rabbitlike animals hung from it on small ropes, and the barbarian tied the *taraan* to this as well, it being not so long that it would drag on the ground.

Tedra was definitely not looking forward to riding on that giant thing to wherever they were going, though the animal's back was so long and wide there would be plenty of room for two or even three people to sit comfortably. But once her companion had finished securing everything, he didn't climb aboard so they could get on their way. He turned to her instead and, after a moment of thoughtful study, reached over to finger the sleeve of her tunic.

"These still offend me, woman."

That was all he said, but he stood there waiting, as if she were a mind reader. And maybe she was. The grin wasn't on those chiseled lips, but Tedra knew it should have been. He'd got his way upside and down, and had gone through a good deal of trouble explaining the facts of Kan-is-Tran life to her so she'd know there could be no more refusing on her part. Either she'd have to take the offensive clothes off, or he'd likely do it for her, and she could just imagine how unpleasant that would be.

And then it occurred to her that if she shed down to nothing, the barbarian might do the same. After all, what lusty male of any culture would pass up such an opportunity? They were alone, and there was a blanket of sorts on the *hataar* that would spread nicely under a nearby tree. It wasn't too farfetched to assume that some pleasant sex-sharing might improve the barbarian's attitude somewhat. A little give-and-take on his part would certainly improve hers.

"Betcha fifty exchange tokens, warrior, that no one's ever accused you of being flexible. But that's all right. Single-mindedness does have its virtues. Lucky for you I know how to give in graciously."

She flashed him a cheeky grin before slipping out of one boot and tossing it to him, then the next. Her utility belt opened with a tug, and, emboldened by the way his dark eyes were attending her every movement, she draped it around his neck, chuckling softly when his lips tightened and he dropped the belt and boots on the ground beside him. The tight neck of her tunic top was designed to give for easy removal, and within moments it joined the other items on the ground. But with the top half of her body stocking now revealed, the barbarian missed seeing her pants slide right off.

He was clearly fascinated by this undergarment that seemed painted on her, it fitted so closely. Made of glittering silver trilon, it covered her skin from the top of her breasts down to her toes, and this fascinated him even more. A tug at the top and it parted down the sides all the way to her ankles, so she only had to step out of it—and now the body stocking was forgotten.

For long, silent moments his eyes examined what the challenge had given him. Tedra became very still, her playful mood gone. No man had ever seen her like this before, and she hadn't realized how disconcerting it would be. And it was impossible to tell what this one was thinking, if he even liked what he saw. Those intense black eyes gave no clue.

"There was more hidden beneath your warrior's clothing than I had thought, *kerima.*"

The color crept up Tedra's chest into her cheeks. She would have known he was referring to her large breasts even if he hadn't been staring at them when he said that. Her body stocking did much to flatten that area, a necessary measure for someone in her profession who couldn't afford a distracting bounce interfering with her job. She wished he hadn't mentioned it. She wished even more that he would take the step that separated them and fold her into his arms to lessen the embarrassment she was now feeling at being naked while he was not.

What was he waiting for anyway? Surely not an invitation?

"This you may keep," he said, picking up the kystral necklace that had come off with her tunic.

He came closer to carefully put the necklace over her head. He even pulled her long tail of hair out from under it, and she thought, Now he'll kiss me. But he didn't. He stepped back to admire the way the two strands caressed the top of her breasts, drawing the eye there, and Tedra could only stare at him in bewilderment. His restraint wasn't normal. It went against everything she knew about men and sex-sharing; she might not have tried it yet, but she knew all there was to know about it. The barbarian had demanded sex-sharing service of her. That had to mean he wanted her, didn't it?

Whatever it meant, Tedra had the sinking feeling she wasn't going to find out any time soon, and her disappointment was suddenly so keen, the sarcasm just dripped from her words. "Kystrals go nicely with this outfit, don't they?"

"Indeed."

She glared at him. "Now *isn't* the time for you to be agreeable, warrior. I didn't strip down to stay stripped down, so give me something else—Stars, what *is* that?" Tedra gasped, seeing a huge white beast loping toward them through the trees. "My phazor, quick, man—give it here before we're on to-night's menu."

She held out her hand for the unit, but her eyes remained glued to the beast that was getting closer by the second. With those visible fangs, she was afraid it was carnivorous, and it was nearly as big as the *hataar,* too big certainly for a barbarian to tangle with. The head was round with tufted ears, the body long, sleek, and short-pelted, the tail about as long as the trunk. Its paws alone were twice the size of her fists, and she had no desire to meet up with the long claws they would contain. But her hand remained empty, and she finally spared a glance at the barbarian, to find he had turned to stare at the beast, but no more than that. His hand hadn't even approached his sword handle, let alone her unit.

With his back to her, the phazor was staring her in the face, and Tedra didn't even think about hesitating. But the moment her fingers touched it, other fingers grabbed hers and lightly tossed her hand away from it.

"Are you nuts?" she shrieked.

The barbarian only looked down at her, facing her again, his expression inscrutable. To the side of him, she saw the beast, still in a lope coming toward them and just ten feet away now. And it roared—loudly.

"Oh, Staaaaarrrs!" Tedra cried and ran for the nearest tree.

She heard the laughter before she even reached the limb which spread out about twelve feet off the ground, though that didn't stop her from gaining a perch on it. It was sturdy enough to support her, but she still gripped it for dear life, tree climbing as alien to her as trees were. Only when she was lying down flat on it and was sure she wasn't in danger of sliding off did she look down to see what the laughter was all about.

It was the barbarian, of course, and he wasn't just laughing, but having a fit of it. She kind of figured out why when she saw the huge feline beast sitting on the ground right next to the barbarian, like a damned tamed pet, which Tedra concluded it likely was. She could hear its loud purring over the noise the barbarian was still making as his laughter wound down to chuckles. And the animal was staring up at her with great blue eyes, as if she were a mere curiosity. She was that indeed, naked and up a tree. She was also feeling so foolish and ridiculous that she was hot pink with it.

"That tree you seem so fond of, *kerima,* would not have served," she was told as her amused companion approached.

"Oh?"

"The *fembair* plays in trees. Had he wanted you on his menu, he would have joined you on that limb."

So that was what a *fembair* looked like. She had gathered from the Sublims that it was some sort of wild animal to be avoided, yet this one no longer looked so wild, just still scary as all hell. It had followed the barbarian, its body as high as his chest when it was up on all fours, and they both now looked up at her from beneath the tree.

"Come down, woman, and we will be on our way."

That was all? No apology for the rotten trick he'd played on her?

"Actually, the view's great from up here," she replied testily.

He ignored her tone and her words. "Drop down and I will catch you."

With the bark on the tree limb irritating the tender skin of her belly and her inner thighs, Tedra didn't offer any more lip. She gripped the limb with both hands, then lowered her body slowly until she was dangling from the limb. As soon as she felt the hands take hold of her calves, she let go and dropped fast—until the barbarian's arms, which had quickly wrapped around her legs, caught on her rear end. For a heart-stopping moment, a hard cheek was pressed to her belly, and then she slid slowly, very slowly, down his body until her feet touched the ground.

This had to be it. That tantalizing body-to-body caress had been deliberate on his part. Hot coils of anticipation were already unwinding in her belly. If he didn't kiss her now . . .

He gave her backside a gentle pat before his arms left her, and then she was watching him walk away. He'd walked away! Tedra felt like screaming and stomping her feet. Of course, she didn't do things like that. Usually when she felt frustrated, she put herself through her more grueling exercises to work it off, to save her friends and co-workers a taste of her foul temper, which was what tended to rise when she felt that way. But she had to admit she'd never felt this kind of frustration before, never having experienced such a keen want of sex-sharing before.

She was standing there naked and wanting him, and he'd just walked away. She still couldn't believe it. Was the man made of stone? Or maybe she was looking at it only from her perspective and he didn't really want her. He'd claimed her, but she had been, according to him, a claimable woman, so what else could he do? He'd even had her in a perfect sex-sharing position earlier when she'd lost the challenge, but he hadn't taken the least advantage of it. Here she had five years of missed sex-sharing to make up for, and what did she get when she decided the time had finally arrived? A man who could take it or leave it, or didn't want it at all. Of all the farden luck.

"Woman?"

A summons? A farden summons! That did it, rubbed her position in good, and snapped what control she had on her frustration. She stalked after the pair, who waited for her by the *hataar*, her aquamarine eyes narrowed and glowing, not the least bit of wariness for the white beast remaining just then.

"I take it that's a friend of yours?" she asked softly, deceptively.

"A very good friend."

Her finger stabbed into the center of his chest. "You could have told me that, you prehistoric jerk, instead of letting me—"

"Woman," he interrupted, half in surprise, a

greater half in disapproval. "Wherever you come from, you are now in Kan-is-Tra. You will abide by the laws and conduct yourself as a woman of Kan-is-Tra."

Tedra snorted. "In other words, I can't cuss you out as you deserve, or point out how infantile your little joke was?"

"You will give a warrior respect at all times."

"Or what?"

"Or you will be punished by he who protects you." He said it calmly, yet there was a promise in those words she didn't care for.

"Some protection," she grumbled, but with less heat. "You don't really think I'm going to miraculously transform into a model of Kan-is-Tran womanhood who will jump to your every little command, do you?"

He stared down at her so long and so seriously that she was regretting that last taunt even before he answered with a soft menace, "You will."

Maybe she would at that—for now. But if she decided she could withstand his punishments . . . Her body was conditioned to take a lot of pain and still function adequately. She'd have to wait and find out.

He must have concluded she was subdued for now, for he said no more and turned to the *hataar*, removing the thin fur blanket from its back. He took his long dagger and made a cut in the center of this; then, before Tedra had figured out what he was doing, he dropped the whole thing over her head, fur side underneath, and even pulled her necklace out for her, and the tail of her hair, arranging both to his satisfaction.

She didn't know whether to thank him or not. The blanket smelled of *hataar*, but the fur was soft against her skin. As a covering it wasn't so great, falling only to the middle of her thighs, front and back, but the width of it allowed it to drape down her arms almost to her wrists. Of course, the bottom line was, it was better than nothing.

She decided not to thank him, since she had been naked under his insistence, not hers. "I'll need a belt," she mentioned reasonably. "Mine will do nicely."

He didn't even glance at her pile of clothes on the ground. He tugged open the long fur sack hanging from the harness grip and pulled out a rope similar to the ones he'd used to secure the animals.

Tedra groaned inwardly. "That's a bit old, and I do mean *old*-fashioned, don't you think? There's nothing wrong with my own belt."

"Likely it is a fine belt—for a warrior," he said in reply; then his dark eyes met hers to add gently, "You need no belt, *kerima.*"

"Then what—" He had grasped both wrists and brought them together in one of his large hands, then began calmly wrapping the rope around them. "Now just a damned minute!" Tedra said with annoyance, but also with some little alarm. "I'm honor-bound to be stuck with you for a month, warrior. This isn't necessary and you know it!"

"Any challenge loser, or captive, too, for that matter, is treated thusly at first, to declare his or her status to all."

"No one's going to believe I'm a challenge loser."

"Be glad of that, *kerima.* Challenge losers are scorned. Captives are merely a curiosity."

"If you'd left me my clothes—"

"Every warrior in my camp would have demanded

their removal. I am not the only one who would find it offensive to see a woman dressed so.''

Tedra ground her teeth together, pulled against the rope now tight around her wrists, and glared at the barbarian. ''I got to hand it to you, babe. You really know how to make a girl love the hell out of you.''

''This habit you have of saying things you do not mean is confusing, woman. Best do you keep to the truth.''

''I'd love to,'' she said resentfully. ''But it's bound to get me punished, as you've repeatedly told me.''

''And what is this truth?''

''That I'm beginning to hate you *and* your planet, *and* your farden customs. Put that in your hat and eat it.''

He tipped her face around to his when she turned aside so as not to see his reaction to that. But his reaction bewildered her, since there was clear amusement in his expression. And then his words confused her even more, contradicting the amusement.

''You were correct, *kerima*. Such does deserve punishment. This will be seen to shortly.''

''Thanks. I really needed to hear that.''

He shook his head at her, as if her remarks were those of an incorrigible child, and then his gaze dropped to her bound hands. These he stared at for a long moment and even frowned, leading Tedra to believe he was going to change his mind. No such luck. He picked up her discarded pants instead, cut a few inches off the bottom of each leg, making her groan at the destruction of such a costly outfit, and then slipped one piece each over her hands under the ropes. Protecting her skin? How considerate—and again contradictory. Why should he care? He'd tied her to begin with. So what if she got scraped raw from the rope? She was less than a captive. She was a challenge loser, to be scorned.

In a moment of sheer disgust over the predicament her traitorous computer had left her in, she switched to her own language. "I hope you're getting all this, Martha, because the strikes against you are adding up. I'm not just going to sell you when I get out of this, I'm going to demolish you—pull all your plugs and melt down your circuits—and that's just for starters. And just because I'll have to endure this for a month, whether you come to your senses or not, don't think time will be on your side. I won't forget that you could have saved me *before* that farden challenge. A month of barbarian arrogance shoved down my throat will ensure that I don't forget. You've been—"

The cloth shoved in her mouth shut off her words, and Tedra's eyes widened as another strip of cloth came to hold the first one in place and tie behind her neck. Bound hands didn't help to prevent this from happening. All Tedra could do was scream her fury at this last outrage, the sound a mere squeak and too unsatisfying to go on for long.

When she gave it up, he was standing in front of her again, wearing his inscrutable expression. "Thus will be done each time you speak to your Martha in words unknown to me," he told her. "When the lesson has sufficient time to be learned, I will allow you to speak again, in Sha-Ka'ani."

Sha-Ka'ani? Was that what he called the Sha-Ka'ari language she had learned? Martha had said the whole planet spoke a single language, though the barbarian must not know that. Even though Tedra spoke another language, he still believed her to be from another country, not another planet. That would make his planet Sha-Ka'an.

Why Tedra felt she had accomplished something by figuring that out, she didn't know. Maybe because she still didn't know her tormentor's name, only his country, and now his planet. But having a positive feeling at that moment, even about something so minor, was needed to counteract all the negative thoughts bombarding her. Tied and gagged. What next?

Chapter Eleven

*T*hey were miles away from their place of meeting before Tedra remembered her belt and the homing device it contained. She had been so preoccupied with annoyance over the restraints binding her, as well as distracted by her close proximity to the barbarian, she hadn't even noticed that all her clothes had been left behind.

He'd climbed aboard his *hataar* with no help other than the harness post to pull himself up by. Then, still holding one hand to the post, he'd reached down and caught Tedra about the waist, setting her in front of him. With reins attached to the animal's head, the barbarian had flicked them and off they went, the tamed *fembair* following close behind.

Now, a good hour later, Tedra couldn't believe she had been so careless as to overlook something that important. Granted, she'd been gagged and in no position to insist her possessions be brought along. But to just forget? And why didn't the barbarian want to keep them, if for no other reason than as something curious to show his friends? She had assumed he would when she had taken them off; otherwise she wouldn't have been so quick to give in and remove her only open link with Martha.

Without voices to follow—and the barbarian had said nothing in all this time—Martha was likely back with the homing device, locked to its signal, maybe even assuming they were silently sharing sex all this time and gloating over it. Without the voices to monitor, the short-range scanner was useless, the reason that the homing signal was so important. The soft clip of the *hataar* wasn't likely to be picked up by it. And who knew how many other moving creatures were in the area to confuse the long-range scanner?

Martha would be as lost to what was going on as Tedra was to being protected by her. Without a voice to lock onto, Martha couldn't Transfer her back to the Rover. Without the phazor combo-unit in her possession, Tedra couldn't either. Plainly speaking, she would be stranded indefinitely on this backward world without one or the other, and right now she had neither. And it was all *his* fault.

Tedra was still thinking that when her gag was untied and the cloth pulled from her mouth. So sufficient time had passed, had it? And she was to have learned something? The only thing she'd learned was not to attempt to reach Martha while the barbarian was around. But that farden gag hadn't been pleasant. Her mouth was as dry as a solaray bath, and one of the things not hanging from the harness post was a water container, so she'd have to suffer with it until water could be found. Maybe the barbarian's lessons were more ingenious than she had first thought.

After she'd swallowed several times, without much relief, Tedra rasped out, "Tell me . . . some . . . thing. Is my time . . . with you to be . . . one unpleasantness after . . . another?"

He lowered his head until his chin rested on her shoulder. This put his cheek against hers and started her mouth drooling, which almost took care of the dryness.

"There will be no unpleasantness, *kerima,* do you

simply obey me and acquit yourself as befitting a woman of Kan-is-Tra.''

''Even though I'm not such a woman?''

''You will be,'' he said, firm conviction in his tone. ''It will be my pleasure to teach you.''

And how much would she suffer in that teaching? ''Look, warrior, I'm not an ass-kisser, and I'm not one to keep my opinions to myself either,'' Tedra said bluntly. ''Where I come from there's no one who could do to me what you did. That breeds the kind of arrogance and confidence that you yourself possess. You're not going to beat that out of me, no matter this service I owe you. Would I amuse you as much as I seem to be doing if you did, if I become a carbon copy of the women you're used to? Why don't you think about that for a while?''

He didn't answer. He didn't remove his chin either. In fact, he rubbed his cheek a little against hers in a nuzzling caress that sent gooseflesh over her arms and goaded the flame in her belly. Tedra groaned inwardly. She wasn't going to let herself get teased into desiring him again, not when the damned warrior didn't deliver what his subtle actions promised. She had almost changed her mind altogether about wanting him to be her first sex-sharer, not that she had much choice in the matter for the next month, *if* he ever got around to it. But she wasn't sure she wanted it from him anymore, not with the way he'd been treating her.

Her thoughts were interrupted by the smell of water. She could actually smell it, and she turned her head and saw it, a small stream that shot out into the low-grassed meadow they were crossing, then snaked away again.

Tedra sat up straight when the *hataar* was turned

in that direction, and she was lowering herself even as the animal came to a halt, her hands gripping the harness post until her feet touched the ground. Nor did she wait for permission to quench her thirst, but dropped to her knees at the edge of the sparkling little stream and scooped up what she could in her bound hands.

"What manner of men do you have in your country that they cannot beat you at warrior's sport?"

So he *had* been thinking over what she'd said. Or maybe not. It could be just that one remark that had intrigued him.

When she glanced around to see him, she got a close-up view of the *fembair* instead. The monstrously huge feline had come up behind Tedra to sniff her over while she was on her knees and so much lower than it. She wasn't used to any kind of live animals, let alone ones of this size, but as long as she was certain the barbarian would tell her if she was in danger of being eaten, she tried ignoring his enormous pet and leaned to the side to see around it.

"Is warrior's sport what you call weaponless combat?" At his nod, she grinned at him. "Far be it from me to suggest you let your women participate, but in my world they do—and frequently win."

She wiped her chin on the back of one arm and stood up, to find his expression just the tiniest bit annoyed, which meant he must be a great deal annoyed to let that much show. "You keep calling your country your 'world.' You will desist in this, woman."

She knew damned well that wasn't what had annoyed him. It was the idea of women beating men that burned his toes.

"Whatever you say, babe," she agreed, still grinning, but in more of a smirk.

"You will also desist in calling me by the name for an infant."

"It's just a term of affection, sweetcakes."

"You will not call me this word either, or pretend to an affection you do not as yet feel."

Tedra's humor went south with the stream. "You're getting on my nerves, warrior. Must I remind you that you never supplied me with your name?"

"It is Challen Ly-San-Ter," he replied stiffly.

"Well, hurray. And do I have your exalted permission to use it, O master?"

"Get back on the *hataar*, woman."

He didn't shout, but that didn't mean she didn't hear it underneath the tone. She returned to the *hataar* and waited for him to place her on it, having the disgusting feeling that was the proper thing for a Kan-is-Tran woman to do. He'd managed to intimidate her somehow, and she didn't like that at all. She liked his name, however, even if it was only lacking the "G-E" to have it spell "challenge." She wondered if that was symbolic. Whatever, she still liked the sound of it. Challen Ly-San-Ter of Sha-Ka'an, barbarian extraordinary.

They were leaving the meadow and entering another wooded area before Tedra got up the nerve to resume conversation—with another gripe. "Couldn't you at least have brought my clothes along, even if you weren't going to let me wear them? I know you've never seen that kind of material before. Weren't you even curious about where it came from?"

"You claim a country called Kystran. From that place must it come."

How boringly logical. "Wouldn't you like to know where Kystran is, then?"

"No."

"No?"

"Of what use is a country of women warriors, and men who cannot beat them? Warriors will not draw sword against women, nor raid or deal with men who cannot control them."

"Beneath your dignity, huh?" she chided. "But I'm afraid you've got the wrong impression—Challen. We've gone far beyond one sex controlling the other on Kystran. Men and women are equal there, taught the same skills, allowed the same career opportunities. It's true our men don't come anywhere close to you in size, and they aren't sword-wielders, but those in Security like myself use different kinds of weapons, ones that don't require size and strength to handle. You had a taste of them, but there are others much more dangerous, weapons that can kill a thing so efficiently, no trace is left of it." She heard him snort, and knew he wasn't believing her again. "Answer me this, then. You *have* seen and felt what a phazor can do. Have you ever seen one before, or even heard tales about such things?"

"Such would be needful for men who otherwise cannot protect themselves."

"A reasonable conclusion, but not the answer to my question. You haven't heard of such things before because they don't exist on your world."

"There are countries far beyond here that have never been dealt with."

"You have a farden answer for everything, don't you?" she gritted out. "Then how did I get here from these far-off places, and better yet, why would I come here—alone?"

"As you say, for trade."

"And as *you* say, women wouldn't be trusted with such tasks. Are you now allowing that they would—at least in countries you have no dealings with?"

He wouldn't answer, changing the subject instead. "What meaning has this far-den word you use?"

"It's used to express mild disgust, which is exactly what I'm feeling right now." Good thing she wasn't the feet-stomping type, or there'd be holes in the ground to show for it. She sighed. "All right, let's stick to things you do know all about—the service I owe you, for instance. I'm beginning to suspect it's not what I assumed it to be, so why don't you enlighten me—in detail."

"There will be many things you will do for me."

"Such as?"

"This moonrise will you endeavor to work the soreness from my muscles."

"Ah, poor baby," she purred with saccharine sweetness. "Did mean old Tedra hurt the big barbarian?"

She was congratulating herself on that dig, which she knew without looking at him he wouldn't appreciate, when he leaned forward, pressing against her back to reach the harness post in front of her. She watched him tie the reins off there and had the distinct feeling she was in trouble. When his hands were empty, she didn't know what to expect. A beating came to mind, though she couldn't imagine how he would manage it on the back of his *hataar*. But his slipping his hands inside her fur covering and under her arms took her by surprise.

Heat hit her, sucking the breath from her body as those long, masculine fingers moved over and around her breasts, until each sensitive mound was fully imprisoned in a strong hand. That tiny flame that had been fanned earlier now ignited, sending a brushfire of sensation over receptive nerves. Her head fell back onto a hard shoulder, and the pleasurable sound that escaped her throat couldn't have been stopped had she known it was coming.

The sound did penetrate her mind, however, bringing with it the knowledge that the barbarian was doing it again, casually, unfairly, and no doubt deliberately making her body sing, when he had no intention of playing a duet with her. Her reflex was to stop him and she even made an effort, only to recall her bound wrists. She couldn't even get her own hands under her covering, much less remove his.

Defenseless. The feeling was so alien, it brought out her fighting instincts. But all he'd left her to fight with was words, and she was afraid that was going to be the norm from now on, rather than the unusual.

"Did I miss something in the translation, warrior? I could have sworn my service was exclusive to place, with no hanky-panky allowed in any other location. Now, I don't see anything around here that comes even close to resembling a bedchamber. And the last time I looked, this *hataar* wasn't a bed. So either cut it out, fella, or you're in breach of contract."

"Cleverness is admired in a woman, *kerima.*"

"Thank you—I think."

"But your cleverness is wasted on me. Again I must remind you of the words 'where I sleep.' "

"If that's your subtle way of telling me you sleep on this riding animal, try again," she said dryly.

"When time is critical and the distance to travel far, a warrior will indeed sleep on his *hataar*. This I have done more than once, else would your punishment be delayed."

Tedra stiffened and tried to pull away from him, but his hands held her firmly in place. *This* was to be her punishment? Now she knew why he'd been so amused when he told her earlier that she was deserving of punishment for her disrespect, and promised to see to it shortly. The man was diabolical. Who but a barbarian would think to punish a woman by making her want him?

She couldn't let him get away with it. One or two beatings she could likely handle, but this? Desire was too new to her, and she was finding her reactions to it all involuntary. Such loss of control was unacceptable to a Sec, who must always be on top of any given situation. She wasn't here as a Sec, but for a woman of pride, the consequences could be just as bad, if not worse.

Gathering every ounce of will she possessed, Tedra concentrated on ignoring the hands that were now gently kneading her breasts. She could feel the warm breeze on her face, the abrasive, shaggy coat of the *hataar* she straddled on her inner thighs, even the soft fur of her covering wherever it touched her skin, but not the barbarian's hands. Her powers of concentration worked, and continued to work—until one of those clever hands discovered the wide-open junction of her legs, and then every sensation she had been ignoring slammed into her at once, and the new ones . . .

It was like melting, dissolving in hot flames. The finger that slipped inside her was the torch. Stars above, she'd never known such feeling! It stole her breath, took her out-of-mind. She now pressed back against the barbarian, giving him total access to her, willing him not to stop. The pleasure was incredible, deep inside her, spreading, humming for release. But

release wasn't in the scenario. What began as pleasure slowly but surely became an agony of frustration, of nerve-frazzling turbulence that gave not a
moment's respite. She trembled, she groaned, she
squirmed all over that *hataar* and against her tormentor. Soon she'd be literally crying—and begging.

"Noooo!"

"What think you of Sha-Ka'an discipline, woman
of Kystran?" the warrior asked her.

The voice had been calmness itself, grating along
already raw nerves. "It . . . stinks!"

"Yet is it effective."

This wasn't a question, but a statement. Tedra
didn't care. It took enormous concentration just to
hear him through the tumult in her mind. Comment-
ing was even harder.

"Enough, Challen. I—I apologize."

"That is good, but for what do you apologize?"

"For anything . . . everything . . . whatever you
want."

"You must be specific, woman; thus will you remember what earned you punishment."

She wasn't likely to ever forget this, but aloud she
said, "I can't think. I can't take any more either.
Challen, please—"

She cut herself short with a gasp. She still wasn't
ready to beg him to take her, but right about now she
could cheerfully kill him—almost. She'd give anything to be able to at least fight him, and there were
a number of things she could still do, bound wrists or
not. But her honor stayed her hand, forcing her to
endure his will even if it killed her. It just might.

The sob came when he brought his thumbs into
play, one flicking at the hard kernel her nipple had
become, the other against the equally hard nub of

oversensitized skin between her legs. But the moment she began crying, the torment stopped. The agony of wanting him persisted, however, her body still screaming with need. Her crying persisted, too, because she knew only time would relieve the state of desire the barbarian had brought her to. *He* certainly wouldn't.

He did wrap his thick arms around her, however, as if he meant to offer comfort. Tedra was barely aware of it, enough to wonder what he was up to now. Surely he didn't regret what he'd just done.

"What is this hanky-panky you spoke of?"

If he was trying to distract her from her tears, he succeeded. "It's an old Kystran Ancient's word. It means fooling around, as in hands-on practice, but mutual practice, and mutual satisfaction derived from it. What you did was not that."

"Nor was it meant to be," he said simply, then sighed. "You do not take punishment well, *kerima.*"

"You wanted me to beg, didn't you?" she demanded bitterly.

"The sound of it would have been sweet."

"I hate you," she said, and then spoiled it by hiccuping.

He laughed. "Can a warrior not tease his woman?"

Was he serious? "I'm not your woman, just yours to order about for one month. And I give you warning, warrior. The very second that month is up, I'm probably going to kill you."

"Now those are indeed the words of a woman sorely chastised. Truly, you are progressing, to reveal such womanly traits."

She had to see the man who could spout such idiocy and turned to glance back at him. "I threaten to kill you and you call that womanly?"

He grinned at her, and took the opportunity while she was turned to very tenderly wipe the tears from her cheeks. "It is common for a woman to say such when she is feeling abused and has no other recourse. They are merely words, *kerima*, and not to be taken seriously."

"Fine. You just continue thinking like that, babe. When you're dead, don't say I *didn't* warn you."

He gave her a look that said he heard what she'd called him, but was going to ignore it this once. Her second threat he didn't even acknowledge.

"Punishment has a purpose. Do you learn from it, then your mistakes will not be repeated. It is not meant to hurt you, but I think you feel this is not so; thus I must regret the manner chosen to correct you. Had I known how quickly you could be brought to arousal, I would have refrained from touching you in such a sensitive place."

He was apologizing? But she didn't see him offering to make amends by giving her the relief she still needed, so a fat lot of good it did her. He was merely saying it hadn't been his intention to arouse her to the point of tears, just to the point of regret. Big deal. Arousal was arousal as far as she was concerned. And that he'd forced it on her, without feeling the slightest bit himself . . . He really was made of stone. How the farden hell did he do it?

And then she was hit with an incredulous thought that would explain much. "Are you real, Challen? Do you bleed?"

She managed to get a frown out of him. "Explain yourself, woman."

"I have an android on my ship. He's beautiful. He's almost free-thinking, like Martha is. And he's programmed to do anything I want him to do. But he's not real. He's a machine. *He* could do what you just did if he was so programmed, and not feel anything. You didn't feel anything when you touched me. You can't deny it. Your voice was too farden calm. *Are* you real? Or is this planet more advanced than I first thought?''

"Your tales get more and more fanciful, woman." He chuckled. "I must remember to tell Tamiron about your 'unreal' men."

Tedra's brows came together warningly. "Give me a straight answer, barbarian, or I'll have to find another way to see if your blood runs red instead of black lubricant."

"I am as real as you are, *kerima*. Think you a warrior has so little control he cannot see to the proper discipline of his woman? You have seen that it is otherwise."

"I am *not*—"

"You are what I say you are. Is that not so?"

This was asked in such a way that she knew it was a reminder that they were still "where he slept," which translated to "his will was hers."

Tedra gritted her teeth and turned back to face the front before retorting sourly, "Whatever you say—babe."

That got her an arm around her waist pulling her back against his chest, and teeth at her ear that nipped gently before she was asked, "Do you wish to rephrase your last response?"

As a matter of fact, she did.

Chapter Twelve

When Tedra saw the encampment through the trees, she knew why the barbarian had left her alone for the last ten minutes of their ride. His "playfulness" had got her to the point of near screaming, which he couldn't help but notice, and so he'd allowed her a short time to calm down before she was to meet others of his kind.

Those others turned out to be exactly of his kind, a pack of giants, though none quite as big as her giant. They looked like him, too, insomuch as none wore their hair short, nor clothing above the waist, and all wore the tight black *zaalskin bracs* and arm shields of different lengths, set with *Toreno* steel, strapped to their forearms. If that wasn't enough to give them a sameness, their hair ranged in shades from brown to blond, likewise their eyes from brown to amber.

If an enemy raided this country, it sure wouldn't have much trouble telling who was who, Tedra decided as they drew closer. Of course, she was seeing only eight of their numbers. Surely the whole country wasn't made up of golden barbarians. She looked, she really did, to see a little fat, a little slouchiness, but these men were obviously all of the warrior cast, in prime shape, and not bad-looking either.

"I'm glad to see you aren't the only gorgeous hunk

of manhood around here, Challen,'' Tedra remarked, wanting to get back at him a little for all his highhandedness with her. "There are several warriors right here I wouldn't mind begging protection from—as soon as my service to you is over, that is.''

"When your service is over, you will again be a claimable woman.''

"Not if I get the words out first that request protection. You said that's all I had to do this morning to avoid my present situation. I'm not likely to forget that, friend.''

He was silent for a moment, and then she heard, ''If I am the only warrior present when your service ends, then you must say the words to me—if I do not say words of my own to you first.''

Could he do that? It really did seem a matter of timing. If he kept her confined . . . she'd have to see the lay of the place first. This was a primitive village of tents, after all, though she supposed that was better than caves. How hard could it be to slip out of one tent and into another? Then just three little words said to another man, maybe even the *shodan* himself if he was here, and she'd have some rights back and could get on with making this trip worthwhile.

She had some pertinent questions to ask him about this requesting-protection business, but that would have to wait. They were moving into the center of the cluster of tents, and the warriors, who had stopped what they were doing to watch Challen approach, now gathered around, their interest in his "catch" too great to ignore.

Tedra, being that catch, recalled belatedly her near naked state, and a little pink began riding her cheeks.

Challen's arm tightened around her waist at about the same time. She wondered if he might be regretting her lack of clothing, too. More likely it was just a claim-staking thing, of the male asserting what was his when other males were around. Or did he assume she might be frightened, carted in so ignominiously as she was, not knowing what her reception would be, and was offering a subtle kind of reassurance? No, she had to stop trying to pin kind and thoughtful qualities to his nature. He was a barbarian, after all, a dominant, arbitrary male. So what if he'd been incredibly gentle with her in every instance, even to cutting up her clothes to ensure that her wrists didn't get scraped by his scratchy rope. Come to think of it, he hadn't laid a single harsh hand on her even when they'd fought and she'd try to lay him low with every blow. And when he did take hold of her, he was exceedingly careful about it. Was this for her benefit, or just the ingrained habit of an extremely strong man in his dealings with females? She supposed she had a month to find out, one way or the other.

"What kind of meat do you call that, Challen?" The teasing began with a chuckle.

Another man took it up. "Sweet and succulent, with the right preparation."

"Such a waste, to find such a tender morsel while hunting," still another said.

This last generated so much laughter among them all, even Challen, that Tedra had to wonder about the underlying meaning. What difference if she'd been found while the barbarian was hunting? How was that a waste?

"A waste of what, Challen?" Tedra asked aloud,

only to set them all off on another round of guffaws.

This went on for a few more moments; then the barbarian dismounted, rather clumsily since he was still beset with chuckling. His hands were sure, however, when he lifted her down from the *hataar*. That was when she noticed all the dead animals strung up in the nearby trees, some already skinned, some simply strung up to drain blood. It was revolting, but she had known to anticipate such antiquated means of food gathering on other planets. She had even, in the back of her mind, known that the *taraan* and the two smaller animals tied to the *hataar* were destined for consumption. Just because Kystran had stopped killing its animals for food hundreds of years ago didn't mean all cultures had advanced to the use of other food sources.

"Your fear comes late, woman."

Tedra turned to see who had made this comment. She had to look up. This was going to get tedious after a while, but just then she smiled. The warrior had light brown hair and eyes, and was almost as handsome of face as Challen. He was certainly as handsome of body, and she let her gaze move slowly down his, then back up, noting when she met his eyes again that she'd managed to disconcert him.

The other men had drifted back to whatever they had been doing, all except this one. "What fear is that, warrior? If you think I was taking seriously that bit of nonsense about my making a tasty morsel for the stew pot, think again. Besides the fact that you fellas would choke to death on me if you *were* cannibalistic, the barbarian here might object to losing my month of service."

"Of course, you would not object yourself, would you?" Challen put in dryly.

"Me?" Tedra said, wide-eyed. "Argue with barbarians? I wouldn't dream of it, babe."

She saw him stiffen at her persistence in calling him babe, but she was saved by the other warrior's question. "From where does she come, Challen, that she speaks so strangely?"

"An excellent question, that." Tedra grinned. "I dare you to tell him my version instead of yours."

"You may do so yourself, *kerima*. As I told you, Tamiron enjoys a good tale as well as I."

Tedra made a face of disgust. "You're no fun at all to goad, warrior," she complained. "He isn't going to believe me any more than you did, so tell him whatever you like. I'll save the truth for your *shodan*. At least *he* ought to be smart enough to let me prove what I say, unlike some people I know."

"Challen—" the other warrior began, only to be cut off abruptly.

"She is Tedra, a woman of Kystran, which she claims to be a world other than Sha-Ka'an."

"A sky-flyer?" Tamiron said in amazement.

"So she claims."

"Wait just a farden minute," Tedra demanded. "Either I'm dense, or you've just admitted you've heard of other world travelers before. If that's so, then why did you—"

"It is not a new tale, woman, just one that cannot be proved."

"But I *can* prove it. Just give me my phazor and I can—"

"This I will not do."

"But—"

"No."

Tedra ground her teeth together. She knew an adamant, no-getting-around-it *no* when she heard one, and she'd just heard one.

"Have it your way, barbarian," she said sourly. "But when my month of service is up, I'm getting on with the business of world trade and mercenary hiring, and you can bet your farden *fembair* that you won't stop me."

"Again does she mention limited service," Tamiron said to Challen. "Yet is she bound as a captive. Surely you do not mean to relinquish such a splendid prize?"

When Challen failed to answer immediately, Tedra smirked. "What's the matter, babe? Having regrets now that you must admit you fought—"

"There is my tent, woman," he interrupted her with a nod toward the tent behind her. "Inside it is where I sleep. I have no regrets." Tedra was flushing with that reminder as he went on to say to Tamiron, "The woman was claimable, but refused to accept my claim. She challenged me instead, and I did not offer the same refusal."

"She challenged—?"

That was as far as Tamiron got before he burst into laughter. And Tedra knew he wasn't laughing over the fact that Challen had accepted the challenge, but because she had been, no doubt in his opinion, foolish enough to challenge a warrior. That was, if he even believed it. But Tedra had been laughed at one time too many that day.

"How much trouble would I get into by showing him that wasn't a joke?" she asked Challen in all seriousness. "After all, the element of surprise is everything, as you found out for yourself."

He stared hard at her. He must have realized she

was referring to how easily she had tossed him on his backside when he wasn't expecting such a move, for after a moment he took hold of her arm and, without a word to either her or Tamiron, safely remove her from the temptation of causing trouble.

"Was it something I said?" Tedra purred sarcastically before she was ensconced inside the barbarian's tent—and once again in a place where he slept.

Chapter Thirteen

It was a good-sized tent with ample head room and some kind of thick material for walls well staked to the ground. Tedra came to know just about every inch of it as she paced the interior waiting for the barbarian to return. She was hungry, irritable at being left alone the rest of the afternoon with only the *fembair* to keep her company, and even more annoyed that she'd been ordered to remain there.

Because the order had been given in a "place of sleep," she had to obey it. But it had come to her after she was alone that Challen's place of sleep was also his living space, that the tent was just one large room, which meant he could order her about all day long rather than just at night when he retired, as she had assumed would be the case. The only time she wouldn't be subject to complete obedience was outside the tent, but if he wouldn't let her out . . . They were definitely going to have a talk about this, among other things. This finding things out when it was too late for her to do anything about them was not the way she operated.

The white *fembair* had remained, stretched out on the floor in an upright position like the king of beasts it likely was. Occasionally its long tail would swish as those great blue eyes followed her every movement. When her belly had begun to growl, she had wondered if the feline wasn't getting hungry, too, and she developed a definite wariness as the hour grew later and the interior of the tent darker.

When the tent flap did finally open, Tedra felt enough relief to temper the irritation she'd experienced. Seeing a plate of food in Challen's hands further appeased her. But she didn't quite smile in welcome. He had ignored her for several long hours, after all, left her with nothing to do and a great beast to guard her. The guarding had been unnecessary. She'd told him she would honor her service to him, and as she understood the rules, that meant obeying him whether she liked his orders or not.

"Why have you not uncovered the gaali stones, woman?"

"If I was supposed to have uncovered something, you should have said so. I'm not a snoop to go through someone else's possessions when they're not around."

She had been tempted, however, not that he had many possessions to snoop through. A large fur rug or blanket, however you chose to use it, was laid out on the floor; one well-stuffed fur sack by it and a small wooden box were all that sat on the big square of material that covered the floor area, more of the stuff the tent was made of.

"You like the dark, then?" he asked her, coming forward to set the plate down on the floor next to the fur blanket, which he sat down on.

"What's the dark got to do with rocks?" she wanted to know, only to hear him sigh.

"Truly do you try my patience with this pretense of ignorance of everything natural to our world."

"Your world," she corrected. "I keep telling you it's not mine."

"So you say. And I suppose you know not what is a gaali stone box?"

She grinned now. "Sure. That's got to be one there next to you, since it's the only box in here. Now what's a gaali stone?"

He didn't tell her, he showed her, opening the box. Tedra gasped as the tent filled with light. She dropped down to her knees beside him for a closer look and saw the five smoothly rounded stones inside the little box, each glowing with a bright blue light. She could stare at them without her eyes hurting, yet they gave off such light that the inside of the tent was as if it were lit by the sun.

"Amazing," she said in fascination. "It's some kind of energy source, right? I wonder how it would compare with crysillium, which was discovered just a few hundred years ago. Before that, our ships could travel only at hyperspeed. Now we get stellarspeed, which is ten times faster and makes it so much easier to visit neighboring Star Systems. But these stones look like pure energy. Are they hot?"

Challen had been staring at her in vexation as he listened to her, but she didn't know that. He answered her question now by picking up one of the gaali stones and placing it in the palm of her hand. It was actually cool to the touch, which was even more amazing, and seemed almost weightless. And when he closed the box on the other four stones, the tent was then lit only with a dim light by the one stone still uncovered. The more the brighter, obviously, and Tedra had to wonder what a really big stone could do.

She suddenly became all business as she glanced at him. "This is something I could trade for, Challen. Is there a lot of it on Sha-Ka'an? Is it easily obtainable?"

He took the stone from her, set it on top of the

box, and moved the box away from her. "Eat the food I have brought you," was all he said.

"All right, so maybe you don't have the authority to trade with me, but you could at least answer my questions about your gaali stones."

"You will not speak to me of trade, woman. You will eat now; then will you work upon my body as I did earlier mention."

The reminder that she was to give him a massage sent all thoughts of trade right out of Tedra's mind. She felt her body come alive with arousal just from the thought of touching his. She squirmed where she sat back on her heels, glanced at the plate piled high with large chunks of roasted meat and some type of root vegetable, and wasn't hungry anymore.

"Why don't we do the massage first?" she suggested, only to see him shake his head.

Her disappointment was almost palatable. Well, what had she expected? He was made of stone, after all. What had made her think that a massage might arouse him enough to finally share some sex with her? He didn't look any more interested in sex-sharing now than he had all day.

She picked up the plate and stared at the food in an effort to get her mind off the question of whether she was going to get breached tonight or not. There were no utensils to eat with, so she hesitantly picked up a chunk of meat with her fingers, trying to ignore the fact that it had been a live animal not so many hours ago.

Challen had leaned back on an elbow on the fur, but watching her, he couldn't help but see the face she made with her first bite. "You have no liking for *kisrak?*"

"I suppose I'll get used to it since I'm going to be here at the very least a month."

"And where do you think to go when a month passes?" he asked indulgently.

"You told me not to speak of it."

He snorted. "There is other meat roasted if *kisrak* suits you not."

She was surprised at the offer. At least it wasn't in his plans to starve her, which was reassuring after she'd waited so long for this nourishment.

"Thank you, but one kind or another isn't going to make any difference, since it's the meat itself I've never had before. We have stuff that tastes like your *kisrak*. We even call it meat, and it comes in a variety of different tastes, textures, and colors. But it's not real meat. We stopped killing animals for food centuries ago."

"Unreal men, and now unreal meat. What else is unreal in your Kystran?"

She gave him credit for concealing his disbelief behind a bland expression. But she'd take any opportunity she could to tell him of the wonders of the modern worlds. She never knew when she might hit on the one thing that might convince him she wasn't just spinning tall tales for his amusement.

"There are lots of things, I guess, though I pretty much take them for granted. Take pets, for instance. Since many of our animals became extinct during the Great Water Shortage, the few remaining live animals suitable for pets are so outrageously expensive that only the really determined are willing to pay the price, especially when mechanical pets are so much cheaper. Now, I'm not talking about pets like your *fembair* there, but something cute and cuddly, with all the behavioral qualities of the animal it's meant to resemble.''

"You own such a pet?"

"I've got Martha, who gives me all the trouble I can handle. What do I need with a mechanical dog programmed to dump on my carpet every so often?'' At his blank look, she made a face. "That was a little humor, barbarian. Actually, it was a toss-up for me between buying a house in the suburbs and buying a pet. I chose the house, wanting a little privacy more than companionship, since I did already own Martha, who is a companion of sorts, just as Corth is. But I would love a pet as soon as I can save up enough exchange tokens again to afford one."

"A real pet would cost as much as a place to live?" He was no longer hiding his disbelief.

"Just about." She grinned. "Aren't the rare things here more expensive than what you have in abundance? What about your gaali stones? Are they very—"

"Now do we change the subject," he said shortly.

So much for slipping that by unnoticed. "Very well, but I'll change it. I have some questions for you anyway. What would happen if I ask for protection of another warrior before my service ends? Would you two end up fighting over me?"

"Do you seek to cause deliberate mischief, woman, you will be punished."

She smiled at his set look. "I was only curious, babe. How else can I learn the rules unless I ask? *You* seem too content to wait until I break them before telling me about them. That's rather late from my point of view."

He ran a hand through his hair, actually seeming flustered. "It is strange, having a woman not know the laws. *All* women know the laws from the earliest age."

"In other words, you haven't deliberately tried trapping me with my ignorance? Why, barbarian, I guess I owe you an apology, then." This was said too dryly to be taken seriously. "Now let's try this one on for size. What happens if I challenge someone while still under challenge loss to you?"

He sat up, an indication he wasn't pleased with the direction her thoughts were taking. "This you will not do, woman."

"I won't? Who says I won't? For that matter, what if I feel like challenging you again?"

"You will lose; thus will your service be extended for another month."

"But if I won, you'd have a month to look forward to Tedra-getting-even, wouldn't you? Now that's a sweet thought. Would it make you think twice before punishing me again?"

"No."

"You could at least have hesitated a little before answering that," she said sourly.

He smiled at her now. "I have told you what you must do to avoid punishment; thus should there be no more."

" 'Should' is a far cry from 'will.' Now don't get me wrong," she said when his smile disappeared. "I have every intention of obeying you when I'm supposed to. . . . Speaking of which, these living quarters of yours are going to have to be redecorated if this is where I'm to live for the next month. There's going to have to be some kind of divider rigged up to make only one section of this tent the place where you sleep."

"That will not be necessary."

"Then we've got a really big problem, friend, because nothing was said about you keeping me all day long in your bedchamber. If that's the case—"

"It is not. This is merely the camp we have used while hunting in this area. On the new sunrise do we return to Sha-Ka-Ra, the town where we live."

"In houses, I hope."

"Yes, in houses." He grinned. "We are not as primitive as you would make us."

"That's debatable, but I'm willing to reserve judgment," she said, pointedly looking at her greasy fingers.

This caused the barbarian to burst into laughter. "Come, *kerima*, I will take you to the stream where you may wash."

"A cloth will do. Until you come up with one of those *chauri* for me to wear, or at least a belt to make this covering halfway decent, I'll stay in here—if it's all the same to you."

"It is not," he replied, though he wasn't annoyed with her for trying to get out of what had been in effect a command. "You must also relieve yourself."

"Oh," she said, but charged through her embarrassment by adding, "Well, that changes everything. Silly me, for thinking the bathroom was going to pop out of the walls of a tent." At his stare, she grinned. "Never mind. I've amused you enough for one day with the wonders of my—Kystran. Lead on."

Tedra set her plate aside and stood up, but before Challen joined her, he drew to him the fur sack and took out of it the rope he had earlier removed from her wrists. She scowled at it, then at him, but held out her hands anyway. He grinned as he stood up, then wrapped the rope around her waist, tying it together for her, and even pulling the sides of her covering closed so that they would stay closed.

She looked up at him and managed a smile herself. "Thanks. I guess you're not so unlikable after all."

"This I am pleased to hear you say, but you will be bound again to enter Sha-Ka-Ra."

Tedra's eyes narrowed angrily. She had a real urge to sock him one, but since her hand was likely to come out the loser, she restrained herself—just.

"You really ought to work on your strategy, barbarian," she said contemptuously. "A smart man would have waited until tomorrow to tell me that little gem."

He seemed not the least concerned with her pique. "There will be honesty between us, woman, thus do I tell you now."

"And give me the whole night to think about a repeat of the humiliation I was put through today? Thanks a lot. I can do without your farden honesty!"

She flounced out of the tent then, but had to stop and wait since she didn't know in which direction the stream lay. More fuel to grit her teeth on. She couldn't even make a decent exit in this place.

Chapter Fourteen

The promised stream Tedra was led to was reached through a stand of trees and down a short, brush-laden path. A moon had risen, a large yellow thing that gave a hazy light through a mist of clouds. The water glittered and bubbled softly between two grassy banks, each set with small white flowers that looked silvery gold in the moonlight.

It was a romantic spot, secluded, perfumed by flowers, the stream providing a tinkling serenade, a perfect spot for sex-sharing, but all Tedra could think about just then was cutting her escort up into little chunks and feeding him to the fish, if there were fish. But if her mind *had* turned toward amorous thoughts, they would have been wasted, since the barbarian tactfully left her alone to her ablutions, which she made short work of. Roughing it was for the birds.

"If you're picking up any of this, Martha, I hope you blow a fuse laughing. Water. They actually wash with water here. And I'll wager there's not one single toilet on the whole farden planet. If I wasn't a history buff and knew a smattering of how our own primitives managed this sort of wilderness living back on the mother planet, I'd really be embarrassed right about now."

She didn't get an answer, nor would she without her phazor unit. But if Martha was listening, then she had a fix on her and could have Transferred her out of there. Since Tedra remained where she was, Martha either was still playing games or hadn't found her yet. She hoped it was the former. She seriously doubted she could take more than a month of this.

She made her way back to the camp without incident, since there was no one else about, and back to the tent she had spent the afternoon in. The big barbarian was there waiting for her, stretched out on his fur blanket, his arms behind his head, perfectly relaxed.

"You took a big chance that I'd come back after that little bomb you dropped on me about tomorrow," Tedra said abrasively, but her look alone would have told him she was still in a slow simmer about it.

"I have decided to trust in your honor. It is a rare thing in a woman, but a quality you have shown you possess."

She hated that bubble of calm he was cocooned in. She hated his magnanimous gesture at the moment, too. So what if he trusted her to abide by the terms of her defeat? Fat lot of good it would do her tomorrow, when she was being gawked at by a whole town of barbarians.

"Is that why you've sent the beasty away? I didn't appreciate having him for a guard dog today."

"Sharm has grown lazy living with me. He stalks his food during moonrise, when most of it sleeps."

"How nice for him," she retorted.

He chuckled at her expression. "You grow more womanly by the moment, *kerima.*"

"Why? Because I object to being trussed up and put on display for the amusement of your people?"

"Because you sulk over what you cannot change. A warrior does not expect a woman to behave otherwise."

"Doesn't he?" she snarled. "And you call it sulking? I'd call it killing mad, at least in my case, and since I'm a Sec 1 and trained to demolish people with my bare hands, I wouldn't exactly call what I'm feeling right now womanly."

"But so it is when you have no control over it. Or can you control it—as a warrior would?"

"Of course I can. I'm not stomping all over your body, am I? What is that, if not perfect control?"

"Wise restraint, for which I commend you. But can you practice it while you give me service?"

"Service?" She stared at him blankly for a moment, then hissed through her teeth, recalling the massage he had requested. "You must be joking. I'm in no mood to give you service—of any kind."

"But you will," he said simply. "And you may begin now."

She watched incredulously as he turned over and rested his tawny head on his folded arms. He actually expected her to go to him and put her hands on his body, to gently knead the soreness from his muscles. And what if she didn't? Would she be punished again? She shivered, recalling his kind of punishment. She wasn't ready to tempt that again, not when she wasn't guaranteed relief anytime soon.

She slowly approached him and knelt down at his side, but so he wouldn't have any doubt that this was definitely service under protest, she said, "There are massages, warrior, and then there are *massages*. The one you get isn't likely to be the one you were expecting."

"Then you may begin with the one you now wish to give me, but you will end with the one you say I was expecting; thus will I know the difference."

Why the farden hell had she given him warning? Talk about spoiling some perfectly subtle revenge.

And he'd made it an order to be obeyed. She wished she'd never heard of the word "honor."

But she had his permission to have at him for a while, his golden back there for her to work her frustration out on. This she did, pounding, gouging, and giving anything but a soothing, pleasurable massage. The trouble was, her hands didn't last very long giving out that kind of punishment, yet she heard not a single grunt of discomfort from her victim. He should have at least tensed up when she worked over the areas where her blows had landed that morning during the challenge.

"Did I really hurt you today?" she wondered aloud.

"No."

Tedra sat back on her heels, her hands going to her hips, and glared at the back of his head. "Then would you mind telling me why I'm doing this?"

He rolled easily onto his back, and those dark eyes held amusement as they locked with hers. "Why you did what you have been doing is because you are still upset with me. Why I requested a massage was so you would the sooner become accustomed to my body. Do you now show me the difference."

She didn't know what to say to that. The massage had been for her benefit. That was really considerate on his part—if she were leery and intimidated by his size, which he probably thought she was. He couldn't know that his very bigness was one of the things she found so to her liking.

She felt rather petty at the moment for taking her frustration with his customs out on him. He didn't personally make the rules that governed how challenge losers were to be treated, after all. And what was a little humiliation, anyway, if she could eventually get an army of these warriors back to Kystran?

"I'm sorry," she said, willing to make it up to him. "You want the difference, you got it. If you'll just turn over—"

"No."

"No?"

"You will use my chest to show me."

"Oh."

Her cheeks began to heat as she glanced at his massive chest. Before she even touched it, she could feel that same heat coiling down into her belly. When she did touch it, her arousal came so swiftly, she nearly groaned. His skin was so warm, yet gave little under her gentle kneading; was so silky to her fingertips, yet so muscle-hard. Stars, she wanted to lean forward and kiss his chest, to rub her face over it, to bite it, but he gave no indication that he wanted anything other than the massage. She was so hot for him she should have gone up in smoke, but his eyes were calmness itself as he watched her, his body relaxed, without tension—without arousal.

She leaned back slowly to meet his eyes with bewilderment in hers. "Was I wrong in thinking service in your bedchamber meant we would be sharing sex?"

"Sharing sex?"

He didn't know what she was talking about. "What did those warriors call it?" she asked herself. "Oh, yes, use." But he still didn't comprehend, and it dawned on her that the Sha-Ka'ari, being slaveholders and accustomed to taking their pleasure without giving any back, would have a different name for sex-sharing than these warriors would. "What do you call it when a man and woman come together intimately?"

"Fun." He grinned, finally understanding.

"I'll buy that." She grinned back. "But is that your only word for it?"

"There is joining, mating, giving pleasure. You would call it making love."

"I would, but you wouldn't? Why is that?"

"Enough questions for this rising, *kerima*. Now do we sleep."

Stars, even talking about it didn't get him interested. Obviously she was not going to get breached today no matter what she did.

She sighed. "All right, friend, just point me to my bed and I'll—"

"Your bed is here with me. Did you think it would be otherwise?"

"With as little interest as you've shown in wanting to have 'fun' with me, yes, actually, I did think it would be otherwise."

She could have bitten her tongue off for letting that out, especially when it sounded so much like a complaint—and in fact was. But the barbarian chose to ignore it and simply moved over some to make room for her on the fur. There was nothing for it but to lie down beside him, though she wasn't likely to get much sleep with him so close. She wished he would have the same problem, but that *was* her problem, that it wouldn't bother him at all.

"Put your arms around me, *kerima*."

She looked at him askance. "Have you changed your mind about sleeping?"

"No."

"Then I'd rather not touch you anymore if it's all the same to you."

"But you will."

Stars, how she was starting to hate those three words. "Am I being punished, Challen?"

"You are being shown the manner in which you will sleep each night. Because it is not yet the time for joining does not mean I do not want you close to me. Do you now do as you were instructed."

Not yet *time* for joining? Were there customs that must be adhered to in this, too, so many days maybe, that he couldn't take advantage of his challenge win? It made her feel better to think so, which was why she didn't come right out and ask. At least it meant he wasn't oblivious to her charms, that he was only practicing his miraculous warrior's control.

She scooted over and tucked one arm to his side, draping the other over his chest. One of his own arms came around her to hold her there.

"Do you now kiss me."

Tedra closed her eyes as those words sent a thrill down her spine. "Is that to be part of the nightly ritual, too?"

"It is."

"All right, you asked for it."

She squirmed upward until she could reach his mouth, then plastered hers to it, but that was not what he'd had in mind. He stopped her so quickly she barely got a taste of him.

"This was to be a kiss for sleep, woman, not for joining," he chided her.

"I never thought I'd contemplate rape," Tedra growled, but she said it in Kystrani, didn't care if that annoyed him or not, and turned around to give him her back. If he insisted she put her arms around him again, he'd have a war on his hands. He must have sensed that, for he didn't insist. He didn't say another word. But his big hand came to rest on her hip. He was still keeping her close.

Chapter Fifteen

Challen woke with the woman's movement. He had lost count of the number of times she had disturbed his sleep with her sighs, mumblings, and turnings, but fortunately, each time his sleep had easily resumed. He doubted that she had gotten much herself, though. Such was to be expected of a captive or newly claimed woman, but not for the reason that bothered his little challenge loser. She had not lost sleep through anxiety, tears, or simple fear of a new warrior she must obey, but because her need was upon her. He had gone to sleep with the smell of her arousal strong in his nostrils.

Long did he debate whether to ease her need without joining. Such could be done easily. But did she not know this, he would prefer she remain in ignorance of it for now, so he did nothing. Also, she could only benefit by her need still being great when he did join with her. Better a slight discomfort through the night than true pain, were she not ready for him when the effects of the *dhaya* juice wore off.

When he opened his eyes, he saw the sun had begun its rising already. When he turned to find the woman was facing him again, he also discovered, instantly, that the last of the *dhaya* juice had, in fact, worn off even while he had thought about it. His loins filled with need, and as was expected when denied with *dhaya* juice, that need was now so powerful it was painful. It was also worse than it had ever been before, for he had the previous rising's memories to goad him, clear and concise, memories of his touching the Kystrani, of her touching him, of every burning, passion-filled look she gave him from those fascinating aquamarine eyes.

He groaned, closing his eyes again, fighting down the need to draw the woman beneath him and end the pain immediately. He had bragged to her of a warrior's control. Where was it now?

He concentrated on the pain rather than on his need, opening his mind to it so that it surrounded him. It was not intense enough to put him into the trance-induced state that would ignore all feeling, but it was enough to give him a measure of calm, to return some of the normal control a warrior possessed when not influenced by *dhaya*. The urgency was still there, but it was no longer the crazed wildness of a mindlessly driven beast.

Again he looked at the woman still in the deep sleep of exhaustion. Even with dark smudges beneath her eyes to attest to her unpleasant night, he found her incredibly beautiful. She was using his arm as a pillow, but both her hands were wrapped around it, too, as if she felt in sleep what he had also felt, a need to hold tight to what he had found, a fear it might be lost otherwise.

The fear was not unfounded on his part, not that he thought the woman would flee him. He had spoken true when he told her he trusted in her honor. There was not another woman he would have said that to, for Kan-is-Tran women could claim honor, but were known to overlook it when it suited them. He was certain this was not so with the Kystrani, for she was, in fact, a warrior woman. Her every action claimed this to be so, even the arrogance she professed to be as great as his.

No, the fear stemmed from another source, one not imminent, but there nonetheless. He had bound this woman to him for no more than a month, and a month was a very short time. It had seemed the ideal solution at the time, to use her unwise challenge against her, but now he was not so sure. True, he had sensed her strength of will, had known it would be set against him for as long as she resisted his claiming, and he suspected that resistance would be like nothing he had ever encountered before. Not even her attraction to him, which was clear in her bold, warriorlike manner of looking at him, would surmount that resistance. And yet he had decided from the moment he had gotten a closer look at her that she would be his. Had a protector appeared suddenly to prevent his claiming of her, he would have fought for her, such was his desire to have her bound to him. But he did not want her to fight him, so the challenge had indeed seemed ideally suited to his needs, except that it was a temporary solution.

If he could not make her want his claiming within the time the challenge loss had given him, then it was her right to seek protection elsewhere at the end of her service, and that did not please him at all. Already she was thinking of doing just that, if her questions were any indication. And already he had begun thinking of ways to get around it, even if he must trick her into challenging him again. To challenge her himself would unfortunately not have the same effect. She would see it for what it was, an attempt on his part to make her his claimed woman without limitations, which was what she so strongly objected to. It was the nonpermanence of the challenge loss that allowed her to accept it. Of this he was certain.

His gaze moved slowly over her face, noting things that the brilliance of her eyes and vitality and boldness of her expressions had kept him from noticing before. There was color on her cheeks that did not belong there, a very subtle rose tint that was barely discernible. Surrounding both of her eyes was a thin line of black that was not natural. He touched it at the corner of one eye without waking her, but nothing appeared on his finger. He had heard that the women of Mal-nik in the north sought to enhance their beauty with face-coloring, but with colors that did not fade or smear?

His little warrior was not of Mal-nik, but from where *did* she come? This he would not think of, for what he suspected he did not want to be true. And right now his body was telling him that his control was slipping, soon to be gone entirely. Did he not wake her now, she was going to miss their joining, it would be over and done with so quickly. Coming off *dhaya* juice was the one time a warrior lost his arrogance and pride in the skills that never failed to satisfy his woman, for those skills were most times forgotten in the wildness of need. Such must not happen with this woman.

In moments Challen had removed his *bracs,* then had to fight again not to bury himself immediately in the warm, sleeping body beside him. The scent she wore was still strong, filling his nostrils with floral sweetness. But it was the scent of arousal he wanted to smell now, and with that in mind, he made short work of removing her covering, bringing her half awake. His kiss completed the process, deep and compelling, demanding the desire she had known so frequently and with such swiftness on the previous rising.

When he leaned back to judge her reaction, her eyes were droopy but open, her lips smiling at him. "I thought you'd never get around to this," she said with a sigh.

"You do not fear joining with me?"

"Do I look afraid?"

"Your words are brave, *kerima,* but I would expect no less from you. But even Kan-is-Tran women fear a warrior's touch at first, no matter that they might want that warrior for their own. Such fear is normal and continues until the woman grows accustomed to her warrior. Such fear is even more prevalent in women captured or claimed."

"Into which category I presumably fall? Let me take a wild guess, babe. Your women aren't much bigger than I am, are they?"

"This is so."

She laughed suddenly. "It must be hard, being a giant. Poor baby . . . now don't take offense. It really is funny from my point of view. Have you had to be so careful with all your women?"

"Women are fragile and easily damaged," he told her shortly, annoyed with her humor and her ability to completely distract him from his purpose.

"Some women maybe, but I've gone through a rough-and-tumble training. I'm not going to break if you feel like letting go."

Unfortunately, she did not know what she was suggesting. "I fear I cannot be gentle with you whether I wish it or not. Too much do I remember of the previous rising."

"All that superhuman control coming back to haunt

you, huh? Well, I've got no sympathy for that, babe. Your farden control put me through hell.''

And his lack of it now would do the same if she did not be quiet and let him bring her to need. There was only one sure way to silence a woman without gagging her. This he proceeded to do for as long as his control lasted. It was not long.

The fire grew slowly, but when it arrived it was a conflagration that banished all traces of exhaustion from a sleepless night. And no sooner did she feel the full force of it than the barbarian moved to cover her completely. How had he known she was ready? Who cared. At last she was going to be breached, and by a man she'd known for only one day, though it seemed as if she'd known him forever. That was the incredible part, not that she wanted him so much and had waited so long for this to happen, but that she felt such an affinity toward him. Of course, having despaired of ever finding anyone who would suit her probably accounted for it. Going through so many ups and downs with him in the short time since they had met also would contribute to her feeling of having known him much longer. And none of it mattered next to the wild turmoil he so easily set loose inside her.

He was well positioned between her legs now, had risen up to do so, his full weight supported by his arms. The biceps bulged and glistened with moisture. There was so much of him to touch, and Tedra loved touching him, looking at him. But right now she wanted to feel him deep inside her.

"If you wait much longer, Challen, I'm going to—"

She gasped as his heat entered her. Stars, there was such tightness, such fullness. She knew her body would accommodate him, but she didn't think she could wait long enough for it to do so. She didn't think he could either. His great body trembled in restraint, his muscles quivered, sweat broke out all over him. Either he was in as much discomfort as she, or he was putting on another superhuman effort. The effort was wasted. Despite the discomfort of his entry, of knowing there would be greater pain to come, Tedra wanted all of him and she wanted it now.

"Are you waiting for my permission?"

He made a sound between a growl and a moan, and gritted out, "Permission is not needed of a challenge loser."

"It figures," was the best she could say at the moment, unable to take exception to anything just now except his restraint. "So why are you holding back?"

She thought he might laugh at that, but he couldn't quite manage it. "Because you are so small."

"*I'm* small? Maybe I'm normal, and you're just too big."

Challen could not believe he was even having this conversation, though he had to admit it was helping to keep him from savagely letting go. "Think you I have known so few women I cannot tell the difference? Long must have been your journey to come here."

Tedra didn't know what that had to do with anything, nor did she care just then. "Well, I'm not going to get any bigger, babe, until we start doing this on a regular basis. So if you're holding back on my account, don't."

"Patience is a virtue you would do well to practice, woman."

"Like you are? Forget that. If you don't get on with it, I'm going to think you're punishing me again by making me wait."

His eyes closed and his forehead dropped to hers. His straining had become worse. "I do not want . . . to hurt you."

She was filled with a warm feeling of tenderness for him upon hearing that, but there was no reason for them both to suffer. Her hands went to his face to make him look at her as she explained, "This is a breaching, Challen. Pain is unavoidable for me no matter what you do. I could have fixed it if I'd anticipated . . . You don't know what I'm talking about, do you? You will if you'll just fill me, so come inside, my gentle warrior. Do it now. I promise you I can take it."

There was no stopping him after hearing that, but he also heard the scream that ripped from her throat as he plunged to the hilt. Never in his life had he drawn such a sound from a woman, but instantly he knew the reason for it, had felt the skin as it was carelessly breached. Breaching—her word. If he had only known its meaning was literal. And now he understood her unusual smallness, not abstinence because of a long journey without a man at her side, but abstinence her whole life. She had been untouched, a woman of her bold looks and words, a woman, not a young girl. It was the one thing he would never have imagined her to be.

"Forgive me," she said, breaking into his thoughts, her voice not quite steady. "That—that wasn't as bad as it sounded."

"Was it not, little liar?"

"No, really, I think it was a mind thing—you know, expecting it to hurt with a *normal* man, but here you are bigger than big. So my mind would naturally assume it's going to hurt a bit more with you, and when it started to, the old mind thought, 'Look out!' and there you have it, a reaction all out of proportion.''

He almost laughed. The things she said could turn him inside out trying to understand them, but for once he felt he grasped her meaning.

''A mind thing? Women often cry before they have reason, merely in anticipation of a reason.''

''I'm going to let that comparison slide since you got the general idea, but take note there are no tears in my eyes.''

He smiled at her gently. ''I did not mean to sting your pride, warrior woman. Your pain was great, and yet you bravely discount it for my sake. You also attempt to take my guilt from me, for which I am grateful. It is I who must ask forgiveness for hurting you. Your—breaching—need not have been so brutal. Had I waited—''

She put a finger to his lips. ''I don't mean any disrespect, babe, but can we put this discussion on hold? If you haven't noticed, I'm not hurting now. And as much as I like the feel of you inside me, I'd also like to know what comes next, so I'd really appreciate it if you'd get on with it.''

She would appreciate it. A Kan-is-Tran maiden would have spent the rest of the day crying and screaming that she had been torn asunder and must never be touched again. His Kystrani maiden would appreciate it if he would ''get on with it.'' He did just that.

Chapter Sixteen

*T*edra wrapped her arms around her bent legs and laid her cheek on her knees as the soothing motion of the comb gliding through her hair began to put her to sleep. Challen had been at it for nearly a half hour already and gave no sign of wanting to quit.

When he had produced the golden comb after they had finished the evening meal, and ordered her to sit between his spread knees on the fur, she hadn't objected. Her hair was a mass of tangles by then and she didn't know the first thing about removing them herself without a styler at hand. Her warrior had made short work of the tangles, only he hadn't stopped there. She was beginning to think he simply liked to comb women's hair. That he might be fascinated with her own black locks didn't occur to her.

They hadn't left that morning for his hometown as he had planned. Tedra had fallen back to sleep after that first glorious experience of sex-sharing, and Challen had let her sleep the morning away. She had awakened when the sun was high overhead and had immediately been joined on the fur for her second, more leisurely experience.

Challen leaned forward now and bit her bare shoulder, bringing her to instant wakefulness. The man did like to bite. The many nips she had received so far had been hard enough to get her attention, but not hard enough to bruise. Yet the element of suspense was there each time those strong white teeth grazed her skin.

She sighed and glanced over her shoulder at him to see if there was a reason for the bite, then grinned at the look that was in his dark eyes. It was a look she was now able to recognize, one that hadn't been there at all yesterday but had appeared a number of times today, a great number of times. It meant he wanted her again. She didn't mind. She wasn't surprised either. The third and fourth times he had rolled her beneath him today she had been surprised. She'd stopped counting and stopped wondering about it, accepting the fact that she had an insatiable barbarian on her hands. For whatever reason he had denied himself yesterday, he was making up for it today. And how could she object when she was getting so much pleasure out of his need?

"Did you want something, Challen?" she purred teasingly, only to find herself swiftly turned and sprawled over his chest as he dropped back onto the fur. "Do I assume that was an answer?" she asked, planting a kiss on the smooth chin she had earlier watched him scrape a blade over.

Without a word he pointed to his lips and she obliged, lazily running her tongue over their grinning surface. When she did no more than that, however, he nipped—and missed. She giggled, then squealed when he tried again. The trouble with that game was his arms were around her to trap her there. Unable to get away, she was quickly kissing him exactly as he wanted, giving him the joining kiss he had rejected last night.

Before she got really carried away, however, he drew her head back, wanting to know, "Are you sore?"

The question was a little late in her opinion, but she didn't point that out. "No."

"You would not tell me if you were, would you?" She grinned. "No."

"This will be the last time, *kerima,* I give you my word."

"Just don't make the sacrifice on my account—or are *you* sore?" She got a bite on the neck for that insinuation. "Ouch! So you can do this all day *and* night. I never doubted it."

That brought a rumble of laughter from him. The man really enjoyed sex-sharing. Tedra found that she did, too, at least with him. He made her laugh. Sometimes he made her want to scream. And most times she *did* scream when the pleasure came upon her, it was so intense.

Right now he lifted her and sat her down on his lower chest, with her knees bent forward, her feet tucked near his hips. This put her entirely within the reach of his hands, and there was no part of her body that he left alone when he began caressing it. This time he wouldn't let her touch him, making her place her hands on her thighs and keep them there. All she could do was stare at him and watch the passion deepen in his eyes and wonder if it was reflected in her own.

"Give me your breast."

She made a sound like a whimper when she heard that request through the daze his hands had created. "It'll be . . . too much . . . Challen."

"Give me your breast," he repeated, making it an order.

She leaned forward slowly, groaning in anticipation just as he had claimed women do. But she knew she had good reason and she was right. The moment she was within reach, his mouth fastened on her nipple and began to suckle, and she went wild, knowing he was in no hurry, that he meant to take his time enjoying her. His urgency had ended that afternoon after the fourth time. Hers seemed to crop up each and every time they joined, regardless of how soon or how often.

She wouldn't beg him, she wouldn't.

She leaned away, only to be brought right back for her other breast to be suckled. Fire raced along her nerves, skidding from breasts to loins, pulsing in the latter. She trembled, she seethed in need. She forgot where her hands were supposed to be and shoved against him, but to no good purpose. She tried desperately to slide lower on his body to find him without his help, only to gain his hands on her hips keeping her where he wanted her.

Please, her mind screamed, while her teeth clamped on her lips to keep the cry silent.

And then she was under him and he was inside her, deep, deep inside, and she was coming, exploding around him, throb after throb of the sweetest, most glorious ecstasy, continuing on and on for as long as he drove into her, and this was endlessly, tirelessly. Oh, Stars above!

Tedra didn't know how much time might have passed. Her guess was that she had fainted, for suddenly she was looking up at Challen and she didn't remember her breathing having calmed down, or her pulse, but they were. He was smiling with a sort of male superiority that at any other time would have made her want to sock him, but right now she supposed it was completely deserved. He knew what he was about, her warrior. He might have driven her a little crazy wild this time, but the end result had been more than worth it.

"I'm going to sleep like a baby tonight," she announced with a sigh.

"First we will talk."

"Talk?" She blinked. There hadn't been much of that today, but now? "Ah, come on, babe, the moon's getting up there, and I'm feeling too mellow—" With a single tug she was sitting up, her legs were crossed for her, and her hands placed on her knees. A very talkable position. "I guess we'll talk," she said matter-of-factly, but her expression was grumbling.

"How is it you were an untouched maiden, yet you seemed . . . not to be?"

Tedra grinned and relaxed. "Is that the bug in your rug? It's called sex education, babe, and it's a mandatory subject taught to everyone. So just because I hadn't tried it didn't mean I didn't know the hows and wherefores." She suddenly laughed. "And now I can finally understand why Kystrani get a mite touchy when they miss their daily dose." At his blank look, she sighed. "That was a compliment of sorts—never mind. Did that answer your question?"

He shook his head. "What of your manner that bespoke experience?"

"What of it? Was I supposed to pretend I didn't like what I saw? Bold, brazen, and arrogant, that's me."

"Yet with such a manner, a woman would quickly find a mate for joining. How is it you have reached the age you have without joining?"

"Because I hadn't met you yet, sweetcakes."

"Is this another compliment—of sorts?"

"No 'sorts' about that one. I just didn't like what I was being offered—until there was you. Actually, it's a bit more complicated than that. I just didn't feel comfortable being with men I could . . . that I . . .''

"That you could challenge and defeat?''

She thought he would have taken offense at that just on principle for the male species, but he was smiling. "Maybe I should explain something, so you don't get the wrong idea again about Kystrani men. I'm not your average Sec 1 trained in weapons and warfare. I took my training a lot farther than that, studying not only modern combat but the techniques of our Ancients, too. Such things had long been forgotten, powerful weapons making the old ways obsolete.'' She frowned at his expression. "You don't look like you're getting the point.''

"Perhaps because I am not.''

"Then look at it this way. How confident would you feel in my presence if I were sitting here with a phazor pointed at you? Would you feel comfortable trying to seduce me, knowing that at any moment I might stun you? And remember, you're not coming to my bed with a similar weapon on hand . . . well, I mean they aren't. *You,* on the other hand, do have a similar weapon. Now do you see my point?''

"Your weapon is weaponless fighting? This is what your Kystrani men have forgotten the use of?''

"Exactly. Oh, they still know how to punch it out, but that's kiddie stuff next to what I can do. And a Kystrani male wouldn't raise his hand against a female anyway. So do you understand now why I was still unbreached?''

"Why you chose to be so, yes. Why you had not been claimed despite this, no. Does a man see what he wants and it is armed, he will find a way to disarm it.''

"Did you have to bring arrogance into this?'' she

said in disgust. *"You* can take that attitude, but a Kystrani male wouldn't. And your weapon, friend, is your incredible size, and muscles like steel rods." And she added a dose of her own arrogance. "Without that I'd have taken you, just as I did Kowan, a brother warrior of yours."

He snorted. "This Kowan could not have been a warrior of Kan-is-Tra."

"He isn't," she said, deciding not to elaborate if that pacified him, and it did. "Now can we go to sleep?"

"First do you explain your meaning of 'fixing it.' Did this imply you could have lessened the pain of a first joining?"

"Yes."

"Such is not possible," he snorted.

"Such is not only possible, it's become standard procedure on Kystran. All it takes is about five seconds inside a meditech unit, and that little membrane you ripped to shreds could have been removed without my feeling a thing."

"But you called it breaching, which signifies an opening."

" 'Breaching' is an old word, used before women got smart and started visiting a meditech first when they were ready to start sex-sharing. The word now simple means 'first experience.' "

"Then why did you not see to this painless removal when you came of age?"

"Because it would have gone on record as being done and I would have been expected to accept my first man shortly thereafter, and that, too, would have been duly recorded into my files. At least I don't have to worry about the Age of Consent law anymore, though how I'm going to prove an old-fashioned breaching without a computer as witness, I don't know. I suppose I'll just have to do it again for Martha's benefit when she finds me. That farden machine would never take me at my word about it."

"Woman—"

"I know, I know, that went right over your head, but you don't really want to hear about one of our more ridiculous laws, do you?"

"If such law pertains to you."

"But it doesn't anymore."

"It is my right to protect my woman, and this cannot be done properly if she is subject to laws I am unaware of. Thus you will let me judge—"

"So the tyrant has joined us, has he? That's a bad habit you have of letting him out—all right!" she gasped when his hand reached for her breast, and then she glared at him furiously, remembering he had promised they wouldn't share any more sex tonight, and so being, his intent had been to punish her for trying to avoid the topic. "You fight dirty, don't you? Don't think I won't remember—all *right!*" She dodged his hand as it came toward her again.

"Do you now explain."

"It's a stupid law, made by stupid men a long time ago, when it was first decided that sex-sharing was a farden cure-all for all kinds of minor ailments, and there was nothing for it but all women should benefit by it, whether they cared to or not. But it only applies to unbreached females, which I no longer am."

"Was this so difficult to tell me?"

"Yes, as a matter of fact, since it's a subject that has disturbed me for a long time. But that's not the point, Challen. I told you it didn't pertain to me anymore. Why didn't you just take me at my word and drop it?"

"You also said you must prove your breaching. Until such proof is given, are you not still subject to this law?"

He had a point. Her new stats, which listed her as Tamber De Oss and breached, didn't apply to Tedra De Arr, still unbreached on record. Of course, she couldn't resume her own identity on Kystran until Garr was back in power, but she'd still like to have the matter taken care of now that *she* had taken care of it.

"Security isn't likely to show up here to give me to my computer-picked breacher, Challen. And under our new government, I'd end up a slave if they did, but that's another story. And to hell with that gleam in your eye. I'm not getting into that unless you're willing to admit Kystran is another planet, not a country here on Sha-Ka'an."

He stared at her set features a moment and must have decided he'd done enough insisting for one evening. "You should not be angry with a warrior for his natural instinct to see his woman safe."

Was that an apology or a scolding? Or a subtle prod that she ought to be doing the apologizing? She didn't take the bait.

"Common courtesy would be to wait until help is requested," she pointed out.

"Not in Kan-is-Tra."

There was no getting around that little gem of truth. Sha-Ka'ani ways were not Kystran ways.

Chapter Seventeen

*T*edra noticed the mountain about midmorning, when they finally left the wooded region for a stretch of low hills intermixed with flat plains. Mount Raik, Challen named it, and it was a magnificent sight, rising straight up in the south to a pointed peak so high its top was capped with ice even in these subtropical climes. There were other mountains they were leaving behind in the north, the Bolcar Range, beyond which were the unknown lands of which Kystran was supposedly one. A long mass of purple hue, it could still be seen easily above the trees behind them, though there were no impressive peaks to it like Mount Raik, toward which they were now heading.

Close to noon, the green-grassed plains dwindled, and Tedra started seeing cultivated fields of grains and vegetables, but no houses or barns to go along with them. The trees were back, huge stately ones wind-breaking for a flowering orchard, a golden-leafed grove half surrounding a small blue lake, another forest of vivid color, where orange, yellow, and bright red leaves mixed with every shade of green and brown.

This they entered by a well-packed dirt road that wound around tree trunks, showing that nothing had been cut down to make way for it. Natural. Tedra liked that, that nothing had been destroyed to make room for man. In fact, she liked everything about this land, the pleasant weather, the beautiful scenery, and the men weren't so bad either.

Those whom Challen rode with shared a warm camaraderie, joking and ribbing one another, frequently laughing over humor that Tedra didn't quite understand yet, though she would with time. She had experienced a moment of keen embarrassment when she left Challen's tent that morning to find those warriors mounted on their great *hataari*, other *hataari* loaded down with the fruits of their hunt, and all just waiting for them. It was made even worse when she realized that they'd spent an extra day of hunting yesterday because Challen had spent the day with her, and every one of them had to know *why* Challen had delayed their departure.

And Challen, that overgrown lout, hadn't made the uncomfortable moment any easier by being overly familiar with her when he set her on his *hataar*, his hands lingering first on her waist, then trailing down her bare leg for all to see. Of course, he'd just finished sharing morning sex with her and so was still in a mellow, amorous mood. She'd promptly been put back into the mood she'd gone to sleep with, which was one of pure vexation, since Challen hadn't taken her annoyance with him last night into account, insisting she still cuddle against him and give him his good-night kiss after their talk.

But her new mad had lasted no more than half the morning, the day too beautiful, the company too good-humored to savor it any longer than that. Even the rope around her wrists didn't bother her as much as she'd thought it would. That was likely because Challen had left the tent early and come back with another rope, one he turned into a belt for her, which in turn made her brief covering more decent than some warm-weather outfits she owned. She'd been really grateful for that belt, the more so that she'd got it without having to ask. From his high-handedness of the night before to his doing something like that . . . there was more to her barbarian than she'd first thought.

Shortly after midday they stopped next to a meandering stream to share cold meat left from last night, also the small round cakes of a sweet white bread called *crumos*. The area was still well into the forest and amply shaded. Birds chattered overhead, along with small furry creatures that lived mostly in trees. Tedra had noticed at least a dozen new animals that morning, but all harmless, and all quickly disappearing at the approach of the large *hataari*.

She wasn't untied for this short meal, but that was all right, since Challen was then forced to the effort of helping her, thereby slowing down his own meal, which was in a sense poetic justice she found amusing. Stretched out by her side, he used his long dagger to cut chunks of meat into bite-size pieces to hand to her. He'd tried to put the food to her mouth at first, but had got a finger bitten for that demeaning effort. But she wouldn't have felt so smug or amused about the arrangement if she'd known he took pleasure in it. And if she'd realized he was deliberately taking his sweet time to provide an excuse to send the others on ahead, her nose would really have been bent out of joint.

As it was, she didn't suspect a thing, not even to wonder why none of the other warriors offered to wait what she figured would be only a few minutes, since Challen was already cleaning his dagger when the rest started moving on. Before the last man was gone from sight, he stood up; she did, too, moving directly to-

ward his *hataar* so she wouldn't have to be told. But
when he came up behind her, it wasn't to lift her onto
the animal's back.

She accepted his arms coming around her and the
gentle squeeze she received. She was, after all, feeling sated and mellow and all-around good for no reason she could put her finger on. She was also already
accustomed to the fact that her warrior simply liked
hugging and having her body pressed close to his.
But after a moment he turned her around, and she
wasn't even aware her rope belt had been removed
until she felt his large hands beneath her covering,
cupping her buttocks to draw her even closer, then
moving upward without hindrance over the bare skin
of her back.

When she started to ask what he thought he was
doing, her mouth was covered by his and the question
answered, and also forgotten. The warrior knew how
to kiss in a way that was extremely thrilling, bringing
lips, tongue, and even teeth into play, and heat, Stars,
the heat, setting off sparks in all points of her body.
It wasn't long before she was stretched out on the soft
grass, lost to the realm of sensation.

After the excess of yesterday, her body had been
feeling neglected without her realizing it, even after
she had been awakened that morning to dance to this
very tune. But that was hours ago, and so her pleasure
was full when it came, intense enough to wring a cry
from her that set off a cacophony of answering bird
calls from above.

Coming back to reality was slow, but her first clear
look at Challen's expression set off warning bells. He
was a man who had just had a victory of some kind,
and it took another moment for it to come together in
her mind, the fact that they were not in a place "where

he slept," the fact that she could have refused that joining, the fact that she had lost the option from the moment he kissed her, not because it was gone, but because she couldn't think straight when he was setting off fires in her newly awakened body.

"Why did you do that?" she asked, just to be sure.

He didn't try to pretend he wasn't aware of her meaning. "To see if I could."

"You mean to see if I would let you."

"Let us not quibble over a moot point."

"I'll quibble if I want to quibble," she shot back as she wiggled out from under him. "We're talking major advantage-taking here, Challen."

At that he chuckled. "Woman, to what do you object, that you did not think to say no, or that you did not want to say no?"

Color stole up her neck into her cheeks. "That isn't fair. You gave me no chance to think of that or anything else."

"Which was my intention."

"You're trying to turn me into a claimed woman, aren't you?" she accused him. "One you can command anywhere, anytime?"

His look said if-the-shoe-fits, but he answered, "This cannot be done during your service, for while you are challenge loser you have my protection, and only a woman without protection can be claimed."

"That's going round the block, warrior. We both know how the other would prefer it, and you've just proved you'll try to have it as you want it no matter what my official status is."

"Perhaps." He shrugged, then flashed her a purely boyish grin. "But that is the nature of a warrior. Did I not try, we would not have each enjoyed the other just now. But did you not want the pleasure I gave you, *kerima,* you had only to say so.''

''In other words, I can pretty well depend on this happening again?''

''Certainly.''

''And you don't feel that's breaking the rules?''

''When the matter is your decision? And it is your decision. Rules would be broken only if I gave you no choice.''

She still felt she'd had no choice, not after he'd first kissed her. But she saw his point. She didn't have to obey him outside of his ''place of sleep'' if his requests weren't reasonable. Respect was all that he demanded then, and she could tend her ''noes'' with the utmost respect. She didn't have to accept his advances either. He was just making sure those advances were too nice to be refused.

She gave a mental shrug. ''So I was a pushover this time. Don't expect that to be the norm, babe.''

''Yet you enjoyed it.''

''That's beside the point. Too much of a good thing and I might get to like it here. You wouldn't want me to become attached to you, now would you, when our arrangement is only temporary?''

''Yes.''

She frowned at him. ''Why? So you can think of me pining for you when I'm gone? Isn't that just like a man—''

She fell silent as Challen shot to his feet and grabbed up his sword. Tedra got up more cautiously. Though she'd heard nothing to explain his sudden tense alertness as his eyes scanned the area, she didn't think this was a ploy to end the subject. The *hataar* was making noises of restlessness, but . . . maybe it sensed something they couldn't, or that she couldn't.

Challen was certainly expecting something to happen, and she was smart enough not to distract him by asking what.

It arrived with such speed, she didn't see it coming. Suddenly it was just there and leaping for Challen's throat. This was missed, thank the Stars, since Challen moved aside at the last moment. The thing went sailing past him to come to ground a good distance away. But it pivoted instantly to face him again, proving its incredible swiftness, incredible because this was no small beast, whatever it was, but a long, ugly, misshapen thing that stood about four and a half feet tall, had large pointed ears, no nose to speak of, slanted yellowish eyes, and an extended jaw with razor-sharp teeth. It was bottom-heavy, with squat, powerful legs used for leaping at its prey, and a long, spiked tail that gave it protection against attack, since its arms were so short and thin they were likely useless for anything but feeding, though there were claws on each of its stubby fingers and toes, numbering in the threes.

It didn't think long about making another attack. It took only a few steps before those strong back legs thrust it up into the air again, and again it missed, though Challen got in a swipe with his sword this time as the creature sailed past him, but not to do any good, since its gray, hairless, wrinkly hide was so thick and rubbery, the blade seemed to bounce right off it. This went on a few more times before the animal realized it wasn't getting anywhere and changed its tactics.

Tedra had backed away slowly, but the creature wasn't interested in her, barely spared her a glance. It either had come upon man before or was more intelligent than it looked, for it seemed to sense Challen was the danger that must be got out of the way before it could feast on its find.

It came slowly now in simulated stealth, bent over so it crouched low to the ground, a clicking growl coming from it, as if it couldn't make up its mind whether to smack its lips in anticipation or sound its annoyance that it was taking so long to bring down its kill. Tedra held her breath, afraid it was going to leap when it was so close that Challen wouldn't have time to get out of the way. But he must have been thinking along the same lines, for he took the initiative with steady thrusts, moving the beast back, keeping it at bay. It tried circling around him, but the long sword remained extended, giving the creature no opening, which an actual swinging attack might have. And it was no longer making that clicking sound, was just growling now, getting good and frustrated.

This might have gone on indefinitely if Challen hadn't stumbled on an exposed tree root. He regained his balance before he went down, but for that brief unsteady moment, the sword twisted aside and the creature grasped the opening. Leaping for Challen's throat with that incredible speed it possessed, the thing was there almost instantly.

Tedra screamed and even took a step forward, though what she could do to help without a weapon she didn't know. But it wasn't soft neck those sharp teeth locked onto, it was Challen's shield-protected forearm, raised at the last second to ward it off. And before those vicious claws could get a grip on him also, his sword came up and sank into the beast's tender underbelly, its only vulnerable spot. Its cry was horrible but quickly dwindled to silence as the lifeblood poured out of it. Its jaw slackened to release Challen's arm, the only thing then holding it up. It flopped loudly to the ground, twitched pitifully a moment, then was still.

When Challen turned to look at her, Tedra was trying to control a mild case of trembling—belated reaction, she supposed, but she'd prefer he didn't notice. *She* finally noticed that he'd fought the beast stark naked. He was now spattered with blood from the kill, and grinning at her.

"This time you should have made your way up a tree, woman."

His added chuckle really scraped at her nerves. He wasn't the least put out over what had just happened, while her heart was still beating at her ribs.

"You mean that thing wasn't another pet of yours? You could have fooled me. What is it, anyway, or should I say, was it?"

"One of the hunters of the forest that has been with us for as long as anyone can remember, one fortunately that does not eat to excess. *Sa'abo*, it is called. Its speed enables it to be on its kill usually before the victim knows it."

"It sure had a fondness for your neck," she remarked as she came a bit forward for a closer look at the dead *sa'abo*.

"Such is the only way it kills, ripping out the throat of its prey. Were it smart enough to do otherwise, or even use its tail as a weapon, it would be more dangerous."

"*More* dangerous? That was enough for my taste. Any more killers like that I'm likely to meet up with?"

"Not this close to Sha-Ka-Ra. Sharm usually gives warning, but sensing his home ground, he has likely returned to his mate."

"Typical of a pet, not to be around when it could be useful," she said dryly.

"Were you concerned for me, *kerima?*"

"Certainly not," she snorted. "It was big, but you're still bigger."

"Then that was not your scream I heard?"

"Must have been some bird," she quipped.

To her chagrin, Challen threw back his head and laughed at the blatant lie. And then he started toward her, and she was beginning to think she could read minds, for she had little doubt what was now on his.

She put out a hand to stop him. "You can hold it right there, warrior. You're all covered in blood, if you hadn't noticed. And you've done enough advantage-taking for one day, so just turn yourself around and head for the water to clean up. I'd like to reach this town of yours before dark and any more *sa'abon* show up, if it's all the same to you."

He didn't answer, but surprisingly, he did do as she suggested. Yet he was smiling in a very pleased way as he turned toward the stream, and Tedra could guess why. The farden warrior liked the idea that she'd been concerned about him. She, on the other hand, didn't like it at all.

Chapter Eighteen

Sha-Ka-Ra was *not* what Tedra had anticipated. Perched on a flat plateau high up the side of Mount Raik, it was reached by a steep, winding road with barren hillsides on either side of it. This made the town ideally located for defense, especially with a solid mountain face behind it, yet she was relieved to see no high walls surrounding it, so obviously defense wasn't necessary. She hadn't been there long enough to consider that defense might simply be disdained.

Tedra got to see Sha-Ka-Ra from a distance, for it was visible as soon as they left the forest, flat cultivated land stretching for several miles before it. She could judge its size, which was impressive, and the types of buildings, all only one or two stories high, except for one. Smack in the center of the town was a white stone *castle*, for Stars' sake, with some round sections, some square or rectangular, but all seeming to be of different heights and shapes, as if each room inside had to be unique unto itself. A square tower in the center was the tallest section, spiral-roofed with a crenelated walkway at the top. It likely commanded a view of the entire countryside clear to the Bolcar Range, and maybe even beyond.

Tedra had seen computer-simulated castles, created from the Ancients' detailed descriptions of such dwellings from their own times, but nothing like this magnificent barbarian structure that towered over the town like a benevolent guardian. Likely it was cold, gloomy, and dreadfully primitive inside, but that white stone gave it an impression of warmth and welcome from a distance.

It could only be the residence of the town's *shodan*, so Tedra was delighted by the expectation that eventually she would get to see inside this primitive marvel, for surely she would meet with the lordly leader to discuss trade and the hiring of his warriors. But right now, as they approached the first buildings at the entrance of Sha-Ka-Ra, she was feeling nothing but nervous dread to be facing people again, to have them see her as she was, her wrists bound before her, her hair in wild disarray, her feet and legs bare, wearing only a farden scrap of fur. This was not how she had envisioned entering her first town on her first discovered planet, though she had to admit she was going to make an impression anyway, just not the right one.

The warriors who had returned before them must have given notice that something of interest would be coming along soon, for it seemed the whole town was turning out to watch Challen ride slowly down the wide main street. In windows, in doorways, in small and large groups standing about, there were barbarians everywhere. And if she had thought Challen's small band of warriors was unique in height and brawn, she was now shown otherwise. All the men of Sha-Ka-Ra were the same, give or take a half foot in height, and the same golden-to-brown coloring prevailed, too, in both hair and eyes, and this in both men and women.

Her first sight of the women she found of particular interest. She didn't know what she had expected, but it wasn't quite such blatant femininity portraying an image of softness, shyness, helplessness, their thin, scarflike gowns and cloaks floating around them in sections only adding to this image. Many of them might have the height for a Sec, but there wasn't a firm muscle or aggressive bone among them. And children! Stars, it had been so long since Tedra had seen children—in fact, not since she herself was a child. Yet here she saw dozens, of all ages, some held in women's arms, some holding the hands of warriors, some older boys even sporting swords. She stared with as much curiosity as they did at seeing a black-haired, aqua-eyed foreigner.

"What think you of Sha-Ka-Ra, woman?"

She wished he hadn't asked. She saw clean streets lined with trees and gaali stone posts, orderly marketplaces where goods and foods were sold or traded, a lovely green park dotted with shade trees and a small pond where children cavorted. Houses bore beautifully carved arches, large glass windows of different shapes and sizes, some with railed balconies or roof decks open to the sun, and each had its own grass yard, its own garden and stable.

The town was civilized but still primitive, the golden-skinned people handsome, wearing beautiful materials and jewels, yet also still primitive. Every man wore a sword, be he merchant, craftsman, or warrior; every woman and child were accompanied by a man, not allowed to venture forth alone even in the safety of their own town. So how did Tedra answer him, a man who had shown these people's attitudes to be the most primitive of all? Next to Kystran, this was the dark ages.

"Your town is . . . well, it's lovely, of course, open, sanitary, much more than I expected."

"Why do I sense constraint in your answer?"

"That's merely surprise. Remember, I was expecting caves. And at least your women aren't running around in animal skins like you men.''

That was unfair. The *zaalskin* leather of his tight black *bracs* was so expertly conditioned, it could have come out of a factory. The men in town wore the same, but with shirts, or to be more precise, a vest-like garment that was sleeveless in deference to the weather, fell just below the hips, and was merely wrapped and belted closed so that a deep V was left to show off the large round medallions they all seemed to favor. Which brought to mind . . .

''What is it, a warrior thing, that you men go out to face danger nearly naked, but wear more clothes at home?''

''The less restriction the better.''

Didn't she know it, but she said, ''You might not buy this, but most warriors, soldiers, or whatever you care to call fighters prefer a little protection in the way of armor or long-range weapons. It tends to in-crease life expectancy somewhat.''

He chuckled at her dry tone. ''Such warriors must then be lacking in skill.''

''Oh, great. Conceit before preservation. I should have known.''

He ignored her sarcasm this time. ''We carry shields to war or raid. That is enough.''

''You people war on each other?'' But she an-swered her own question. ''Yes, of course you must. How else would you gain the captives you mentioned, those poor creatures that your rules demand you bind up like you have me?'' The bitterness was back, but she couldn't seem to help it. ''I should be grateful,'' she added. ''At least the rule doesn't say naked *and* chained. Our own Ancients used to do that, drag the defeated through the towns in such an ignoble fashion.''

''So too do we.''

The color drained from her face as her eyes scanned the crowds so avidly watching her arrival. ''Are—are you going to do that?''

''If such had been my thought, *kerima,* it would have been done already.''

She swung around to look at him in surprise. ''You're breaking that rule for me?''

''You are not a normal challenger loser. Never before has a woman been such.''

Now if that didn't beat all. ''So you couldn't break two rules to let me arrive free of restraints?''

''And leave the Sha-Ka-Ran in doubt of what you are to me?'' he replied.

''Oh, sure,'' she said in disgust. ''We certainly wouldn't want to leave anyone in doubt. They might think I'm from another planet, after all, here to improve the quality of their lives if they're interested.''

''What they would think is that you are a claimed woman—mine. No other thing would occur to them.''

''Not even that I'm a free woman under your protection?'' she demanded.

She thought she had him there, but he disabused her quickly of that notion. ''A free woman would not be seen in public dressed as you are. She would insist I supply her with the *chauri* of my household before she was brought into town.''

And he'd do it, too, which showed her more clearly than anything else could the difference between a free woman of this world and a claimed one, who couldn't get away with making demands like that any more than a captive could, and *she* was lower than them all.

Chagrined, she heard her tone turn surly. "Have you people never heard of public announcements? A single statement from you would clarify what I am."

"Is this what you would like me to do?"

She started to say, "Of course," but his reasonableness gave her pause. And then it occurred to her that he still didn't believe anything she'd told him about herself, that all she was as far as he was concerned was a challenge loser, and *that* was what he was being magnanimous in offering to announce, even after he'd told her how challenge losers were scorned and treated worse than captives.

"You really are a jerk sometimes, warrior," she spat out before looking stonily ahead.

"Because I tease you? Announcements are made only for concerns of war, raids, or the safety of the town. They are never made for the sake of clarifying the status of a woman."

"Because we're so farden unimportant?"

"Because a woman's status is of concern to no one but her protector and his household."

"That's not exactly true in my case, but I'm not going to belabor the point. Let me ask you this instead. What if one of these warriors you're parading me before likes what he sees and wants to offer me double occupancy?"

"Double what?"

"The equivalent of a man and woman sharing their life together. The Sha-Ka'ari didn't have a name for it because all their women are slaves, but you must call it something when two people join up for exclusive sex-sharing."

That got a laugh from him, which she didn't appreciate. "Yes, we have such unions. But you are bound as a captive would be, and captives are rarely offered such union.''

She had a feeling *this* was the reason he broke only the one rule for her. He didn't want to be bothered by offers for her that would require the explanation of her true status.

"So I don't keep harping on this, why don't you give me the whole of it for once? Sorting out these subtle little differences between your women is driving me nuts, especially the difference between claimed and captive, which only seems to be the matter of a farden rope about the wrists.''

"A woman claimed is one who had no protector. Is she offered for, she becomes a free woman with all rights returned to her. A captive is one who is taken from her protector; thus is her stay to be considered only temporary.''

"Why?''

"This should be obvious, woman. If she is desirable enough to be taken captive, it is almost a certainty her true protector will seek her return, either by theft or by purchase. Thus would a warrior think long and hard before offering for a woman who is likely to be stolen from him, whom he must then steal back again if he still wants her, and such can go on indefinitely, year after year.''

"You mean you mighty warriors would rather play tug-of-war with the poor woman than settle the matter with swords?''

"Women are not fought over, *kerima.*''

"Oh, excuse me. I keep forgetting how unimportant we are.''

"Warriors have enough reasons to fight without adding—''

"Forget it, Challen,'' she interrupted coldly,

though she wasn't certain why his words upset her. "Explanations aren't going to improve on that statement. Even we Kystrani, who think nothing of sharing sex with a different partner every day, still occasionally fight over a woman, or a man, for that matter. Not to the death. That would go against the laws of Life Appreciation. But we get the matter settled. So I commend you for having conquered such a basic emotion as jealousy. Few other cultures can say the same.''

If she hoped he would tell her she had somehow misunderstood, she was doomed to disappointment. He said nothing more, so she didn't either, brooding instead on this unusual revelation. From what she had observed so far, it could well be that barbarians lacked many of the more frustrating emotions suffered by the humanoid species, such as anger, jealousy, disappointment, exasperation. And if that were so, then mightn't they also lack some of the nicer ones—such as love? Did they have living down to the animal instinct of survival, procreation, and nothing more? But they did possess humor, a purely human emotion. She clung to that thought.

Chapter Nineteen

*T*edra's mood perked up a bit when they made a turn and there at the end of the new street was the white castle. It was set behind high walls of the same white stone, with a wide arched gateway spanning the street and presently open to the public. It was an opportunity she couldn't pass up, for who knew when she'd find another?

"Why don't we stop by and pay our respects to your *shodan* before you take me to your home, Challen? I'd really like to meet him."

"Why?"

The question was a mere formality, since they both knew he already knew the answer. So she didn't feel she had to spell it out, just offer reassurance.

"I promise I won't mention a word about my origins, trade deals, or mutual benefits. I just want to meet him."

"Is your promise as good as your sworn word?"

"Good enough," she replied indignantly, annoyed to have her integrity again questioned. "I'll even swear to be a model of Kan-is-Tran womanhood, obedient to the letter."

"For that alone I would grant your request."

"Very funny," she retorted.

He must have thought so, for he was chuckling as they passed under the arched gateway. Tedra ignored him, her interest caught by the goings-on inside the wide walled-in yard that circled the castle, and her first close-up glimpse of the castle itself. It really was a spread-out conglomeration of uniqueness, with different-shaped rooms or buildings sitting one on top of another, with square or round towers separating or flanking them, or simply open spaces between that could be roof decks or upper courts. The castle climbed, almost in pyramid fashion, with the tallest, conical-roofed tower at the center.

There was a long rectangular building at the front of the castle that faced the gate, with a flat, crenelated roof that could be considered battlements. Six wide steps stretched across the whole front of this building so they could be climbed from any point, but they led only to a single set of double doors made of, if she wasn't mistaken, *Toreno* steel.

Likely there were other ways of getting inside such a large structure, but Tedra didn't see them right off. The doors were closed. Two warriors stood at attention on either side of them, and this was where Challen rode to. But other people who had come through the gate, either on *hataari* or driving vehicles pulled by large beasts of burden and laden with foodstuffs or goods, were all heading around toward the back of the castle.

There was a stable in the front yard, with a large fenced and partially shaded area beside it that contained a dozen or so unburdened *hataari* feeding from big troughs. Tedra actually recognized a few, or thought she did—Tamiron's animal, for one. But she was almost surprised into not mentioning it by her first sight of a *small* man coming quickly across the yard to them. He wasn't really small, just not warrior material by any means. Nor did he wear leather like a warrior, but a thin white material in both pants and shirt that looked cool and comfortable, but was otherwise unremarkable.

This could be no other than a Darash male of the servant class Challen had mentioned, and one who apparently worked in the stable, for it was the *hataar* he was after. He didn't speak, but he didn't behave in a cowed or servile manner either. Challen got a nod and a smile from him. Tedra didn't even get a curious glance, bare legs and feet or not.

She found that unusual enough to ask Challen, "He's not interested in women?"

"In Darash women, yes," the warrior replied easily. "All others are forbidden him."

"So he doesn't bother to look. Smart of him, I suppose, but does that work both ways? Are Darash women forbidden to warriors?"

He grinned quite unrepentantly as he said, "No."

"It figures," she said with disgust. Then, watching the servant head back toward the stable, she noticed those other *hataari* again. "Tell me something, Challen. You had to come here anyway, didn't you, to check in or whatever?"

"It was necessary I come here, yes."

"Couldn't you have just said so?"

"You seemed to prefer making bargains, *kerima.*"

"Sneaky as well as a jerk," she mumbled, only to get another chuckle out of him as he took her elbow and escorted her up the stairs.

Neither of the two sentinel warriors moved to open the double doors, but this proved unnecessary, for one side was opened from within before they were reached. The two warriors must have recognized Challen, since they didn't question his business for being there or anything. They didn't say a word, but, like the servant, offered him a smile and a nod. Unlike the servant's, their eyes were all over Tedra until she passed through the doorway, making her feel things were back to normal. Then every thought went right out of her mind with her first look inside the castle. Castle? Maybe the place looked like one from the outside, but inside it was more like a farden palace.

She was in a very wide, very high-ceilinged entrance hall that was as bright and airy as the outside. A blue carpet ran down the center, about a dozen feet wide, and on either side of it were shining, white marblelike floors. Walls that were barely walls but great open archways were also on both sides of this hallway, revealing rooms beyond spread with long, backless couches, low tables, small flowering trees in great urns, and tall open windows accounting for the airiness and light. Dining or gathering areas, she guessed, but the reason they were divided? Segregation of the classes—or the sexes?

Tedra was about to ask Challen when she became aware that he was being greeted by the man who had opened the door for them. With a warrior's height and dress, but much older than any she had so far seen, he bore a marked resemblance to Challen and was as incredibly tall; he had the same aggressive chin, the same strong nose and dark eyes, eyes so dark she still wasn't sure if they were brown or black. Only the hair was different, shorter, and not Challen's rich gold, but a chestnut hue.

"Then all has been peaceful?" Challen was asking the older man.

"As well as can be with so many women under one roof, yet here you bring us another." There was frank disapproval in this warrior's expression, and he went on to add, "Best to see to the disposition of—"

"I know, Lowden, I know," Challen interrupted with a sigh. "And it will be seen to when there is time for such things. But this woman is special and not to be treated like the others. She is a challenge loser."

"A—"

That was as far as Lowden got before the rumbling laughter started. An exact copy of Tamiron's mirthful reaction forced down Tedra's throat again. She stood there tapping one foot and wondering how much wallop her bound hands would give if she used them as a club. The very idea that this fellow should think she was being gifted to the *shodan*. And her grinning warrior hadn't said anything to the contrary, except that she was to be treated differently. If he dared . . .

"I'm going to get mighty tired of being the butt of this particular joke—"

"He laughs at *me,* woman, not you," Challen said before she could work up a good steam. "To be a challenge loser, challenge had to be accepted. This is what amuses him, that I would accept."

Well, that was all right, and she was even magnanimous enough to point out, "What choice did you have after I tossed you over my head?"

Lowden stopped laughing abruptly, but Challen picked it up after seeing his incredulous expression. "Best—best you explain—"

Challen couldn't get it out, but she caught his drift. "I think he wants me to admit that I took him by surprise," she told the older warrior, then lowered her voice to a conspiratorial whisper. "Of course, it takes a real lummox to get caught by that particular move—"

"Woman!"

That from both of them, although only Lowden seemed indignant over what she'd said. There was still laughter in Challen's eyes, and as Challen was the only one she cared to worry about just now, she widened her eyes at him before asking, "Was it something I said?"

He tried to look stern, he really did. "You know exactly what you implied. What has happened to the respect you promised?"

"It'll be there when you—Stars!" she gasped. *"He's* not your *shodan,* is he?" She turned her wide-eyed look on Lowden, who in turn looked even more indignant.

"Me?" Lowden snorted. "Woman, it was the *shodan* whose skill you belittled."

"Now how do you figure that, when I was talking about—" She paused, swinging back to Challen, her eyes narrowing the tiniest bit, not much indication of the temper about to erupt. "I hope I'm drawing the wrong conclusion here, babe. You wouldn't neglect to tell me you were the *shodan* if you actually were the *shodan,* now would you?"

"The matter was of no import to our dealings, *kerima,"* he stated calmly.

"Don't *kerima* me, you son-of-a-cracked-tube!" The rage broke free. "How dare you not tell me who you were when you knew I had business with the *shodan,* knew I'd eventually be seeking him? You even had me promise my best behavior so I could meet him! Well, that's off, if you hadn't noticed. In fact, I farden well ought to challenge you again!"

He stood there taking her abuse, but when she paused for breath before continuing, he grasped her bound wrists and bent to place them over his head.

When he straightened, she was pretty much locked in place against him, with no way to get her arms out of that forced embrace around his neck. It was no position to rant and rave in, which was what he had probably counted on, and in fact, she was done yelling. But she wasn't in the least bit cowed by this new restraint.

"There's something you should know, warrior," she said quietly now, looking up at him without expression. "When we fought, I didn't take advantage of certain moves because I felt, you being a man and me being a woman, it wouldn't have been sporting. I've changed my mind."

That was all the warning he got. Her knee came slamming up between his legs, instantly freeing her as he doubled over in pain. Lowden, watching this, quickly grabbed her arm, thinking she had done it to escape. But since she had no intention of going anywhere, nor could she if she meant to honor her challenge loss, which she still did, she objected to being restrained by another warrior, one to whom she owed no obedience or anything else. And just as Challen had been easy to surprise before he knew what she could do, so too was this Lowden.

With a sharp twist and a foot placed behind his knee, that knee collapsed, bringing him enough off balance in her direction that she was able to send him the rest of the way simply by his hold on her arm. He went down, but didn't stay down, was back on his feet almost instantly and facing her again. He might be older, but he was still a warrior, and still as big and brawny as Challen. And the look on his face said he'd like to see her try that again. She wasn't *that* dumb.

"Tell him to back off, Challen. I'm not going anywhere, and I don't kick a man when he's down, so he had no need to restrain me."

Challen had straightened partially, but was still experiencing a good deal of discomfort. "My uncle . . . did not see it . . . so."

"Is that my fault?" she retorted. "And by the way, if I *had* challenged you, I'd say you just lost." A well-satisfied smile came with that remark. "Be glad I only said 'ought to' and leave it at that."

When he didn't answer immediately, Lowden did. "The woman needs be punished."

"Says who?" Tedra demanded, rounding on the man with baleful eyes. "And what's with all this farden interference, anyway? This is between me and the warrior here, who got exactly what he deserved for the dirty hand he dealt me by not owning up to who he is."

"Woman—"

"Forget it, Lowden uncle," she cut him off. "Punishment is uncalled for in this case and won't be accepted, so keep your suggestions to yourself, why don't you. And *he* can get away with calling me *woman*, but to you I'm Tedra De Arr."

Challen stepped between them at that point, recovered enough to take command. "Leave be, Lowden. The woman feels she had good reason for her anger, and in part she does. I cared not to discuss with her what she has to discuss with the *shodan*, so she was not told that I am he. Such was not the doing of a *shodan*, but of a warrior more interested in other things." The way he looked at Tedra just then, no one had to ask, "What other things?" "I admit my wrong, woman," he then said to her. "Has your honor been satisfied?"

Had he used any other word but "honor," she

would have stubbornly said no. But he was in essence calling forth her own sense of fair play with that word, so what else could she do but concur?

"As for wrongs, I suppose one canceled out the other—as long as I don't hear any more talk of punishment."

"For this there will be none," he assured her, only to add, "Whether you earn future punish—"

"I get the picture!" she snapped, her temper right back up there with that unnecessary reminder. It goaded her enough to tell him, "And when my service is up, I'll find another *shodan* to speak my piece to, so you don't have to worry that I'll bother you with discussions you're not interested in. You aren't nearly open-minded enough to suit my needs, anyway."

"As you wish," he said, but she had the feeling she'd just hit a nerve. She just wished he'd *show* it.

Chapter Twenty

The route to the state bedchamber, or whatever it was called, was direct, up a grand set of stairs and to the right, down another wide hallway also centered with a soft blue carpet; and there were the doors, two gigantic carved wooden ones that Tedra had the uneasy suspicion only a warrior's strength could open. Her warrior had no trouble doing so and she was ushered inside, and immediately found out why the older warrior, Lowden, had accompanied them.

"Do you now apologize to my uncle," Challen told her in a no-nonsense tone.

She almost laughed. She did grin. There was no way she could have missed the large bed right upon entering the room, so she couldn't mistake where she was, and that he meant to take advantage of it.

"What's the matter, babe? Didn't you think that request would get results outside this room?"

"That thought had occurred to me, *kerima*. Do you now do as you are instructed."

"Sure." She shrugged. "Why not?" And she gave the stony-faced Lowden a cheeky grin. "Sorry for dumping you on the floor, Lowdy, and for whatever other disrespect you feel I showed you. Things like that tend to happen, though, when strange men put their hands on me."

"*This* is an apology, Challen?" Lowden asked, indignation still heavy in his voice.

Challen sighed. "In her way, yes. She is different,

not from Kan-is-Tra or even a country known to us. This must be taken into account when dealing with her, else a warrior can easily find his control threatened.''

''If I'm such a trial to you, warrior, why don't you end my service and send me on my way?'' Tedra suggested.

''You are no trial to me, since I have your complete obedience, do I not?''

She wasn't about to get tricked up by a word like ''complete.'' ''In this room you do.''

''So this is her challenge-loss service,'' Lowden said, that knowledge for some reason lightening his mood. He even chuckled. ''You should have made this clear, *shodan*. Her conduct is then yours alone to see to.''

''Why does that amuse him?'' Tedra wanted to know.

Challen also chuckled, now that he understood Lowden's earlier disgruntlement. ''He thought you would fall to his jurisdiction. He has governance over the women of this house, you see.''

''Governance?''

''He sees to their proper behavior.''

''Ah, the whip-wielder. So that's what an uncle is.''

They both looked at her strangely upon hearing that. She thought it was her derisive tone, but Challen's question said differently.

''How is it you know not the word 'uncle'?''

''I'd learned the word, just not its meaning, since we have nothing to compare it with on Kystran. It's like the food and animals I told you about. I have most of the words, but until I can see them to make the connection . . .''

He was still locked on her first disclosure. ''No

uncles? Then what do you call the brother of your father?''

"The what of my—wait a minute. Are you talking about relatives?''

"Indeed; family, relatives, kin.''

"You don't have to rub it in the ground. I've made the connection. And don't look at me as if I should have known right off. I told you, we have nothing like that on Kystran—at least we haven't had for centuries. But I recall now it was a subject in one of the few history lessons required by all.''

Neither man appeared to have understood a word she said, and Lowden verified this. "I will take my leave, *shodan*. The woman makes my head ache trying to grasp her meanings.''

As soon as the door closed behind him, Tedra snorted. "I happen to know I speak excellent Sha-Ka'ani. What wasn't to understand?''

"He has not had the opportunity I have had in deciphering your shortened words, but what you have just said still makes no sense, woman. People cannot survive without family.''

"Sure they can. We manage to just fine. It's just one more of the many differences between our planets, differences I know you don't care to hear about, so I won't bore you with an explanation. Details like that can wait for the *shodan* I finally get around to dealing with, if he's interested.''

She had to turn away from his look of chagrin before she laughed out loud. Talk about your subtle revenge. He was dying to question her further, but he wouldn't, not after what he had admitted to his uncle Lowden about deliberately avoiding such talk with her.

An uncle, imagine that. Challen must also have

real parents, or did have, maybe even siblings. She should have realized that sooner, primitive culture that this was, and she herself had some questions she'd like to ask now. But having effectively closed the subject in the way she had, she couldn't ask either.

She didn't let the lost opportunity bother her, however, and busied herself looking over her new sleeping quarters instead. Here she was a little more than impressed. The sheer size of the room nearly made her drool. This single chamber the *shodan* used only for sleeping was twice the size of her whole new house. Of course, there were no movable walls here to section off individual rooms for separate needs. What you saw was what you got. But she liked what she saw.

Like the meeting rooms below, this room was also extremely light and airy, with tall arched windows along one long wall, even taller arched openings on another that led out to what looked like a large garden balcony. Sheer white curtains stirred with gentle breezes over these openings, blending in with the white-and-silver-veined, marblelike walls and floors. There was more of the soft blue carpeting in certain areas, under and around the mammoth bed, under low, backless couches that surrounded a large square table, also low to the floor, and made of some kind of highly polished dark wood. Another fancier piece, a good ten feet round and with white designs running through the blue, was smack in the center of the room, for show obviously, since there was nothing on it.

There were a number of great carved chests in the same dark wood up against another wall, each a good five feet long and several feet high, with padded tops in the same white material as the couches making them suitable for sitting on. Chairs were conspicuously absent, but there were more of those comfortable-looking backless couches set before two of the open windows, with smaller tables about them, and what Tedra imagined to be gaali stone stands.

What she found the most impressive, and personally delightful, was a ten-foot-high tree in the corner between the windowed wall and the balcony, fully green-leafed though well contained, sitting in a beautiful black glazed urn. Smaller plants sat beside it, filling that corner with greenery in differing heights, and before all of this was a sunken pool, perhaps eight feet round, with bright red flowers floating on its surface.

"A pool in a bedroom?" Tedra turned around to locate Challen and found him where she'd left him, by the doors, doing nothing else but watching her. "It's kind of small, isn't it?"

"It is for bathing, not swimming."

"Oh, that's right." She turned back toward the water before he could see her grimace. "I forgot I'm going to have to do without a decent bath for a while."

His chuckle was close and getting closer, telling her he was moving up behind her. "My bath is one thing you will not find complaint with, *kerima,*" he said, misunderstanding her comment. "So which do you care to test first, the bath—or the bed?"

"I'd opt for the bed if that pause was meant to be significant, but are you really up to helping me test it out—after what I did to you?"

She turned to catch his rueful smile. "Perhaps not."

Guilt stirred, but she quickly stomped it down. "I'll wait to test out the bed, then. I'm afraid I'd get lost in it by myself, it's so big." The thing had to be

at least ten feet square, and was covered with a soft,
billowy blue spread that looked like it might swallow
her up if she lay in the center of it. "But I'd rather
pass on the bath, if you don't mind. It'll take some
nerve building before I'm ready to experience *that*
novelty of your world."

His humor returned when he heard that. "It is true
it is not a normal means for bathing, but it is not so
deep you need fear it. And it has been prepared for
my arrival."

"I wasn't worried about the depth, though I suppose I should have been. But don't let me stop you
from enjoying it. I'll—watch."

"You will do more than that, *kerima.*" He was
chuckling again, which should have given her warning. "You will join me."

She hadn't felt him untying her rope belt, but she
couldn't very well miss the fur blanket being lifted
off her. "Now wait a—" She was picked up in strong
arms and on her way toward the sunken pool before
she could complete that protest. "Put me down,
Challen! I mean it! I don't want—no!" She found
herself dangling directly over the water, held out at
arm's length. "Don't you dare . . ."

He did; simply let go of her. Tedra screamed on
the way down, but it wasn't that far a drop, and he'd
been right about the water not being very deep, only
hip-deep for her. Her scream of fright quickly turned
to several more of rage as she held her arms up and
away from the now swirling, lapping, clinging water—uck!

Challen was laughing outright, watching her. "Did
I not know better, woman, I would swear you have
no liking for water. Is it not warm enough for you?"

She noticed it now that he mentioned it, warmth,

clinging to every inch of her that it touched, surrounding her, seeping into her pores. It wasn't as terrible as she had thought it would be, kind of like standing in a vat of thin gel or thick air, but it would still take getting used to.

"Is is supposed to be warm?" she asked, finally looking up at him.

"Is it supposed . . . you would prefer a cold bath?"

"I would prefer a solaray bath, but that's beside the point, since I'm not likely to get one here. My question was legitimate, warrior. Warm, hot, cold, what's the norm?"

He didn't answer. He started taking off his sword belt, still without answering. She finally got the message that she'd annoyed him somehow, and she figured she knew the "how."

"You know, warrior, things like this are going to crop up now and again during our time together, you thinking I'm taking you around the block or teasing, when I'm not. When one person has never been in water before, but the other has, it's kind of natural for the one to ask questions about temperature and such—"

"Enough, woman. You have not a body that has never known water. Think you I could not *smell* the difference?"

She nearly choked. She did laugh. "Somehow, some way, before I leave this planet I'm going to get you on my ship and into a solaray bath. You won't be touched by water, but you'll be cleaner than you've ever dreamed of being, and it only takes about three seconds. That's modern technology, efficient, quick, and easy. And I'd say by that expression of yours that you think I've just handed you another 'tall tale.' That's all right, babe. To each his own."

He gave no reply, but he did extend his sword toward her raised wrists. Fortunately that disgruntled expression of his didn't intimidate her, so she knew it was the rope he was after, not her heart. She positioned her wrists, slid the underside of the rope along the blade, and was free of restraints at last, hopefully for good.

She tossed the severed rope to the floor by his feet, then waited for him to join her. If her questions about bathing were going to bother him so much, she'd just wait and watch, thereby learning how to go about it without asking.

There was a bench of sorts nearby that she hadn't noticed sooner because it was tucked in among the plants, even with several small ones resting on one end of it. A tall stack of towels sat next to this, and Challen used the other end to sit on and remove his boots. He was still watching her rather than what he was doing, and slowly but surely, the annoyance left his expression.

"Sit down, *kerima*," he finally told her.

"And drown? If it's all the same to you, I don't mind standing."

"There is a ledge behind you, there for sitting on." This with a sigh.

"I'm sure it's a fine ledge," she allowed, glancing back at it. "I'll still stand."

He made a sound she could have sworn was exasperation-caused, and then the *bracs* were being peeled off his long legs. Tedra was suddenly feeling more warmth than from just the water, more like real heat as she watched him put a hand to the floor to lever himself over the side of the pool. But then the water rushed at her, distracting her as it slapped against her stomach. Yet in the next moment Challen was standing before her, and it wasn't only water touching her now.

"These you could have covered with the water," he said, his large hands circling her breasts.

That was an outright lie she couldn't help making a rude sound over. "Get off it. You can see through this water."

"Not as clearly as I see you now. But I do not mind the invitation, woman."

"I wasn't . . . So that's why you wanted me to sit? Well, why didn't you say so? I can be more adventurous if it's for a good cause, and I'm sure this is a good cause . . . or are you feeling—better?"

The large hands on her breasts slid around to her back to draw her up against him, and she caught his smile just before his mouth moved over hers in a very delicious way. That was really all the answer she needed. Her own arms moved up to lock around his thick neck, and in the course of the next few hours, she found out that a primitive bath had other, more enjoyable uses than just bathing.

Chapter Twenty-one

*T*edra rolled over to find herself tangled up in covers in the center of Challen's huge bed. She had known she'd feel lost in the farden thing, and without the big barbarian there beside her, she did. However, she hadn't realized the bedding would try to strangle her.

When she finally got one elbow loose, enough to lean up on it, she glanced around to find what had awakened her, hoping it was . . . it wasn't. Challen hadn't returned. He'd left her at dawn with a very sweet parting, but obviously he'd meant it when he said he'd be so busy today that he wouldn't likely see her until this evening, or in his words, this moonrise. He'd ignored several summons yesterday for his time, instead devoting the rest of the day to making her feel very welcome in his home, or at least in his bedroom. But today was back to business as usual, and if she felt deserted, that was just too bad.

The one who had disturbed her sleep was the young Darash female she had met yesterday—well, not actually met. Challen hadn't bothered with introductions when the girl had brought them a meal last evening. And the girl hadn't made any comments in the serving of it, had simply left quickly, a warrior waiting at the door for her and closing it after her. Tedra remembered her suspicions rising upon seeing that door-opening warrior, and had immediately got up to test the door herself. But she *could* open it, she was relieved to find, though not easily, for the thing really was heavy, but she could do it. It had been opened and closed for the servant simply because her hands had been full with the large tray she carried.

She carried another tray now, a much smaller one, and the door to the room had been closed behind her this time. Tedra watched her place the tray on the large square table with the couches around it, where she and Challen had eaten last night. That had been a study in decadence, lying stretched out on those couches so they met at one corner, she on her belly on one, Challen on his side on another, eating with fingers, but not their own fingers. The barbarian got to feed her as he wanted to, and because of where they were, she couldn't refuse or bite his fingers. He also insisted she feed him, and after a while she didn't half mind doing it, and getting her fingers sucked in the process. It got so erotic, in fact, the meal was interrupted for an hour and had to be finished cold, Tedra refusing to let him call for fresh food since it would be too easy for anyone to figure out how the first batch had got cold. She accepted the fact that everyone *would* know what she was doing in Challen's bedroom, but she didn't care to be thought so insatiable she couldn't even take time out for a farden meal—whether it was true or not.

The girl didn't depart immediately as she had done last night. She approached the bed, smiling, making eye contact, in no way obsequious or appearing slavish in manner. A step above a feudal-type serf, but a step below being actually free, the Darasha had a strange relationship with the ruling class. They were simply servants, subject to certain rules just as the women on this world were, but apparently not disliking their lot. Coming from a world that had no servants, since things mechanical made them unnecessary, Tedra knew it would take getting used to, being waited on by an actual living, breathing person.

This living, breathing person was maybe a few years younger than Tedra, a somewhat pretty girl with brown eyes and hair. That coloring was as close as she got to resembling those women Tedra had seen on the street yesterday. The girl's skin tone was dark, not golden, and like the Darash male from the stable, she was much smaller than the average citizen of this world, probably no more than five feet and one or two inches, if even that.

"Would the mistress like a bath after she eats?"

Tedra glanced at the small pool, empty this morning. These barbarians had plumbing, for Stars' sake, complete with hot and cold running and draining water, not exactly a primitive accomplishment. She was finding that, like the Sha-Ka'ari, the Sha-Ka'ani were advanced in some ways, archaic in others, especially the clinging to old beliefs and customs.

"No, no bath, thank you." She wasn't likely to enjoy it without the barbarian there to make it enjoyable.

"May I then select a *chauri* for the mistress?"

Tedra frowned, hearing herself addressed like that a second time. "Look, you're not a slave and I'm not your mistress, so why don't you call me Tedra?"

"That would not be properly respectful."

"Is everyone mistress or master to you?"

"Yes, mistress."

"Doesn't that bother you?"

"For what reason should it do so?"

Tedra sighed. "Well, that was a pleasant trip around the block. How about if I order you to call me Tedra? Would that do the trick?"

"Trick?"

"Would it work, an order? Or don't the wishes of a challenge loser count for much around here?"

"Challenge loser? The mistress is teasing me?"

"Yeah, I'm a great kidder," Tedra said with a derisive snort, deciding hearing her name on the girl's lips wasn't worth this kind of aggravation. "You can fetch me some clothes while I fight my way out of these farden covers—that is, if clothes fetching is part of your job."

The girl had trouble nodding, she was trying so hard not to laugh. It probably was funny, seeing a grown woman wrapped up in a blanket tighter than a gift-wrapped box and not too clear on how to break out of it, but so Tedra was. She could have said something about the convenience of air blankets, which turned off as soon as you sat up in bed, leaving nothing to tangle your feet in, but discussing the advantages of her world that she was having to do without would only get her more aggravated.

"If I may?"

The girl crawled onto the bed, found the corner of the blanket that was tucked under Tedra's hip, and pulled it loose; then the rest of the blanket followed. Tedra started blushing immediately, having forgotten her state of complete undress, but the girl didn't seem to notice. Having helped with the immediate problem, she left the bed to take care of the next, heading toward a door Tedra hadn't even noticed yesterday, probably because it was without a doorknob of any kind and stood between two of those great, long chests. It merely pushed open, revealing a room beyond that Tedra was curious enough about to investigate for herself, if she could manage to find the sheet that had become lost under the blanket.

When she arrived at the room some minutes later, draped in the light blue sheet and trailing a good eight feet of it behind her, it took her a moment to grasp that she was looking into an old-fashioned closet, something she'd never seen before. What she thought of as a closet was a mechanical rack that came out of the wall with whatever outfit she had dialed for. She had never thought to wonder where her clothes were kept, or where they went when her robocleaner disposed of them for cleaning—just more of the things she was discovering she took for granted at home.

As closets went, she had a feeling this one was larger than most, just like the bedroom it was connected to. Sight of a long mirror, a wide shelf topped with bottles and jars, and even a couch in one corner indicated it was also used as a dressing room. A number of chests and one entire wall of drawers, some too high for even Tedra to reach, suggested it might also be a place for storage. But there were clothes in evidence, a great many clothes, hung on pegs on the walls, on stands with sticklike arms extended from them, draped on funny-looking racks that stood upright but curved at the top to lay spread-out *comtocs* on. The setup made everything just about visible at first sight, eliminating the need for an inventory list.

Among the male attire of boots, sword belts, dozens of *bracs*, all in black *zaalskin,* and *comtocs* in some really fantastic, glittering materials, the few *chauri* looked out of place where they draped over some of the racks. Tedra recognized the female outfits like those she had seen the women wearing on the streets yesterday. They were exactly the same, in thin, gauzy cloth, appearing to be no more than square-cut scarves double-draped and tied together.

"These three have been prepared for you, mistress,

but if these colors do not suit, I can prepare you another. There are pieces in any color you could wish for.''

''Pieces'' should have given Tedra warning, but even when she moved over to where the girl stood by the three outfits, she was still brought up short. The things really were nothing but scarves—''pieces,'' as the girl called them—a top with a skirt, tied together and designed to just hang about the body.

Actually, they were a little more complicated than that, as Tedra saw when she picked up the top of the white one. It was made of a total of twelve scarves that would fall to about mid-thigh. ''Prepared'' meant the scarves were already tied together in tiny knots where they were supposed to be tied, a knot of six for each shoulder. Individually, each scarf was totally transparent; draped one over the other, they became less so, but not by much, except over the breasts, where they would cross over for an extra layer.

The skirt, now, was another story. It too had twelve square scarves to it, with about three inches of a corner from each scarf sewn to a narrow elastic-like band, one draping over the next to form an even circle around this band that would fit around the waist, and made the scarves lie partially open. None of these scarves were tied together or sewn together in any other way. They hung down the legs, the bottom points falling just short of the ankles, leaving gaps halfway up the calves between each one, and ready to part and expose shin, knee, and some thigh with the least wind or brisk walk.

There was a tie belt in the same material to fit over the top, to add form to the body, and probably to help keep the scarves covering what they were supposed to cover. Tedra couldn't have cared less as she tossed the one she had examined back on its rack. She had only two words for the girl awaiting her decision as to which one she would wear.

"Forget it."

"Mistress?"

"I wouldn't be caught dead in one of those things, kiddo—what *is* your name, anyway?"

"Jalla, mistress. If these colors—"

"It's not the colors, Jalla, though I've never been partial to pastels. It's that peekaboo material, not to mention the farden things look like they're designed for removing, not putting on. There must be something else I can wear."

"But—"

"Something like what you're wearing." The white, sleeveless tunic and skirt were exactly like what the male Darash had worn, the only difference being he wore pants, and Jalla, a full, ankle-length skirt. "Now that looks cool and comfortable, and I wouldn't feel like I'm playing watch-closely-and-you-might-see-something."

"But this is not a *chauri.*"

"So?"

"So the ladies of Kan-is-Tra wear only the *chauri.* You can wear only the *chauri.*"

And the servants did not, obviously. Nor did Tedra miss the fact that Jalla had included the whole country in that, not just the town.

"What happens if I refuse?"

Jalla actually grew alarmed at that question. "But you cannot. The *shodan* would not allow it."

Tedra gritted her teeth. She didn't want to wear that damned *chauri,* but she didn't want to get into a blowup with Challen either, when things had been going so smoothly with him. She looked wistfully at his clothes all around her, but knew she didn't dare borrow any, that the first warrior she came across would demand she hand them over, and she didn't care to go through that again.

"Farden hell," she fairly snarled, but pointed a finger. "That one."

She'd picked the light green, since she had a feeling the blue and the white were somehow symbolic with the *shodan,* likely his colors, if the color scheme of the castle was any indication. And right now she was too displeased to want to please him by wearing his colors.

"Whose *chauri* are these, anyway?" she asked as Jalla began helping her dress, and she saw how easily the top could become hopelessly tangled if it wasn't put on carefully.

"Yours, mistress."

"But whose were they before?"

"Yours—"

"Never mind," Tedra cut in, her patience gone with her irritation.

The clothes had been there before she was, so they couldn't be hers. And she didn't really care to know who had shared Challen's closet before her. But he'd be hearing what she thought of wearing someone else's *chauri.*

When she looked down at the finished package, she groaned. When she caught her image in the mirror, she groaned louder. It was much worse than she'd thought it would be. Now she knew why the women she had seen on the streets looked so soft, shy— helpless. There was no other way to look in one of these outfits.

Tedra wasn't one to object to a little skin showing. It wasn't that, for she had bodysuits that showed off more. But she'd never worn anything that was so dainty, so blatantly feminine, so farden delicate-looking. In it, she felt strange, exposed, vulnerable.

"The *shodan* will be pleased, mistress," Jalla offered nervously. She hadn't missed those groans. "You look beautiful."

"I look like a Sex Clinic worker," Tedra replied in disgust. "But as long as Martha can't see me in it, I suppose I'll survive the wearing of it."

Chapter Twenty-two

Tedra got her revenge for being forced to wear the *chauri*, and was it ever sweet in being so unexpected.

Jalla had taken her on a tour of the castle after she had finished eating. It was really interesting, and she even forgot for a while the way she was dressed, especially when she began seeing other women dressed exactly the same, and none of them feeling the least self-conscious about it. Jalla introduced her to a good number of them, explaining who they were and why they were there. She learned a great deal that morning about the women of Sha-Ka'an, very little of which she liked, but then she wasn't there to change their world, just trade with it, and hopefully enlist aid from it.

One of the rooms she wasn't supposed to go near was where Challen was conducting business, but when had "wasn't supposed to" ever stopped her. She slipped into the back of this room despite Jalla's protests, the girl flatly refusing to go with her. It was long and cavernous, the walls and floor in that shiny, marblelike substance, in this case light blue veined with dark. There was row after row of those low couches all white, with an aisle down the center of them, and at the far end of the room, sitting behind a desk and looking like no more than a Goverance Building official, sat Challen.

Expecting a throne, at the very least a raised dais piled high with pillows, Tedra was surprised by the normal-looking desk. But she supposed this was just one more of the little abnormalities of Sha-Ka'an that made it so different from what she knew of the history of her own people.

The room was crowded with men, just about every couch filled with two or three of the big guys. They were probably waiting their turn to speak with the *shodan,* who was presently speaking with a group of four men who stood before his desk.

Tedra couldn't hear anything that was said from that distance, and she was about to slip back out of the room with no one the wiser that she'd intruded in this strictly male domain, when Challen made eye contact with her and stopped whatever he had been saying. She supposed she was in hot water now, watching him stand up, come around the desk, and start down the aisle toward her. He'd given no excuse for his leaving so abruptly, so heads started turning to see what drew him, and very quickly Tedra had every eye in the room on her.

She wanted to leave before Challen reached her, she really did, but that smacked of cowardice, and so she stood her ground. Being brave was a pain sometimes; so was pride nudged with stubbornness. All she could do was hope Challen wasn't too angry with her for being where she wasn't supposed to be.

But as he got closer, she could see that the fire in his eyes had nothing to do with anger. She relaxed, and even began to be faintly amused, recognizing that look by now. The barbarian was inflamed with lust, and Tedra had little doubt that it wasn't just her but the *chauri* that had inspired it. He liked her in the farden thing, oh, did he ever. His eyes told her so as they moved all over her.

When he reached her he didn't say a word, just

took her elbow and led her out of the room. He didn't stop outside it either, but started off down the wide corridor, her elbow still in his hand.

"Where are we going?" she asked with a knowing grin that he didn't turn around to see.

"To my chambers," was all he said.

"Now why would I want to go there?"

"Woman—"

"No, I mean it. Will you hold up a minute?" When he stopped to look back at her, she stated flatly, "I've got no reason to go to your room, Challen."

"I do."

"Then go ahead. I'm not stopping you."

He had his desire under control, but in no way had it diminished. "You will come with me, *kerima*," he said in a reasonable tone.

"Why should I?"

"Woman, you know very well why." This in a less reasonable tone.

It was all she could do not to laugh at this point, but her expression didn't reveal how amusing she found this situation. "Maybe I do, but you have to look at it from my viewpoint, babe. Your sudden need of me isn't at all flattering. It's actually insulting, since I know very well it's not me who brought it on, but this damned outfit I'm forced to wear. If I were able to dress in something of my own, which I could retrieve from my ship, by the way, if you'd just give me back my communicator, you wouldn't have been willing to leave your business for a little sex-sharing break. You'd probably have just barked at me to leave the room, instead of leaving it yourself."

She waited a moment while it dawned on him that he *had* left a room full of warriors awaiting his attention. It was comical, really, to see exasperation and chagrin mix with desire, but still she didn't laugh. This was "getting even" in a splendid way, and she didn't want to spoil it by letting him know she *was* getting even.

"And another thing," she continued, "is that I'm presently acquainting myself with your castle and really enjoying the tour, so I don't see your request as being at all reasonable just now. You did tell me I had the option of refusing unreasonable requests, didn't you, as well as being able to refuse you my service if we aren't in a place where you sleep? Now, if you're going to tell me you've slept in this hall—"

"Enough, woman," he cut in, for once doing nothing to hide his displeasure. "Do I carry you to my bedchamber, the matter will be settled."

"Well, yes, you could do that," she said, feigning surprise before she closed the door on that option. "But if you did, I'd see it as a breach of our agreement, which it would be, and that would release me from my service as far as I'm concerned. So if you want to find out what it's like to have a fight on your hands every single time you get near me, go ahead and carry me off."

He stared at her for a long moment, and she suddenly knew without a doubt that he was remembering the last time he'd joined with her in a place other than "where he slept," and how she'd admitted to him that she hadn't been able to even think of refusing once he kissed her. Warily, she tried to pull back, but he was still holding her arm, which meant she could forget about getting loose until he decided to release her.

"Now you can just get those thoughts right out of your mind, warrior."

"What thoughts?"

"You know farden well what thoughts. I'm going

on record right now as saying no, so any advantage-taking on your part would still be breaking the rules this time." At his sigh and the release of her arm, she relaxed again, enough to say, "Cheer up, babe. It's not so many hours until moonrise, and then I'll be right where you want me."

"The thought of this does not help at the moment, *kerima.*"

He said this so wistfully she almost changed her mind. His wanting her made her want him, too, which was strange when she considered that other men had wanted her without having that effect on her. But she wasn't going to lose this opportunity of getting even for being forced into wearing the hated *chauri*. She'd just have to see that they both made up later for the loss of mutual enjoyment now.

She stepped closer to him now that he wasn't holding her, and was even so bold as to run a finger down the center of his chest, from the base of that large golden medallion to the point of the V of his *comtoc,* just above the rim of his *bracs*.

"You should be glad I made you see reason, Challen. Wouldn't you be embarrassed returning to that room so much later that every man in there would know why you had kept him waiting? Now they'll only think you took me out of there to chastise me for showing up where I wasn't supposed to be."

"No warrior awaiting me would have thought I left him for any other reason than the one I had, woman, not after seeing you for himself. But do you mean to tell me you were aware you had trespassed where you did not belong?"

She thought about lying, she really did, especially with him suddenly looking like a man who had found the means for some "getting even" of his own. She stepped back, frowning, but she had hesitated too long in answering, leading him to assume the correct one.

"As you do so well at remembering rules a warrior could wish you had forgotten, I will do as well at remembering rules broken."

Tedra's mouth dropped open, then snapped shut for some teeth grinding. "If you mean to punish me, Challen, you can farden well do it right now. It's not my fault you got all heated up because of this damned *chauri*, which I hated wearing in the first place!"

He chuckled, his humor returned now that hers had flown. "Much as you assumed otherwise, *kerima,* this had no bearing on my sudden need for you. I see women every day dressed as you are, but none have ever given me such a powerful urge to fill them with my heat, not as you do."

"But that urge came only because you saw me as *you* deem proper, in clothes *you* insist I wear. Admit it, Challen. It's still the fault of the *chauri.* "

"I cannot deny I find you both beautiful and desirable in the clothes of Kan-is-Tran women, but no more desirable and beautiful than when you wear no clothing at all." Hot color stole into her cheeks, but he wasn't finished. "Nor can I deny I still wish you would reconsider and come with me to my bedchamber now."

"If I did, you'd forget about punishing me for trespassing, wouldn't you?" she said, thinking darkly that blackmail was prevalent on all worlds.

"No."

She hadn't expected that answer. "At least you're honest," she replied grudgingly. "But under the circumstances, you'll understand why I'm not in the mood to reconsider."

"Of course." He nodded and started to return to his business.

"Wait a minute." She caught his arm. "I meant what I said. If you're going to punish me, do it now. I'm not going to have the rest of my day ruined by worrying about it all afternoon."

At that a single golden brow rose to taunt her. "Did you not tell me it was not so many hours until moonrise? That is when you will be seen to, *kerima*, not before."

She gave him a fully loaded glare he couldn't mistake before turning on her bare heel to stomp away, noting with disgust that Jalla hadn't waited around to receive any of the punishment being doled out. Smart girl.

"Woman?"

"What?" she snapped, swinging back around, her glare still in place.

"Had I warned you against entering the petitions chamber, you would not have disobeyed, would you?"

That was debatable, but all she said was, "So?"

"So it was not a warrior you ignored, only a Darash, a small matter that will require only minor correction. You have no reason to look with dread upon that correction."

Having said this, he disappeared back into the forbidden-to-women room. Tedra stared at the closed door incredulously. He had given her as much as a promise that her punishment would be no more than a slap on the wrist, or the Sha-Ka'ani equivalent. He had no reason to tell her that except that he didn't want her to worry about it. She smiled, filled suddenly with a warmth that threatened to bubble over. She wanted to laugh in sheer pleasure. She wanted to call Challen back and say she'd changed her mind after all. She did neither. She savored his concern for her peace of mind, but didn't lose track of the fact that if she didn't make her displeasure felt over the things she seriously objected to on his world, at least those things that directly affected her, then they would just continue. Now he knew how strongly she hated the *chauri,* and now maybe he'd make an exception in her case and find something more acceptable for her to wear.

Chapter Twenty-three

*J*alla never did make a reappearance, so Tedra continued her tour of the castle by herself. But she soon got bored without the servant's input to explain what rooms were for what purpose and who was who of the people she happened to come across. She was left with few choices to fill the rest of the day: either return to Challen's bedroom and do nothing, or return to that large room she had passed through earlier that seemed to be a gathering place for the women, the free women at any rate. There the orphans, young widows, and old women who had outlived their children and husbands, all now under the protection of the *shodan,* sat around gossiping while they applied needle and thread to cloth.

Tedra couldn't see herself doing the same, especially after the less than friendly welcome she had received from those free women, several of whom had been downright frigid during the introductions. And out-and-out doing nothing had never appealed to her, so she elected to do neither. She'd seen the castle. Now she'd see the town.

That decision was easier made than done, but after a little more exploring, she finally found a room on the ground floor with no one in it and access to the outside by some handily open windows. Next to negotiate was the gate, but having left the castle from a room near its rear, she quickly discovered another gate, one not so wide or heavily trafficked. In this back area of the castle, where deliveries were made, were mostly Darasha; the males determinedly didn't notice her, and the females only looked at her curiously.

Tedra wasted no time in crossing the wide yard and slipping out the open gate. It didn't take long before she was wishing some type of footgear had gone with her outfit, but she didn't think of turning back. If knowing full well she was doing something she shouldn't hadn't stopped her, sore feet certainly wouldn't.

There was a market of sorts outside the back gate. It was a street of merchants, apparently, and each one had at least half his goods on sale in front of his shop, on tables and carts, in baskets or whatever was handy, or just spread out on blankets on the sidewalks. Of course, there was more to see inside the shops, probably the more expensive stuff, but a glance in all directions showed a wide variety of goods being offered, from food and cloth to jewels and weapons.

She was relieved to see again mostly Darasha here, doing both the buying and the selling, but there were some free women shopping, too, moving casually from shop front to shop front, their brightly colored cloaks tied at the throat and set back over their shoulders. Tedra would have personally used a cloak to cover up if she had one, but she supposed it was a matter of pride for these women to let their *chauri* be seen clearly, since the *chauri* was a mark of freedom. Some freedom, when they all had a warrior or two escorting them. The fact that she didn't shouldn't be a problem, though. As long as she stayed reasonably close to a woman who did, who was to say the woman's escort wasn't hers as well?

She picked one couple and kept up with them. She

even took into account that the warrior with the woman would know he wasn't guarding her, too, so she managed to keep to his back and out of his notice while still seeing what she wanted to see of the marketplace.

This went on for all of five measly minutes before a big hand fell on her shoulder and turned her about, and she knew even before she looked up to see the two warriors that her tour of the market was over. One was grinning down at her, the other displayed disapproval. Both were unknown to her but were typical giants, though not of Challen's caliber—just lots bigger than she. Tedra still figured she could take them, if it came down to that. What she wanted to know was how they had found her out when she had stayed so close to that other warrior and his lady. So maybe they hadn't found her out. Maybe they just wanted a little friendly conversation.

With that thought, she said, "Yes?"

"Yes, she says," the grinning one replied to no one in particular, but then, to her, "Woman, you were given enough time to make your choice. Since you have not taken that time to ask protection from one of us, I now claim you."

"Oh, for Stars' sake, do I have to go through this again?" Tedra said in disgust.

Her tone didn't get rid of that grin. It was still firmly in place as the warrior reached for her. Instead of his hand connecting with her arm, however, her hand caught his, and with one swift turnabout, she had his digits twisted in an extremely uncomfortable position.

"Don't take this personally, warrior," she said calmly to the big guy, not even having to strain to keep him from moving an inch. "But I've already been claimed, so to speak, or at least my time's all booked up for the next month. So you understand why I can't go with you, don't you? My own warrior wouldn't like it, and that leaves me honor-bound to stop you from trying to make off with me.''

''Bullan!'' was all he said to this, but he said it quite loudly and in the way of requesting aid.

Bullan had to be the warrior's disapproving friend, and Tedra turned to warn him off, only to find he'd gone. Where he'd gone she discovered in the next instant as steellike bands wrapped around her from behind, getting her upper arms inside that circle to more or less immobilize her—or so he thought.

''Release him, woman,'' Bullan told her in a voice sharp with anger.

''And if I don't?''

There was a long pause, as if the man were struggling to overcome shock or just plain disbelief that she wasn't jumping to do his bidding. ''Do not make me hurt you.''

That warning got her just a little bit mad. ''Hurt me? Oh, no, warrior, you aren't going to ease your conscience by putting the blame for hurting me on *my* shoulders. I didn't ask you two clowns to detain me, and I've already told you I'm not available for claiming. So any hurting you do to me is your idea, not mine. Of course, that goes both ways,'' she added magnanimously. ''Any hurting I do to you I'll take full credit for.''

''Bul-lan!'' the no-longer-grinning warrior cried out again.

He was already the recipient of some of the hurting she could dish out, and he'd just as soon it ended. His friend started seeing about ending it, slowly tightening those massive arms around her. But Tedra had already guessed that would be his move, to steadily apply the pressure until she either released his friend or blacked out. Before that pressure got too bad, she shoved up a bit more on her victim's wrist, eliciting a moan from him that worked to distract Bullan into easing his hold on her just long enough for her to twist her free arm back and behind her where her fingers locked onto something soft.

With just the tiniest squeeze she got released right quick. The trouble was, she might have both men at her mercy now, but both her hands were tied up keeping them that way. As far as she was concerned, being in control of things had not improved her situation very much. Frankly, she had no idea what to do next.

Chapter Twenty-four

"And how long do you think to hold them like that before some other warriors notice and come to their aid?"

Hearing "some other warriors" made Tedra think this new voice behind her belonged to a Darash male. No such luck, as a glance over her shoulder showed her. She hadn't recognized the voice, but she certainly recognized Tamiron, Challen's friend. She just didn't know if she was now extricated from the vexing situation she had got into or was in more trouble. Likely the latter, if the cold look he gave her was any indication.

She decided to be prudent and release her victims. Maybe an apology was in order, too.

"Sorry about that, fellas, but Tamiron here can verify what—"

The words were choked off abruptly. She hadn't actually hurt the warrior Bullan, just made him nervous as hell. So he was quick to react as soon as her hand let go of his soft parts, and his reaction was to put her out of commission. Only one arm circled her this time, but so tightly her breath was cut off. The other hand made sure her own couldn't reach anything else he held dear, not that she had much strength to try, fighting for breath as she was.

The other warrior, meanwhile, was shaking the circulation back into his wrist and numb fingers, and glaring at her with murder in his light brown eyes.

Fortunately, Tamiron stepped between them at that moment, before the fellow could put thoughts to deeds. But if he didn't do something quickly, she wouldn't care one way or the other. She was already seeing spots before her eyes.

"The woman has a protector, Kogan."

"You lie, Tamiron Ja-Na-Der! She wears no colors."

"Through her own ignorance." Tamiron's voice seemed unnaturally calm after the heat of Kogan's. "She comes not from Kan-is-Tra, so knows nothing of our customs. She also has ways much different from our own, as you have both found out for yourselves. Think you a Sha-Ka-Ran woman would dare behave as this one has?" Tamiron didn't expect an answer or wait for one. He gave Bullan a level look and said quietly, "Best you release her now, before we must bring the matter to the *shodan.*"

"There is no reason to involve the *shodan.*"

Even Tedra, as groggy as she was becoming, could hear the nervousness in Bullan's reply. And damned if he didn't let go of her. Trouble was, she nearly fell on her face, and would have if Tamiron hadn't been near enough to catch her.

"Are you all right, Tedra-de-Arr?"

She was too busy dragging in lungfuls of air to answer just yet, but when she did, it was to complain as she pushed away from him. "You sound just like my android, calling me by my full name. De Arr happens to be my classification, not a last name as you know it, so just Tedra will do if we're friends. If not, you might as well call me woman. I'm getting used to it."

"It is good to know you are accepting *some* things of our country. Were you as wise to accept all things, you would not have been claimed by a warrior who thought he had every right to claim you.''

"I knew I was going to like you, babe, if that's the extent of your scoldings.''

"Scoldings? I think you will receive much more than that, Tedra.''

"Oh, come on, you're not going to tell *him* about this, are you?''

Before she got an answer, Kogan interrupted quite insolently. ''I would know who her protector is, Tamiron, or must I take your word that she has one, when her presence here alone says she does not?''

Tedra glanced from one to the other, expecting to hear a challenge issued. She hadn't yet learned that warrior arrogance allowed for a certain belligerence that all warriors accepted as normal, so this in itself was no cause for insult. The way they saw it, every man had the right to doubt, argue, and disagree, no matter who was involved.

"There is no need to take my word,'' Tamiron said, but he was grinning when he added, ''You need only come to the castle and ask anyone there where the woman sleeps. You will be told she sleeps in the bedchamber of the *shodan* himself.''

"That was rather crudely put,'' Tedra said as she watched her two would-be claimers hurry away after hearing that.

"It was said to embarrass you, but I see you are not embarrassed. Best I leave the disciplining of you to the one who has the right.''

She took his arm and started him back toward the castle. ''But I like your idea of disciplining so much better. Do keep it up, and then you might not feel the need to file any extra reports for the day.'' She waited for him to say he wouldn't be telling Challen about her little escapade, but was met only with silence. She gritted her teeth, telling him. "Look, all I wanted was to see a little of your town. I wasn't going to go far, and I wasn't trying to escape, if that's what you think."

"I believe you have discovered that to leave Sha-Ka-Ra by yourself would be no easy task, but no, the thought that you were attempting such had not occurred to me." And then he chuckled. "Likely you would have drawn no notice had you been properly cloaked. Of course, I would not have let you venture too far from the castle without stopping you."

"You followed me?" she said accusingly.

He merely nodded, showing not the least embarrassment that he hadn't interfered before the situation got sticky. Likely he thought she wouldn't have learned her lesson so well if he had. It came to her suddenly why she had been noticed so soon, so she didn't tear into him over his delayed rescue.

"It's the farden cloaks, isn't it? And since they're different colors, that's the colors that warrior was talking about, the colors of the cloaks."

Again he nodded, then elaborated. "The Ly-San-Ters' family color is blue, but the color of the household of the *shodan* is white. Either color or both combined are recognizable as Challen's. To leave the castle without cloak and slippers is to become claimable. Were neither supplied with your *chauri?*"

She looked pointedly down at her scanty outfit and bare feet with a grimace. "If they were, don't you think I would have used them?"

He smiled to acknowledge her attempt at humor, but still shook his head at her in what could only be considered disapproval. "The lack could be no other thing than Challen's wish that you not leave the castle until he could escort you himself; thus your disobedience of his wishes must be made known to—"

"Now hold on," she cut in anxiously.

This was no minor thing to call for minimal correction. If Tamiron hadn't been there, the matter could have got serious. Serious, too, was likely to be her punishment if Challen found out about it.

"What if I swear it'll never happen again?" she continued hopefully. "Couldn't you see your way clear to keep it between ourselves, then?"

"And have Kogan or Bullan get up the nerve to apologize to the *shodan* for attempting to claim his woman?"

"I'm *not* his woman," she snapped, but only because she saw Tamiron's point. For Challen to find out about it later would be much worse, for then she would be guilty also of keeping secrets from him *and* involving his best friend in them. "You know," she added conversationally as they reached one of the doors at the rear of the castle, "I'd forgotten for a while that I don't like this world very much. I should be grateful I'm going to be reminded of it in a really big way, since one of the main precepts of a World Discoverer is to remain aloof and indifferent to the world they discover so they won't be tempted to stay. Explorations naturally frowns on losing its pilots that way."

Chapter Twenty-five

Tedra spent the last few hours of the afternoon working herself into a fine case of nervousness tinged with anger, the anger because she had no business being nervous. Whatever Challen did to her she had to accept for the simple fact that she'd known she would be punished if she were caught leaving the castle, but she'd left anyway. If you were going to flaunt rules, you couldn't cry over the consequences, now could you?

Tedra couldn't. But she could farden well complain about such ridiculous rules being forced on her in the first place. She had never before been stopped from coming and going as she pleased, not since she had become an adult. So she couldn't go far, but had to stick around for a while. She accepted that as part of her challenge loss. But the service that loss demanded didn't take up every hour of every day, just a few in the morning and evening, and maybe a few more if Challen happened to catch her in his bedroom in the afternoon. That didn't amount to more than half her waking hours, and being confined to the castle for the other half smacked of imprisonment no matter how she looked at it.

Oh, yes, she had her complaints lined up, but Challen was going to punish her anyway, because he was a barbarian and they seemed to think punishment was the answer for everything around here. So all right, she'd already accepted that, but what she needed was a this-for-that list so she'd know what it was she was accepting. Every other woman on this world probably knew exactly what punishment would be given for whatever wrong she committed. Not having that knowledge herself was what Tedra couldn't stand and was causing her such nervousness as the sky darkened outside and Challen's return became imminent.

Taking what precautions she could, Tedra placed herself as far from the entrance to the bedroom as she could get, which was out on the balcony. She wanted plenty of opportunity to observe Challen before he reached her. She could determine then how angry he was and if jumping off the balcony to disappear for a while, at least until he cooled down, might be the wiser course. She wasn't likely to do that, brave fool that she was, but she still wanted that option. Maybe if she broke something on the way down—these individual rooms *were* twenty or more feet in height— he'd forget about punishing her.

The balcony would have been a balm to her senses under any other circumstances. There was a view of a good portion of the town seen above the outer walls, of the castle grounds below, even of the street through the wide front gate, left open until late at night. She could see gaali stone tenders using the long poles that flipped open the covers on the posts along the street as the daylight departed.

She had done some cover-opening herself, having watched yesterday how Challen did it. Each wall in the bedroom had a narrow ledge at about a seven-foot height, with a wooden top that rolled back into the wall at the turn of a lever. Concealed inside these ledges, of course, were layers of gaali stones; with five adjustments on each lever, light could be had anywhere from dim to superbright, shining up the white walls and onto the ceiling, reflecting off the marble as if a sun had been let into the room. She had also opened all the gaali stone boxes on their stands throughout the room, leaving alone only those out on the balcony; there was enough light spilling from the room that the balcony was well lit anyway.

Tedra spent only a few minutes taking in the view before turning about to face the bedroom so she could watch the door. It was a long time before it finally opened, but she didn't desert her position. And Challen wasn't alone. He held the door open for a Darash to enter with a tray of food and waited to close the door upon her leaving. Then he looked for Tedra.

It wasn't hard to find her. There wasn't anywhere to hide in the large room except maybe under the bed, but they both knew she wouldn't stoop to hiding. Besides, she was visible on the balcony. Not as visible as he was inside the room, but visible enough. And all her waiting and careful positioning proved useless. The barbarian wasn't revealing any of his emotions as he crossed the room to stop in one of the arched openings. He was the picture of calm control. But maybe that was revealing in itself. No smile of greeting. No rekindling of the burning look of passion she had had from him at their earlier meeting. Just a quiet perusal that lasted several tense moments.

"Come inside, woman."

Even his voice contained not the slightest inflection. "Are we going to eat?"

"We are going to talk. I am going to eat."

"So I'm to be sent to bed without my dinner?"

"That—among other things."

For a second there she had been filled with such relief. No dinner. A barbaric child's punishment, but so minor. Now she came forward with extreme wariness to accept the hand he held out to her. She didn't think of rejecting it. They were, after all, in the place of his complete power over her.

He led her right to the table where the platters of food had been deposited. There were both red meat and white meat, cut in neat little chunks with a dark sauce over them; what could be either vegetables or pared fruits; a basket of sweet *crumos* rolls; some kind of baked dessert with a glazed topping and a really delicious smell to it; and a carafe of *yavarna* wine. There was enough for two, maybe even three, people.

Tedra hadn't felt the least bit hungry until now, looking at all that food and knowing she couldn't have any. Challen stretched out on one of the couches, but didn't indicate she should do the same. But no matter where she went in the room while he ate, knowing he was eating was going to play havoc with her belly. Going without dinner when you didn't see or smell the food first was one thing, this quite another.

She started to turn toward the window couches when Challen's voice stopped her. "You will remove your *chauri* now."

A glance at him showed he wasn't making a move to remove his *bracs* or the fancy blue metallic *comtoc* he wore. Well, how many times today had she thought to herself she'd rather be naked than wearing the damned *chauri?* And it wasn't as if she hadn't stood naked in front of Challen before while he remained clothed.

With a shrug she said only, "You're the boss."

She untied the belt, and with a lift here, a tug there, she stood beside his couch unclothed, the *chauri* in a fluffy pile on the carpet next to her feet. Again his eyes moved over her in a calm study, reminding her of the day they met, which gave Tedra her first suspicion of the kind of hell she was in for tonight.

"Do you now sit here," he said.

The "here" was his loins, which he indicated while watching for her reaction. She didn't disappoint him, flushing with bright color. Her eyes brightened, too, as they locked with his, but with irritation at her own embarrassment. If she had had a few years of sex-sharing behind her instead of only a few days, she could have taken this in stride, but not even all they had done in those few short days had prepared her for straddling his hips naked while he was still clothed.

She did it, however, and tried for an unconcerned tone. "Is this how we're going to talk?"

"This is how you will feed me. We will talk while you do so."

Double whammy, feeding him, which had been such an erotic experience just last night, and she couldn't very well not remember that while sitting on him, *and* being forced to handle and smell the food she couldn't have. Talk about your cruel and unusual punishments. Or was this merely a little extra thrown in as they discussed what a bad girl she'd been?

"Let me take a wild guess," she said, reaching for the platter of meat and thinking about dumping it over his head. "Your good buddy Tamiron spilled his guts to you, right?"

"His guts remain where they should be. He had words with me, if that is what you ask in your Kystrani way."

"But you're not interested in my side of it, are you?"

"Your reasons for earning punishment will not keep that punishment from you."

"Is that so?" she said, shoving a chunk of meat

into his mouth. "What if I told you someone forced me to leave the castle grounds at the point of a knife?"

"Is this true?"

"No." She jammed two more chunks of meat past his lips. "I just wanted to see if *all* reasons don't matter, or only the ones you assume to be true."

He frowned at her then, and stopped the next meat chunk coming at him by grabbing her wrist. "This is no matter to treat lightly, woman."

"Oh, I wholeheartedly agree. It's a matter that has given me considerable anxiety, which I'm willing to bet now is just another part of the punishment. But let me tell you something." She set the platter she was holding on his chest so she could use her other hand to fill his mouth with food and keep it full, long enough to say her piece. "Your rules might apply to all your women, but I'm not one of them. I'm a visitor here and so should be allowed immunity from your rules, especially since I find them totally barbaric, not to mention offensive. Where I come from, women can go wherever they want, do whatever they want. be whatever they want, *and* wear whatever they want. They aren't treated like children half the time and slaves the rest of the time."

"Are you finished?"

By his very tone she knew that nothing she had said made one bit of difference to him. "No. For the record, I never agreed to obey your farden rules, just you in this room. But since that doesn't matter any more than anything else I've said, you better tell me now. How many different ways do you big, brave warriors have for punishing us poor, helpless women?"

He had the gall to grin at her derisive tone. "There

are too many to name. A woman learns by experience.''

"Experience, huh? That had better be your idea of a joke, babe, because if you think I'm going to go through this kind of anxiety every time I step a little over the line, you're crazy."

"The rules for our women are for their protection. You will obey them for your protection."

"Even when I can protect myself?"

"You cannot set yourself against warriors, woman. Do you go alone among them, you will be claimed. Do you challenge them, you will lose. Here a woman does not go where she pleases, do as she pleases, be what she pleases, or wear what she pleases—not in a country where warriors will not have it so. You have learned this truth once in challenge loss. Now you will learn it again in punishment."

"Just like that?" She took the platter from his chest and dropped it loudly back on the table. If that didn't let him know she'd finally got angry, the furious gleam in her eyes did, as well as the finger she jabbed in his chest. "I'm supposed to let you abuse me, you arrogant jerk? Just lie back and take it? All I was was bored and wanted to see a little of your town. You call that a crime worth punishment?"

She rose to her knees with the intention of getting up. A hand high on each thigh forced her back to her seat. Both hands then slid down to her knees to push her legs flush against the sides of his chest, so she was hugging him with her thighs. For a moment, Tedra forgot what she was angry about. Challen was quick to remind her.

"You left the household of your protector without escort, something no woman in Kan-is-Tra may do. For that you will be punished."

He said this quietly, but she could detect no trace of regret in his expression, no reluctance to mete out the punishment. He was simply stating the way it was. And he wasn't finished.

"Also, did you leave without wearing the colors of the house that would identify you. For that you will be punished."

"I didn't know about that," she interjected curtly.

"Ignorance can be no excuse, since you would have been given the proper clothing had you requested the escort as you should have done."

"But would I have been given the escort? Tamiron seemed to think not."

Challen didn't deign to comment about that, probably because he still wasn't finished. "You used your skills against unknown warriors, thereby inviting them to a showing of the same, which you may not have survived. For that you will be punished."

"Tell me something, Mr. Judge and Jury. Was I supposed to just let those two brainless wonders steal me away?"

"Had you done what you were supposed to do, they would not have bothered you."

Tedra crossed her arms over her chest, glaring at him. "As long as we're at it, let's not forget my trespassing this afternoon in your petitions hall."

"I have not. For that you lost your dinner."

Simple. Everything so simple and tied up in a neat package of barbaric logic for her edification. Well, the only enlightenment she was getting out of this was that she would be wise to get off this farden world at the first opportunity, to hell with trade and honor. But she was forgetting the mercenaries she needed, those very same warriors for whom she was fast developing a strong case of dislike, but who still seemed to be the only answer for the liberation of Kystran. She could close her eyes to honor with enough provocation, but not to all those Kystrani women-turned-slaves on Sha-Ka'ar who were suffering worse fates that she was right now.

"All right, barbarian," Tedra said tonelessly. "If you're done listing all my heinous crimes, break out your whips and do your worst."

"You *want* to be beaten?"

"Yes," she said, and meant it. *But if you think everything is going to be the same between us when it's over, think again.*

She didn't say it aloud, and not because a strange tightness was closing around her throat to make speaking difficult. She simply wouldn't give him a reason to reconsider. No, right now she wanted him to hurt her. She wanted pain to remember, to make her fear him, to make her dead inside when he touched her, to make her hate him for real, because even now she didn't. She should, after all those calmly stated "for thats," but she didn't. All she felt as the moment was . . . was a need to cry. Stars, what a horrible realization!

She missed his sigh during her contemplation, but she couldn't miss his sitting up, since it brought his face mere inches from hers, his chest touching hers.

"Do you lay yourself across my upper legs, woman. You may rest your hands on the floor if you wish."

"What?" she said, distracted by his warm breath against her lips. And then, "Oh, sure. Across the legs."

She was still distracted, but managed to get up and reposition herself before she realized what she had done and reared back up, or tried to. A hand in the center of her back wasn't letting her up, and both her hands pushing against the couch weren't changing that. Her breasts just reached the edge of the couch, but her head didn't quite reach the table she was facing.

There was nothing for it but to place her hands on the floor in the space between the two pieces of furniture. She certainly wasn't distracted any longer. She was, in fact, thoroughly indignant.

"This won't work, warrior. You'll have to tie me down, or I won't be responsible for what happens if I go nuts in reaction."

"No."

"No?" She twisted her head around until she could just see him. "I wasn't kidding. I've got some techniques so deeply ingrained that they're automatic reflexes. And you've given me your right side. I can do serious damage from here to your liver and kidneys, and if I manage to turn over, I could well kill you."

"You really think this is possible, woman?"

He was humoring her, she could tell, which only made her madder. "Of course it's possible. I can take a lot of pain, but I've never been put through anything extreme, so I can't know how I will react. Don't be so farden arrogant in thinking I'm not dangerous when pushed, warrior. With the right provocation, anyone can be dangerous, but I've been trained to be especially so. I don't want to end up killing you by accident, no matter how much the thought tempts me right now."

"I appreciate your candor as well as your concern for my safety, but you will not be tested beyond the limits of your endurance. What you will do is remain still and quiet, and accepting of what you asked for. Is that understood?"

"You're making it an order that I have to control myself?" she asked incredulously.

"I see you do understand," he said gravely.

But Tedra could have sworn he was fighting to contain his own control—not to laugh. She turned back to face the table. The cooling food spread out there should have disintegrated, her look was so hot and murderous.

"Get on with it, damn you," she snarled low.

"As you wish."

His open hand came down of her bare bottom with that last word, and stayed there to await her reaction. That he was awaiting her reaction should have stirred her suspicions, and if not that, then the measly strength behind that first smack should have. It didn't. She was just annoyed that it didn't hurt, when what she still wanted was the pain that was going to permit her to hate him.

"Give me a break," she said slowly and with thick scorn, trying to prod him to anger. "A mosquito bite carries more impact than that love tap. I thought this was to be a punishment, not an insult."

"Is this better?"

The next blow was a little harder, but still nothing to blink at. Again his hand remained on her backside until she commented.

"Will you stop with the kid stuff and get serious?"

"As you wish."

The next wallop had quite a sting, but wasn't even close to drawing forth the tears.

"Why don't you try your right hand?" Tedra suggested dryly. "You're obviously lacking strength in the left."

"As you wish."

She gritted her teeth now, expecting quite a difference, but all she got was another sting identical to the last. Now both his hands rested on her only slightly warmed bottom, again awaiting her reaction. That reaction was quick and furious, and with no hand pressing her down, she twisted half around to give it to him full blast.

"Just what the hell do you think you're doing? I dust my *bracs* off harder than that!"

"When you have had enough, woman, you need only say so, since this was your idea, not mine."

"What?!"

"You asked to be beaten," he reminded her and could no longer keep from grinning. "I thought it a strange request, but since your punishment was not to begin until after I had finished eating, I decided to grant your wish."

She screamed in pure rage and swung at him, only to miss completely from such an awkward position. "You miserable son of a diseased *sa'abo!* You knew what I thought! How dare you play on my assumptions like that?"

"When a woman has such silly assumptions, a warrior cannot resist teasing her with them."

All those "as you wishes" took on a different meaning now, the literal meaning, and she screamed again, and swung again. This time her wrist was caught, and with total ease on his part, he rearranged her until she was positioned exactly as she had been before he decided to play games with her.

"Now you will be still, woman."

He released her wrist to see if she would obey him. She did for the moment, though she wasn't done frying him with her eyes.

He had the nerve to laugh at her anger. "Do you now begin to accept the truth that a warrior does not give actual pain to a woman? Such is not needed to teach proper behavior when there are ways to punish that cause little harm. I told you this when first we met. You should have remembered."

"Just what do my terrible misdeeds warrant, then? A night on my knees facing a blank wall?"

"Again you make assumptions and mistake the seriousness of what you have done."

His humor was gone now. His hand came to her cheek, and this time she saw the regret in his eyes. It frightened her as nothing else on this world had.

"No, *kerima,*" he said softly, sadly, using his pet name for her for the first time that night. "Make no more assumptions. Before the next rising, you will swear to obey all rules. You will not only beg for mercy, you will cry. But your tears will not be heard by a warrior bent on his duty. A warrior's control forbids it."

She shook her head, denying his words, knowing by that word "control" exactly what he meant to do to her. But it wouldn't be like before. This time he wouldn't stop until she did beg, did cry, did swear to anything he wanted, and he probably wouldn't stop even then. What he was going to do was designed to humiliate, to smash her pride, to turn her into a malleable, obedient Kan-is-Tran woman. It wasn't going to hurt her. No, it was just going to drive her crazy.

Chapter Twenty-six

*T*edra lay perfectly still on the narrow couch inside the closet, wishing she could go back to sleep to escape her discomfort. But she'd already slept the morning and half the afternoon away. Sleep wasn't ready to come to her rescue again.

It was hot and stuffy inside the closet, but she had discovered the very moment she awoke that the nightmare wasn't over. Her skin was still so sensitized from her ordeal that even the slight breeze today inside the bedchamber was an irritant. She had immediately shut herself away in the closet, where the air didn't stir, quickly finding that the only relief she could get was in lying perfectly still, keeping even her breathing shallow.

Stars, what she wouldn't give to have Corth there for five minutes. She was so primed for sex-sharing, she could likely experience a dozen orgasms in that short a time. Five minutes in the Rover's meditech would do just as well.

She wasn't going to get these wishes short of a miracle, or the hundreds of others she had made, most of them dealing with the disposal of the barbarian. But one in particular she had made she was going to accomplish on her own. At the first opportunity she was going to find her communicator and get out of Kan-is-Tra. There had to be warriors in other countries on Sha-Ka'an whom she could deal with more easily than Kan-is-Tran warriors. And the next time she wouldn't make the colossal mistake of losing her phazor to one of them, or of giving, accepting, or even discussing challenge.

Stars, she was hungry, but she'd rather lie there and suffer the hunger pangs than go into the other room, where food had been left for her. Maybe she would starve herself. That would stick a bone up his nose but good. The thought gave her only a moment's satisfaction before reality intruded to spoil it.

The barbarian wouldn't let her starve. He'd just order her to eat, and refusing orders wasn't an option she had, and not because of her honor. That got damned last night and wasn't a part of this anymore. No, she'd do whatever he ordered because he'd punish her again if she didn't, and she wasn't going to go through that again, not ever.

She shivered with the memory of it, then moaned as that brought her nerve endings to life again. She had done a lot of moaning last night, and everything else he had said she would do. He'd wanted her to finish feeding him first, and she'd wanted to, just to buy time. But knowing what he was going to do to her had started it happening before he even touched her. She became so bothered from sitting on his loins, her hands started trembling and he had to finish the meal on his own. But once he was done . . .

It really was the most horrible experience of her life. Challen had brought her again and again to the point of hysterics, to where her need for him was so great she would have raped him if she could, to where she would have done anything, promised anything, for just one moment of the relief he could have given her. But relief wasn't part of the deal, only the constant need for it, and he never let that need diminish even a little. He'd leave her alone for a few minutes while she prayed and prayed that it was over, but then he'd draw her back into his arms and start all over again.

She hadn't known her body could be played like that, that it could be made to override her will, her instincts, her pride. Another part of it was that Challen made her *think* there would be an end, that relief would come before the night was over. His kisses said so, passionate. His caresses said so, in no way indifferent. She had assumed he himself was aroused and merely using his phenomenal control. But she finally came to understand that was just another aspect of the punishment, hope raised and then destroyed.

He hadn't been aroused by what he did to her, not even a little, or by anything she did or said. She flamed with shame every time she thought of how she had crawled all over him, kissing him, begging him to join with her. But nothing she did could shake his control. That was perhaps what hurt the most, not the agony of sexual frustration he put her through, but the fact that she just didn't have what it took to play the same game. To want a man so desperately but be unable to make him want her back was worse than demoralizing. It made her feel inept as a woman, worthless, totally undesirable, and so miserable she could cry again, remembering it.

Stars, how she wanted out of there, and immediately, before she had to face the barbarian again. She couldn't bear the thought of that, especially with this need still upon her.

But even if movement wasn't still a physical reminder of what she had experienced, she couldn't go searching for her communicator yet. Her punishment wasn't just finding out what hell was like for a single night. Sometime during those many hours that Challen had devoted to her, he informed her that she was also confined to his bedchamber for a week. And an added little bonus to that was that she was to remain in the room without benefit of clothing.

She supposed this was to make her long to wear the *chauri* she claimed to hate. At the very least it was to keep her regret for earning punishment uppermost in her mind. But that wasn't necessary. She wasn't ever going to forget what had been done to her. Challen had the results he wanted out of the punishment. She wasn't going to break any more rules. But she had what she wanted out of it, too. She had thought she needed a bad beating with lots of pain to make her hate him. He had accomplished it without a single blow.

Chapter Twenty-seven

Challen rode his *hataar* deep into the woods before dismounting. Fog was trapped in pockets low to the ground, making it a gloomy place well suited to his mood. He wasn't there to hunt, though the area teemed with animal life. Two plump gray *curaki*, likely mates, cooed down at him from a nearby tree. A *karril* slithered around the limb of another. *Kisraki* bolted when the *hataar* grazed too close to their warren, but the well-trained animal merely swished his tail.

Challen chose the tree the *karril* was hunting in to sit under, almost hoping the slimy thing would drop down in his lap. He watched its slow progress along the tree limb without really seeing it, looking inward instead and not liking what he saw, any more than he had when his thoughts and lack of control had driven him from the castle earlier.

He had come so *close* to challenging the *shodan* of Sha-lah for some ridiculous reason he could not even remember, and all because a woman had his emotions twisted in coils of regret, anger, confusion, exasperation, guilt, frustration; and, Droda help him, it was not lessening one bit. Half those emotions had been with him since the previous rising when Tamiron first told him of the woman's misconduct.

He had felt anger, more anger than he could ever remember feeling, that she had put herself in danger by the use of her strange skills. Also present, but more unusual still, was a feeling of strong annoyance that she had not worn the colors that would proclaim her as his, regardless that he had not explained the necessity to her. It was a rule meant to avoid confusion and keep warriors from claiming protected women if they should happen to become separated from their escort for any reason. But Challen realized it was more important to him that Tedra De Arr simply not be bothered, that he wanted no other warrior getting close to her.

Confusion came next, because he was feeling things he did not understand, but mostly because his duty was suddenly abhorrent to him. The woman had to be punished. There could be no exceptions in this, and it was his responsibility to do it. But he wanted not to do it. And this reluctance was also something he had never felt before.

He had been punishing women since he had become old enough to be responsible for them, mostly for behavioral reasons, not for the breaking of rules. Women obeyed the rules that pertained to them because they knew those rules were for their protection and benefit. They also did not like punishment and tended to avoid it with proper behavior, so he had not punished many women. Doing so had never bothered him before. It was simply something that had to be done. But he had punished only a few women in the way he had punished his Kystrani, and only because they had been sharing his bed at the time.

Yet it was the most common form of discipline for a warrior to give his own woman, the one he most preferred to use if he felt more than normal concern for her, since it in no way did her harm, and it was quickly over with. Denying sustenance only made a warrior worry for his woman's health. Giving total

solitude only made them both suffer, as did other punishments such as Darasha labors, which caused exhaustion, discomfort from rarely used muscles, and
any number of other lingering adverse effects. Arousal
without release was the punishment women preferred,
too, if given a choice, and for the same reasons, but
also because they knew if their need had not diminished by the next day, it would be seen to, to their
complete satisfaction.

Because it *was* preferable to women, he had thought
Tedra would think so, too, but still he had not wanted
to do it. That reluctance had led to his stupidity in
thinking a double dose of *dhaya* juice would make
punishing her easier. It did. It also affected his mind
somewhat, and now his memory, in that there was
little he recalled of the actual punishment other than
that he had been totally lacking in concern or mercy
during the administering of it.

He did remember that, and not even caring that it
was so, when both feelings were a prerequisite of
discipline. But also absent had been all sense of time,
only he did not know it until the *dhaya* juice had let
go some of its hold near the new rising, enough for
him to realize the punishment had continued much,
much longer than it should have. And therein lay a
guilt so strong, he wondered if he could ever face the
woman again.

The *karril* dropped suddenly from the tree, landing
a few feet from Challen's bent legs. It was best not
to startle the poisonous thing as it had startled him,
so he remained still until it slithered off into the brush.
But it had brought him back to an awareness of his
surroundings, and to the Kystrani voice box he held
in one hand.

He was not sure why he had brought the box with

him. He fully intended to examine it, but there was no hurry to do that. Perhaps he had hoped it would speak to him, that he might learn from it a better understanding of his woman. But he knew not how to make it speak, or if it even would speak to anyone other than Tedra.

The box was white, with small gray things rising on its surface, some round, some rectangular. There was a smooth square black surface on one flat side, with a circle below it that contained many holes. In one end there was a deeper hole like an inverted cone, and all over the box were tiny raised markings similar to the scribbles in the scrolls kept by the Guardian of the Years.

Challen shook the box, but that did not wake the voice. He had seen Tedra point the box to give stillness to the *taraan* and himself. Stunning, she had called it, but how she had made the red line that had touched them both come out of it he knew not. He had also seen her hit the box to make the voice silent. Could that also wake it?

He hit the box, and was so startled by the red line that shot out of it to touch the tree limbs above his head, he immediately dropped it to the ground. As soon as he had let go, however, the red line disappeared. He stared at the box now, unwilling to touch it again, but knew he would. He had managed to stun a tree. He would get the box to speak, too.

He picked it up again and carefully pointed the coned hole, which the red line had come out of, away from him. Then he began touching the gray shapes to see which one had made the line when he hit it. The first shape did not depress, but slid up and down, moving no more than an inch. Nothing happened in either direction. The second shape depressed and brought the line back. He played with that for a moment, intrigued because the line stayed on only while the round shape was depressed. The next shape was round with a line on it that pointed to markings. This turned, but did nothing that he could see. The next shape also depressed, and the noise that then came out of the box was so loud, Challen was again startled into dropping it.

"Where the hell have you been?!" the woman's voice screeched up at him from the ground, and then there was silence.

Chapter Twenty-eight

Challen knew the woman inside the box was waiting for him to answer her question. But the question had not been meant for him, surely, so he said nothing. And also, he was not so sure now that he wanted to speak with her. What could she tell him, after all, that could assuage his guilt or aid him in making amends for what he had done?

And then the voice came again, in a much calmer tone.

"I retrieved your belt. I don't have to tell you how disturbed I was that you weren't in it." Again there was the waiting silence, then, "Tedra, can't you talk?"

The next silence worried him, being much longer. If he didn't speak, the voice might go away, and he wasn't sure if it had come by itself or if he had brought it.

"Tedra is not here."

Immediately he was asked, "Who are you?"

"Challen Ly-San-Ter."

"A lot that tells me," the voice grumbled. "Look, fella, be a good sport, why don't you, and give the unit back to Tedra. You do know who she is, don't you?"

"Yes."

"And you know where she is?"

"Certainly."

"Certainly? Why do I get the feeling that word has a wealth of meaning in it?"

"Are you Martha?"

"Ah, I thought so. So you know Tedra well enough for her to tell you about me. That's good. That will make things much easier. But why don't you pick up the unit and turn it around now? The grass on your world is interesting, but I'd rather see whom I'm talking to."

"Are you inside the box?"

"In a manner of speaking, yes. At least a small part of me is inside the box, which lets me speak to you and see you. If you'll just turn the unit over, you'll see what I mean. Go ahead, it won't bite you— not if you don't touch any of the buttons and switches." After a long moment of nothing happening, Martha gave her best imitation of a sigh. "That was a joke, kiddo. What was Tedra thinking of to let you have the unit without telling you how it works?"

"She did not. I took it from her."

"I see. Well, that certainly explains a lot, and tells me who you likely are. So pick up the unit and let's see if my deductions are as accurate as always. It doesn't bite. The worst it does is stun, but I think you already know all about that, don't you?" The sound of chuckling was unmistakable—and challenging.

Challen picked up the box and turned it over so the flat side with the colored things was facing him—and almost dropped it again. The small black square was no longer black. There were tiny, needle-point lights flashing from it in what looked like another box in what looked like a miniature room. Inside the small box-unit? Impossible. But a voice inside it was also impossible, yet he heard it, spoke to it, and had it answer him.

"I knew it was you, warrior," the voice said smugly now. "Probables is my forte, after all."

"You can see me?"

"Quite clearly."

"Then why do I not see you as well, woman?"

"That's rich, doll. Don't you know you're talking to a computer? Computers don't have gender in anything but voice. And you are seeing me. I'm the gorgeous machine with all the flashing lights you're frowning at. No, don't turn the unit away again. You haven't told me where Tedra is, or how she is, for that matter."

Challen's expression turned inscrutable. He didn't answer. He was wondering himself how Tedra was now, if she was still in need, if she would let him see to that need when he returned. He wanted to explain it all to the—the voice, or whatever it was, to tell it what he had done. Probables? Deductions? It could tell him if he would be forgiven or not.

"Come on, warrior, I want some reassurances here." The voice came out sounding impatient. "Fair is fair. I let you have Tedra for the month of service she owes you. I didn't have to do that, you know. I could have brought her back to the ship that day, and there wouldn't have been anything you could have done about it."

That possibility enraged him, that he might have no control over keeping the woman or not, but there was no indication of it when he asked, "How do you know of her service to me?"

"I was there, remember? She turned me off so I couldn't see or comment on what was going on, but I still had a fix on you both and could hear everything that was said and done. And hearing for a computer that is expert in probables is just as good as seeing is for you humans. Did you breach her?''

He almost took insult at the impropriety of that question, until he recalled what Tedra had told him of the need to have her breaching proved. ''Are you the one who will record that it was done?''

''Yes.''

''It was done.''

''Did she like it?''

''Yes.''

''I figured she would. She'd been waiting a long time for someone like you to come along, but you never did. She had to go to another world to find you. So tell me, are you willing to return with us?''

''Return?''

''To Kystran,'' Martha clarified. ''To wrest control back from those Sha-Ka'ari warriors you people bred about three hundred years ago.''

''I know nothing of which you speak.''

''Hasn't Tedra told you *anything?*''

''I cared not to discuss the reason for her being here.''

''Well, don't get all out of joint about it. I suppose that's your privilege. And you're just what she's needed, so her stay with you isn't a waste of time as far as I'm concerned, though I doubt she'll see it that way. The woman takes life too serious. Work, and train so she can work better, that's all she's known. And now she's set herself up to be the salvation of Kystran . . . but that's not your problem. As long as she's enjoying herself with you, I'm satisfied I made the right decision.''

''And if she is not?''

''Now why would you ask that, unless she was not?

What's happened, warrior, to have you looking so guilty?''

Challen flushed, startled that the voice could read him when he was being so careful to school his features to blandness. Deductions and probables again. He would have to watch his words as well as his reactions if he did not want the thing inside his head, knowing his every thought. And he did not. Answers were all he wanted from it, but he would not get them unless he was honest now.

"The woman disregarded certain rules, a matter demanding punishment. This she was given by me.''

There was a short silence, then, "I think I'm going into what you humans call shock. I've made a mistake, but I'm not programmed to make mistakes. How the hell could I have been so wrong about you, warrior? I thought you wanted her!''

Challen did not know whether to feel insulted by the contempt coming out of the box or guiltier. "You were not wrong in that,'' he said stiffly.

"Then how could you hurt her? More to the point, how badly have you hurt her? Does she need a meditech?''

"I know not what such is, but the woman was not hurt. She was made to feel great frustration and physical need, with no relief to ease it.''

"That's what you're feeling guilty about? And here I thought you'd half killed her. Well, that's different, but if that's all you did to punish her, what's with the guilty conscience that threw me off the track?''

"I—took something to make my duty less a burden.'' He went on to briefly explain the rest of it. "But I have not returned to her since I left her near the new rising. I know not whether she will accept the matter as finished and welcome me as before, or whether she will now abhor my touch.''

"You've got yourself a problem all right, kiddo. First off, you don't punish a Sec 1," Martha told him plainly. "They're a law unto themselves."

"Here she is no more than a woman, one who must obey rules as all women must."

"Oh, I bet she just loves that." The voice came out exceedingly dry. "And only a barbarian would think to use a woman's body against her for a means of punishment. But I suppose you great big fellas had to come up with something to keep from killing your women off with those mighty fists." There was a short span of chuckling here, not at all sympathetic to the difficulties of a Sha-Ka'ani male. "So are you asking me what you can expect, now that you've given Tedra a more thorough taste of your world?"

"It comes to me that you likely know her better than I," he replied.

"Smart of you to figure that out."

Challen stiffened at the unmistakable sarcasm. His need to instruct the voice on the proper respect due a warrior was strong, but quite impotent. How could he enforce that instruction when the one needing it was hidden inside a box which he knew not the workings of, much less how to open? The voice was safe from retribution, which only proved that such impunity encouraged objectionable behavior, whereas the promise of swift discipline prevented it.

Challen controlled his vexation long enough to demand, "If it is true you know the woman so well, you will give me the probables you claim skill in so I may determine how best to deal with her."

"Will I? If you use commands instead of requests with Tedra, it's no wonder she's breaking rules. But you're right on the nose, doll, in supposing you need my help. I've been programmed to know her better than any human ever could, and I can tell you there's only two ways she'll react to what you've done. If she hits you with a broadside of verbal anger, then you've got nothing to worry about. She'll swear up and down she'll get even with you, and any number of other things you won't like hearing, but that's her way of getting all that bruised emotion out of her system. That's not to say her fury won't be very real.''

"It was my hope you could suggest a means of defusing it," Challen reminded the voice.

"My suggestion is you not even try. If you cajole her out of it *before* she's had a chance to let you know how misused she's feeling, then you're only asking for more trouble. You should have discovered by now that she's easy as computer basics to provoke, with that quick temper of hers. But the thing you aren't likely to figure out on your own is that she doesn't *like* to be angry at people. That's one of my purposes, channeling her anger and frustrations in my direction, since it's easy to yell at a machine without feeling guilty about it afterward.''

"So I am to allow her to be disrespectful?''

"If that goes against the grain, warrior, you might as well give her back to me right now. But I thought you were looking for a way to make amends for that guilt you were feeling," she reminded him.

"But to allow—''

"You can't make amends without giving a little, big guy, and it seems to me you owe her all the disrespect she cares to dump on you.''

There was a long hesitation before Challen asked, "Do I allow it, how long before she puts her anger to rest?''

"If you weren't just bragging and she really has liked sharing sex with you, then count yourself lucky. The most she's stayed mad was two days, and that only because no one was smart enough to talk her out of it after she'd had her blowup. But she's looking at her stay with you as temporary, so she won't want to waste much time nursing resentment."

Challen knew very well the woman thought in terms of temporary. That he had no intention of losing her after her challenge service was ended was best kept to himself, certainly not to be disclosed to one who claimed such powers as this Martha.

"Did you not mention two possible reactions that may be anticipated?"

"The second one's more simple, kiddo. It's silence. If Tedra's got nothing to say to you, then you can bet those overdeveloped muscles of yours that it's because she's decided the only thing she wants from you is your blood. If that's the case, I want her back now, since she'll be of no further use to you in that state of mind."

"No."

"Why do I get the feeling you don't think the second possible reaction will be a problem? It wouldn't be because you found it so easy to defeat her in the challenge, would it? I hope you're not so arrogant that you haven't considered the possibility that you came out the winner in that fight only because the woman wasn't trying to kill you, merely defeat you. There's a world of difference in what she's capable of doing when it doesn't matter to her if her opponent gets seriously hurt or not, even more difference if she's actually trying to kill him."

"Perhaps this is so if the opponents are the non-warriors of Kystran. The woman has told me they know not the art of weaponless fighting. And perhaps you yourself are unaware that weaponless fighting is the sport of warriors. There is no arrogance involved when I tell you the woman cannot defeat me, no matter the level of her skill.''

''Be that as it may, I think you've missed my point. If she's out for your blood, you'll have to fight her every time you get near her, and confine her otherwise. You won't be having any more fun with her, and I mean that both ways. The probables in that scenario tells me it's just going to get her more and more punishments, and I didn't leave her with you so you could abuse her. If I determine it's necessary, I *will* get her out of there.''

Again a rage reared up, that it might be possible the voice could do as it claimed, and this time he didn't even try to control it. ''The woman is mine for one month by her own word. I will have *your* word you will not interfere.''

''That's rich, doll. You keep forgetting I'm a computer. I'm not programmed for integrity.''

''Does this mean you would not keep your word did you give it?''

''It means I do whatever I think is best, regardless of anything.''

''And if I destroy this box?''

''Tedra needs it to come back on her own. I don't need it to bring her back if I get a fix on her as I now have on you. And you can lead me to her.''

''Your threat lacks substance, computer. Could you follow me to her as you say, you would not have lost this fix on her you claim to need to take her back.''

''Picked up on that, did you? But you don't think I'd give away information like that without a reason, do you?''

"And your reason?"

"It's true I can lose you in a crowd and be unable to pinpoint your position again without a great deal of luck, and computers don't deal in luck. And you'd know I'd lost you if you abuse Tedra and nothing happens from my end. So I'll make a deal with you. I've already determined you'll keep your word if you give it, so I want it that you *won't* abuse the woman if she foolishly tries to kill you."

Challen suddenly burst out laughing. "By the stones of gaali, the gall you have is astounding."

"Only a gentleman would put it so nicely. Do we have a deal?"

"For what are you dealing?"

"I get your word, as well as being kept apprised by you of her reactions to your arbitrary way of doing things down there. In return I'll practice hands-off and allow you the full month she owes you before I demand her return. I'll even throw in free advice if it's needful, and if I know my Tedra, it'll be needful a great deal."

"You have already told me you cannot be trusted. Do I speak with you when she is near, the matter of luck becomes more a matter of probables and deductions for you in the 'fixing' on her location."

Chuckling came out of the box. "You've got me there, warrior. But you're overlooking a couple of things. If Tedra's only good and mad, but not enough to want to kill you, then chances are she'll get back to thinking she's got to honor her service to you. If that's the case, it won't matter if I decide to take her out of there. She'd only get a new Transfer unit and come right back to you to complete her service. Now that's what she'd likely do. But what I can do, if you don't care to deal with me, is create havoc on your world of the like you've never dreamed of. Whole towns can be demolished, making your people think the world is coming to an end. Of course, I wouldn't do that without knowing in what town you have Tedra stashed. But destroying your crops would accomplish the same thing, causing widespread panic and fear. Actually, just showing myself would probably do it. To appreciate that, you should know the Rover is the size of a small town. What impression do you think it would make on your people to see it hovering threateningly over your towns and cities?''

"It is easy to make claims that cannot be proved," Challen scoffed. "If what you say is true, show yourself to me."

"If I do that, someone else is liable to see me, too, starting the panic I've just predicted." There was a short pause, and then, "How about this instead?"

The ground suddenly exploded twenty feet away, sending dirt and grass flying, and Challen diving for cover. "Droda," he whispered, shaken. "You are indeed as God-like as the woman said."

"No, I'm just in control of the Rover's attack-and-defense systems. And that was no more than a repulsion beam, a blast of air used mainly just to clear away space debris from the Rover's path. I've entered your atmosphere to use it, since it's not as far-reaching as the Rover's actual weapons. But a lazor blast would have left a much, much bigger hole, as well as set the vegetation around you afire. As long as I've got this cloud cover to conceal me . . . you don't look too well, warrior. Hadn't you begun to suspect yet that Tedra had told you the truth about her origins?"

Certainly he had, but this was not something he would have admitted to anyone, least of all to Tedra. He had wanted her to be of his world, unimportant, claimable. If she were otherwise, then she would be of interest not only to himself but to every *shodan* in Kan-is-Tra.

"Never let it be said a Mock II can't do a perfect simulation of mercy and compassion." The voice broke into his thoughts with a drawn-out sigh. "I've probably blown a circuit I'm unaware of, but I'm going to let you in on a little secret, warrior, that ought to make you feel a whole lot better. I happen to be on your side. You may not believe that after everything I've told you, which was just my strong-arm tactics program running on convince-at-no-expense. But the bottom line is, you're just what Tedra needs in her life, and one of my priorities is seeing that she gets what she needs."

"She is in *my* possession, computer, not I in hers," he stated stiffly.

"Arrogance doesn't impress me, kiddo, so why don't you put it on a back burner for now? I *know* you already consider her yours, but you have to accept that fact that first she is mine. I was created for her, my purpose none other than to see to her health, her ultimate happiness, her well-being. Everything I do is for her benefit. Do you know how many worlds I passed up that she would have felt a marginal satisfaction in discovering? But I don't deal in half measures. I knew long before she realized it what would be necessary to accomplish the goal that's become so important to her. So I found her the mother planet of the warriors she's determined to defeat, and let me tell you, finding it was no easy task. I gave her the opportunity to complete her goal, and I'll do everything I deem necessary to help her complete it. Which means, warrior, that she's got to go back to Kystran, whether you like it or not. That doesn't mean you have to lose her. You're welcome to come along. What happens afterward will then be a matter you can settle between you."

"If her goal is so important to her and to you, why have you allowed it to be delayed by her challenge loss? She says you could have intervened to prevent it from occurring."

"Sure I could have, but it wouldn't have seen to a goal of mine, which was to give her something she's needed for a long time, her own wishes in the matter notwithstanding. Sometimes I must help her despite herself, stubborn and contrary as she is. And I've already told you that you're the 'something' she needed."

"But you knew not my mettle, computer. You knew not the character of the warrior you left her to."

"Are you kidding?" There was laughter here. "You accepted her challenge and let her pound all over you without returning a single bruise. That told me all I needed to know about you. Besides, her sexual libido went crazy at her first sight of you. That alone decided the matter as far as I was concerned. Now, your restraint puzzled the hell out of me, and why you didn't breach her immediately. Probables tells me you weren't yourself that day, any more than you were last night. And that concludes you were on the same 'something' you admitted to taking yesterday, or a similar agent."

He thought to deny it, but saw no point. "Yes."

"Does she know that?"

"No."

"Stars, how I'd love to be there when she finds out, but that's another scenario. Do we have a deal on this one? I still need your word you won't abuse her if things get out of hand. And I still want her back if she's now dead set against you.''

''The giving of my word is unnecessary. Warriors do not abuse women for any reason. And I will do the deciding if I must give her up.''

''Fair enough. Then you'd better get back to see if you have a decision to make.''

''How do I—send you away?''

Chuckling came up at him again. ''And here I thought you were going to blunder by forgetting about that. Very well, press the round button just below the monitor and I'm gone. Press it again and I'm back. And don't forget I want some progress reports, at your convenience, of course. But before you turn me off, I should warn you that you're in danger of taking a long time to get back to Tedra if you don't slide the safety on on the phazor—that's the rectangle that moves up and down. My readings show me the phazor is still on max, the setting Tedra last dialed, since she wasn't going to take any more chances with you that day. If you accidentally stun yourself, you'll be out of commission for a good ten hours. And accidents are very probable when the safety isn't on and the user doesn't know what he's doing. Have you got all that?''

''Yes.''

''Then good luck, warrior. You're definitely going to need it, if I know my Tedra. And I do.''

Chapter Twenty-nine

"*A*re you comfortable, mistress?"

"Sitting in water? Getting wet? Am I *supposed* to be comfortable?"

The sarcasm was unmistakable, but it didn't bring the miserable expression to Jalla's face. That had been there since the girl arrived with more food, and stayed to draw Tedra's bath and urge her into it.

"A bath is said to be soothing after certain punishments," Jalla offered.

That brought a rigid frown from Tedra. "Does everyone know I was punished?"

She realized that was a stupid question when she recalled how loudly she had screamed with frustration during the worst of it. But Jalla nodded anyway, and that made Tedra glower even more.

"That's just great, just what I needed to know, that I'm more humiliated than I realized. And you're no help, Jalla, so why don't you absent yourself? You're good at doing *that*, aren't you?"

The miserable expression got worse, causing Jalla to drop some genuine tears. "I know it was my fault, mistress. You may punish me if you wish."

"Don't be ridiculous," Tedra snapped, further annoyed that she'd been taking her anger out on the girl. "My actions are my own responsibility. If I didn't venture out yesterday, I'd have done it sooner or later. So stop giving me that hangdog look. It doesn't help to know you feel guilty. But why *did* you take off yesterday? Were you afraid you'd lose your dinner, too?''

"Lowden Ly-San-Ter would not have been as lenient as the *shodan* if the matter were brought to his attention. For no less than seven risings, I would have been assigned the chores I most dislike the doing of.''

"Is that all?''

"You scoff, mistress, but it is no pleasure being driven from your bed in the middle of the darkness to bake the bread for the first meal. Before the sun rising you have wilted from the heat of the great ovens, and your arms feel as if they will fall off, they are so sore from so much grinding and kneading. There are Darasha with thick muscles who love the baking of bread. To them go chores they do *not* love when punishment comes to them. Master Lowden is wise in knowing what chores are most hated and by whom.''

Tedra could only shake her head. Barbarian reasoning was so fascinating. Trust them to find such harmless yet despised means for discipline.

She could not help grinning as a sudden thought hit her. "What happens if there's a chore *everyone* hates doing? Does it ever get done?''

"There are many Darasha in the castle, mistress, as well as many women under protection of the *shodan*. Thus is there always someone or other in need of punishment.''

"Almost guaranteeing that the one thing barbarians won't want to trade for is robocleaners.'' And that idea made Tedra laugh out loud.

Which was how Challen found her when he entered the room. This was not exactly what he had been expecting, but he got the expected the moment she noticed him. Her humor vanished instantly, and worse, she turned her back on him without the slightest acknowledgment of his presence.

Challen found himself at a sudden loss. He had been prepared to deal with the angry words the computer had promised would be his, not the damning silence it had also predicted. That silence sat on his shoulders, pushing them down in defeat as it continued.

He dismissed Jalla with a nod, but he made no move toward the bath once the girl was gone. Watching Tedra was out of the question. He was fully prepared to see to any remaining need she might have, now that the double dose of *dhaya* juice had finally worn off. But her need must also be gone, and gaali stones could lose their light before he would force his own need on the woman, with her feelings for him so altered.

Tedra remained in the water, but certainly not because she liked it. It was more that the punishment denying her the use of clothing or even a covering made the bath slightly preferable just then to getting out of it. Or would the barbarian consider the water a covering? Ha! Just let him say so and she'd have an excuse never to get disgustingly wet again.

She had known Challen would show up eventually, and she'd been so afraid he would come before her body was hers again to command. She had thought he would want to take advantage of that, but he'd surprised her. Whether intentionally or not, he'd given her enough time to return to her normal inclinations and urges, instead of those he'd created. Her need for a man was gone. What she hadn't counted on was its coming right back at the first sight of him. But it was controllable. It had farden well better be controllable.

"Do you intend to spend the whole darkness at your bath, *kerima?*"

The question drew her attention no more than to say, "I was considering it."

There was a silence while she sensed him moving across the room to the table where food and wine awaited him. "I know you dislike the water. Come out."

"Is that an order, master? If it is, I will certainly obey it. If not . . ."

She deliberately scooped up two handfuls of water and only cringed a little as the slippery stuff poured over her breasts. But one scoop was enough to get her point across—if he was watching. She wasn't going to look to find out.

"It was no order, woman. You may do as you please."

"Well, aren't we accommodating tonight," she replied dryly. "In that case, I'll get out. I'm not one for making subtle statements anyway, or spiting myself to make them. I much prefer spelling things right out."

"You are welcome to do so."

That got her attention, swinging her around so fast, a wave of water hit the side of the sunken tub to splash back at her. "And get myself punished again if I do? No, thank you."

She watched him warily as he came forward then, but it was only to pick up one of the waiting drying cloths to hand to her. She took it as she stepped out of the tub, damning the fact that she wouldn't be able to keep the cloth once she was dry. Prancing around naked in front of the barbarian was not her idea of fun, Kystran-style fun, anyway. Now, if it would get him wanting some Sha-ka'ani fun, that'd be another story, worth a little revenge when he found out she didn't want the same anymore. But he'd proved beyond a doubt last night that her nakedness didn't affect him. All it was doing was giving her further punishment by the means of embarrassment.

That embarrassment was extreme just now, with Challen simply standing there watching her. And the way he watched her, with an alertness that seemed anticipatory, as if he were waiting for something in particular to happen.

That annoyed the hell out of her. He'd as much as said she could be frank, but she wasn't buying that. Her frankness would sear his ears off, and she wasn't forgetting for a minute what such disrespect to warriors would get her. His offer had to be a trap, and that suggested that he'd had such a good time punishing her last night, he was now going to hunt for excuses so he could do it again.

She wouldn't help him toward that end. She'd keep a lid on her temper if it killed her. But it made her absolutely furious that she had to, enough to throw the drying cloth down before she was completely dry. She walked away, heading toward the closet, refusing to remain in the same room with him unless he ordered her to.

His voice came before she was halfway there. "You will join me for the meal."

Thank Heaven's Stars she could say to that, "I've already eaten."

"Then you will sit with me while I do."

She turned, forcing mere inquiry in her expression. "Is that an order, master?"

His jaw clenched, hearing her call him that again. "It is a request."

"Then I decline."

"Then it becomes an order," he gritted out.

"Then certainly I will obey."

No matter how sweetly agreeable she sounded, her movements told another story. Stiff and stomping, she stalked to the table. Challen got there first, swinging her around to face him.

"If you are so wishful of obeying, woman, then speak to me your thoughts. I have given you permission to do so."

Was that frustration in his expression? If it was, it was nothing compared with her own.

"Permission to do so? Very well, you asked for it, warrior, and I'll start with that. I shouldn't need permission to speak my mind. Freedom to say what I think and feel has always been mine—until I came here. I don't even curb my opinions with my boss, and he's got power over a job which is very important to me. Here all a woman can say is what *you* want to hear. Well, you can stuff that where the sun won't reach it, warrior. I'll never say only what you want me to."

"I would not ask that of you."

"Wouldn't you? Haven't you? What the farden hell do you call your demand for respect at all times, if not that? Has it never occurred to you beef-witted louts that you can't force respect, that it has to be earned or it's worthless?"

"What you say is well known, woman. What is also known is what happens if a woman so angers a warrior with her careless tongue that he loses all control and strikes her to silence. Thus do they both suffer, she with serious hurt, he with the guilt of causing it. Respect demanded of women is for their own protection."

She wasn't interested in the sound logic behind that

bit of reasoning. "Lose control? Get angry? You've got to be joking," she sneered derisively. "You people have control down to a science. You've got about as much emotion as robots, and I speak from experience."

"Warriors *can* lose control. They strive not to, but the loss is not beyond their capabilities."

He was grinning when he said that. And that was all Tedra needed to see for her own control to snap.

"Why don't you show me, then?" she said just before she slapped him for all she was worth. "Now show me how hurt I'll get when you hit me back."

Challen fingered his cheek as he stared down at her. "I am not a callow youth who can be so easily provoked."

The grin was gone, but there was still something about him that said he was amused, even delighted by what she'd done. Tedra wasn't positive. She could be reading him quite wrong. But when had that ever stopped her temper when it wanted out?

"Then let me try harder." And she hit him again, hard enough to turn his face with it. *"Now* will you hit me back?"

"You can do this the whole darkness, *kerima,* and I will not retaliate."

"Not even if I want you to?"

"What you want is the guilt I would feel if I did so," he answered softly. "Such is not necessary. There is no room for more guilt to join that which I already possess."

"Liar!" she all but screamed, and slapped him twice more. And then she was pounding on his chest with both fists. "Damn you for a lying, insensitive jerk! You wouldn't know what guilt was if it knocked you over. And what could you be guilty about? You were doing your *duty!* You said so! And don't touch me!'' She pushed out of the arms that had started to close around her. ''Do you think I could ever want your touch again?''

''Yes,'' he replied with supreme confidence. ''You want it now, if for no other need than comforting. It is the stubbornness inside you that denies it.''

''Fat lot you know,'' she retorted, but in a more level tone. The first heat of her temper had passed with the pounding she gave him. She was now choking on what was left. ''I don't need comforting. All I need is to get out of here and never see you again.''

''No.''

He didn't exactly shout it, but there was more feeling in that word than she'd heard from him before. ''Oh, don't worry, warrior. I'm not forgetting the challenge loss. For a while there I thought I could, but honor's got a way of hanging on with a death's grip even when you try to shake it off. I'll stick around until my time's up. I'll even jump when you say jump. But I'll hate every minute of it.''

''No.''

''No, again? What's with you today?'' she demanded in exasperation. ''Aren't I getting my point across? I don't *like* you anymore, warrior. Do I have to hit on you some more before that registers?''

''Why have you not used your skills on me instead?''

This inquiry was accompanied by another grin, which had her shouting again. ''Because what you did, you did to me, not to a Sec 1—to *me!*''

''And you are, after all, a woman?''

''I hate you,'' was all she could think to reply to that observation, but the words came out with difficulty through the knot in her throat and sounded tepid even to her ears.

"Enough to want my blood?"

"Don't be ridiculous," she snapped automatically. "If I wanted your blood, I'd have had it by now."

Her eyes widened the moment she said it, the reason dawning on her finally why she was lacking conviction in her words. She still didn't hate the farden jerk. Damn! Why did the effects of the punishment have to wear off completely, leaving her nothing to support and sustain her fury with? The fact that the effects were gone only proved the punishment had been terrible while it lasted, but nothing to warrant true revenge over.

And yet she wasn't forgetting that it *had* been terrible, that he'd made her beg and cry and forfeit her pride totally. The worst of it was that he could remember everything she'd done and said; that every time she looked at him from now on, she'd wonder if he *was* remembering it, and gloating over it. But she could view it objectively now, even allowing that what he'd done was normal and acceptable from his standpoint, the Sha-Ka'ani way of doing things. That she couldn't accept those ways was her problem. That they had ruined what she felt for the warrior was also her problem. She just wished she didn't regret it so much.

But *he* wasn't likely to care one way or the other, as long as he got his service from her. Or would he care? For some reason, she had the feeling he thought she was just blowing off steam, that nothing had really changed between them. That would account for his amusement, and for the fact that he didn't seem to be taking anything she said seriously.

She didn't *need* to convince him. He'd find out the way it was soon enough, when he got only unwilling service from her from now on. But he'd said she could speak her mind, and she hadn't yet told him even half of what she was feeling. So maybe the rest of it would get through to him, and maybe a calm approach would help.

"Look, warrior, to be honest, I don't actually hate you. You can't help being an insensitive brute any more than I can help not liking it. None of us are perfect, and I'd be the first to admit I don't even come close to the mark. So I still owe you service. Well, I'll be here for you to take it, but note the key word is 'take.' You won't be getting willing service from me anymore."

This merely raised a golden brow. "Perhaps you have forgotten what your service is, woman. It is to *deny me nothing*. If I demand your willingness, will you deny it to me?"

Tedra flushed with chagrin, and felt her temper returning. "There's a difference between willingness given and willingness forced. I gave it to you before because I wanted to . . . because I wanted you. But I don't want you any longer, so now you will indeed have to demand it from me. I won't fight you. That's not what I meant at all. No, I'll obey you, just like I'll obey all your farden rules around here, because, believe me, you *did* make your point last night, warrior. You made it about an hour after you got started. The other five hours' worth of your barbaric punishment only made me appreciate my own world, my own culture, where women aren't subjected to a man's whim. They made me see how stupid I was all these years, looking for a man I couldn't beat, thinking that's what I wanted. I suppose I should thank you for making me see that's not what I wanted after all. I'd much rather break the fingers of a guy who tries doing to me what you did. I won't make the mistake of losing that option the next time around."

"Does this mean you will try to break my fingers?"

He was still amused! Still grinning! "Not yours, beetlebrain," she fairly snarled, "I was talking about the next guy I'm dumb enough to think I want. Stars! I just love wasting my breath, I really do!"

"So I must believe, since most of what you have said is patently untrue."

"All right, I'll bite. Just what does your barbarian reasoning base that assumption on?"

"You still want me."

It took a moment for the sheer arrogance behind that statement to hit her. He *couldn't* know. He was guessing. Even she had been able to ignore what his closeness was doing to her, so how could he know?

"I don—"

"You want me now."

"No!" she cried.

She took a step back, only to come up against the couch behind her. She was shaking her head, reinforcing the lie. But she didn't know he could smell her arousal, so it was little wonder he reached for her despite her denial. And once she was enfolded in those massive arms, and those firm lips took fierce possession of hers, there was nothing left to say. She was still shaking her head mentally, but only for her own sorry sake. She did still want the big jerk. Her mind might deplore it, but her body was all too happy to make a fool of her.

Chapter Thirty

It was several hours, and a whole lot of pleasure later, before Tedra was thinking clearly again. But before she could work up any indignation over the way she had been defeated this time, the barbarian was leaning over her on the bed, and there was nothing in the way of amusement about him now. He was languorous. He was sated. Yet his expression was totally serious.

"Thus is it proven," he said.

She didn't have to ask what was proven. Injured feelings and wounded pride hadn't stood up very well next to his kisses; neither had determination, anger, or anything else. She had to face it. She was simply a sucker for a gorgeous body. It was contemptible, deplorable, but there it was, proven without a doubt. She was only surprised Challen wasn't gloating over it. But he wasn't. There was no triumph in his expression, only a kind of reluctance to say more, but he did have more to say.

"It is now time for me to speak my thoughts as you have done. I will endeavor to be more truthful in the doing."

This came with a halfhearted smile, an attempt at gentle teasing, minus the mood for it. She doubted he knew how to really gloat over something, everything was so black and white for him. He was positive in all his beliefs, and that didn't leave room for doubt or rubbing things into the ground. She wished she could be just half as decisive.

"All right, warrior, I'll listen," she said with a sigh. "But first I should point out that the only thing that has been proved is that my body likes sex-sharing. That doesn't mean I was untruthful in what I said, only that my body doesn't have its priorities straight just now."

And *right* now was a good example, she thought, wishing he'd move away from her if all he wanted to do was talk. He was in full contact with the right side of her body, lying there facing her, she on her back, he on his side and raised up with the support of one arm, so that he seemed to be looming over her. His chest was so wide he'd only have to drop one shoulder to completely cover her upper torso with it, and although his hands weren't touching her, the one he had resting on his hip had all the pertinent parts of her body within ready reach. The position was distracting, nerve-racking, and cleverly dominating, all of which were likely intentional on his part, forcing her to work twice as hard to concentrate on what he was saying. Resenting his subtle tactics helped her to do that.

"Generally a warrior finds amusement," he was saying now, "in the sayings and excuses his woman offers when he knows her to be displeased with him. Truly do I wish I could find such amusement in your words."

"You *were* amused," she reminded him.

"I was relieved, *kerima*, and happy that I had not done such damage as could not be corrected."

"There you go again, dismissing everything I've said. What's been done can't *be* corrected, Challen. You took a simple lesson in discipline and turned it into a demonstration of barbarian mercy—the lack thereof. You overdid it."

"I know."

Tedra frowned up at him, sure she had heard him right, but also sure she'd missed something. "Come again? What do you mean, you know?"

"Your punishment continued much longer than was called for."

"You're confessing you're a sadist, right?" she quipped sarcastically. "Somehow I'd already guessed."

That brought a frown to match her own. "I am confessing that I so abhorred the duty that was mine, aid was needed to see it done. I took that aid without knowing what the actual results would be."

"Wait a minute. Aid, as in agent? Aid, as in character-changer? You took a farden drug?"

"It can be called such, yes."

She could only stare at him, not sure whether she wanted to laugh or be furious. The big, brave barbarian needing help to discipline the little woman? That was funny. It was also kind of touching, if the reason was really what he had said—whoa, auto-reverse that. She wasn't actually going to let that make a difference, was she? Not farden likely.

"So you didn't like the duty that was yours? You could have fooled me, babe. I was still punished, as I recall, so your hating it or not doesn't cut ice from where I sit."

"Nor did it, as you say, 'cut ice' for me either. I regret there was a need for discipline. That does not mean I could ignore that need."

"Don't give me that. You're the head honcho around here, the *shodan*. You can do anything you farden well please."

"And it pleases me, *kerima*, to see to your safety.

If this includes assuring you obey rules made for your safety—''

''I think I'm done listening, warrior,'' Tedra cut in frostily. ''When you make up your mind which it was you felt, pleasure or abhorrence, let me know and we can discuss it again. On second thought, don't. This subject's about thirty feet underground already.''

''You *will* listen,'' he said, annoyance with her attitude making his voice stern and commanding. ''I have yet to beg your forgiveness. I do so now.''

''That's a little barbarian humor, right? You want forgiveness when you've just admitted you're not at all sorry? You'll pardon me if I don't feel like laughing.''

Frustrated, that hand she'd been worrying about came up to place a finger over her lips. ''Not another word from you until I have finished.''

He waited for her to nod in compliance. She didn't feel like nodding, but he wasn't going to go on until she did, and his patience was infinite compared with hers, which had already expired. So she nodded, but that didn't get her lips unsmashed. He wasn't taking any chances.

''A warrior will do what must be done regardless of his feelings on the matter. Do you require additional discipline, make no mistake, woman, you will receive it. But it will not be done again with the carelessness and lack of regard shown you the previous darkness. There can be no excuse for that lack of concern, for my being so unaware of what I was doing that the doing went far beyond what was required. The irresponsibility was mine in not facing what was required without aid, but more in not knowing the full consequence of that aid beforehand. The blame is mine. The regret is mine. It is doubtful even your forgiveness will relieve me of all the guilt I feel, yet do I earnestly beg it of you. Will you give it, *chemar?*"

He removed his finger from her lips and waited, but Tedra truly didn't know what to say. The nightmare hadn't actually been deliberate on his part? Could that really be true? Would he say it was if it wasn't?

He was admitting to being imperfect, to having made a mistake. That surprised her enough, but he was also admitting regret, and damned if he hadn't sounded sincere. Yet he hadn't said there wouldn't be any more punishments—quite the opposite. In one breath he promised more; in the next, he begged forgiveness for that already given. And that was another thing. He begged forgiveness. *Begged.* Was that supposed to be a sop for her lacerated pride? All it did was remind her that he wasn't any more likely to forget all the begging she'd done than she was. Of a sexual nature, how *could* he forget it?

And she'd made a stand. She didn't like having the foundation knocked out from under it. Was she to let him think he could get away with anything as long as he offered up a sweet apology afterward? And yet— and yet he'd called her *chemar.* Love. Of course, to a Sha-Ka'ani warrior, the word was no more than an endearment. But she'd still liked hearing it, had put her own meaning behind it—for a moment anyway— and . . . and was she really going to let him talk her out of her mad?

In self-defense, she demanded, "How could you be unaware of what you were doing, yet retain the memory of it? That sounds impossible to me, Challen, no matter how I look at it."

"It is impossible. I remember very little of what

was done. I have judged the seriousness of it solely by your reaction, and in knowing the new rising was almost upon us before I returned to a semblance of awareness and left you.''

''Are you actually saying you don't remember what you did to me?'' she asked incredulously.

''I do not . . . yet is there a certainty that what was intended to be done was done.''

That arrogant certainty that he had done his duty as he had intended was merely annoying at this point. ''Let me rephrase that, then. Are you saying you don't remember *my* part in the evening's agenda?''

''Nothing beyond your last attempt to feed me. I recall your anger before that, and everything else from the time I joined you until then, for the aid had yet to take full hold of me. But I cannot recall even beginning your punishment, or any part of it.''

And she was supposed to buy that just on his say-so? ''Then you don't recall my threatening to jump off the balcony, to take my life, to cut off that useless piece of flesh . . . between . . . your—?''

She didn't finish. The horror of his expression said he actually believed she'd said those things last night, proving he didn't recall the things she had really said and done. She might have been tempted to say those things, but she'd been too busy crying and begging him to make love to her to even think of threats and bluffs.

She felt now as if she'd had the breath knocked out of her. Her foundation of anger and resentment toppled from its last thread of support. Merely assuming he had done as he meant to do, and that she had reacted as he had promised she would, was not the same as having actual memories of it. He had no memory of her shame, he could only imagine it, and a man could imagine all he liked and never come close to the reality.

She could even console her pride by the certainty that she could probably have held out for the normal length of time devoted to such punishments—except that if Challen hadn't been under the influence of a character-changer, he wasn't likely to have stopped until she at least did a little crying and begging. And even a little crying and begging would have changed what she was feeling now, which was an urge to laugh because she *could* forgive him now, *could* still enjoy him until her service ended. So she could actually be grateful that he had taken the farden aid, even if it did prolong her misery at the time. The shame and humiliation that had been the worst of it were only hers to recall, and how long would such a memory last when it wasn't shared?

But was she going to let him off the hook so easily? His mistake was no worse than hers, but she'd been punished for hers. Who punished a warrior when he erred? She could, she thought with a measure of keen satisfaction, and by no more than using his guilt against him. But she didn't have to lie to do it. In fact, it bothered her that he still looked mighty upset thinking she'd been moved to violence, not only against him but herself, too, when she hadn't.

"Don't you recognize anger talking when you hear it, warrior? I never said those things to you last night. I didn't even think them."

"This was a means to add to my guilt?"

"No, just to see if you were telling the truth."

"And if you are still angry, I must conclude the truth has made little difference to you. If you cannot forgive me—"

"I didn't say that," she cut in, making sure she sounded grudging about it.

But he took her literally, that if she wasn't saying she couldn't forgive him, then she would, and his relief was instantaneous, flowing through him. She hadn't realized how tense he'd been until she felt him relax against her. She didn't appreciate the grin that came with the relief, however.

"You're asking for a lot without any compensation at all, warrior," she grumbled, hoping to knock a dent in his returned good humor.

She didn't. "This is so." He tried to look grave again in agreement, but just couldn't manage it. "Thus I have brought a gift for you, to make amends in a small way."

That arrested her curiosity, especially since he had shown up without anything but himself. And she had to wonder what a barbarian's idea of an amends-making gift could be. But whatever it was, it wasn't what she had in mind.

"Gifts might appease your Sha-Ka'ani women, but not me. Where I come from, it's tit for tat."

"This you will have to explain."

"It means equal retaliation, babe, but I might settle for simply changing places—say for the rest of the evening."

"You wish me to lie on my back while you face me at my side?"

She almost laughed at his confusion. "No, not physical places."

"Ah, a status change." He concluded next, and with some amusement, "You wish to be *shodan.*"

"No . . . I had in mind me being the victor, you the challenge loser, giving me all rights and privileges that that entails."

He became so still, she thought he'd stopped breathing. He didn't have to try looking grave now. Actually, he looked kind of shocked.

"You want me in a position where you may order and I must obey?"

"Now you got it, babe, but there can be no balking if you agree to make amends this way. No matter what I might have you do, or do to you, there can be no halt-calling. You'll have to take it like a true challenge loser, owing the same service I owe to you."

"And then you would forgive me?"

"Completely."

"And give me willing service?"

"Unconditionally."

He asked for no more clarification. Long minutes passed while outwardly he did no more than stare at her. But she knew instinctively that inwardly he was doing a lot more, that he was fighting with his desire to appease her and his total reluctance to do it in this way. She almost changed her mind, knowing it would be an alien experience for him to take orders from anyone, much less a woman. And to agree to obey those orders, not knowing what they would be—she wouldn't have to change her mind. He'd never agree to that.

"You may have your 'tit for tat,' *kerima.*"

Chapter Thirty-one

*T*edra's eyes flared, experiencing as much shock as Challen had earlier. Had she heard him right? He was actually going to give her complete power over him?

"You . . . agree?"

"Did you not wish me to?"

"Well . . . yes, but—"

She clamped her mouth shut before she stuck her foot in it. She would have wagered every exchange token she earned over the next ten years that he would have flatly refused, or, at the very least, tried to talk her into asking for something else instead. Had she missed something, some slyly inserted word in his questioning that would give him an out?

"Are you sure you understand the rules of this scenario, Challen? You'll have to do whatever I tell you to, no matter what. You can't refuse to do it, and you can't use your strength against me, for instance, to keep me from *giving* you orders. Is that understood?"

"It is."

"And you still agree?"

"Yes."

He didn't hesitate with his answers, but had a man ever sounded so miserable? And she'd have to be blind to mistake the look of utter defeat about him. This wasn't surprising, since being dominated would go against the grain for someone domination came naturally to. But suddenly she knew it was more than that. In fact, it came to her quite clearly that he expected her to humiliate him, to shame him, most likely to punish him in the same way he had her. And expecting it, he'd given her the power to do it anyway.

Stars above, was he *that* guilty? Or was he just so desirous of having things the way they once were that he was willing to do anything to make it so? He'd begged her to forgive him. Did he really think he had to do this before she would? Well, it wouldn't hurt him to think that for a while. It wouldn't hurt him to expect the worse for a while either. She had no intention of exacting that kind of revenge, but she also had no intention of passing up this delightful opportunity to have the upper hand with him.

"Now that I've got you at my mercy, warrior, I think the first order of business should be a little protection insurance for myself. Give me your word right now that there won't be any reprisals tomorrow or at any other time for what happens here tonight."

That shook him out of his dejection, as if what she was insinuating was an insult to him. "Such had not occurred to me," he said stiffly.

"Maybe not," she allowed. "But just in case it does—your word?"

"You have it."

She grinned at the way he gritted that out. "Poor baby," she purred, knowing how he hated being called that. "If that was so hard for you, you're going to have a hell of a time complying with the rest of my demands. But since you don't have any choice, why don't we go on to the next one? Lie down for me, baby, on your back."

For a moment she thought he would balk, but he must have recalled he'd given up that option. She helped him to recall it by pushing on his chest and coming up as she did, switching their positions after

WARRIOR'S WOMAN 299

all. Now she was looking down on him, and what she saw was a very stiff and wary barbarian, dreading her next outrageous order.

Not to disappoint him, she said, "Open your legs a little, sweetcakes."

Again he looked like he was going to balk. His jaw clenched. His fists clenched, too. Long moments passed before he raised one leg and slammed it down a few inches away from the other. Tedra almost laughed. He hated this, he *really* hated it, and any other man would have fire blazing out of his eyes by now, but not her barbarian. He gave a few paltry signs of his feelings, as powerful as they must be, but his eyes remained inscrutable. She'd have to see what she could do about changing that.

"You're not to touch me tonight, warrior, unless I tell you to. And so you won't forget yourself and disobey me, you will place your hands behind your head and keep them there."

This he did without hesitation, probably because he was already thinking about putting his hands on her—around her neck. But she was safe and knew it.

She took a moment to observe him as she had arranged him, in a position he usually assumed for himself, the difference being he wasn't at all relaxed in it now. Being forced to lie just so wasn't the same, making it her idea instead of his, thereby making it objectionable to him, so objectionable that he probably wasn't even aware that it *was* a preferred position of his. But she wasn't going to point that out to him. Giving him a little taste of the suspenseful, sexual teasing he liked putting her through wasn't going to hurt him at all. And having his big, gorgeous body in her power, even for a little while, was heady stuff.

Stars, how she loved just looking at him, at his

massively muscled chest and shoulders, twice the width of hers; at those mighty arms with more strength in them than she could possibly guess at, the biceps bunched and deeply ridged in their present position, the forearms thicker than her calves. Smaller ridges stepped down his abdomen like a steel casing, and she knew firsthand how little damage could be done to that area. Solid rock couldn't be much harder. And those long, powerful legs were in perfect proportion to the rest of him.

His size never failed to thrill her, and now was no exception. Having command of him was a particular turn-on, putting them on the equal footing she could expect from a normal sex-sharing relationship on her world. She was ready for him again, despite having experienced no less than six explosive orgasms just a short while ago. This didn't surprise her anymore. He had to no more than walk into the room she was in for it to happen, her body reacting with embarrassing swiftness to the mere sight of him. She didn't like his having that kind of effect on her, but there didn't seem to be anything she could do about it. It wouldn't even be so bad if she had the same effect on him, but it had been drummed home to her in a maddening way that she didn't.

Recalling that, and with the evidence before her, a dent was put into her smugness. Challen having earlier attained satisfaction three times himself, his flesh was soft and sated, not at all the way she wanted it just now. Also brought home to her was the annoying fact that he could keep it that way if he so chose.

The plain truth was she *couldn't* punish him as he had her, even if she had meant to. To command him to readiness was ludicrous. It couldn't be done and she knew it. Unlike a woman, a man had to feel desire to be accommodating, and under the circumstances, Challen wasn't likely to be feeling anything of the sort. But the barbarian also had one up on that. Unlike normal men, he had complete control over his flesh. Farden hell. This wasn't going to be a bit of fun if he exercised that control, and she had little doubt that he already was. And worse than that, she hadn't even tried to stem her own arousal, expecting it to be seen to at her own convenience. For Stars' sake, had she gone and maneuvered herself into self-punishment?

"Relax, warrior."

The sudden anger in her tone startled him, but only for a moment. "This I am powerless to do."

"All right, I'll buy that. Let's try this one, then. You are not to use your superhuman control tonight, not even a little. I want honest reactions from you, and I want *every* reaction, not just those you're willing to show me."

He started to growl in answer, and she blinked in surprise herself. Was it that easy to get around his control? She immediately put it to the test, leaning down and biting his nearest nipple, and not too gently either. His growl turned to a groan, proving how quickly his flesh could come to life when he was powerless to control it. She'd made him powerless by ordering him to react, and he'd agreed to obey any order she gave, no matter what it was. His eyes were no longer inscrutable either. He wasn't pleased that she'd snatched away his only defense. *She* was, immeasurably so. She'd got upset over nothing.

She laughed low, and bent to make amends to his nipple, swirling her tongue around it. She kept her eyes on him as she did, but he closed his, as if that would stop what she was making him feel. She grinned and changed her position, crawling up him until both arms were resting just below his neck and she could look down at him, her face only inches above his. She was lying half on him to do it. She could feel her nipples harden with the contact.

"Look at me, babe."

She smiled when he did. There was hot passion in his eyes now, but whether from anger or desire, she couldn't tell. Not that it mattered, when any reaction from him was gratifying.

"Now give me a joining kiss, and make it so hot it'd blow my circuits if I had any." He started to bring his hands into play to do this, so used to having things come to him, like lips and breasts and such. She shook her head at him. "No-no, you still can't touch Tedra."

"How then may I kiss you?"

"With your lips, sweetcakes, just your lips."

She grinned at the scowl he gave her, and waited patiently for him to catch on that his head was going to have to come up if he was going to obey her. It wouldn't be a very comfortable position for him, but she wouldn't prolong the kiss. She already had other ideas about what was next on the agenda.

When he finally raised his head, it was to capture her lips quite thoroughly, so thoroughly all thoughts of a short kiss vanished. In this he dominated as usual, his lips demanding she return their pressure, which she did, demanding she open her mouth for him, and she did that, too. Heat snaked to the pit of her stomach, but that was only one of the reactions her body was telling her about. There were others, just as powerful, and they all escalated when his tongue slipped in to caress and play with hers.

Stars, how she loved the taste of him. Intoxicated,

she unconsciously slipped her hands behind his neck to support it. Not that those thick neck muscles couldn't have done the job on their own, but she wasn't taking any chances on having that kiss end before she was ready. She also wasn't aware of his hands slipping around her wrists to hold them there, since he was in no hurry to have the kiss end either.

It went on for a very long time, because, as usual, she couldn't think when his mouth was joined to hers. But finally she broke contact out of sheer self-preservation. She was going up in flames. She wanted him every bit as much as she had last night. And all he'd done was kiss her!

But then she became aware of his hands clamped firmly around her wrists. Also that her hands were holding his head up. Immediately she let go. So did he. Mentioning the breach was out of the question, even if she could find the breath to do it, since she'd practically put her wrists in his hands, trying to give him support he didn't need.

She sat up, facing away from him. She felt like fanning herself, but she was sure his eyes were on her, so she didn't. She did, however, take as much time as was needed to get her breath back to normal before turning back to him, only to have it catch in her throat when she did. There was no doubt now which passion burned in his eyes. His body gave hard evidence of it—very hard evidence.

She almost said to hell with everything else she wanted to do to him. It wasn't fair that his need could fan her own. And the ease with which she had made him want her—was that another attempt at appeasement on his part, after his total lack of desire last night? She had demanded he relinquish control, but she knew very well he could retain as much of it as he liked and she wouldn't know the difference. He could have merely told her he felt nothing and she'd have to believe him, since that was the one thing she couldn't do anything about if it were true. And she wouldn't even have doubted it after he'd already come not once but three times. Yet he'd allowed her to arouse him, giving her the response he thought she wanted from him even when he suspected she meant to leave him high and dry. Or did he know her well enough by now to know she couldn't do that even if she wanted to, that her body would demand its own release, thereby giving him his? Maybe he did know it, or at least suspect it, and that was enough incentive to make her keep him in doubt a while more, and to add to that doubt.

She smiled at him quite wickedly. "I don't know about you, babe, but I'm really enjoying myself. In fact, the next time I challenge you, I'm going to have to try much harder to win, now that I've had a taste of the power that comes with it."

She ignored the frown that got her, and leaned over until her cheek rested against his chest. She brought her hand down next to her face and began to play with the nipple in front of her, watching it get as hard as hers already were. When he groaned she left off there and began to torment the rest of his skin, using both hands now, spreading her fingers wide to reach more of his chest, feeling the muscles jerk and ripple under her fingertips, hearing his heart pound beneath her ear.

"Stars, touching you is such pleasure, babe."

She hadn't meant to say that thought aloud or with such feeling, but she wasn't sorry that it slipped out when she heard his much louder groan. She turned her head to place a kiss in the center of his chest, then looked up at him as she licked the same spot. He wasn't having an easy time of it. His face was shades darker with a reddish hue. Beads of sweat had appeared on his brow, and his arms had bulged half again in size, indicating his hands were locked together behind his head and straining to stay that way. She had to give him credit. He didn't close his eyes this time, but gazed back at her with such intensity, she had to look away herself or end it right now.

She wasn't ready to do that, even if her body was all for the idea. No, she wanted him to have at least a little taste of what she'd gone through last night. But not to the point where he would hurt with need or beg for release. She couldn't do that to a man like him, didn't even want to. But she would make him worry a bit more.

"After last night," she said as she began kissing her way down his chest to his belly, "I've discovered just how long I can delay the inevitable, even that I won't perish if it doesn't come to pass."

"Woman—"

"No!" she cut in sharply, then bit his lower abdomen to emphasize her displeasure at his presumption. She knew he'd been warning her off the direction she'd taken, but she wasn't going to be warned off. "You aren't to speak, warrior. Didn't I mention that before? This is my time to play with you, and Tedra wants to play . . . with *all* of you."

She tried sucking on the spot where she'd left her mark, but the skin was so tightly drawn there she had to settle for licking to take the sting out of the bite. And licking on his lower abdomen really got him nervous. She heard a half groan, half growl, and smiled to herself. Was he doubting he could take much more? He'd have to.

"Don't worry, babe," she said as she licked her way closer to the most sensitive part of him. "I'm not going to do anything to you that you haven't done to me."

She knew very well that that would *not* reassure him. In fact, the sounds coming out of him now sounded suspiciously like choking. She would have laughed if her own breath wasn't suspended with what she was about to do. She delayed it, running one hand down his leg, moving to the inside of his thigh, coming up gently with her nails. She felt him tremble where she rested across his stomach. Her own body answered with a spread of gooseflesh.

She cupped him where he was soft. She leaned over what was so hard and throbbing. Her barbarian had become very still. She guessed he was holding his breath. After all, she'd given him enough clues about her intention.

It fascinated her, this part of him that could give her such pleasure. Big and long and full of power like the rest of him, it usually responded only to his will. Tonight it responded to hers, and it responded so well.

"I love this body of yours, Challen," she felt compelled to admit. "I love its strength, its gentleness. It amazes me that you've never hurt me with it, even unintentionally. I know you could . . . you know you could. But you're very careful when you're with a woman, aren't you? The only time you're not exactly gentle is when you make love, and then it's deliberate. It scares me sometimes, how—ungentle—you can be. But it excites the hell out of me, too. And I think you know that. I think that's why you do it . . ."

That was all the warning he got before she bent and raked her teeth slowly down the length of him, just as he had done to her breasts on several occasions. But it wasn't an exact imitation, since she couldn't have covered as much ground if she'd taken him into her mouth to scrape him as he'd done to her breasts. And she stopped short at biting the tip a bit harder as he had done to her nipples—not that she could have with the way he reared up, nearly unseating her.

"Easy, babe," she chuckled. "You ought to know by now that I'm not done yet."

And still giving him back some of his own, she followed the path her teeth had taken, but this time with her tongue. His moan was more a shout. His body went from stiff to trembling to stiff again. But his reactions, those same reactions she had demanded he give her, were having an unwanted side effect—on her. Driving him wild was driving her wild, and she had less endurance than he did. In fact, she couldn't stand another minute of it.

She rose to her knees, faced him, and reached the unpleasant realization that she didn't want to impale herself on his ready flesh, she wanted to *be* impaled. She could command him to make love to her, but she was afraid that wouldn't do it either. She wanted his arms around her because *he* wanted them around her, not because she ordered them there. The plain truth was, she had become addicted to his special brand of domination. The helplessness it engendered was what took her outside herself and joined her to him, making her feel totally possessed . . . making her feel—loved.

That was what she wanted, but she'd backed herself into a corner where she wasn't going to get it, unless . . .

"I—I think I've played enough, Challen. I thank

you for obliging me, but I now give you back your challenge win, my challenge loss. You can—"

She didn't get to finish, he came up onto his knees so fast and immediately dragged her against him, locking her in the vise of his arms.

"Have you forgiven me, woman?" he demanded.

"Yes," she gasped, gasping because he was already thrusting into her.

"Place your hands behind your head."

She didn't even hesitate.

"You will now drop back," he told her.

Would she? His thighs were spread wide to support her buttocks, hers clasping his hips. He was deep inside her, and the exquisite sensation of that almost made her miss the feel of his hands gripping her waist. If she dropped back, she wouldn't drop far.

She dropped, and instantly realized why he'd wanted her to. The vulnerable position thrust her breasts up at him, and he swiftly bent to capture one. He didn't bite, but he sucked so hard she thought he meant to swallow her. She cried out. He surged into her, and she exploded, dissolved, exploded, ah, Stars, the incredible beauty of it, the incredible ecstasy.

It left her so dazed, she wasn't even aware of being gently laid down on the bed a while later, or of giving him the good-night kiss that had become a ritual between them. And only he noted that she first curled her limbs against him before she gave herself up to sleep.

Chapter Thirty-two

A pleasure, to wake feeling so marvelously refreshed—or so Tedra thought until the happenings of yesterday crashed into her consciousness. She flushed with the vivid memories and felt a distinct uneasiness that would have had her squirming, except she didn't want to wake Challen, whose arm lay heavily across her upper chest.

Where in Stars' universe had she got the guts to do what she did to the mighty barbarian last night? Was she nuts? A glutton for punishment? And where in the farden hell had the idea come from that she *liked* being dominated by a man so insufferably arrogant and inflexible in his ways that he was on the close side of being an absolute tyrant? And she had thought to give him a little tit for tat, when he was an expert at it?

She had his word there would be no reprisals, but in point of fact, she'd forced him to give it. She wouldn't honor a swearing given under duress, so why should he?

She made a sound in her throat, and Challen's arm moved, his hand coming up to turn her face toward him. "Do you not feel well, *chemar?*"

"I . . . did I wake you?"

"No," he said simply, leaving her all kinds of things to wonder about—like had he been watching her all this time?

She stared into his dark-as-midnight eyes, hoping

they would tell her something, but they were back to being inscrutable. Not for the first time, she wished she had his warrior's calm, his ability to appear unruffled even if he was hopping-around mad on the inside.

"Have you stuck around for—for a particular reason?" she ventured.

"No."

There was no help for it with such enlightening answers. "Are you mad at me, Challen?"

It was funny from that angle, seeing one of his golden brows arch. "Should I be?"

She felt like telling him what a great communicator he was, but pushed down the urge, wondering where this suicidal tendency kept coming from. From one of her donators, no doubt, those two unknowns who had supplied the genes for her tube. One of them must have been unbalanced—probably the male.

"If you aren't mad, warrior, I'm not going to bring up a subject that might change that. But if you are mad, I'd like to discuss it."

"A sound strategy," he replied, laughing.

"Well?"

"I will leave it for you to decide, whether I should be mad or not."

"Do I look stupid?"

"You look, as always, very desirable."

She frowned for about two seconds, then broke into a brilliant smile. "You really aren't mad, are you? I'm glad, since I can't say I didn't enjoy the—ah—uniqueness of the experience. And if you didn't mind it all that much, maybe we can play switching places again sometime."

"Absolutely not."

"Oh?" She grinned as she watched him sit up on

his side of the bed with a degree of stiffness. "Need I remind you that there wouldn't be any play to it if I decided to challenge you again—and won?"

"You are welcome to try," he came back with supreme confidence.

"Well, thank you—I think. And as long as you're being so generous, how about throwing in a handicap? Considering your size and gender, I'd say that's only fair."

He turned toward her, interested if nothing else. "What is a handicap?"

"An edge. A head start, so to speak. Or to put it another way, it'd be the same as if you had one hand tied behind your back to make the odds more even."

He thought about that for a moment. "Very well, what then is the handicap you request?"

"The element of surprise would do nicely. That would let me attack without giving you prior warning. Would you agree to that?"

"You have already given me prior warning in the asking. How then do you perceive an element of surprise?"

"I didn't mean I was thinking of challenging you this minute, babe. And you can't be on guard every moment of every day, now can you?"

The warrior frowned, wanting to know, "You would attack while I slept?"

"No, I'd draw the line at that."

She had the feeling he was actually considering it when he didn't answer right off. She hadn't expected that. She'd really been no more than teasing him. But, of course, if he wanted to be foolish enough to even up the odds between them, she wasn't about to stop him from doing so. She was feeling quite pleased with her barbarian just now, but that could change so easily, and having him handicapped would definitely be a blessing if her feelings did change.

"I find your reasoning sound, *kerima*." He actually looked pleased that he could say that, which Tedra didn't appreciate one bit. "Thus you need not declare your intent to challenge beforehand, if such is your intent." He leaned down then to give her a short, sweet kiss before adding, "It is my hope you will find no reason to challenge me again."

"You keep that up and I certainly won't."

They grinned at each other before he sat up again. She hated to see him go, especially when she had confinement in this room stretching out before her for the whole day.

She caught his hand when he started to get up. "You've been full of surprises this morning. And as long as I'm being surprised, I believe there was mention last night of a gift you had for me?"

"Indeed," he said, and hauled her across the bed until she was sitting beside him. "Dress yourself and I will take you to it."

"Dress myself, as in putting clothes on?"

Both of those golden brows shot up. "You find the suggestion unreasonable?"

"Sure it's reasonable. I'm all for it. But I'm not setting myself up for further punishment just because you seem to be forgetting that already given."

If she was annoyed at his obtuseness, he was fast catching up. "Woman, explain," he demanded curtly.

"Explain what? I was only reminding you of the rest of my punishment. No clothes, remember? For the full duration of my confinement here?"

She expected him to look shamefaced at forgetting, not sigh and shake his head. "I begin to see you were not deliberately flaunting your body before me last darkness."

"Flaunting?" she gasped indignantly, but ended snorting, "As if I would."

"No, I see now that you would not be so brazen, though a warrior could wish it were otherwise."

"Challen . . ."

"I do but tease you, *kerima,* which I will not apologize for. But for the rest, in truth, I remember not the giving of additional punishment, nor was such called for. I have admitted what was done was overdone, thus would further punishment make it more so. You will ignore those additions and accept my apology that they were given."

"I'll ignore them, but accepting your apology should be mine to do."

"As giving my word last darkness was mine to give?" he reminded her.

"Quits!" she cried quickly. She could debate commands later, when those she had given him weren't so fresh in his mind. "Let's bury this one and plant a tree on it, okay? Apology accepted as ordered. Now what was that about taking me to my gift?"

He chuckled even as he dragged her onto his lap, holding her loosely, but only for the moment. "You have sat too long beside me, *kerima.* The sight of you in your brazen nakedness has decided the matter. The showing of your gift will have to wait until other matters are seen to."

"Such as?" As if she didn't know.

He didn't answer. He demonstrated instead.

Chapter Thirty-three

Tedra was still smiling over the barbarian's bemusement as he escorted her down the wide hallway. She'd decided to wear her kystrals with a white *chauri* today, after Challen informed her they would take food with the rest of the castlefolk this morning. He'd given her enough clues, without actually admitting it, that he wanted her to make friends in his household. The warrior was looking at the long term, while she was still working on the temporary—which included *not* getting involved with the Sha-Ka'ani. She'd already made one colossal mistake in that area. It'd be foolish to make any more. But when the master spoke, the challenge loser had to obey.

So putting on her kystrals was for morale. But having them change color in front of Challen was "getting even" for this latest high-handedness she was annoyed with. And she was quite satisfied by his reaction.

His expression, watching the clear red rocks transform into a brilliant aquamarine, was truly comical. He simply didn't know how it was done, but he was determined to find out. He'd taken the necklace off her without asking, without even sparing her a glance, and proceeded to examine each and every kystral. He spent a good long while doing it, too, but couldn't find a single mechanism or device for operating them.

"How did you do it?" he finally demanded of her.

"Where were your ears, babe? Didn't you hear me request the color to change?"

"The necklace is a computer, then, like your Martha, progalled to do as you say?"

"That's *programmed.*" She grinned, assuming she must have mentioned the word to him at some time or other. "And no, it's not a computer, or any other type of machine that you can turn off or on. Kystrals will change color for you because they know they're beautiful and they love to show off. They're alive, sweetcakes."

His expression said, "Sure they are." But he wasn't going to call her any more of a liar than that look did, nor was he going to ask again how the color changing worked. Yet he really wanted to know, was really fascinated, and holding that curiosity in check was amusing to watch. She might try again later to convince him that she'd told it the way it was, but right now she let it pass into the realm of tall-Kystrani-tales-not-to-be-discused.

They hadn't walked all that far from Challen's room when he stopped before a door that was only a mere eight feet in height, which was small as barbarian doors went around here. This he indicated she should open herself, which she did, finding she didn't have to shove against the wood to accomplish it. Inside, there was the familiar blue carpeting of the castle, the usual white walls with their gaali stone ledges. That was where familiar ended.

It was the smallest room she had yet seen in the castle, no more than a quarter the size of Challen's chamber. Of course, that still made it a pretty large room by Kystrani standards. The soft carpeting ran from wall to wall. There were several couches in muted lavender that actually had backs on them. And there were chairs, also with backs, and looking really comfortable with thick padding.

In a corner stood something that could have passed for a musical instrument, though Tedra had never seen the like. The recently absent *fembair,* Sharm, lay stretched out on the floor in front of one of the couches. She was surprised to see him, but more surprised by the miniature copy of him curled up asleep on the end of the couch above him. In another corner was an apparatus like what she had seen in the women's gathering room, which Jalla had called a cloth maker.

There were shelves on one wall filled with vases in varying sizes and shapes, a few appearing to be made of gold. On the floor beneath them was a long chest, left open, and stuffed with the materials to make flowers for those vases: colored stones, colored metals, colored jewels. There were more jewels in another smaller chest, with silver and gold mountings and chains, and the tools necessary to create jewelry. In still another chest were small bottles and vials, some filled, some empty, and it didn't take much to assume everything was there for the making of perfumes.

"It's a hobby room, right?" Tedra guessed as she finished with her examination of the last chest. "The only things lacking are a computer terminal and a collection of Ancients' tapes, since history is my hobby."

"Perhaps you can find another to amuse you, since the room is now yours."

"Mine?"

"A place where you may come to be alone or not, as you like. You may also make use of what is here for the occupying of your time. Did you not tell me once that a place of privacy was important to you?''

''Yes.'' She was surprised he remembered that, but more surprised by his thoughtfulness. ''It's a wonderful gift, Challen. And I'd been wondering what I was going to do to keep from going nuts without my work to keep me busy. But I have to tell you, I've never in my life made anything with my own hands. I wouldn't even know how.''

He smiled. ''You now have the opportunity to discover hidden talents. The women will show you how. But this was not my gift to you, *chemar*. This you need to keep you from mischief when I cannot be with you.''

''Is that so?'' she snorted, aware he was only half teasing. ''All right, I'll bite. What can be better than all this?''

''Sharm's son.''

''Sharm's wha—?'' It hit her before she got the question out, and her eyes flew to the couch where the little *fembair* still slept. ''Ooooh.'' The tears started, but she couldn't help it. ''A pet, you're giving me a pet, a live pet. Oh, Challen,'' she whispered softly.

She threw her arms around his neck, hid her face against his chest, and sobbed her eyes out. Challen's arms came around her, but hesitantly. He was totally confused.

''This was to make you happy, *chemar*.''

''I am!''

''Then why do you cry?''

''I don't know!'' she wailed.

Now he understood. ''Ah, a woman's response. I had not expected to find the soft female inside you and set her free this soon.''

"I'm having a breakdown, so give me a break." She pushed away from him to give him a reproachful look. "I'm a Sec 1. A Sec can't be soft or womanish. The job doesn't allow it." She wiped the tears off her cheeks, then glared at the wetness on her fingers. "I don't believe I did that."

He was trying to keep from laughing. "Women often cry when they are happy. I must confess I assumed it would be otherwise with you."

"That's right, rub it into the ground," she grouched. "One little slip . . ." She broke off with a gasp, having forgotten the reason for it in her upset with herself. "Oh, Challen, is he really mine, mine to keep?"

This time he did laugh. "Yes. He has just been weaned from his dam, but as you see, Sharm has developed a fondness for this cub of his. It will not be easy to separate them."

She missed the implied meaning in that statement, too eager just then to examine her wonderful gift. "What shall I call him?" she asked, bending over the end of the couch to pick him up. This brought another gasp. "Stars, is this supposed to be a recently born animal?" The baby filled her arms and then some, and weighed at least thirty pounds.

"Does his size matter?" Challen frowned, not having considered that. "He will get bigger, much bigger."

She glanced down at Sharm, who was watching her hold his son with a very attentive eye. "As big as that, huh? Well, I'll make room for him. I do live in the country, you know."

She would not have to make room for her pet if Challen had anything to do with it, for there was ample room right here, but he did not mention that. He watched her put her cheek to the baby *fembair*'s head, making weird little sounds of getting acquainted. The cat stood this abundance of affection only for a short while before squirming to get down.

Challen had to smile at Tedra's reluctance to let the cub go. But then she was looking at him, and he caught his breath at the tender warmth in her eyes. There *was* a soft and womanly female hiding behind her gruff exterior. He understood this about her, and someday he would understand everything about her. Droda, how the woman fascinated him with the complexities of her nature. And how he wanted her to be the mother of his children, more than anything he had ever wanted before.

She had closed the distance between them, was standing before him now, and there was moisture in her eyes again. "I thank you for my gift, Challen."

"It was my pleasure to give it, *chemar*," he said deeply.

Her hands came to his cheeks very gently. "You're such a sweet barbarian. No wonder I . . ."

"What?"

She dropped her hands, dropping her eyes, too, from his intense gaze. "Never mind."

He didn't press her. She was not yet ready to admit her true feelings for him. But soon . . .

He placed an arm around her to lead her from the room. "Come, we will take food now; then I must leave to inspect the gaali stone mines. Perhaps you would like to come along?"

She glanced at him in amazement. He knew her interest in the gaali stones. She'd never tried to hide it. Was this even more appeasement on his part?

"Sure, I'll tag along. And I promise not to take notes," she teased.

But she was still amazed at the extent of Challen's generosity. When a barbarian got a guilty conscience, he *really* got a guilty conscience.

Chapter Thirty-four

"Who owns these mines?"

"I do."

Tedra swung around in surprise. They'd come about a hundred feet into the mountainside on what was a gradually downsloping path. Challen had been filling her with information about how the gaali was cut, transported, sold, the dangers involved. She'd been amazed to learn all the miners were men who had for some reason or other lost their eyesight. Understandably, there weren't that many miners, for unlike a few cut stones, a large vein of gaali was bright enough to blind. And the Sha-Ka'ani obviously hadn't devised a way to get rid of that risk yet, or maybe they just didn't want to. Gaali stone mining was a good-paying job for the handicapped, after all.

"What do you mean, you do?" she asked. "Or do you control them as the *shodan?*"

Challen laughed at her assumption. "Being *shodan* does not have great rewards, other than the living in a fine house. The mines belong to my family, who have long owned the northern face of Mount Raik."

"But the town faces north, doesn't it? Does that mean your family owns Sha-Ka-Ra, too?"

"Most of it, yes."

"Well, hell, no wonder you're *shodan.* How come you never mentioned you're a powerful landlord?"

"It was not a thing needing mentioning. But you are wrong in this assumption, too, *kerima.* The *sho-*

dan is chosen for his strength alone, or he assumes the duty does he defeat the current *shodan.*''

"Which was it in your case?"

"A little of both. I had warriors who followed me who wanted the title to be mine. The last *shodan* became angry, hearing rumors of this, and so challenged me."

"That must have been a pleasant win for you."

"Not wholly. When I had fewer duties, I had more time for fun."

It was his look that made her blush, not his reference to sex-sharing. "Poor baby," she purred defensively. "I haven't noticed you depriving yourself of fun lately."

"Nor will I with such a beautiful challenge loser tempting me."

Tedra turned away from the possessiveness in his eyes that warmed her clear to her toes. "We're steering into an inconvenient subject here, babe. After all, you haven't slept in these mines."

"Does that still matter?"

It didn't, not in the least, but she wasn't going to admit that to him. As lusty as he was, it could get embarrassing if he thought she'd let him make 'love to her in just any old place. Their warrior escort was waiting outside the mines for them, and how long before they would decide to investigate if the inspection took too long?

She latched onto that thought. "What is it you have to inspect if you can't go into the actual area where they're cutting the stone?"

She heard him sigh before he answered. "These tunnels, the support beams. There are warriors who do this daily, but twice a year I like to see to the matter myself."

The ceiling and the left wall were boarded up to cover the residual remaining of the main vein of gaali that ran through this area; otherwise it would be too bright. The thick beams he mentioned ran down the center of the ceiling and were supported at six-foot intervals by narrow wooden posts.

"Is it really one of those inspection times now?" Tedra asked.

"No," he confessed, not at all embarrassed about it. "I merely decided to satisfy the curiosity previously revealed by my challenge loser."

She grinned, glancing back at him with soft eyes. "What am I going to do with you, warrior? You really have to stop being so nice, or I'm going to want to take you home with me." She didn't give him a chance to respond to that, was chagrined that she'd even said it. "Come on, you're here to inspect, aren't you? I'll help." She moved on to the next post. "This one looks as sturdy as the rest."

She kicked the base of it with her slippered foot, not hard, but the farden thing moved. Tedra jumped back as dust filtered down from the ceiling. Fanning the air in front of her, she said, "Sorry about that—"

Challen yanked her away before she could finish. "Return to the entrance, woman, *now!*"

He shoved her in that direction. She took about two steps before she turned back to see Challen moving toward the post she'd kicked.

"What about you—?"

The groaning overhead drowned her out. The mountain was pressing down on the ceiling planking. The dislodged post couldn't take the weight at its present angle and cracked. With the support entirely gone, the planking overhead started cracking, too, and

Tedra stared in horror as a large section of the ceiling dropped. The whole thing had taken only seconds.

Tedra was hit with the blast of disturbed dust and dirt and immediately started coughing. The cloud was so thick, she couldn't see anything in front of her, even though uncovered gaali lit the whole area, particles of it sparkling in the dust cloud like floating glitter.

"Challen, I can't see anything. Come out of there. Challen?" She went cold with the realization that he wasn't coughing like she was, that the only other sound she could hear was more dirt and small rocks falling—and that he'd been directly under that collapsing ceiling. "Challen!"

In a panic, she entered the bright cloud, stumbled on something, fell forward onto a high pile of debris—and heard the groan from under it, just barely. She immediately rolled to the side to get her weight off the pile. It was so high, so much weight!

Like a madwoman, she started frantically digging through dirt and rock, crying, choking, calling his name repeatedly, screaming it when she couldn't get even another groan. She couldn't see what she was doing. She knew when she reached wood only by the feel of it. And then something tried to pull her away and she turned to attack it.

"Easy, Tedra." Hard arms wrapped around her before she could do any serious damage. "We can work more quickly than you."

Tamiron, and the rest of the escort. Thank the Stars! Either they'd heard her screaming, or some of that dust cloud had reached the entrance to alert them.

"Go out now—"

"I'll wait."

Her tone was emphatic enough that he didn't try to

insist. He only moved her out of the worst of the area while the others went to work.

After agonized moments, there was another groan. Tedra almost collapsed with relief, her worst fear put to rest. Challen would be all right. He wasn't hurt badly. *Oh, Stars, please, please don't let him be hurt bad!*

And then he was being carried out. The six warriors it took to do it didn't stop so she could see him. Tamiron almost got his fingers broken when he didn't release her quickly enough so she could follow. But even when she caught up with the bearers, she couldn't see Challen clearly around the large warriors carrying him. She tried getting in between two of them, and was yanked out of the way again.

"Are you determined to delay them?" Tamiron demanded sharply, none too pleased with her at the moment with his fingers smarting.

"No, I just—"

"Do you stay out of the way, woman, the sooner he will be seen to."

She knew that on a rational level, but she wasn't working just then on a rational level. Tamiron must have concluded that for himself, for he kept hold of her arm to make certain she didn't get in the way again. So it was that Challen had already been laid on the ground outside the entrance by the time she left the tunnel.

She shook off Tamiron's hand to rush to Challen, but one of the warriors who had carried him turned and prevented her from getting close. One look at the man's face and Tedra screamed, very nearly fainting with the anguish that filled her chest almost to suffocation. But she didn't faint. She went wild, attacking the warrior, dropping him in seconds and the next who came to help him. It took four of them to finally throw her back, and they stood there like a steel wall, refusing to let her pass, refusing to let her see what was left of her barbarian.

"I just want to hold him!" she screamed at that solid wall, dropping to her knees, pounding on the ground with her fists until they were bloody. "Ah, Stars, noooo! Nooooo! Don't take him! Give him back, please, please, pleeeease!"

"Tedra, you must stop." Tamiron went onto his knees beside her, pulling her into his arms. "He hears your voice and is trying to wake. Do you want him to suffer even more before he dies?"

She pushed back, staring at him in shock. "He's not dead yet? You've kept me from him when he's not dead yet?"

She shoved Tamiron over in her haste to rise, but he caught her foot as she passed him and she went down. He had to roll on top of her to keep her down. It was almost next to impossible, since she had gotten closer to Challen and knew it.

"Enough, woman!" he had to shout to make her hear him. "You can do nothing for him, do you understand? Nothing! He will be dead before the sun sets. Let him die in peace, without your hysterics waking him to the pain."

"Oh, you fools!" she screamed up at him. "I can save him!"

"You have not seen him," he said more gently.

"Because you won't let me!"

"Woman—Tedra . . . he has bones crushed. He has a mortal wound in his chest. Nothing can be done, no matter that you wish it otherwise."

"It can—it can!" she cried. "I tell you I can save him, if my communicator can be found before he . . .

Tamiron, please, you have to believe me. Challen has a small box of mine. Where would he put it—hide it? Where would he hide something?''

"This you will not be told."

She couldn't believe her ears. "Don't . . . be . . . an . . . idiot!'' she screeched at him. "I have to have that box. It has to be found, *now!* Or do you want him to die?''

"Do not be foolish—''

"Damn you, why won't you believe me? With that box, I can save your friend. If you have any feeling for him at all, how can you take the chance that I'm not telling the truth?''

"How can the box save him?''

Thank the blessed Stars, he was finally listening to her. "It will—''

"No.''

Tedra gasped to hear that voice, sounding so weak, but still commanding. She craned her neck around to see him, but couldn't.

"Challen, you don't understand! You have to tell me where—''

"No,'' he repeated, but he wasn't speaking to her. "She is not . . . to have it, Tam. She will . . . leave and not . . . return.''

"I won't!'' Tedra cried, struggling again with Tamiron to let her up. "Challen, I won't leave you. I'll take you where you can be healed, and I'll return with you. I'll even give you back the communicator, I swear!''

"He heard you not,'' Tamiron told her. "He has lost wakefulness again.''

Tedra groaned, and then growled, "Get off me, warrior. I'll return to town myself and find my unit.

But I swear if he dies, when you could have given me a clue to shorten the search, I'm going to kill you.''

"You heard him, Tedra. You may not have the box. His orders are to be obeyed, despite—''

"He didn't know what he was saying! He doesn't know he's dying—or that I can save him. If he knew it, it wouldn't matter to him if I left or not, would it? But I'll tell you what does matter. I caused that tunnel to collapse. If he dies, then I killed him. Are you going to let a helpless woman live with that on her conscience?'' When he started to smile at that, she growled, "That was supposed to get through to your barbarian mentality, not make you laugh. And if you don't get off me right now, I'm going to hurt you.''

"What could this box of yours do for him?''

Was he finally thinking for himself? "It will Transfer us to—where I come from. It will Transfer Challen directly into a meditech unit that will make him whole again.'' She couldn't blame Tamiron for his skeptical look, but for once she couldn't afford to be doubted. "Damn it, I swear I'm telling you the truth. If you don't trust me, you can come along, too, but don't waste any more time, Tamiron. Return to the castle and find that box for me before it's too late.''

"This will not be necessary. I have it.''

"What?''

"Challen gave it to me with the warning that it was to be kept from you. Knowing your penchant for going where you do not belong, I felt the safest place for it was on myself. Serren,'' Tamiron called to the nearest warrior not nursing some hurt she'd given in her earlier loss of control. "Bring to me the sack on my *hataar.*''

He let Tedra up finally while they waited, but tried

stopping her again from going to Challen. "You still should not see him—"

"Don't get foolish again on me," she snapped. "It doesn't matter how he looks now, because he'll be whole again before the day ends, without even a tiny scar to show for it."

"That would be a miracle," he said with total disbelief.

"Yeah, well, we have a lot of things where I come from that will seem like miracles to you."

"Are you truly, then, from another world?"

"Not just another world, but a completely different Star System. With any luck you might see it one day. But you'll see the proof of it in just a few minutes, so be warned, warrior, not to be surprised by the strange things you see."

She ignored him then to turn to Challen, and didn't move another muscle. They'd tried to spare her this. Tamiron hadn't told her the full extent of Challen's injuries. There was damaged muscle, skin scraped raw, skin slashed open, even his face . . . blood everywhere. And sticking out of his chest was a two-foot-long spike of wood nearly four fingers around. Oh, Stars, the pain he must have felt when he woke, yet all he was concerned with was her leaving him.

The tears started again and ran unchecked. She reached him, but was afraid to touch him. She wanted to cradle his head in her lap. She wanted to hold him, but was filled with so much emotion she was afraid she might hurt him even more. How much time did he have—was he even still alive?

"Hurry up, damn it!" she threw over her shoulder.

Tamiron was already at her other side, and placed the communicator in her hand. Tedra almost kissed him, but all she spared time for was to swipe at her cheeks with the edge of her cloak before she hit the audio button.

"Martha, I've got an emergency here, so spare me all comments for now. Are you there?"

"What's the problem, doll?"

"My warrior is . . . he's dying. I want you to open the meditech and Transfer him directly into it as soon as I say. Have you got that?"

"Sure, two to Transfer."

"No. I've got my unit, so I'll Transfer up myself and one other. You just concentrate on Challen. Have you got a lock on him?"

"If he's the one with the low energy level," Martha answered. "But you'd better get everyone else away from him so there are no mistakes."

"In a moment. I have to remove something first." To Tamiron, "Tell your buddies not to go into shock when we disappear."

She said it only to distract him, since she had a feeling he'd try to stop her if he saw what she was going to do, had to do. But she was so loath to do it, Tamiron had returned before she got a grip on the long spike of cracked beam.

"No." He drew her hand back. "It stems the blood. Do you remove it, he will last no more than moments."

"In less time than that Challen will be out of danger. It has to come out or the meditech unit won't be able to close over him and do its job. And there's no one up there who can do it except Corth, but he could be clear on the other side of the ship."

"A ship . . . up there?"

"Don't ask me questions now, Tamiron. There's no time. And let go of my hand."

"No, I will do it. It is wedged between his ribs. You would not have the strength to remove it."

"Thank you," she said with some relief. "But the second you have it out, step away from him."

He nodded, though reluctantly. He was putting his trust in her, and well she knew it. She wasn't sure if she were in his place that she'd believe even half the things he'd been told. She knew she wouldn't.

In another moment Tamiron stepped back, Tedra with him. "Now, Martha!" She took Tamiron's hand in hers, telling him, "All you'll feel is a little tingling, warrior, so don't let it disturb you."

She didn't bother to ask if he was ready. She was too anxious to follow Challen, who'd already vanished. And then they did as well.

"Welcome home, kiddo."

Chapter Thirty-five

*T*edra had forgotten that the coordinates of her unit were set to Transfer her back to the same point from which she had left the ship. And the Control Room was a long way from Medical. She'd also forgotten how clear and strong Martha's voice could be when it wasn't coming through a link. The louder sound of it had startled Tamiron, but that was before he opened his eyes and saw where he was. "Shocked" didn't even come close to the way he looked now, but hopefully the warning she had given him would help him function.

"I'm only visiting," Tedra said in answer to Martha's greeting.

"I'd already figured that out. Who's your guest?"

"He's called Tamiron Ja-Na-Der, a friend of Challen's. Be a good girl and answer his questions while I—"

"There's no point in your rushing off to Medical, kiddo. The big guy's closed up tight, and let me tell you, it wasn't easy fitting him into the meditech. It will be quite a while before the unit's finished with him, though, as bad shape as he was in."

"I still need to know that we weren't too late."

"Then why don't you ask me? Or are you forgetting the extent of my powers?"

"Stop trying to impress the warrior," Tedra said in irritation, having indeed forgotten that Martha was

335

linked and in ultimate control of everything in the ship. "He's not even listening to us."

It was true. All Tamiron was doing was staring, in awe and fascinated horror, at everything in the room. Sirens could have gone off, and he wouldn't likely have noticed.

"Well?" Tedra said impatiently now. "What are you waiting for, permission? Link up."

"I'm already linked, kiddo. I've been monitoring the unit since your warrior arrived." For once Martha didn't make Tedra pry every little piece of information out of her. "He's already out of danger, since the worst wounds have already been sealed, and his body tolerated the transfusions, which he needed a great deal of. That was the only question mark, if he could accept alien blood. Right now the damage is being repaired from the inside out. His vitals are good, major organs sound, and that punctured lung is no problem."

"His lung was punctured?" Tedra asked in a small voice.

"You want a full inventory of injuries?"

"No—that won't be necessary. Just tell me, can everything be fixed?"

"In your line of work, you ought to know there isn't much a meditech can't do, except bring the dead back to life, and the scientists are working on that one. Your warrior will be good as new."

Tedra sank into the nearest adjustichair, the relief making her weak. "Thank you," she whispered.

"All I did was bring him aboard."

"I wasn't talking to you, Martha," Tedra snapped, her old impulses returning now that she could breathe easier. "Stars, I need a bath, a decent bath," she said, noticing for the first time how filthy she was, her *chauri* and cloak not only stained but hanging on her in shreds after that demonstration she gave of a woman gone nuts. "I'll be in my quarters, if there's any change in Challen's condition. And keep an eye on Tamiron here."

"That's all you have to say after that disappearing act you pulled down there?"

"Oh, that's a good one. You abandoned me, but now it's my fault that you lost track of me?"

"Still want to melt my circuits?"

"Maybe." She might not regret being abandoned to the barbarian's mercies anymore, but now she faced an even worse dilemma.

"You're worrying over nothing, doll," Martha said, able to guess her thoughts accurately as usual. "You won't lose him. He wouldn't allow it."

"You don't know what's been happening, Martha, so don't speculate when you don't know the facts."

"You don't think he'll return to Kystran with you?"

"He won't believe anything I've told him. He won't even let me prove it. The man is totally close-minded."

"He won't be after he wakes up here." Martha chuckled.

"No, that'd be taking advantage in the worst way and I won't do that to him. I don't want him to know he's even been here. Have the meditech keep him under until he's returned to the planet."

"And who's going to keep his friend there from relating every detail?"

"You mean if Tamiron doesn't think he's dreamed the whole thing?"

"Don't be cute."

"It won't matter. Challen wouldn't believe him anyway. I tell you, the man invented stubbornness."

"Well, it's your call. I assume your 'only visiting' means you're still determined to honor your challenge loss."

"Why would you think that was in question?" Tedra asked suspiciously.

"Oh, no reason. I was just wondering how you're liking it down there."

"Well, you can keep on wondering. I—"

"To whom do you speak, Tedra?"

She turned to see that Tamiron had returned to the world of hearing, and he was busy looking for a body to go along with the voice he'd heard. "You, me, and Challen are the only people on the ship, Tamiron. Martha has a voice, but no body to go along with it."

"I beg your pardon," Martha cut in dryly. "I'm rather fond of my body."

"Don't confuse the issue, Martha." And to Tamiron, "She's talking about her casing, this grand console here in the center of the room, and it's not even hers, but belongs to the ship's master computer, which she's hooked up to. You could say she's the heart and soul of the ship, since she operates everything on it. But she's just a computer, albeit an advanced model, a free-thinking machine, which is why she sounds so human. Does that make sense to you?"

"No, but—nothing here does."

Tedra grinned. "Don't worry about it. It's not necessary to know how things work, just what they can do. Martha will answer any questions you have about the ship or anything else. And I'll be back shortly."

"You go to see Challen?"

"No, he can't be seen while the meditech is working on him. But he's already out of danger and is being patched up in high-tech style. He's going to be just fine, Tamiron."

"If you are no longer concerned, then it must be so."

Tedra blushed. She'd really given herself away with her farden hysterics, hadn't she, and she a Sec trained to retain control under any circumstances. But at least Challen hadn't been awake to witness her falling to pieces.

"Yes, well, as I said, I won't be gone long. I'm just going to clean up a bit. So relax and enjoy your little adventure into space. As soon as Challen is completely healed, we will return to Sha-Ka'an."

Tedra headed for the exit, leaving Tamiron wide-eyed again as he watched the sliding doors open and close without being touched. But if she thought she'd have a few minutes of peace, she was mistaken. Martha's voice followed her down the hall through the ship's intercom system.

"You shouldn't have left him alone. He could well damage something if he doesn't listen to me and starts touching what he shouldn't."

"Don't be too surprised, Martha, but the man isn't stupid."

"He's a barbarian. Every known source states quite clearly that they're an aggressive breed who do exactly as they please. And you've left him in the Control Room. If we end up in deep space, don't blame me."

"Stop exaggerating. You're supposed to be entertaining him with your vast knowledge, not bothering me."

"I can do a thousand different things at the same time, and you know it. He's getting his questions answered, and *you'd* be surprised at what interests him."

"You, no doubt."

"Not at all," Martha replied with only a slight touch of pique. "His questions are devoted to the ship, how much it costs, how many men it takes to operate it, how long it would take them to *learn* to operate it."

"Well, he is a warrior. He's no doubt already contemplating conquering other worlds."

"You're being sarcastic, but I think you've hit it right on the nose, doll."

"He can contemplate that all he likes, but he doesn't know what's out there. When he does, he'll settle for much safer trade instead of aggression."

"Speaking of which, is there anything worth trading for down there?"

"They're a strange culture of old and new, nothing advanced to our level, but for primitives, they don't lack for comforts. And yes, they've got something to trade all right, an energy source that could well rival crysillium."

"Well, congratulations, kiddo. How's it feel to do good on your secondary-choice job?"

"I just want my old job back. And I didn't say I'd closed any deals, Martha. I told you, my barbarian won't discuss worlds outside his own, much less the possibility of trading with them."

"So is he the only one down there?"

"As far as I'm concerned."

When she reached her quarters, it was to find Corth sitting in an adjustichair and looking like he'd been there since she left. "Well, hello, Corth. What are you doing here?"

He came immediately to his feet. "Missing you, Tedra De Arr. You have been gone a long time."

"I've been gone less than a week, not long at all."

A week? Stars, was that all the time it had taken her to fall head over heels?

"Will you stay?"

"No, I've—ah—still got business to take care of on the planet. And actually, I'd like a little privacy now."

He took the hint almost like the old model, before Martha had tampered with him, though he did display a good deal of disappointment on leaving. She was going to have to have another talk with Martha about changing him back to her original specifications, but she had too many other things to think about right now.

After giving orders to her robocleaner, she stepped into the solaray bath—what heaven! But Martha was back, her voice still reaching her.

"You're having those rags you were wearing cleaned? What's wrong with changing into something of your own as long as you're here, complete with utility belt and homing signal?"

"Because Challen wouldn't like it, and for now, I'm just a challenge loser, forced to accede to his wishes."

"So I'm to lose track of you again?"

"You should have considered that before you refused to send down Corth so I wouldn't have had to challenge the barbarian in the first place."

"And you could have tried a little harder to win that challenge."

"Go *away*, Martha."

Chapter Thirty-six

They were Transferred back to the mine entrance, though Tedra had asked Martha to put Challen down in a different spot, away from the one soaked with his blood. With any luck, Challen wouldn't even know he'd left his planet—except all his warriors were still there, awaiting his return, and looking as amazed as barbarians could look upon seeing something materialize out of the air.

"Could you talk to them, Tamiron, and ask them not to mention to anyone what they've seen here today?"

She wasn't sure Tamiron had heard her. He was staring with some amazement himself at Challen's unmarked chest, this being the first he'd seen him since Transferring to the ship. There was no trace of a scar, nothing to show Challen had received a wound that would have killed him if not for the wonders of another world, one so far advanced, it still boggled Tamiron's mind.

"What of his bones?"

"What?" Tedra frowned. "What bones?"

"Those that were crushed."

"Everything has been fixed, Tamiron. I told you, he's as good as new, and will be waking up any minute to prove it. Now didn't you hear what I said about his warriors?"

"Certainly, but the matter should be decided by the *shodan*," he replied.

"Actually, the one I didn't want told *was* Challen. Does he really have to know he was injured? Couldn't he just think he'd been knocked out for a little while?"

"Why?"

"I don't want him thinking I saved his life."

"But you did."

"I didn't. I just had the means available that could."

"We do not keep secrets from the *shodan,* woman."

She was learning fast what was a say-no-more-on-the-subject expression and what was not. "Well, how about letting me tell him, then? I'd like one more chance of getting him to believe me on my own, without you or your buddies backing me up."

"Does he ask—"

"For Stars' sake, just give me the rest of the day," she said in exasperation. "You guys could leave, go on back to town. You won't have to lie to him if you're not here to be questioned, and that's not keeping secrets."

Instead of answering, he looked down at Challen again, and she knew it would drive him nuts to have to wait to confide to his friend all the wonders he'd seen. She also knew he still wanted assurance Challen was all right, assurance that wouldn't come until he could speak to him. And none of that was going to get her another opportunity to convince Challen that she'd never told a tall tale in her life. And it was so important that he take her word for it.

"He's breathing, isn't he?" she said now in irritation. "You trusted me earlier, Tamiron, so why can't you trust me now? I'll have him back to town before moonrise. A couple of hours. Is that too much to ask when I've saved his life?"

The warrior's brows shot up when he heard she was now taking credit for it, but Tedra wasn't adverse to using any means to get what she wanted if she thought it might work. And it apparently worked this time.

"Very well, but no longer than the darkness," Tamiron told her.

"No problem," Tedra grinned, well aware his gratitude had taken a part in that decision. "You can even send out a search party if we're a little late arriving back—due to unforeseen circumstances, of course."

"Such would be pointless, do you make use of your going-to-the-ship box. This I will have back now."

She handed it over with a shrug, but asked curiously, "Aren't you worried about his reaction when he's told you let me have it? You did disobey a direct order, after all, even if it was for his own good."

"Were you not here and still his to command, then I would worry. But all was done as you claimed."

That "his to command" got her goat, enough to admit, "I hate to burst that bubble of satisfaction you're wrapped up in, warrior, but until I leave this area, Martha's still got a lock on me and can Transfer me out of here just as she did to Challen. So you're just going to have to take my word for it that I have no intention of disappearing until I've paid my full challenge loss service."

"The *shodan* has called you a warrior woman. He would not do so did you lack a warrior's honor, thus is your word on the matter sufficient."

Tedra was chagrined to find herself glowing with pride over that left-handed compliment. "When you decide to trust, you go all out, don't you? Thanks, Tamiron. But you'd better get going, or there won't be a further need for trusting."

He nodded and left with the others. She watched them until they'd passed around the jutting arm of the mountain that concealed the mine from Sha-Ka-Ra, only a short distance away. Then she turned to glance down at the big barbarian, looking so peaceful *and* harmless under the influence of the meditech's sleep-inducer.

A shiver ran through her, thinking how close she had come to losing him. And now that she had him to herself, she was impatient for him to wake, also needing the reassurance that speaking to him would bring. She paced a few minutes, but finally sat down and lifted his head into her lap.

He sat up instantly, as if she had disturbed him from no more than a light sleep. With a swift glance around, he asked, "What do we out here?"

"Enjoying the late afternoon sunshine? You don't buy that? Well, I'd tell you that you were just napping and I was just sitting here watching you nap, but I suppose you remember the tunnel collapsing on you?"

"Indeed."

The meditech had cleaned him up, even his *bracs*. Since she was clean, too, maybe he wouldn't recall that they ought to be dirty. And it wasn't necessary to lie to him to temporarily avoid the truth.

"What can I say, babe? Your head's not as hard as I thought it was."

This got her a quick, reproachful look, but the man wasn't dense, and he had a memory to rival that of a Mock II computer. "I recall pain, *kerima,* but not in my head. Why is it I feel none now?"

"Divine intervention? No? All right, I confess you got a little banged up, and since I can't stand to see anything suffering, even you, I convinced your good buddy Tamiron to let me speak to Martha. You remember Martha, my God-like computer who can perform all kinds of miraculous feats? Well, she took you up to my ship and performed some, then sent you back down here, minus your bruises. Will you buy that one?''

Instead of the usual condescending doubt she always got, Challen immediately scooped her up and carried her to his waiting *hataar*. She didn't know what he was up to, and he didn't tell her, but in moments they were riding back to town, and his haste was unbelievable. All she could do was hold on as best she could, though she managed to get out an "Are you nuts?" before the barbarian's hand covered her mouth. And it stayed there until they were threading their way through the traffic on Sha-Ka-Ra's main street.

By then, Tedra had forgotten all about convincing Challen she was from another world. She wasn't sure she wanted to ever speak to the crazy barbarian again, about anything. And he still didn't give her any clue about what had sent them racing back to town. He went straight to the castle, but even then he didn't release her, carrying her inside and all the way to his bedchamber. Only there did he finally let go.

Tedra began to pace immediately. Her arms crossed, her movements stiff, she marched back and forth in front of the warrior, who only now seemed to have relaxed.

"There was another *sa'abo* sneaking up on us, right?" she offered first, to be fair. "It even followed us back to town. No? Then maybe some fire sirens were going off that only you could hear? Or have you simply lost your mind?"

"It was necessary for the peace of my mind to

enter a crowded place so the 'fix' on you would be lost," he replied quite calmly, as if he weren't shocking the hell out of her. And in the next breath, "I did not need to visit your sky-flyer to know it was there."

"What?!"

"I have spoken with your Martha. She gets her points across with blasts of air. I did not need to visit—"

"I heard you the first time!" Tedra cut in, shouting. *"When* did you speak to my Martha?"

"After your punishment. I needed advice from someone who knew you better than I."

"And did you get it? Yes, of course you did. No wonder I got so many gifts."

"She mentioned no gifts, *kerima.* She suggested I allow you to release your anger, no matter how disrespectful that releasing might be. It was good advice, for which I am grateful, but I trust your Martha no further than that; thus have I removed you from her 'fix' on you."

Tedra's eyes narrowed on him. "Why do you suppose she had a fix on me?"

"Did you not say you had spoken to her at the mine?" he replied.

"And you believed me? I suppose now you'll tell me that you accept everything else I've told you as Stars' truth, simply because you've spoken to Martha. *She* could convince you, but I couldn't?"

"For what reason are you angry, woman?"

"You wouldn't believe *me!* I show you what a phazor can do, I show you what *I* can do, I even show you live kystrals, all proof enough as far as I'm concerned, but no, I'm still spinning tall tales. And yet all Martha does is show you the blast of a puny repulsion beam, and whammo, you're convinced. Well, thanks a farden lot, but I no longer care what you believe.''

He came over to her to draw her into his arms, despite the struggle she put up to prevent him. Thus drawn, she began to think of other things, hating it, but it happened every time he held her like that. It wasn't fair that he could chip away at her mad so easily, but she had to face it. *Nothing* was fair for women on his world.

"I have no liking for what I have admitted," he told her in his usual calm tone that never supported or disproved what he was saying. "I so dislike it that I would not have admitted it did such not happen that it could no longer be denied. Now I must make known to the *shodani* of Kan-is-Tra your existence, your reasons for coming, what you offer, and what you want in return. Thus are you no longer of interest solely to me, but to all of Kan-is-Tra. This is what I object to, woman, what I have attempted to avoid in the denying of your origins. Not even to your Martha would I admit that I suspected from our first meeting that you spoke true."

"You—ah—haven't said why you object," Tedra pointed out, grinning, appeased, and light-headed with what she hoped was the reason.

"I had assumed it would interfere with your challenge loss service. I have just decided it will not."

She leaned back to look at him, her expression disgruntled. "Is that so? And is that your only reason?"

"You wish to hear that I wanted you to be of my world, and therefore claimable?"

"I think I've already figured that one out," she bit out. "What else?"

"You wish to hear that I have discovered in myself a possessiveness unusual in warriors?"

She hoped he was only teasing her, but there was only one way to find out. "That's better. And since you've admitted that much, I'll do some admitting of my own. I've fallen in love with you, Challen."

"I know."

"You *know?*"

"It was inevitable, but it pleases me that it has happened in so short a time."

She stared at him incredulously. That was it? He was pleased? Actually, he did look pleased, but that wasn't what she'd wanted to hear. And she realized she'd never hear the words she craved, that she'd forgotten a major discovery she'd made shortly after arriving here, that barbarians weren't capable of strong emotion, at least not of the softer variety. A fine time to remember that, after she'd let that soft emotion get a grip on her.

"You can forget that silly confession of mine, warrior. I lied."

He had the gall to show he was amused by that. "Such is the reaction of a woman of high expectations. Best you know now, *kerima,*" he added gently. "Women experience love, warriors do not. Sha-Ka'ani women give their love freely, accepting that no more than protection and caring can be returned. You will also come to accept this."

"Wanna bet?" She shoved out of his arms and turned her back on him. "Look, it doesn't matter one way or the other," she managed to get out over the lump in her throat. "What we got going is only temporary anyway, so it's no big deal. Now, can we forget the nonsense and get on with what's important? I'd like to have all negotiations settled before my service is over so I won't be further delayed here."

His arms came around her again from behind,

squeezing so hard she was fast approaching pass-out. "Such is not nonsense that causes you hurt, *kerima*. I will not allow you to feel this hurt."

"Won't allow?" She choked on a laugh. "You're killing me!"

The pressure eased, but only because he turned her around to face him again. "You will cease these thoughts of the temporary, woman. When your service is over, you will not be quit of me. I will return with you to your world to do what must be done there that has importance to you, but then you will return with me here, and here you will stay."

"And if I refuse?"

"Then you will not have the help your Martha claims you need."

"You're making it a farden condition?" she asked with rising temper.

"Yes."

She stared at him, fighting the urge to scream with an equal urge to laugh. Had she gone nuts in the past few minutes?

"Do you even know what you're bargaining to get yourself involved in?"

"It matters not. Do *you* understand that I will never let you go? You gave me your love—"

"I took it back—" she tried inserting, but uselessly.

"You gave it; thus is it mine to keep, not yours to take back. In return, I give to you my life, yours to keep until the day I die."

She had a feeling those were formal words that somehow were committing. She also had a feeling, which thrilled her to her toes, that the big jerk loved her and didn't even know it. If these barbarians needed anything, it was reeducation in their beliefs, especially the belief that warriors didn't have feelings. Her warrior had put enough feeling into what he was saying to melt her bones. And why had she given up, anyway, she who never gave up? If he *didn't* love her now, she'd just have to work on it until he did.

Chapter Thirty-seven

A craving for something tart drove Tedra to the kitchens late one afternoon several days later. Since she had apprised Challen of the situation on her world and what was needful, she hadn't seen much of him. His days were filled with clearing away all business that couldn't await his return, for his planned trip to meet with the other *shodani* was scheduled for tomorrow. Messengers had been sent out to gather them all together, but it would still take days to reach the meeting place, and days longer until all the *shodani* showed up, if they did. Transferring could have cut that time in half, but Challen had refused to consider it.

Tedra hadn't pressed the matter because she assumed she would be going along, and was frankly looking forward to seeing some more of the planet. But she had been disabused of that notion this morning. She wasn't needed on the trip, not as long as the warrior had Martha to do any convincing and demonstrating, and Martha was apparently willing to cooperate fully.

To say Tedra wasn't pleased with Challen's decision was putting it mildly. She was, in fact, furious with him. The meeting would determine whether or not she would be getting the mercenaries she needed, whether or not the *shodani* would even agree to trade with sky-flyers. She had every right to be there. But not as far as her barbarian was concerned. No, he didn't want her coming under such close scrutiny of other warriors as powerful as he. His possessiveness was acting up and he didn't even know it, but this was no time for it when the matter was so important to her.

She still meant to have another go at changing his mind tonight, if he managed to return to his chambers before the late hour guaranteed she'd be sleeping. Right now she tried putting the matter from her mind. The strange craving she was having helped to do that.

The kitchen was busy at this time of day in preparation for the evening meal. Tedra wouldn't have admitted it, but she found the place fascinating, all the human labor involved, the Darasha camaraderie, women enjoying what they were doing, though what they were doing were jobs considered obsolete on Kystran. But she wouldn't spoil their fun or feelings of usefulness by telling them that. Besides, it hadn't become common knowledge yet who she really was; only Challen's warriors were privy to that information. The women still thought her to be a captive, the story of her being a challenge loser unanimously doubted by them all.

Tedra had made one sort-of friend besides Jalla, that day Challen had insisted they eat with the household in the gathering rooms at the front of the castle. Those rooms weren't exactly segregated, as she had first supposed, but they could be if a meal was to turn into a warriors-only discussion, as sometimes was the case. That day, the lady sitting to Tedra's right had struck up a conversation with her about, of all things, gardening. Nothing could have endeared the woman to Tedra more, the subject being of keen interest to someone starved for all things of a horticultural nature.

Her name was Danni Hal-Dar, a widow of nearly two years, and from her Tedra had learned things that Jalla wouldn't have thought to mention, such as there being not a single job in all of Kan-is-Tra that would pay a woman a wage so that she could support herself. *This* was the reason all orphans and widows had to seek protection of a warrior, but then this was also the reason a warrior could not refuse a woman his protection, and the household of the *shodan* was, of course, the most prestigious household to be protected in.

Tedra could have laughed at the idiocy behind that ancient law, for the *shodan* was the one with the headaches of having so many idle women under his roof. And to think of the newly colonized worlds out there starving for women, and how most of these women might delight in an opportunity to go where they might be useful again, or be trained for jobs that were scarce and paid high wages. Of course, as she had already determined, something like that would take some heavy reeducation in the way these people looked at things, but it wouldn't hurt to mention such an option to Challen—when she was no longer annoyed with him.

Danni wasn't in the kitchen, but then this was the domain of servants, not of ladies of the household. Yet Marel, one of the younger ladies, was there, and it didn't take much to realize she was being punished, her task that of peeling a vegetable called *falaa,* a strange one that was horribly odorous when raw, but cooked up into a sweet-smelling, delicious side dish.

If Marel's expression was any indication, she was hating the punishment, as Master Lowden no doubt expected her to. Tedra didn't bother to ask what she had done to get punished. Marel was of that large group of ladies who looked on Tedra as beneath their contempt, if not with outright hostility. This had never bothered Tedra one way or another, but Danni had thought to explain, confiding that many of them had hoped to win the *shodan* for themselves, that some of them had in fact shared his bed in that effort.

Now *that* bothered Tedra, though she hadn't let on. Just let any of them try catching his notice now and they'd get a swift trouncing by a Sec in full fury. Finding the prettier ones mates was going to be Challen's first order of business when they returned from Kystran—Stars, what was she thinking? Come back to this backward madhouse of a world? No, Sha-Ka-Ra could find itself a new *shodan*. She was going to talk Challen into staying in her part of the universe—when she was no longer annoyed with him.

"Are you looking for one of these?"

Tedra deftly caught the small purple fruit Jalla tossed at her, grinning. "How did you know?" Her mouth watered just looking at the sweetly tart thing.

"It is my job to anticipate a mistress's wants and needs," Jalla replied.

"Of course, my going nuts over these *vechem* yesterday had nothing to do with accurate guessing."

"Certainly not," Jalla said primly, then spoiled it by giggling.

Tedra joined her at the cabinet where she was arranging tall, jeweled goblets on a tray around a bottle of chilled *yavarna* wine. "More guests to impress?" she guessed.

"Merchants from Sha-lah," Jalla admitted. "The rumor is, they have just been denied a very large order of gaali stones, for which they are most displeased. They will have to go many *reyzi* out of their way now to find another supplier, and no one can guess why the *shodan* refused to deal with them. The chest they brought with them was filled with *tobraz* to make the purchase, and you know how valuable are those light blue gems."

Tedra didn't know, but she could guess why Challen had refused the offer and she couldn't help but smile delightedly. They hadn't actually got down to talking trade yet, but he knew what she was most interested in, and obviously was making sure he would have a sufficient supply available.

"You find that amusing?" Jalla asked, perplexed.

Marel had overheard their conversation and interjected snidely, "That one finds everything amusing since the *dhaya* juice has been put back on its shelf. But it is not likely to stay there overlong."

"If that was supposed to be a dig, Marel, I'm afraid it missed its mark, since I haven't the faintest notion of what you were talking about. Nor do I care. But perhaps the Lowden uncle should be made aware that you haven't got enough to do to keep you busy and minding your own business."

The younger woman turned a bright shade of mortification when a good many Darasha laughed at Tedra's remark. Tedra hadn't meant to shame the girl in front of others, though, so she said no more and left the kitchen. Jalla caught up with her in the hall, her tray of jingling glasses announcing her, if her giggles didn't.

"That was no more than she deserved, mistress. Lady Marel has ever been a sour mouth to anyone she is jealous of, and she is jealous of most everyone."

"Another emotion only women feel the sting of?"

"What?"

"Never mind. But what *was* that nonsense she was muttering about? What's *dhaya* juice being shelved have to do with my good humor? And I thought *dhaya* was a potent wine only warriors are allowed to drink.''

''That is so, but . . . how is it you do not know the purpose of *dhaya,* as juice or wine?''

''Is this another one of those things every woman should know? Well, consider me dense and enlighten me so I can join the club of knowing-it-all.''

Jalla shook her head with a smile. ''What you say sometimes makes no sense to me, mistress, and yet strangely, it does. But there is no mystery to *dhaya* juice, and likely you know it by another name. It is what a warrior takes when he goes to raid or war so he—''

''That again,'' Tedra interrupted. ''It seems mighty unusual that, with as much as I've heard about raiding around here, I haven't seen any proof of it.''

''Why, the *shodan* raided Kar-A-Jel just this last full moonrise,'' Jalla said, surprised Tedra didn't know that either. ''But of course, the *shodan* of Kar-A-Jel, Falder La-Mar-Tel, he is no more than a pest. He snips at our feet, raiding the farms in our valleys. He has not the courage to face our *shodan* in challenge.''

''Just a regular pain in the ass, huh?''

Jalla giggled again. ''This is true. So our warriors usually go twice a year to retrieve the women and *hataari* that are stolen.''

''But what if a warrior's life-mate is taken? Must he wait months to get her back if Challen retaliates only twice a year?''

''He can go alone to retrieve her, or buy her back. Or he can wait, since there are others to take her place, there being no lack of available women in Sha-Ka-Ra.''

"I would have to ask," Tedra said in disgust. "Now what was that about the *dhaya* juice?"

"It is taken for raiding so a warrior will not lose himself in the lust of the moment and do harm to a woman. It is what a warrior takes when he goes off for many rises to hunt, so he will not be distracted by thoughts of a woman. It is what a warrior will take if he journeys far from his own woman and wishes to be tempted by no other. And it is what a warrior will take if he must punish his own woman."

"Just what is it supposed to do for these mighty warriors, particularly in the matter of punishment?" Tedra asked in a barely controlled tone, afraid she knew, but to be fair, she had to be sure.

"Think you a warrior could bring you to your need without it?" Jalla grinned, missing the signs of the explosion about to take place. "Warriors are too lusty for that. The juice removes all desire, no matter the stimulation or provocation. It gives a warrior the control he would lack did he try to punish a woman in that way without it."

Control? Whammo! That farden liar! That farden braggart! A warrior's control? A dose of impotency was more like it!

Tedra let loose with a screech of fury and a string of invectives a mile long. By the time she was done, she'd cursed the barbarian in seventy-nine languages, but felt not one bit better for it. And then she recalled the day she had met him, and how it had driven her nuts wondering when he would breach her, all the way up until she slept, unbreached. And the remark by that warrior about her capture being a waste while hunting. It had been a joke among them all, one she finally understood, and she cursed the barbarian some more.

When she finally noticed Jalla staring at her in wide-eyed alarm, she calmed down, but only long enough to ask, "Does *dhaya* juice work on women the same way?"

"I do not know, mistress. For what reason would a woman need to take it?"

"What reason, indeed." Tedra smiled.

Chapter Thirty-eight

"*W*hat have you done to the *shodan* now, woman?"

Tedra turned around on the balcony, where she had been waiting unconsciously for a glimpse of Challen as he departed on his journey that morning. Tamiron stood in one of the arched doorways, doing nothing to conceal a strong vexation, and by the sound of it, his irritation was with her.

"Aren't you supposed to knock or something before entering this chamber?"

"That was done, repeatedly."

"Oh, well, I've got a lot on my mind, so I probably didn't hear—or you just weren't knocking loud enough. What was it you wanted to know?"

He did not like her nonchalance. In fact, his teeth likely lost their sharp edges, they were ground together so hard.

"I was just informed that my friend passed the darkness with a bottle of *yavarna*," he gritted out. "If that was not strange enough, he has also called off his trip. He sits and stares at nothing, and will answer only when prodded. He—"

"I get the picture, warrior. It's called depression."

"I care not if it has a name. I wish to know its cause."

"And naturally you think I'm the cause?"

He didn't mince words, but came out with a resounding "Yes," his expression daring her to deny it.

Tedra shrugged to show an indifference she wasn't actually feeling. Her memories of last night were mostly vague around the edges, but those she did have weren't pleasant. What she had wanted to happen had happened. But Challen's expression, when he finally realized she had absolutely no desire for him, almost killed her. If that was supposed to be getting even, it had backfired in the worst way. And yet she was justified in what she'd done. So feeling bad about it was annoying, to say the least. It put her on the defensive as nothing else could.

"You want to know what I did?" She glared at the warrior. "Well, all I did was take some of your *dhaya* juice. Of course, I didn't bother to tell Challen that, any more than he ever saw fit to inform me of the help he was getting to resist me. He, in fact, let me think the control it gave him was all his own. He lied to me!"

"Lied, when every woman knows the use of *dhaya?* He but teased you, assuming you would know he teased. It is a common joke that a warrior will claim *dhaya* control as his own. It tells a woman that he has not the power to resist her without it."

"And she's supposed to feel complimented, I suppose? Give me a break, warrior. There is no compliment that can make that kind of punishment easier to take."

"For you, but you are not Kan-is-Tran."

"No, I'm Kystrani, and I'd never heard of your farden *dhaya* juice. And I won't apologize for what I did. If you men can make use of that stuff, you deserve to find out what it's like being on the receiving end of it at least once."

"So you thought to punish me?"

Tedra turned toward the new voice, to find that

Challen had quietly come to stand in another archway. Her chin went up, her defenses rising even more, especially since he wasn't trying to hide his displeasure with her any more than Tamiron had.

"Now how do you figure that?" she demanded, coming to stand in front of him. "All I did was give you a taste of indifference, the same kind you gave me the day we met. That can't be construed as punishment no matter how you look at it, for the simple reason that there's no comparison. Indifference for you turns off the whole farden machine, so nothing can be done. For me, it merely turns the motors down. But that doesn't prevent *you* from still having fun, does it?"

"This I would not do to you."

She knew it. Deep down, she'd known it all along, that he'd never make love to her unless she wanted him to. So in a way she had actually punished him, and he had every right to be angry about it, *was* angry about it. He'd also spent the night thinking she didn't want him anymore, and that was what was choking her up inside.

"I will *not* feel guilty about this! I won't! You let me think you were an emotionless, inhuman jerk, with the ability to turn off your feelings at the blink of an eye. So you got a little tit for tat, and the operative word is 'little.' You weren't made to cry or plead like I was. I didn't even try to turn you on. So what's the farden big deal?"

"You feel no remorse at all?"

"I'm not apologizing, if that's what you mean," she maintained stubbornly.

"Then there is no more to say here."

He turned away, leaving her with the guilt she'd denied, leaving her to suffer because she was too proud to admit she might have done wrong, especially if his control claiming *had* been only teasing, as Tamiron had suggested. He turned away, when he could have forced her to say she was sorry, forced the guilt out of her like he forced her to do everything else around here. But not this time. No, when *she* wanted him to force her, he played Kystrani and gave her rights and courtesies that she couldn't care less about at the moment.

Tedra's reaction to that was pure impulse. She attacked. The running leap put her in position, the neck hold was secure. With the momentum gained, the barbarian should have gone crashing to the floor, and she would have skillfully rolled out of the way. Of course, nothing was going right for her this morning, and this was no exception. Despite there being no warning, despite the perfect execution of the move, Challen wasn't budged, and the momentum gained ended up carrying Tedra right over his shoulder.

She landed flat on her back. By the time breath had seeped back into her lungs and she opened her eyes, Challen was very casually lowering his big body to cover hers.

"Thus are you defeated."

Tedra blinked. He was no longer looking angry or disappointed in her. He was looking rather smug, as if something he'd done had worked out exactly as he'd hoped it would. She didn't have to beat her brains to figure out what.

"Very clever," she said, but her lip curled to taunt, "But you won't be here to collect, will you? Or are you going to keep all those *shodani* waiting for you indefinitely?"

"You assume I mean to demand another month of the same service? This is not my thought at all, *che-*

mar. No, I will instead have of you women's duties of the more laborious kind, and enough to keep you so busy, you will not have time to even think of new ways to bedevil me—nor will you have time to cause any other mischief. The while I am gone, you will be under my uncle's direction. You will follow his orders, and do you disobey him, it will be his lot to punish you. This will be your new challenge loss service, to continue until such time as I return. Is this understood by you?''

"But you could be gone for weeks!"

"That is indeed possible."

"So I'm to be punished the whole time you're away? Do you call that fair?"

"You will be punished only do you disobey my uncle, woman. Your labors, Darasha labors to be sure, are no more than the service you just lost to me. I see no unfairness in that, since the service is mine to name, yours to do. Is that not so?"

"If you think I don't know I'm being punished for last night, you're nuts. So don't think I'll be waiting here with open arms for you to come back."

"You *will* be here, woman—"

"Sure I will," she cut in, giving him a tight little smile. "But my first service to you will be over by the time you return, or just about. And you can bet your farden weight in gold that I won't be challenging you anymore, so you can forget about all future service, of any kind. I'm getting my rights back and keeping them, and that includes the right to tell you to—"

He shut her up the way he'd found to be the easiest. After a few minutes of having her lips pleasantly mashed along with the rest of her body, she was no longer thinking of her rights.

"I hope that was a preview of what's on the morning's agenda before departure. If it is, shouldn't you tell our audience to leave?"

"He has already gone. Does this mean you want me again?"

"I always want you, babe. It was only your damned *dhaya* juice that temporarily changed the program, for which . . . I'm sorry. I shouldn't have done that to you, but doing it, I should have told you about it last night."

He kissed her again, then picked her up and carried her to his bed. Her apology didn't get her new service changed, but the taunting she'd done before it almost guaranteed the barbarian would hurry home.

Chapter Thirty-nine

*T*edra would never have admitted it to a soul, but she was having a great good time performing her new service. Challen's uncle, like her, had assumed she wasn't to particularly enjoy her labors, so he didn't set her to easy tasks like serving meals or even cooking, though she'd have made a nice mess of that if he'd insisted she try. No, he set her to more strenuous work like washing dishes all day, or scrubbing down walls and floors—there were enough in the castle that she could have worked for a month and not finished—or beating rugs, or cleaning leathers.

Oh, she got tired after a full day of doing everything she was supposed to, but it was a good tired. What Lowden uncle didn't know was that there wasn't anything he could come up with that would be more strenuous than the kind of exercises she had put herself through for most of her life, exercise she had been missing since meeting up with the barbarian.

It did confound him, however, and that really gave her a kick. Some of his expressions were priceless, like the day he'd told her to rearrange some heavy furniture so it could be cleaned under. He'd come back after about a half hour, probably thinking he'd gone too far this time—the furniture really was heavy—only to find everything moved and the floor already cleaned.

She hadn't wilted over the hot sink as he'd expected. She hadn't balked at having to go up and down ladders to wash the high walls, or getting on her knees to scrub the floors. She'd caused such a dust cloud in the back court from beating the great oval carpets that everyone at the front gate was coughing from it, and Lowden had to find someone else for the job who didn't put so much effort into it.

But no matter what he had her do, he wasn't getting the results *he* was looking for, which were some complaints, at least some signs of exhaustion. And then he thought he'd hit on something she'd really object to: getting her delicate hands dirty working in the vegetable gardens. Stars love him, she certainly did after that one. But she'd never tell.

Even her status dropping several notches with the women, Tedra found amusing. They, too, thought she was being punished with Darasha labors, and Marel, for one, figured to have some fun while she had the chance. She waited until Tedra was scrubbing the hall outside the women's gathering rooms before she came out with some of her cronies.

Tedra would have ignored them altogether, except that Marel was carrying a long switch. Tedra had no doubt any longer that women here weren't switched, for punishment or otherwise. Neither were Darasha. There was no need for that kind of discipline when there were so many other kinds. But when Marel started complaining loudly that Tedra wasn't working fast enough, Tedra knew what direction this scenario was supposed to take, and she was having none of it.

Before the young girl could get up the nerve to actually hit her with that switch, Tedra took it away from her and broke it, not just in half but into little pieces, no easy task since it was green wood. Marel, of course, started screaming for Master Lowden. By the time he arrived, the rest of the ladies had come into the hall to watch, but only Marel was making any noise. She was in for a surprise, however, when she made her complaints to Challen's uncle. What could the man do, after all, regarding the charge that Tedra had been slacking off in her work, when she was nearly finished with what should have taken her all day to do? As to the charge that she had then attacked Marel, *Tedra* was the one surprised upon hearing a good many of the ladies take her side by denying it. And since not one of Marel's cronies supported her in the claim, the poor girl got herself punished for causing trouble—back in the kitchen peeling the *falaa* she hated.

That was the day Challen returned. That he was back in only five days surprised everyone except Tedra. She'd figured that he wouldn't drag his feet at the meeting, and now she still had two weeks remaining on her first service to him. But hearing that he was approaching the castle ended her second service, and she quit what she was doing to go with everyone else to the courtyard to greet him.

But her first sight of him coming through the gate ended the good humor she'd retained in his absence. Sitting in front of him on his *hataar* was a very pretty blonde wearing—nothing. And from what Tedra could see around the shoulders of the warriors in front of her, the woman seemed to be crawling all over Challen, and *he* didn't appear to be doing anything to stop her from making such a spectacle of them both.

"Another captive, *shodan?*" Lowden asked in greeting.

Challen laughed at his long-suffering look. "You need see to this one only until Tamiron returns, uncle. Since it was his suggestion I steal her, I have decided he may have her.''

"But, *shodan—*" the girl in question began to complain.

She was cut off sternly. "Enough. I have told you, Laina, that I have a woman, the very one spoken of at the meeting. I need no others, nor would the mother of my children welcome another into our chambers.''

"Your *what?*" Lowden asked, more than a little surprised.

"Forgive me, uncle, but I had thought to save the telling until my parents returned. Have they yet?''

"No—no, but, Challen, why would you have her punished so harshly if you have taken her to mate?''

"Punished?" Challen became very still. "Uncle—''

But Lowden was in the throes of remorse that had to come out. "Droda, she has been worked hard enough that any child she may have conceived could well be lost," he said in horror. "If such happens, your mother will never forgive me, she has waited so long for you to choose your life-mate. Why did you give her into my keeping, if not to be punished?''

"Did I *tell* you to punish her?''

"You told me to keep her busy, yet she is a challenge loser and so not under my care. I could only surmise one reason for—''

"Be easy, uncle." Challen placed a hand on his shoulder to calm him. "The fault is mine for not explaining more fully. You did not have to—punish her more severely when she complained, did you?''

"Complained?" Lowden snorted. "I wish I had even one Darash who would work as hard and efficiently, and with not a single complaint.''

"No doubt she has saved them all for my ears. Where is she now? Perhaps my good news will take the edge off the anger she has likely reserved for me."

"This rising she has the scrubbing of the halls."

But she was not where Lowden had left her, and although this did not surprise him, she could not be found anywhere else in the castle either. Challen was almost beside himself with anxiety when Serren was carried in to him and was able to confess, before passing out from a wound received in his shoulder, that Tedra had convinced him to escort her to the market. There they were set upon by Kar-A-Jel warriors, Serren to be wounded, the woman, captured.

Challen was no longer worried. He was furious.

Chapter Forty

*F*alder La-Mar-Tel was not the pest Tedra was expecting, after Jalla's description of him. She had pictured a barbarian gone to pot, slovenly maybe, petulant surely, with a dose of greed and craftiness thrown in. She had *not* imagined a giant's giant, a warrior at least seven and a half feet tall, a solid, immovable powerhouse of a man. This was the pest who feared to face her barbarian in challenge?

But she'd seen his town on the way to his house, which was no more than a normal-size dwelling with a large hall. The town was also small in comparison to Sha-Ka-Ra. It could be assumed, then, that the *shodan* of Kar-A-Jel didn't have a great many warriors under his leadership. It could also be assumed that he wasn't very smart, if he kept nipping at the heels of a greater power to no purpose. But Jalla had said that all these two *shodani* did was raid each other back and forth, neither of them attacking in force that would have the makings of war behind it. They likely just supplied each other with the excuse for some warriorlike fun.

So what was behind her capture? It had been deliberate. The warriors sent after her knew whom they were taking, had heard all about her at the meeting, and she'd made it easy for them to get at her, leaving the castle like that with only one warrior to escort her. Of course, she hadn't made the actual capture easy. Even though Challen was to have told the council of *shodani* that she was a warrior in her own right and what he had witnessed of her capabilities, the four warriors who set upon them had been worried only about Serren, not her. Little wonder she walked into Falder's hall while her escort limped.

But what *was* behind her capture? Merely a strike at a favored nemesis? Or did the *shodan* of Kar-A-Jel simply want the distinction to be his of possessing the only alien on the planet? Whatever he wanted, he wasn't pleased to see four of his mighty warriors nearly out of commission.

"Could you not have lured her out of his stronghold?" he demanded when they stood before him, two on either side of her. "Was it necessary to fight his entire—"

"The woman *was* outside his castle," the warrior on her right said in their defense. "You told us not to harm her. You did not tell us how to keep from being harmed in the process."

"Do you tell me *she* did this to you?"

When he got no answer but chagrined expressions, the big giant threw back his head and laughed uproariously. Tedra, bound only at the wrists, and that not even at her back, just loved how easy it was to surprise these barbarians before they took her seriously. Without even thinking about it, she hooked her foot behind Falder's and gave him a little push. It sounded like he broke the floor. Likely it was cracked. But he wasn't laughing anymore. He wasn't angry either. He just looked up at Tedra from his prone position with a good deal of awe.

"So he spoke true," Falder said as he got to his feet, slowly dusting off his *bracs*.

His warriors just looked on smugly as he moved to stand out of Tedra's reach. She realized then that

Challen must have done some exaggerating at that meeting. This giant of giants actually thought she could take him. Well, she'd brought him down while she was tied up and looking helpless, so she couldn't blame him for making that assumption. And she wasn't about to disabuse him of it.

And then a thought struck her that should have sneaked up sooner. "That pretty blond captive Challen came home with wouldn't happen to be yours, would she?"

He heard only what he wanted to hear in that question. "So he has already returned home? Then it will not be long before he joins us."

"To exchange captives?"

"Not at all." The big man smiled at her now. "Laina he can keep. It is the Ly-San-Ter gaali mine that will be exchanged does he want back his woman; thus will the sky-flyers come to this warrior to trade."

Tedra didn't like the sound of that, not at all. "I'm the only sky-flyer there is around here, *Shodan* La-Mar-Tel, the only one who's discovered your planet, so I'm the only one who'll be making the trading deals. And what makes you think I want gaali stones?"

He kept right on smiling. "It is the only thing of true value in all of Kan-is-Tra. Living jewels you possess. What can you want with ours? Wondrous weapons you possess. What use our *Toreno* swords to you?"

"Didn't Challen tell you guys that every town would benefit?"

"He lied and so I told the council. Towns without wealth will benefit nothing."

"I get the feeling you didn't stick around until the end of the meeting."

"After he stole my woman nearly out of my hand? Indeed I left."

His affronted look was really amusing, but Tedra didn't laugh. She came up with some half-truths instead. "I hate to put a dent in your conclusions, babe, which were really quite brilliant, but gaali stones are just raw energy, and we've got so many sources of energy it's not funny. I'm not saying we wouldn't like to have some to study, but there are many other things I'll be trading for as well, some things I see right here in your hall. For instance, those goblets on your table. Aren't they made of gold?"

"Think you I have no sense, woman? No one would trade for cheap metal dishes."

"Then they are not of gold?"

"Certainly they are," he snorted. "But it is a soft, useless metal, good only for the making of jewelry and shiny vases—and dishes."

"Ah, but that's only your opinion, and perhaps that of your entire planet, because it's something you people have in abundance here. Where I come from, it's not so plentiful. My planet doesn't need it, but there are other worlds out there whose entire economies are gold-based. You find it useless. They use it for money. And that's not all. Once I report the discovery of Sha-Ka'an, you'll have representatives here from every planet in the Centura League to make offers for everything from food and wine to jewels and minerals to plants and trees. Even your dirt is valuable to planets with contaminated or burned-out soils. So don't think gaali stones are the only things worth trading around here."

"Dirt, trees, and gold?" He laughed. "Flowers, too, maybe?" He laughed some more, then sobered, showing a new face, one out of patience. "We are not fools here, woman, no matter you seem to think so," he growled, and then to his men, "Chain her up—and watch those alien feet of hers!"

"I would not do that were I you, Falder."

This from a new voice, one Tedra recognized very well. She turned as the others did, to see Challen standing in the doorway to the hall with a neck-lock hold on one of Falder's warriors, obviously one who'd tried to stop him from joining the party. As they watched, the man was released, to fall unconscious to the floor at the barbarian's feet. Even before he landed, Challen's great sword was drawn. And then he was walking forward quite purposefully, heading straight for Falder.

He wasn't alone. He had a handful of warriors with him. But there were a good deal more than that inside the hall, Falder's men, and they didn't just stand around waiting for the enemy *shodan* to reach their own. Tedra got her first true demonstration of why the barbarians called themselves warriors. If she thought those weighty swords were just decorations, she was wrong. And Challen, Stars, she'd never seen him like this. He barely paused in his determination to reach her—no, to reach Falder, who'd dared to take something of his. Swords that could have cleaved him in half were brushed aside with little effort, men literally thrown out of his path.

Falder got the message, was losing too many men by just standing there doing nothing. His options were two. He could lay hands on Tedra to use her as a leverage, or he could try reasoning with what appeared to be a madman. Naturally he looked toward Tedra. But she'd been keeping half an eye on him, and when he made his move toward her, she back-kicked him clean in the gut, then with a fast dive and

a roll got well out of his reach. She even got an unexpected bonus, taking down two of his men whose
feet, unfortunately for them, got tangled up in her
roll. They happened to be the last two barriers between Challen and his target, except maybe for her.
And although they were fast getting to their feet, she
was faster to rise. Challen finally paused, with her
standing right in front of him. But it was only a brief
pause, long enough to look her over to see that she
hadn't been hurt, and then he was going to set her
aside . . . not farden likely.

"Enough, Challen!" she had to shout above the
noise still clanging in the rest of the hall. "He thought
he wanted your gaali mine, but I think I've convinced
him he doesn't need it. If you have some other reason
to kill him, though, then go ahead. But *don't* make it
on my account."

Falder was close enough to hear that. "You are
willing to die for her, Ly-San-Ter?"

"Yes." Challen finally spoke, his eyes still on
Tedra. "I have given her my life."

"By the stones of gaali, why was that not mentioned at the council?"

Challen glanced at the surprised man in disgust,
reminding him, "You were there to doubt everything
I had to say, despite the proof I brought with me."

"I doubted that all could benefit as you claimed,
but . . . the woman has made me rethink the matter.
Thus do I relinquish all claims of capture. You may
have her back. She is too dangerous to have around,
anyway," the giant added, rubbing his belly.

Of course, they were good buddies after that, much
to Tedra's disgust.

Chapter Forty-one

*T*edra sat stiffly before Challen on the ride back to Sha-Ka-Ra, silently brooding and seething in a general all-around bad mood. She was furious at that muddlehead Falder for going to the trouble of capturing her, then just blithely letting her go. And she still wasn't sure why the fight had ended so suddenly. Certainly not because of anything *she'd* said. There shouldn't even have been a fight. Hadn't she been told warriors didn't fight over women? Buy back or steal back, but Challen hadn't come to make an offer.

And then he'd behaved as if he'd merely come for a visit! The two *shodani* had discussed the council meeting, so she got to hear all about it—secondhand. Falder even offered up a number of his warriors for the contingent of mercenaries already volunteered and ready to leave for Kystran. It would have been nice if she knew what those mercenaries were going to cost her, but *that* wasn't mentioned. Challen had taken it upon himself to arrange it, and so it was done. Get her input? Find out if she even needed so many men or if the Rover had room for them? Oh, if she *didn't* need them, how quickly she'd tell them all where they could stick their high-handedness.

Challen had wisely kept quiet on the three-hour ride, but there had been no privacy for a heated discussion, and Tedra's mood told him plainly it was going to be heated. He waited only until they reached his chamber, though he'd practically had to drag her that far. There she went straight to the couch where her *fembair* slept and pulled the cat onto her lap.

"You have every right to be angry with me, Tedra."

"Damned right."

"Best you speak of it—"

"Martha isn't always right, warrior. *Best* you leave me alone right now."

He came to sit next to her, only to have her move to the end of the couch, pulling the heavy cat with her. He tried a different tack.

"You are not pleased you have your army?"

"You mean your army, don't you, in your command?"

"So it must be. Warriors will not fight for a woman."

"Just like they won't fight *over* a woman?"

"You are angered by that, too?"

"I didn't ask for your life! You think I saved it so you could throw it away fighting a behemoth like that? And I'd already defused the situation. Falder would have accepted a cart of dishes for me!"

"Now you make no sense."

"I told you to leave me alone, didn't I?"

"*Chemar—*"

"Don't call me that. If you can't give it the meaning I want, then I don't want to hear it at all."

Challen ran a hand roughly through his hair in exasperation. "Remain where you are, woman. I will bring my uncle here to explain, since you will not listen to me."

"Don't bother. All he can tell me is where you've stashed her. But let me tell you something, warrior. I don't go in for threesomes. You try bringing that woman near me and I'll tear her eyes out!"

"Who?"

"Oh, that's funny. Who else was crawling all over you today, and her naked?"

"Laina?" Challen suddenly smiled, then he laughed. "All this because of Laina?"

He laughed again, so hard he didn't even see Tedra get up to push him right over the backless couch. But even sprawled on the floor, he still chuckled.

"Keep it up, warrior," Tedra growled, "and I'll do to you what I did once before. *That* will shut you up, won't it?"

"Tedra, *chemar.*" He grinned over the couch at her. "You have no reason for female jealousies. Have I not stopped drinking *dhaya* wine? Have I not given my life to you?"

"What *is* it with this life giving? It didn't stop you from bringing home a new captive, did it?"

"She was taken merely to end the dissension Falder was causing, not because I wanted her. I do *not* want her. She is to be Tamiron's."

"Then what was she doing on *your* lap?"

"She rode with me only because Tamiron went to arrange for the food supplies for the journey to Kystran. Now you have your army, there is no reason to delay the leaving."

"The Rover has all the food necessary to feed two armies," Tedra replied, but with a lot less heat and a good deal of feeling horribly foolish.

Challen came around the couch and drew her unresisting into his arms. "This Martha told us, but you have nothing of real meat, which a warrior must have. Our supplies will be included, else you will not get my warriors on your Rover."

"The Food Processor won't know how to cook it," Tedra said softly, kissing his neck, his bare chest.

She didn't see the couple who came in from the balcony at that point, but Challen did. What Tedra saw was her barbarian looking suddenly ill at ease, extremely so.

"Before this becomes more embarrassing than it is, best we make ourselves known."

Tedra turned with a start, but then she thought she understood what was wrong with her warrior. She'd blown it but good.

"I didn't know we had an audience," she said. "Maybe I should apologize for pushing you over."

"No," he choked out.

"For screaming at you, then?"

"No."

Now she frowned. "Then what *are* you disconcerted about? That's just your uncle. Do you think he doesn't know what we do in here?"

He merely groaned in answer this time, and Tedra turned to glare at Lowden and the woman with him. The woman was smiling. Lowden was for once not looking disapproving. Tedra could have sworn, in fact, he was trying not to laugh.

"Haven't we seen enough of each other this week, Lowden uncle? Much as I enjoyed it, I've got other things to—"

Challen's hand cut that off, plastered flat to her mouth. "Woman, that is *not* my uncle. Those are my parents!" he hissed in her ear before letting her go.

"But he's identical to Lowden," Tedra pointed out, as if Challen couldn't see that. "You do cloning here and never bothered to mention it?"

"Lowden is my twin brother," Chadar Ly-San-Ter interrupted at that point. "And may I make known to you Haleste, the mother of my children. We welcome you to our family, daughter."

"Thanks, but I don't need parents at this late date."

The older couple laughed, but the woman said, "She speaks very strangely, Challen."

"It is a long story, mother."

"Mother?" Tedra cut in, startled. "She's your *mother?* An actual mother?" And then to Haleste: "Oh, you poor woman."

"Challen?" Haleste, asked, confused.

"A *long* story, mother," Challen repeated, thought about putting his hand over Tedra's mouth again, but tried jarring her memory first. "Parents? Relatives? You remember when you first met my uncle and we spoke of this?"

"I've made the connection, babe. I just forgot for a while that that kind of stuff goes on down here."

"Stuff?"

"Women having babies. It's—"

"What you will do as the mother of my children," Challen finished for her.

"The wha— Oh, no." She shook her head, wide-eyed. "Women don't do that where I come from."

Three pairs of eyes looked at her as if she'd gone off the deep end. "Then who does?" Challen finally got out. "Your men?"

"Real cute," Tedra snorted. "No one does, of course."

"Then how can your race survive?"

She finally realized where they were coming from. "Don't get me wrong. We have children, we just don't have to bear them."

"Challen, *where* does this woman come from that this can be so?" his father wanted to know.

But Haleste replied, taking his arm and leading him toward the door. "It indeed must be a long story, Chadar, as he has said, and we will hear it soon enough. Best we leave them alone now to decide the matter of our grandchildren.''

Challen hardly noticed their going. He had about lost his patience, but not the topic under discussion. ''Woman, you contradict yourself. You cannot have children without bearing them.''

''We can,'' Tedra said smugly now that they were alone. ''An adult female can produce two or even a dozen babies a year, depending on how many are needed—Population Control is strictly monitored. All she has to do is donate the cells when she's asked and then has nothing more to do with it.''

''Have *you* done this?''

''No. Only cells from the most intelligent females are requested. I don't fall into that category.''

''I will not believe you lack intelligence.''

''Thanks, but when I said most intelligent, I was talking certified geniuses. It doesn't guarantee a child genius. It just betters the odds.''

''But how—who, then, bears the child?''

''Not who, what. If we can make a perfect simulation of a man or woman in android form, don't you think we can simulate a perfect womb? Babies are the jurisdiction of Population Control. They go through gestation in an artificial womb we still call a tube, where their growth and development are under constant surveillance. Their education is begun even before they are 'born' from this, and continues in the Child Centers until they are old enough to have their interests and talents established and matched, between the ages of three and five. This is when they are sent to the appropriate schools for training in their life-careers.''

''This is how you were raised, in these centers and schools?''

"Certainly. It's how every Kystrani is raised."

"It is not how *our* children will be raised."

She knew that this-is-the-end-of-the-discussion look. "All right, if it's so important to you, when we get to Kystran we can donate our gene cells together. It's never been done before, but I'm sure something can be worked out so the child can be turned over to you when it's ready."

"*You* would not want it?"

"What for? I told you, Population Control raises babies, donators don't."

"No," he said flatly. "It will not be done this way. It will be done as it is meant to be done. You will carry my child inside you. You will bear it. You will be its mother."

"Are you nuts? I'm supposed to be the first Kystrani in centuries to bear a child? I'm not dumb, you know. The reason we stopped doing it that way was not just because it's dangerous, it also hurts like hell."

"So you took away a little pain, but you also took away a child's right to know its parents' love."

What she had always felt the lack of, love, any kind of love. Tedra sat down, feeling suddenly confused. "I—I need to think about this, Challen."

"This you may do, certainly, but the matter is decided." He drew her gently back into his arms to hold her before he told her, "You already carry my child, *chemar.*"

Chapter Forty-two

Challen was exploring the ship. That ought to keep him busy for hours, or so Tedra hoped, and keep Martha busy, too. They'd Transferred up together. He'd have it no other way. Sometimes she got the feeling the barbarian didn't trust her. Maybe he had good reason.

Tedra locked herself in Medical and stared at the meditech unit, which would give her the answers she needed—no, not answers, just one. She'd already figured out *how* she might have got pregnant, but not the technicalities of it. Like so many other things she was learning she'd always taken for granted, birth control was just one more. On an automated world, however, such things weren't left to chance. Birth control was administered to *everyone* whether they wanted it or not. It was in the food, in everything Kystrani consumed. But Tedra hadn't been eating Kystrani food lately, not since she'd met up with the barbarian. And if she was supposed to have been taking some other sort of precaution while she was off ship, that must have been a subject her World Discovery class hadn't got to before she changed careers.

She could be pregnant. Challen was certain that she was. And he based his belief on the fact that he'd stopped taking birth control, too. Talk about your double whammy. But she'd found out a lot of new things in the past few days since he'd dropped that bomb on her. Barbarians' birth control was in their *dhaya* wine, something only warriors drank, so only warriors controlled it. But there was a reason behind that, since once a warrior chose the mother for his children, they were hooked up for life, and *that* was the meaning behind those words that had sounded so formal to her when he told her his life was hers. They were formal. Challen had married her barbarian-style, and she hadn't even known it!

She could be pregnant. She likely was. The meditech would tell her for sure. But she was afraid to get in, afraid to know, because then she *would* have a decision to make, one the barbarian didn't know she could make, one she didn't want to make. Stars, there was no decision to it. She couldn't go through something as barbaric as giving birth. It was terrifying even contemplating it. Women died. But that was then, centuries ago, a common-sense voice reminded her. Would it be so dangerous now, with the modern advances in the past two hundred years, with a meditech on hand? But there was still the pain. Why should she go through that when Challen didn't even love her— yet? But she loved him. And he wanted her to have his baby. *His* baby.

She got into the unit before she lost her nerve, pressing Gen. Ex. before closing herself in. It didn't even take a half minute before the lid was opening again, her health stats coming across the screen at its base. But she couldn't look yet. She'd have a printout delivered to her quarters later, when she wasn't so paranoid about it.

"You might as well look now, kiddo." Martha's voice came in over the intercom, making Tedra grab for her heart. "It's not a word we see every day. I'm surprised I even have it in my data banks, it's so obsolete.''

"Am I supposed to be a mind reader to know what you're going around the block about?''

"No, I'm the mind reader around here. You're the Sec 1 who got herself pregnant. So are you going to have the seedling transferred to a proper container?''

Tedra crossed the room to glare at the viewer on the intercom. "Actually, it's in its proper container. Tubing is an artificial means we've come to accept as the norm, but I've been reminded it *is* artificial.''

"And none of that answered my question. Kystrani don't bear babies.''

"Sha-Ka'ani do,'' Tedra retorted

"Ah, that's right, and you're going to be a Sha-Ka'ani, aren't you? In fact, you already are, if I can believe everything that barbarian of yours has been telling me. By the way, he just mutilated one of our adjustichairs. He sat down in it, felt it adjusting to his great girth, and thought it was very much alive. He'd hacked it to pieces before I could tell him it was only doing its job.''

"Oh, stop.'' Tedra began giggling. "He didn't do any such thing.''

"He did. Of course, he was properly apologetic afterward, but that didn't save the poor chair. You should have seen his face, kiddo, when that thing started moving under his backside. I've never seen anyone move so fast as he did coming out of that chair.''

Tedra had to hold her sides, she was laughing so hard. "We're going to have a problem, then, when I take him to bed tonight. It's going to do a *lot* of adjusting to accommodate his size.''

"And will you be doing some accommodating for his son?" Martha asked.

Tedra sobered, staring at the viewer in wonder. She hadn't realized she could learn *what* it was.

"The unit listed its sex? It's a boy?"

"Makes it harder, doesn't it?"

"No." Tedra grinned. "I'd already decided to keep it. It'll just be nice knowing something the big guy doesn't know for a change, if I can keep a secret that long. Stars, how long *does* it take, anyway, to have a baby?"

Martha got a chance to use her exasperated voice. "Honestly, you'd think I'm supposed to know everything."

Chapter Forty-three

*T*edra was still grinning later when she entered her quarters. She'd located Challen, teased him about killing the furniture, then left him looking disgruntled, yet bewildered that she should know about that when she hadn't been there. She supposed she ought to warn him that Martha was a busybody who had eyes and ears in every room.

He wouldn't be joining her for a while, for his warriors were still being Transferred up, and he had his hands full dealing with their different degrees of shock and wonderment, not to mention his own. They'd all been briefed about what to expect, but seeing was believing, and that didn't even do it for some of them. Fortunately, the warriors would have a few weeks to adjust before they reached Kystran.

Corth was waiting on her. So was her *fembair,* prowling around and feeling caged in a room so much smaller than it was used to. In the short time she had had him, he'd already grown, and now reached halfway up her legs. At that rate of growth, she was worried about how big he would be by the time the ship landed. But she couldn't leave him behind. She still had ideas of talking Challen into staying on Kystran with her.

"Has Martha told you what's going on, Corth?"

"Yes. She suggested I stay out of the way. I am pleased you have accomplished your goals, Tedra De Arr."

"Yes, well, I suppose getting an army *was* the hard part. Defeating the Sha-Ka'ari and Crad Ce Moerr ought to be easy after that. Dial me something to eat while I change, will you? You know what I like, but add something tart for dessert—wait a minute. Martha, are you there?"

"Always, doll."

"Check with Medical about the food, if it's safe for someone in my condition?"

"It's safe, but fresh is healthier."

"But fresh is so—fresh," Tedra said in disgust. "It *bleeds*, Martha. And I was looking forward to some normal food."

"Like I said, it won't hurt you, but the warriors' supplies would still be healthier for you."

"And I suppose you'll tell Challen that?"

"Certainly."

"Thanks a lot," Tedra grumbled, heading for the utility wall to dial the closet.

She made her selection, but frowned when the ship's uniform came out on the rack, for she'd dialed it automatically. She'd never get away with wearing it, even if she was back in her own territory, so she sent the one-piece suit back and dialed a skirt and blouse. Her humor returned at seeing how really skimpy both pieces were. And while she was at it, she changed her eye and hair coloring to look more Sha-Ka'ani.

She laughed then, picturing how surprised her warrior was going to be when he saw her made over. Her shiny gold-and-black skirt was only about a foot long, in the design of a wide belt, and just barely covered her from hip to mid-thigh. The sleeveless blouse stopped just below her breasts, though the top of it dipped enticingly low and, like the skirt, buckled together. Her hair was as golden as Challen's and swept up and out of the way in a hair-tail. Her eyes were a soft amber and still filled with laughter when she removed the bathroom walls.

"What is so amusing, Tedra De Arr?" Corth asked, coming up behind her.

"Do I look warriorlike to you?"

"You look like you should be in bed."

Tedra's mouth dropped open just before she yelled, *"Martha!"* but as she might have expected, the troublemaker didn't answer.

"Was that not an appropriate response?"

"No, Corth, it was not," Tedra gritted out. "Didn't Martha tell you that I have a man now, one of the warriors?"

"Yes. Challen is his name."

"Well, if she told you that, why in the farden hell didn't she adjust your programming while she was at it?"

"I would not let her."

"You *what?*"

"That was a joke." Corth grinned. "The Martha has given me humor."

"Oh, the metal lady is having a grand old time experimenting with you, isn't she? But *I don't like it!*"

"You wish my new humor removed?"

"Don't play dense, babe. You *know* what I want removed."

"But my drive to satisfy you will not be a problem, as long as the Challen satisfies you."

She might have laughed if she weren't so exasperated. It wasn't easy arguing with perfect reasoning, but she'd been doing that ever since she'd brought Martha home. But Martha was the one who needed arguing with over this fiasco, not Corth. What could that warped computer be thinking of, to deliberately leave the android in his new, sexually aggressive mode when she knew the situation with Challen?

"All right, Corth, it's not your fault." Tedra moved over to the dining area that had been ordered up, but the several selections waiting for her didn't look all that tempting just now. "I think I need to work up an appetite, babe. Come and defend yourself. With a full ship, it might be better if we do our workouts in here for the time being, and I've missed them."

The android obliged and Tedra attacked. The *fembair* ran for cover when the first body hit the floor. Tedra rebounded quickly, grinning. Corth had the strength to demolish her, but he wouldn't use that strength against her. For workouts, he was programmed to her skill level, which meant she took as much punishment as she gave. She couldn't beat him, but that wasn't the purpose of the exercises.

When the door slid silently open, Tedra was in the process of blocking a high kick and swung around for one of her own. Seeing Challen standing there looking like something a thunderstorm might deliver threw her timing off, and the arm Corth raised to block her caught her in the back instead. She went stumbling, Challen went berserk, and Corth, naturally, defended himself. By the time she turned around, her barbarian was fighting for breath. Corth had him in a bear-hold, and was having to expend extra strength to hold him. But hold him he did, much to Challen's confusion.

"Release him, Corth."

He obeyed her instantly, of course. Challen, on the other hand, couldn't be controlled like that. No sooner was he released than he drew his sword. Tedra had never moved so fast as she did to get between them.

"He's a machine, Challen. You're not going to kill another machine, are you?"

That didn't do it, if Challen's expression was any indication. Corth didn't *look* like a machine, that was the problem. And Challen wasn't looking at her, but at Corth, still with every intention of hacking him to pieces, which would have been done already if she weren't in the way.

In a firmer tone, she tried explaining. "Now, look, warrior, you can't go around destroying things just because you don't understand yet how they work. Corth wasn't doing anything I hadn't told him to do. We were exercising, something I like to do daily. You understand practice-makes-perfect? *You* exercise with your sword, don't you? Well, I have to exercise my skills, too, and Corth's the only one I can do that with where no one gets hurt."

He took his eyes off Corth only long enough to say, "You were getting hurt, woman."

"No, I wasn't. And you're wasting that look on a machine, Challen. He couldn't care less that you're angry. He's programmed only to please me. And since when do you show *anyone* that you're angry? Where's your control gone lately?"

That got her a grunt and a disgusted look, though he did sheathe his sword. "A warrior cannot be expected to maintain his control when he has such a one as you for his woman."

"Oh, that's cute. Blame me for every—"

His hand caught her face suddenly. "What have you done to yourself?"

"I changed—"

"You will change back, and you will do it now."

"Now just a—"

"Now, woman!"

"And leave you two alone in here? Not on your life," she said, crossing her arms over her chest in an I'm-not-budging pose.

He looked around until his eyes caught the bed. "Is this not the place where I will sleep?"

Her arms uncrossed. "Challen!"

"You will do as you are told, *kerima*, will you not?"

"All right!" she snapped. "I'm going. But I'd like to know what you're going to do for kicks when my challenge service is over and I no longer have to jump when you say jump."

"In a lifetime, think you that you will never challenge me again?"

She started to deny it, but what was the use? At the rate they were going, she'd be challenging him every other month at least!

Fortunately, it didn't take but a few minutes to get her own coloring back. She decided Corth could hold his own that long, especially since Challen got distracted by his first encounter with movable walls, walls that enclosed completely and were without doors. By the time he had figured out that there was no way he could get into the room that had just formed itself, Tedra sent the walls back out of sight.

"Convenience, Challen, remember? Getting a lot out of a little space is just another aspect of it. And don't worry, we've got lots of time to show you everything so things like this don't throw you when we get to Kystran."

This got her another grunt. "Best you bring those walls back, woman. You have not finished changing."

"But I did," she protested.

"You will also remove those clothes and wear what is appropriate."

She smiled now. "I didn't bring any *chauri* with me, babe." But an "I did" got rid of her smile. "If you think I'm going to step one foot on my world wearing one of those—"

"When you needs be a Sec 1, you may dress accordingly."

"Stars, who's the captain around here, anyway?" she grumbled.

"Martha claims to be."

"Well, Martha is still answerable to me, though she likes to pretend otherwise. And I know farden well you haven't had time to unpack anything yet, so how about compromising a little and letting me wear what I want to until you do?"

"When a warrior begins compromising—"

"Challen! Be reasonable for once, dammit!"

"If the Challen is displeasing to you, Tedra De Arr, I will—"

Tedra rounded on the android. "Stay out of this, Corth!"

"No," Challen said menacingly. "I would hear what the man would do."

Tedra rounded back on the warrior. "He isn't a man. Why can't you grasp that simple concept? He's a machine, a companion, an entertainment android. He's here to amuse me, and nothing else. He's like a pet, Challen. Does *that* make sense to you?"

"I am also a fully functional sex-sharer," Corth pointed out, much to Tedra's horror.

"Now, Challen . . ." she said when he started toward the android again. "I've never used him in that capacity. You, more than anyone, ought to know that."

"Nor will you be able to when I am finished with him," the warrior growled.

"Will you stop! You can't be jealous of a machine." And then Tedra's eyes widened at what she'd said. "Can you? Are you jealous, warrior?"

The look he gave her was priceless, full of chagrin, exasperation—and bewilderment. Warriors weren't supposed to experience jealousy. That was a woman's emotion. Yet he felt it, and couldn't deny it, and Tedra was so delighted, all she wanted to do was shower him with kisses.

"Why don't you go visit Martha in the Control Room, Corth," Tedra suggested, doing her best to keep an idiotic grin off her lips. "I think she's just got the results she masterminded and needs someone to crow to. Don't you, Martha?"

"Sure do," came the smug voice out of the large audiovisual console against one wall.

The voice and turned-on screen temporarily distracted Challen, and Tedra shooed Corth out while he wasn't looking, then came up behind the warrior to wrap her arms around him. "You know, I swore a long time ago that one day I'd get you into a solaray bath. But you aren't dirty, not even a little sweaty. But I know a way to get you sweaty. Wanna hear about it?"

He turned around so he was the one doing the holding. "Best you show me instead."

That idiotic grin got loose as she unbuckled her blouse to drop it over the console screen. "Just remember, babe," she said as she wrapped herself around him and was picked up in his arms, "if the bed moves—ignore it."

Chapter Forty-four

"*O*h, my Stars, they've brought in the big guns and haven't even bothered to dress them appropriately," was Rourk Ce Dell's alarmed comment before it dawned on him that the giant was standing in his living room. "Wait a minute. How did you get in here?"

"He's with me, babe," Tedra said, stepping out from behind Challen.

"Tedra!" And she was pounced on for a hug that swung her around the room. "Oh, babe, it's good to see you! But when did you . . . why are you . . . dammit, Tedra, it's too soon. Nothing's changed yet."

Before she could answer, she was separated from Rourk, who was still holding her, the entire span of Challen's arms. Rourk, understandably, lost his train of thought. All he could do was stare at the warrior, who was giving him a don't-touch-my-woman-again look.

Tedra shook her head, snapping her fingers in front of her friend's eyes. "You'd be surprised what *has* changed, Rourk. He's not one of them, he's mine, and there's more where he came from."

That got Rourk's attention back real quick. "What do you mean, yours? Who *is* he, Tedra?"

"Challen Ly-San-Ter, *shodan* of Sha-Ka-Ra on the planet Sha-Ka'an."

"You mean Sha-Ka'ar?"

"No, I mean Sha-Ka'an. You suggested I do a little

world discovering while I was gone, remember? Well, guess what I discovered?''

With another glance at Challen, who looked nothing at all like the uniformed warriors still in control of Goverance Building, Rourk hit it on the nose. ''Their mother planet? You actually found their mother planet? Where?''

''Not in Centura Star System, that's for sure. I believe we named their system Niva, but they don't call it anything, not knowing too much about other worlds, theirs or anyone else's. I was only the second sky-flyer to pay them a visit, you see.''

''The first being?''

''Those miners who made the mistake of thinking captured Sha-Ka'ani would make good slave labor. By the way, according to Challen's father, who is a Guardian of the Years, it was a penal village that got taken. All they knew was the entire village disappeared three hundred years ago. Naturally, they weren't too upset to have their worst element taken off their hands.''

''Criminals?'' Rourk laughed. ''Sha-Ka'ar founded by criminals? No wonder *they* kept no records of where they came from.''

''Yes, well, they might have been criminals, that original bunch, but they were still Sha-Ka'ani warriors to start with. And their descendants might be familiar with advanced worlds, but they haven't advanced all that far themselves. They're still sword-wielders, and what better way to defeat sword-wielders than—''

''With sword-wielders,'' Rourk finished for her, beaming. ''Do you really have more like this one?''

''This one has a name,'' Challen said stiffly.

"Ah, sure, Challen," Rourk said uneasily. "You've just been so quiet, I—ah—"

"Don't stick your foot in it." Tedra chuckled. "If my warrior's not saying much, it's because he's suffering a little cultural shock. He saw visuals of modern cities on the Rover, but it's not the same as actually being inside one with air cruisers and fleetwings flying all over the place. We Transferred down right to your front door, but that one brief look really—"

"You have made your point, woman," Challen complained gruffly, a little too gruffly as far as Rourk was concerned.

The Kystrani forgot Challen's earlier annoyance over his familiarity with Tedra and pulled her aside to whisper, "Are you nuts, teasing him like that? The man's a farden gia—hey!"

He got picked up this time, and held up, and Challen was about to shake him, too, when Tedra got mad. "Dammit, warrior, that's my friend you're scaring the hell out of! Put him down right now!"

"Tedra, really, it's all right," Rourk insisted, more alarmed by her ready-to-fight tone. "Let him do whatever makes him happy."

"It would make me happy did you keep your hands off my woman." But Challen set him down as he said it.

"Sure. Whatever you say. I don't even *know* her."

"Cut it out, Rourk," Tedra said in disgust. "And as for you"—she poked a finger in Challen's chest—"you've got to get this thing under control before someone gets hurt. Now, I love it that you're capable of feeling jealousy, but it's groundless. Rourk is to me what Tamiron is to you, no more, no less, so I think you owe him an apology."

Rourk almost choked on that one. "Tedra please—"

"For Stars' sake, Rourk," she cut in, exasperated "will you stop thinking the man's going to flatten me? He's not, you know. He'd die before he'd even put a bruise on me."

"He would?"

"Certainly I would," Challen said indignantly.

Rourk frowned then, at both of them. "What the hell's going on here? And what is it with all these possessive 'mys'? Did you adopt him, Tedra?"

"Real cute, babe. Give the man a little reassurance and he gets nasty. No, I didn't adopt him. I signed up for double occupancy."

"You didn't. You did? With *him*?"

"I don't know if I like your tone, Rourk."

"But, Tedra, he's—"

"Yes?" Her tone got menacing.

"He's—"

"Yes?" Her tone got really menacing.

"Well, I don't know how you could miss it. He's a farden giant."

"No kidding? My, how *did* I miss that? You see how blind love can be."

"You love him, too?"

"You know, I think I'm going to kill you tonight, Rourk."

Challen chuckled and pulled her to his side to wrap an arm around her waist. "I think I will believe now that you are only friends. He would not tease you otherwise."

"*You* tease me all the time," she pointed out "And we're much more than friends."

"You will not attempt to provoke my jealousy again, woman."

"You just can't break that habit of telling me what to do, can you, even though my challenge loss debt has been paid in full."

"Do you wish to challenge me again?"

"I just might."

"I don't believe I'm hearing this," Rourk said, looking on in amazement. "Tell me you didn't really challenge him, Tedra."

"Of course I did. He's not much bigger than that warrior Kowan was, and I took *him* down, didn't I?"

"Not much bigger?" Rourk grinned. "Only about a foot, I'd say. How quickly did you lose the fight?"

"Oh, shut up."

"Who is this warrior Kowan?" Challen wanted to know, the signs of jealousy back in place.

Tedra rolled her eyes, while Rourk put a hand over his mouth to pretend he was coughing. But Challen was still awaiting an answer.

"Didn't I tell you about Kowan, babe? I could've sworn I mentioned the handsome warrior who wanted to make a slave of me. But if you want to get at him, you'll have to get inside Goverance Building, so why don't we get down to discussing that, instead of all this nonsense? That is why we came here, remember?"

"Stars, Tedra, it's just occurred to me that if we had a few more like Challen here, we might be able to get inside Goverance—"

He ran, but Challen held Tedra back. "Very funny, you jerk." She glowered at her friend. *"Now* can we get serious? What is the current situation? Has Crad Ce Moerr relaxed enough to come out in public yet?"

"No, he's still playing it very safe. And the situation is about what we anticipated. The bulk of the women were taken in the first three weeks. It's slowed

down, with a ship leaving for Sha-Ka'ar about every
other week now, the cargo being kept at Goverance
Building until departure.''

''And the rest of the female Secs from the outer
areas?''

''We were able to warn only four. I'm sorry, Tedra
but they got the rest.''

She waved that aside. ''We'll get them back, and
every other Kystrani.''

''How?''

''I've got an idea, but first we have to free Garr
Have you had word on him? Is he being treated
okay?''

''They don't dare harm him. He's their only lever
age for keeping the male Secs in line, those in the
city anyway. They've still got communications in a
blank-out, thanks to the Mock II in Goverance Build
ing. And they're still only letting traffic in, not out
It's too bad that computer was never programmed to
a single individual. If it had been linked to Garr a
Martha was to you, Garr would have been freed a
long time ago.''

''And we might have had an all-out war and a hell
of a time winning it, or are you forgetting how easily
those warriors defeated us with their *Toreno* steel
weapons?''

''Ah, that's a good point, and I guess the next ma
jor question is, do *your* warriors have *Toreno* steel?''

''Where do you think the Sha-Ka'ari armorers
recipe came from? What I've brought back are sword
wielders to defeat sword-wielders, and mine are
bigger, stronger, and they don't particularly like slav
ers.''

''Even though they are in a sense related?''

''I think three hundred years has pretty much bro

en the ties," she replied dryly. "Besides, they fol-
ow Challen, and he—"

"Follows you?"

"Not exactly." Tedra grinned. "Things this big
lon't take orders easily—unless they give permission
irst to be ordered around."

"I beg your pardon?"

"That's a private joke, Rourk," she said quickly,
earing the barbarian's rumble. "But Challen is here
ecause he has this thing about pleasing me. He really gets a kick out of it."

"The woman is 'going around the block' to say
what is important to her is important to me," Challen
explained.

"Isn't that sweet, Rourk?" Tedra beamed.

"Any sweeter and we'll get fat," he teased, then
added sincerely, "I'd say you hit the jackpot, babe."

"I know."

"So you've brought us an army. Now to figure a
way to get it inside Goverance Building. *That* isn't
going to be easy. Crad has just about all his warriors
securing the place, except those who still go out to
collect the lawbreaking females. No one gets in without a *very* good reason."

"You're forgetting the Rover, babe. Martha is going to simply Transfer us inside the building."

"Not us," Challen clarified. "You, woman, will
come nowhere near where warriors will be fighting."

"Chall-en!"

Chapter Forty-five

It took three hours of shouting and arguing and coming close to challenging before the barbarian could be budged from his stand. But when Tedra tried a long shot and got Martha on line to ask her opinion, her contrary computer actually backed her up. She wouldn't be doing any Transferring unless Tedra was included, and that took care of that.

Challen was not happy about it. He had to war with his need to keep Tedra safe and his desire to let her be herself, which he had come to realize was what had attracted him to her in the first place, her difference from other women. It was important to her to be part of the fighting. Martha's compliance reminded him of that. But he liked it not.

Tedra wasn't taking any chances that he'd change his mind again. She quickly concluded arrangements with Rourk, who would contact all their people who had been working toward liberation without success. Fortunately, there was no need to involve them in the fighting at Goverance Building, but there would still be warriors out in the city who would need to be taken care of, at least kept track of, and they could do that.

So it was less than another hour after leaving Rourk that Martha Transferred them all to different points inside Goverance Building. Tedra, Challen, and six others made their appearance right inside the Director's office. And it was fortunate that Molecular

Transfer was instantaneous, for Crad Ce Moerr was not alone, but was in conference with some of his warriors, ten to be exact, and all armed. Had Transferring been any slower, Tedra's group could have had swords pointing at their throats before it was completed.

As it was, the opposite happened. The Sha-Ka'ari were too surprised to draw their weapons with any degree of swiftness, and were disarmed in a matter of minutes. Only one resisted, and he was made to regret it when Tamiron engaged him and made short work of it. Crad Ce Moerr, on the other hand, managed to sound an alarm. Tedra could have kicked herself for not anticipating that. So much for making the rest of it go easy.

"I don't know who the hell you think you are," Crad said with full confidence even though his warriors were throwing down their weapons. "But you're not getting out of here alive."

"It sounds like that should have been my line," Tedra replied, coming up to push the dictator back down in his seat. "Except I know who you are, you slime ball, and your fun's over with here."

"Because *you* say so?" he sneered. "Maybe you don't know what you're up against. I happen to have hundreds of warriors right here in this building."

"So . . . do . . . I," Tedra was delighted to tell him. "But you won't be around to see the outcome. Martha?" She opened the link of her lazor. "Transfer this jerk to the Rover's lockup. Garr can have the pleasure of disposing of him later."

"You can't—"

But the dictator blinked out before he could say any more, and although it gave Tedra a great deal of pleasure to have done that, she was reminded by a glance about the room that they weren't finished yet.

"Where do you have Garr Ce Bernn?" she asked the nearest Sha-Ka'ari.

"The alarm was given, woman. He will be dead by now."

"You're lying," she said angrily. "He's the only bargaining power you guys got, or are you too stupid to know that?"

"Why does a woman speak for you?" the warrior demanded of Challen, who stood directly behind her.

"This is her world, thus is this her concern. I am here merely to see that she is protected in the doing of what she must do. Best you answer her now."

"Protected?" Tedra snorted, swinging around to the barbarian and, in the process, letting her elbow connect with the belligerent warrior's windpipe. "I don't need protecting from jerks who don't know what to do with a woman unless she's a slave. Protected?" she snorted again and looked at another Sha-Ka'ari. This time she merely snapped, "Garr Ce Bernn?"

"Below," the man answered immediately, his eyes on his friend rolling on the floor choking. "In the detaining rooms below."

"Thank you," Tedra replied on the way to the door. "Well, come on, *protector*. This isn't over yet."

"You have no reason to be angry, *chemar*," Challen said as he stopped her from opening the door before he could see what awaited on the other side. Nothing did.

"I'm not," she admitted while she hurried her pace down the empty corridor. "I'm sorry. I'm just worried and needed to take it out on someone. They wouldn't really kill Garr just because that farden alarm sounded, would they?"

"I would like to reassure you, but I cannot fathom the minds of warriors such as these."

"Who can? Oh, Stars, I want to rush down there, Challen, but if they were going to kill him, it's been done already. But if he's still alive, then that alarm got him surrounded, so we'd be smart to gather our forces before we go any farther. And from the look of it, all the Sha-Ka'ari have either deserted the building or—"

"Or they have gathered below for a united defense."

"Exactly."

The latter proved to be true, much to the Sha-Ka'ani warriors' delight. They'd come here to do some fighting, but hadn't got much in so far. There had been some sporadic engagements throughout the building, but the bulk of the Sha-Ka'ari warriors had headed straight for the lower levels. Tedra could have gladly left them down there to rot, since there was only one way in or out, if Garr wasn't down there with them.

Standing there looking at the six lifts that wouldn't fit all of them at once, Tedra was ready to pull hairs. "It won't work. The area in front of the lifts down there is as big as it is up here. They'll be lined up ten deep just waiting for the doors to open. I ought to have Martha Transfer them all into deep space."

"And have your Garr go with them? He has not a signal on him that Martha can recognize, as do we," Challen pointed out.

Tedra stopped her pacing to gape at him. "I must have left my brains back on the Rover. You expected to pop in on them all along, didn't you?"

"Certainly. Why else were we each supplied with the homing device?"

"So we could all Transfer into the building at the same time," she replied, grinning. "And if we can do it once, why not again? Oh, Mar-tha?"

It was done in a matter of moments. The scene before them now was a solid wall of Sha-Ka'ari warriors facing the lifts as Tedra had assumed they would be. What she hadn't counted on was their numbers.

"Stars, I think we're outnumbered," she said beneath her breath, but Challen heard her.

"Best we even the odds, then."

He chuckled deeply, which had the Sha-Ka'ari turning en masse. Tedra would have preferred figuring out some other option, but it was too late for that. She was shoved behind Challen, then behind the next warrior, then behind the next, until she was in back of them all whether she wanted to be there or not. She couldn't make use of her own weapon with her own warriors all in front of her. She just had to stand there and listen to the racket they were making as the battle joined, doing nothing to help, unless . . .

"Martha, how about getting me from one side of this area to the other?"

"Forget it, kiddo. I didn't put you down there to die."

"You didn't put me down here to twiddle my thumbs either!" Tedra snarled

"So why don't you see if you can't find Garr while your friends are busy?"

Tedra made a face. "You really did forget to send my brains down here with me, didn't you?"

Her answer was one of Martha's best simulations of laughter. But Tedra wasted no more time on self-disgust. She turned to face the closed doors that surrounded the circular area. They opened into rooms of different sizes, she knew, and she also knew which one was the largest and most likely to have been turned into permanent living quarters for a valuable prisoner. She approached it now, and sure enough, a special security lock was in evidence. Tedra smiled to herself. The dum-dums had used what was on hand. Similar to an identilock, it worked on visual identification, voice verification, *and* handprints, and gave clearance only to guards—and all Goverance Building Sec 1's. And since the Sha-Ka'ari hadn't figured on any Sec 1's showing up, she'd wager just about anything the locks weren't modified.

Sure enough, the door slid open at her command. And Garr was there, seated in a chair in the center of the room. A warrior stood behind him holding a sword across his throat, a *Toreno* shield raised to protect him. Tedra leaned against the doorjamb and crossed her arms over her chest, which pointed her lazor at the ceiling. It wasn't going to do her much good against *Toreno* steel. And she still didn't want to kill this particular warrior.

"Well, hello, Kowan. Fancy meeting you here."

The poor guy was doubting his sight as well as his hearing. He wasn't expecting a woman to come through the door, certainly not one wearing a Sec 1 uniform, and certainly not one he thought he knew very intimately. Garr, on the other hand, wasn't a bit surprised.

"You certainly took your sweet time, Tedra." He grinned at her.

"I had to make a detour to another Star System." She grinned back.

Kowan had recovered by then, enough to say, "You will put down your weapon, woman, or I will kill him."

"Oh, come on, warrior, you're not going to play

stupid, are you? Take a look behind me. Those are barbarians making mincemeat out of your friends. Not Kystrani Secs, but warriors from your mother planet. Sha-Ka'an ring a bell? No? Well, no matter. But take my word for it, you guys don't stand a chance. Besides, I've already captured your fearless leader and put him where you'll never get him back, so the slave farm is closed. Why don't you play smart and surrender while you still can?"

"To a woman?" he snorted.

"Well, if that's your only difficulty, I can get a Sha-Ka'ani in here for you to hand your sword over to. But I'm a Sec 1 before I'm a woman, and I hate to tell you this, Kowan, but I already took you down once—or haven't you ever wondered why you have no memories of our time together after we arrived at our destination?"

"You lie. I became drunk."

"I drugged you, babe, but *after* you were already—"

"Tedra, look out!" from Garr.

"No!" from far behind her.

She turned, but all she saw was the flash of blue steel coming at her. She had time to do no more than keep her head from leaving her body. She had no time to avoid the backlash of the blade as it bounced off the doorjamb. It knocked her flat. Pain lashed across her chest. She suddenly didn't feel like trying to get up. The Sha-Ka'ari didn't care one way or the other. He was desperate to get his hands on Garr, assuming him to be his only protection now. She'd merely been in his way. But he didn't reach Garr. Challen came charging through the door right behind him, roaring like a man gone mad. His sword buried, lifted, and actually threw the Sha-Ka'ari across the room. That was the last Tedra saw before she closed her eyes against the pain.

And then she was being lifted carefully, so carefully, but the movement still hurt like crazy. She tried holding it in, but the groan got out anyway. The movement stopped instantly. There was another groan, not hers, but it managed to get her eyes back open. Only she doubted what she was seeing: Challen leaning over her with tears in his eyes, tears running down his cheeks, Challen crying?

"Hey, don't . . . babe."

She raised her hand to his cheek, but it dropped back before it got there. Stars, she felt so weak—and cold.

"Do you . . . do you die, so too will I. Please, *chemar*, please! You will *not* die! You cannot!"

"No . . . I won't."

But he thought she was only trying to tell him what he wanted to hear. He was looking at her blood-covered chest and dying inside. She realized that at the same time it became clear he'd forgotten all about meditechs.

She tried reminding him. "Just get me to a—" But the awful sound of anguished rage he made drowned her out. Garr would have to tell him, she decided. She didn't have enough strength left to break through all the noise Challen was making. But she wouldn't have missed this for the world.

Her last thought before she lost consciousness was, *That man is definitely in love with me.*

Chapter Forty-six

Challen gave her still another frown. Tedra chuckled this time. She felt wonderful, actually close to ecstatic. Her barbarian loved her, and before they left her old quarters at Goverance Building, he'd tell her so.

"I tried to remind you about meditechs, honestly, I did. But you were too busy grieving over me to listen."

His frown got worse. He was holding her in his lap, in an adjustichair that had made plenty of room for them. She was curled around him, wearing not a stitch of clothes, and feeling not the least bit embarrassed that she wasn't and he was. But that was the first thing he'd done as soon as she'd brought him there, strip her down and completely examine her body. There was no sign left of her wound, not even a pink mark. The meditech had spit her out with a clean bill of health and the assurance that her son hadn't been bothered at all by the ordeal. No wonder. He was going to be a warrior after all, just like his father.

His father told her now, "Warriors do not grieve."

"Oh? Then what would you call it?"

Suddenly his arms closed tight around her, his face buried in her neck. "I thought I was losing you," he said deeply, with a wealth of feeling. "Woman, you must never leave me!"

"I won't," she assured him, holding him just as

417

tightly. Yet after a moment she smiled to herself. "But why is it important to you that I don't?"

"Why?" He looked up, and back came his frown. "Did I not tell you?"

She ran a finger across his chin, not at all discouraged. "You said something about dying if I died, but . . . why do you feel that way?"

"Because I treasure you more than my life."

Her finger stilled as the warmth flowed through her. She forgot about hearing the words she was seeking. What he'd just said was quite good enough.

"Oh, Challen, I love you so—"

"Am I intruding?" Rourk Ce Dell asked innocently from the doorway.

"Hell, yes," Tedra half growled, half groaned. "How did you get in here?"

"Obviously no one was in a hurry to change your identilocks when you moved out, babe, but then, of course, we were invaded not long after that. I gave it a try and found my prints were still on record."

"Then let me put it another way," Tedra replied. "What do you *want?*"

"Just to congratulate the heroes." He grinned. "By the way, that is a stunning outfit you're wearing."

Tedra's face went up in flames. "You jerk, you farden jerk," she gritted out before she stomped off to find something to wear, leaving both males laughing behind her. When she came back in a convenience robe, she was still glaring, and they were still laughing. "That wasn't funny."

"Yes, it was. You didn't even *know* you were sitting there—"

"You'll change the subject, Rourk, if you know what's good for you."

"Very well." But he really had to fight to get that

grin off his lips. "I hear you've got at least two hundred prisoners, and more coming in by the hour with your warriors sweeping the city. Did Garr reward you properly?"

"He was very generous, to both of us. Didn't you stop in to see him, to find out what he has in mind for you? I told him that I would never have escaped without your help."

"You did?" He was surprised.

"Come on, Rourk, without you I'd probably be a slave on Sha-Ka'ar right now."

"Instead of a double occupant on Sha-Ka'an?"

"Who says I'm going back there?"

"Well, aren't you?"

"Yes, but I hate it when people take things for granted," she grumbled. "I really do."

"I'm guilty." He sighed.

"So am I." She finally grinned at him.

When they both looked at Challen, he snorted, "I never take anything for granted."

"The hell you don't," Tedra scoffed, but she was still grinning. "You never had a single doubt that your warriors wouldn't win the day. Admit it."

"This is so, but I did not take it for granted, since no other thing could have happened."

"Arrogant, isn't he?" Tedra said to Rourk.

"It sounded like just plain confidence to me."

"Oh, he's got barrels full of that, but who can blame him? They don't come much bigger than he is, you know, at least not in Centura."

"So what's the word on getting our women back?" Rourk asked to distract the frown Tedra was getting from the big guy. "Has Garr made contact yet?"

"Certainly."

"Well? Is there going to be a problem? There

shouldn't be, when you have their warriors as hostages.''

"Actually, they were willing to sacrifice these guys to keep the women. But Garr pulled a bluff at my suggestion.''

"What?''

Tedra chuckled. "They were told to return the women or Sha-Ka'an would make war on Sha-Ka'ar. A few of them remembered where they came from, and so they decided not to chance a hostile visit from barbarians of their mother planet.''

"*Was* it a bluff?'' Rourk asked Challen.

"No. All must be finished here before I can take my woman home. Does this mean we must go to Sha-Ka'ar first, then there we would go.''

"Well, I *thought* it was a bluff,'' Tedra said, smiling at her warrior. "Would you really make war on a whole planet for me, Challen?''

"Do you not know I would do anything for you, does it make you happy?''

"I—ah—think that's my cue to be going,'' Rourk said.

"Good-bye, babe,'' Tedra said without looking at him, already crawling back into Challen's lap.

"Have I said something to please you?'' Challen asked, settling her back into her previous position.

"What gave you that idea?'' she teased him. "By the way, Garr is letting me keep the Rover.''

"I thought the Rover was yours already.''

"No, Martha and I stole it. Now it's mine, which means we can go anywhere in the universe. And World Discovery *was* my second career choice.''

"You will not miss being a Sec 1?''

"I'll always be a Sec 1, babe. I just won't be working at it anymore. After all, there's this barbarian I know who gets nervous when I think of fighting—other guys. Of course, he's delighted if I want to fight him.''

Challen chuckled. "Best you remember what happens when you fight him."

"All I can seem to remember just now is his very gentle way of making me cry defeat. Why do you do it that way?"

"Because it gives me pleasure to cover your body with mine, *chemar*. I see it gives you pleasure to know that."

"Not at all." She managed the aloof sound she was trying for, but just barely.

Challen grinned wickedly. "Woman, you lie. I can smell your heat."

"You can not! Can you? Now that's not fair, warrior. You give so little away, and I give *too* much."

Challen shook his head. "And this displeases you? You wish to hear that you have captivated me, bewitched me?" He started taking off her robe. "You wish to hear that I am whole only when you are near, nothing when we are apart?" He got his *bracs* off without disturbing her position, but then he repositioned her. "You wish to hear how much I yearn to join with you, how much I need you?"

He entered her slowly, exquisitely, and Tedra couldn't hear another thing. She melted around him. He melted into her. Fused, joined, without separation—his. Stars, how she loved him, and loved loving him. But he knew that, the beloved jerk. And he had a right to be arrogant and cocky, didn't he? Look at him. Where in the universe was there another man like him? And he was all hers.

She stayed right where she was, even after her breathing returned to normal. She'd like to go to sleep like that, with him still inside her, his strong arms about her, his heart beating under her cheek. But she wasn't tired. The day had been too exciting.

"That wasn't fair of you, warrior. You did that to distract me, didn't you, because you know what I'm fishing for, and you just won't say it."

"Perhaps if you tell me what you wish to hear, you will hear it."

"I want to hear only that you love me."

"But warriors do not love."

"That, warrior, is worth a challenge!" she growled, coming up to glare at him.

But he caught her head in his hands, and his mouth fastened on hers before she could say any more. It was a kiss worth a thousand words, filled with all the passion they felt for each other.

And then she had her words, whispered against her lips. "Warriors do not love . . . they should not . . . but here is one who does. I love you, woman. My heart cries with how much I love you."

"Oh, Challen!" Tedra cried.

He sighed. "This was to make you happy."

"I am!" she wailed.

"As you were at the giving of the *fembair?"*

"Yes!"

The warrior could only shake his head, grinning, but Martha was laughing her head off as the viewing screen behind them went blank.

The Sizzling *Night* Trilogy by
New York Times Bestselling Author

CATHERINE COULTER

NIGHT STORM
75623-4/$4.95 US/$5.95 Can

Fiery, free-spirited Eugenia Paxton put her heart to the sea in the hands of a captain she dared not trust. But once on the tempestuous waters, the aristocratic rogue Alec Carrick inflamed her with desires she'd never known before.

NIGHT SHADOW
75621-8/$4.50 US/$5.50 Can

The brutal murder of her benefactor left Lily Tremaine penniless and responsible for the care of his three children. In desperation, she appealed to his cousin, Knight Winthrop—and found herself irresistibly drawn to the witty, impossibly handsome confirmed bachelor.

NIGHT FIRE
75620-X/$4.50 US/$5.50 Can

Trapped in a loveless marriage, Arielle Leslie knew a life of shame and degradation. Even after the death of her brutal husband, she was unable to free herself from the shackles of humiliation. Only Burke Drummond's blazing love could save her ... if she let it.

KAREN ROBARDS

THE MISTRESS OF ROMANTIC MAGIC WEAVES HER BESTSELLING SPELL AGAIN AND AGAIN...

MORNING SONG
75888-1/$4.50 US/$5.50 Can
Though scorned by society,
theirs was a song of love
that had to be sung!

TIGER'S EYE
75555-6/$3.95 US/$4.95 Can
Theirs was a passion that could
only be called madness—but
destiny called it love!

DESIRE IN THE SUN
75554-8/$3.95 US/$4.95 Can
Love wild, love free—dangerous,
irresistible, inexpressibly sweet!

DARK OF THE MOON
75437-1/$3.95 US/$4.95 Can
The sweeping tale of a daring woman,
a rebellious lord, and the flames
of their undeniable love.